T0274029

"Rich prose, exotic world-building, and compelling characters will make this novel an instant favorite and leave readers clamoring for more. This is a mesmerizing debut!"

— DANIEL SCHWABAUER, award-winning author of
Operation Grendel and *Maxine Justice: Galactic Attorney*

"Briggs bypasses typical fantasy tropes to create a unique and excellent story. Forbidden treasure, a curious priestess, and a gate that may or may not bring judgment on the world. I could not put this book down!"

— MORGAN L. BUSSE, award-winning author of
THE RAVENWOOD SAGA and SKYWORLD series

"I read through *The Eternity Gate* with my 13-year-old son so I got to see it both from my perspective and that of a younger reader. In both cases, we found the story to be told with a fresh voice in an emotive style. Seyo's struggles were ones which were easy to relate to as she struggled to find her place in the world.

Speaking of the world, Briggs does a great job fleshing out a world which beckons to be explored. The motivations displayed were both complex and believable and this provided for a very real feel while still providing the wonder of a magical world.

I look forward to seeing more of what the author has to show us in this delightful world."

— SEAN OSWALD, author of the LIFE IN EXILE series

THE

ETERNITY

GATE

THE ETERNITY GATE

KATHERINE BRIGGS

The Eternity Gate
Copyright © 2023 by Katherine Briggs

Published by Enclave Publishing, an imprint of Oasis Family Media, LLC

Carol Stream, Illinois, USA.
www.enclavepublishing.com

ISBN: 979-8-88605-066-0 (printed hardcover)
ISBN: 979-8-88605-067-7 (printed softcover)
ISBN: 979-8-88605-069-1 (ebook)

Cover design by Emilie Haney, www.EAHCreative.com
Typesetting & map design by Jamie Foley, www.JamieFoley.com

Printed in the United States of America.

To Mom and Dad.
Thank you for reading to me,
teaching me how to write,
and leading me toward
the True, Good, and Beautiful.

VEDOA

THE TERROR LANDS

NAZAK

LAIJON

AI'BIRO

HANDPRINT OF GOD

PIRTHYIA

1

THROUGH THE PAPER WINDOW, lingering stars winked against a cold sky, the morning my eighteenth winter passed and I, Seyo, came of age. The temple had given me blue skirts and overlays, a rare color among its helpers. One didn't wear blue for long before graduating to a priestess's yellow, or not. And I would stick out in a sea of yellow when I served my first midnight vigil that evening, my soul stained by a mountain of confessions.

I burrowed into my too-short quilt and counted the rules we planned to break that night. Two temple statutes and a king's law shattered, all so I could see the Heart, the forbidden cave weaving through our hills. I would drag my friends Kiboro and Jorai along, and I was too excited to feel guilty. What was wrong with me?

Qo'tah. They lived for after-curfew adventure, and I had dreamed of seeing the Heart since we were children. But this was my last escapade. Tomorrow I would live up to wearing blue. Kiboro would understand, but Jorai wouldn't. I imagined that conversation and groaned.

The straw cot creaked. Princess Kiboro, who I served as attending maiden, rose for sunrise prayer. She crouched by my pallet and shook me. "Happy birthday, Seyo. Ready for tonight's ghost hunt?"

Did she have to say it that way? I remembered the gravelly voice of our first tutoring priest and mumbled into my blanket, "Indulgences, such as birthdays, weaken the will. They lead to

memory lapses during recitation, and snores interrupting teaching."
I hesitated. "Also leading one's friends astray."

"Stop worrying." Kiboro grinned and snatched the quilt.

Chilly. I uncurled from the pallet and crossed our cramped quarters in three long strides to light a candle and retrieve clothing. Kiboro almost squealed seeing my new garments. I shushed her, had her sit, and bent to braid her dark hair into a crown.

As Kiboro preferred, we arrived early for prayer, before the other temple helpers and even the presiding priest or priestess. The day raced in a routine of prayers, chores, lunch, instruction, ignoring the extra glances my blue overlay earned, and dinner. Back in our room, we laced our boots and opened the window to shimmy to the grounds and find Jorai. But then Kiboro received a knock at the door from a young priestess, the one who lived inside the helpers' compound as guardian. The woman bowed and extended a letter bearing the queen's seal.

I closed the door after our courier, and Kiboro tore the seal. Her spine straightened as she read. "Mother is ill."

Headaches. Queen Umoli must have quarreled with the king again, and faithful Kiboro would care for her mother at the palace. As attendant, I would accompany her, and my chest squeezed as I gathered shawls. How could this happen now? This night? Please—

"No. You're going with Jorai to see the Heart. It was your only coming of age wish, and I've never seen you look forward to something so much. Besides, you have a vigil afterward." Kiboro sighed in disappointment. "I promise to make this up to you."

I blinked. It was my place to remain at her side, but despite being friends, I didn't dare argue with her, the princess. And I didn't want to.

Kiboro tugged a shawl from my arms and left to join her bodyguard.

I stood in silence. Alone. It felt wrong. If Jorai and I were caught without her, there would be no protection for either of us, a disgraced nobleman's daughter and the king's despised second-born son. But if I didn't see the Heart now, I never would.

From the opened window, frigid air teased my face. So much for spring. I climbed through the hole and scrambled to the darkness covering the grounds. Rule against sneaking outside after curfew—broken.

Shafts of moonlight pierced cloud cover and dripped across the forest and hills of Laijon. In the west, distant mountains rose. I jogged east, toward cliffs guarding the harbor and sea beyond. Evergreen trees made for better cover than their seasonally skeletal companions as I crept near the temple.

Washed with night, the temple rose in severe lines, sloping roofs, and bright glass windows. Dormant gardens sprawled everywhere, and I skirted these to a fenced thicket, Laijon's holiest site, called the Handprint of God. Hidden among wild brambles and bushes, a covered stone well stood. Only the high priest or priestess passed the wooden gate to draw water from the well, and only once a year after the spring rains. Within the pages of the holy Nho, it was written that the Handprint of God was where the Father of Light first formed the world. Many believed the water still pulsed with dangerous, divine power. I bowed toward the site and looked around.

A form paced between clusters of trees. One foot dragged. The young man folded a hand behind his back and gripped a cane with the other. He wore an ordinary cloak, but his fancy tunic and trousers defeated his disguise. Oh, Jorai, second prince of Laijon, will you never learn?

When he saw me, Jorai's striking golden eyes brightened. He tucked his cane under his arm, stepped into a puddle of moonlight, and reached for my hands. "Seyo, may light guide your path—"

"The temple can see." I pushed him into the shadow of the trees. Metal jangled under his cloak. I ignored that and bobbed a bow. "May light guide your path, too, but are you trying to get caught?"

Jorai laughed and looked over my head. "Kiboro?"

"Queen Umoli is ill."

"My sympathies." He stated this without emotion, but it wasn't his mother. Jorai, born to the second queen, towered over Kiboro and Crown Prince Huari, and even me. He would be a portrait of Laijon's ancient kings if he'd stop knotting his ebony hair like the Nazaks, our rebellious southern neighbors. It increased the king's contempt for him. Jorai, why?

"Oh, well. I'll make up Ki's loss in your celebration." Jorai beamed and caught my hands. "Happy coming of age."

I dipped my head in thanks. Rule against meeting a man without a chaperone—broken. What scene did we suggest without Kiboro? Lovers keeping a tryst? Ridiculous. Jorai was like a brother, except I felt more like myself with him than with my literal brother, or even Father. Jorai was my best friend, but also a thrill-seeker, which reminded me that I needed to make him swear that we would return in time for the vigil.

Jorai pulled me deeper into the woods. His lame foot dragged, cane plodded, and supplies clanked under his cloak. "Shall we be off?"

"Yes. But . . ."

Jorai raised his brow.

"I have been assigned to my first vigil."

"I'm sorry."

I rolled my eyes. "It's an honor, but it begins at midnight. Unfortunately."

He frowned. "Are you changing your mind about our plan?"

"Never. I just need to arrive on time." So don't cajole me into doing something foolish, especially without Kiboro to bully you into cooperation.

"Understood and relieved. Honestly, I'm impressed that you're going through with this. Remember all the schemes you've begged us to abandon? And now we're about to break the king's law. Trespass through the forbidden tunnels."

He didn't name the consequences. The terrifying legends were a more effective deterrent than imprisonment, anyway. Besides, this was only a game to him. Another chance to rebel against the king. Again, I wished Kiboro, who held their father's favor, were with us, just in case something went wrong.

"How can we ever top this? Storm the treasury? Hijack a royal ship? Take horses and roam the continent like gypsies?" Wistfulness tainted his theatrics.

"Those ideas don't deserve answers."

"How about a serious proposition, like stealing into the city to watch the street players? I think it's my turn to plan our next meeting."

My stomach twisted. I wouldn't attend our next meeting. I couldn't. Should I tell him and get this over with? "I can't."

"That's the Seyo I know. Maybe we can see if the lake's warmed up and swim, instead."

"No. I can't meet anymore because I need to start keeping the temple rules if I am going to graduate to priestess."

Jorai slowed, and I almost plowed into him. "What does that mean? What rules? You're becoming a priestess right now?"

"Not yet, but I have come of age. I now wear blue." Was I lecturing a child? But Jorai had not vowed himself to the temple as Kiboro and I had. Far from it.

"I noticed, and you should wear blue more often. It suits you. But why do you want to become a full-blown priestess? I thought you became a temple helper to visit the Archives. Isn't that enough?"

Yes and no. "I can't remain a helper forever. When Kiboro comes of age, we plan to graduate together. But the temple won't accept me if I don't purify myself."

Jorai snorted. "So we'll only see each other inside the temple? We'll never speak freely again, of course."

Agitation bit at me. "We'll find a different way. I want to still see you, but I can't continue bending so many rules."

"Kiboro bends rules all the time."

I didn't answer. She was princess, but she would have become a priestess, regardless. And I had marks against me. Secret ones even he didn't know about.

"So you'll wed yourself to the temple in the hopes that it will find you worthy?"

I bit back a gasp. But he was right.

Jorai opened his mouth and shut it. Thank goodness. Why was he so annoyed and, frankly, mean? I wanted to wrench my hand from his, but he didn't let go of mine and quickened his pace.

Just as the trees grew thickest, we reached foothills rising into cliffs. The palace crowned their summit. Kiboro would have reached her mother by now. Jorai hunted around slopes and boulders for the mouth of the cave until the crevice gaped before us.

We passed within the shadowy stone walls and followed the narrow corridor to a metal gate. Jorai rummaged in his cloak for two candle lanterns and a tinderbox. Warm, flickering light revealed rust devouring the bottom half of the gate.

How many times had we brought lanterns and peeked through the bars to the passages beyond? Quieted our breaths and hearts to hear rivers flowing through the veins of the cliffs? The whispering of imagined specters? Yet Jorai's sulking consumed my focus now.

He thrust a lantern in my direction. I took it, and he stooped to examine the lock. After a moment, Jorai reached into his cloak and extracted a metal ring with two clanking keys. Both were ancient, one small and ornate, the second an eye-catching, jagged key the length of Jorai's palm. "They were tucked into an old book, of all places," he said. "A nightmare to find."

I did not want to know how he had managed to steal these from the king's chambers. If King Zaujo found out, would Jorai be able to bear his wrath? And Jorai took these risks for me. Shame squirmed inside me again.

He singled out the smaller key. It fit, and the gate squealed open. A breath of stale cave air wafted over us.

Jorai hid the keys within his cloak, dusted his hands, and stepped backward to glower at the night sky. "We'll let the candles burn halfway before turning around. Then you can have your midnight vigil."

"Jorai, thank you. This means. . ." I struggled over words, "everything to me. I shouldn't have let you go through with it."

His posture softened. "You've only talked about seeing the Heart your whole life."

"I'm indebted to you."

"Good. I'll remember that." He extended an arm toward the cave. "Shall we go ghost hunting?"

He sounded like Kiboro. Many thought spirits and curses prowled here, but a priestess wouldn't believe that or go searching for them.

I lifted my lantern and stepped into cool shadows. The royal decree that no one enter the tunnels—violated.

Jorai shut the gate and followed. "Let's find your Heart."

It wasn't mine. But I crept into yawning sightlessness and avoided brushing the rock walls. They were rough, damp, and slick, and the tunnel narrowed. The ground rose, fell, and twisted endlessly, like the throat of a snake. I stumbled once and slowed for Jorai.

He drag-stepped close behind. "When's the last time someone entered the tunnels?"

"The gates were installed three centuries ago."

"Go on, historian."

I shook my head. "You know my father was the historian." But Jorai's humor had returned.

"My school learning is rusty. Not everyone has the opportunity— or desire—to pore over endless, dusty records with their historian father."

Everyone's learning was lacking because the Archives' shelves were half-empty with lost manuscripts. And my days of researching with Father were long gone.

"You've only told me that a battle occurred here. So what are we looking for? A pile of bones?"

I shivered. "I had a nightmare about finding the remains of that ancient war. Colossal, warped skeletons and rust-eaten armor. But all of that would have been cleared out before the gates were installed. Anything that remained would have been washed away by the monsoons." I bit my lip. I was looking for a different type of ghost—answers to Laijon's lost past.

The passage curved. I touched the slimy wall for orientation, and imagined pages of the Archives' manuscripts covered in descriptions of this labyrinth. All maps of the Heart had been destroyed. "These underground tunnels have several openings, including a secret passage into the palace. Centuries ago, before the Occupation, these acted as escape routes for the royal family."

That snared Jorai's attention.

I continued, "During the Occupation, our enemies made these tunnels into a stronghold and used it to overtake Laijon. Our country's treasure, artifacts, and precious manuscripts were hoarded here, along with the wealth of other conquered nations. Records written after the war say that the battle that ended the Occupation occurred at the Heart, and Laijon's stolen wealth and history were destroyed by our enemies before their defeat. Street tales say our precious metals and gems were melted or vanished by evil magic. Either way, the people of Laijon were left like refugees within a ravaged country, with our past stolen."

"The Heart is where Laijon's wealth was destroyed? That's far more interesting than ghosts." Jorai's voice echoed against the stone corridor. "Maybe I'll find a gold coin or something."

"Anything valuable that survived would have been taken before the gates went up," I informed him.

"You would make a fantastic historian. And you don't need to become a priestess to do that."

I stiffened, but then cold water splashed my ankles. I lowered my lantern to see water rippling across the tunnel.

Jorai sloshed after me. "This is dry season? Your coming of age is well timed. I don't want to be down here after the spring rains begin. How far are we from the Heart?"

I eyed the height of the candle. We were moving too slowly. "I don't know. My eyes won't adjust. It would be so much brighter if Kiboro were here." Because she, like almost everyone else of Laijonese descent, possessed the gifting to scoop light into her palms. Neither Jorai nor I were gifted with light, one of many things we shared in common, and so brought candles. I secured my skirt under my knees.

"Kiboro would have been helpful, but I'm happy to have you to myself." Jorai studied my efforts. "Can't arrive at the temple with a soaked hem? What's the penance for that?"

I ignored him and waded in ankle-deep water.

"About the temple, Seyo, can I speak honestly?"

Hadn't he already? But before he could say anything more, the tunnel split into three paths. Heart quickening, I lifted my lantern to illuminate the cave ceiling.

Jorai held his candle high too. "What is it?"

"Look." I pointed. "See the soot smudges? When the enemy claimed the tunnels, they carried torches going back and forth. The walls are smoother here, too, from their passage. Following the soot will lead us to the Heart."

We kept going. The water level rose and then disappeared. Jorai tapped his cane, and the candles burned down.

Jorai's shoulder brushed mine in the dark. "Back to our previous conversation. We've known each other for a long time, yes? Since you, me, and Kiboro played together as children in the palace. Don't I know everything about you?"

I didn't answer. He knew almost everything.

"Then may I speak plainly?"

Could I refuse him, a prince? I turned right at the next intersection and forced myself to nod. "Of course."

"Seyo, you aren't going to be a priestess."

I missed a step. "What?"

"You're too full of life. Priestesses surrender their freedom to confessions, pretending to be perfect, greeting unrepentant people who only visit the temple to appear pious. And for what? To grow old staring at the altar? You'll regret it."

I fought for breath. How was I supposed to respond? What was wrong with him?

He grunted. "You'll be too good for everyone else. Or me."

Hang his position as prince. "That's ridiculous."

"Think of everything you can do if you leave the temple. Like finding work among the Archives that you love so much?"

I wanted to scream. "That's half of why I joined the temple, because the priests maintain the Archives since the king dismissed the historian's position. Now can I be a priestess?"

Muddled in candlelight, Jorai ran a hand through his hair. "You're of age now. Don't you want your own life? You could gain an apprenticeship in something useful. Travel the continent."

When would this interrogation end? And was he talking about me or himself? Did he forget that I was Kiboro's attendant? Maybe he didn't understand what that position meant to someone of my heritage. I would never be able to do better for myself.

"Or you could marry."

Marry? I failed to hide a chuckle.

Tension crept into his shoulders. "Why is that funny?"

"I'm hidden among an army of young women, and we almost never cross paths with to-be-priests, let alone anyone else besides Kiboro's bodyguard." She and I joked about this all the time, and I adopted a sarcastic tone. "Who would I marry? Besides the temple itself, of course?"

He did not answer. Shallow water lapped against the walls. Candlelight bounced across our narrow confinement, until all of a sudden, the cave walls ended and we spilled into an enormous chamber.

Thick gloom swallowed our lights. I couldn't see the ceiling or across the space, but our hesitant footsteps echoed from afar. I extended my lantern, then my toe caught on something and I toppled to my knees. Jorai helped me stand, and we looked down at a slab of cut stone laid across the cave floor. Smoothed by time and flood, carvings blossomed across the rock. My heart beat faster, and I bent to lay my palm against the markings, all religious depictions like those within the temple. "Yes. This is the Heart." Unseen for centuries. Where Laijon's former glory had been hoarded, yet today it was empty. Bare. The Heart portrayed Laijon's present as well as our past, and I had finally seen it. Tears pricked my eyes, and I carried my lantern to walk across the slab, dropped down to the cave floor, and circled the cavern. Seven openings, including the one we came from, interrupted the walls. I drew closer to the nearest passage.

Stonework framed the natural doorway. Delicate symbols of first-century Laijonese snared my gaze. I devoured them, translating around carvings too faded to read. They sang Laijon's praises and the power of her kings, favor, and wisdom. Then I looked higher and shuddered.

A chiseled, stone monster crouched above the arch. Its wings and claws spanned the length of a man. In a humanlike face of rock, its mouth stretched in an infinite scream.

"You found a monster after all. What is that?"

I jumped at Jorai's approach. "A Shadow." And this statue was as awful as the sketches within some of Laijon's older manuscripts. "It is written that Shadows were so evil, none could pass Heaven's gate."

"Our nanny used to tell stories about those." Jorai suddenly bounced with energy. "Perhaps my gold coin lies beyond. Let's explore."

"Some paths are dangerous," I warned. "They might lead to bottomless eddies and mazes. And there isn't soot on the ceiling." I wanted to study the Heart. But hadn't I already seen everything?

Jorai pressed a hand against my lower back. "The treasure of three defeated nations was kept here during the Occupation—don't look so surprised. I paid some attention during my studies. No destruction is thorough enough not to leave something behind."

I sighed and followed. The water deepened. "The candles are almost half-burned."

"Let's make a bet. If I don't find something during our remaining time, fine. If I do, you'll leave the temple and I'll become a wayfarer, we'll run away from this prison of a country, and travel the continents."

"Jorai, that's madness."

His voice lowered. "Only if you don't run away with me."

Run away with him? Wait—

Something snapped under my shoe. I cried out.

Jorai swept me behind him and peered into the water. Pale, jagged bones broke the surface. I scrambled back. Had we actually stumbled upon the lost carnage of a battle? No. It was the ribcage of a river serpent picked clean.

"Wide-jawed devourers," he said. "How did it end up here?"

"I've read that river serpents are flexible enough to compress their bodies and pass through the thinnest crevices." I looked around. "There might be live ones."

Jorai faked a cough. "Historian." Then he patted his silken trouser leg. "I brought a dagger." Jorai lifted his lantern, and we stared.

A graveyard of river serpent skeletons glutted the narrowing passage. So many lay before us, piled one on another, they blocked the tunnel. All the bones were bare, thanks to their living brethren, but death lingered in the air.

"Why are there so many?" I froze. Underwater, the cave floor sparkled.

Jorai lowered his lantern toward the bones. His eyes grew. "Seyo." I saw and sucked in a breath.

Artifacts of glittering metal shined from inside the bones. Our lanternlight illuminated water-tarnished silver, green bronze, and gold. Jorai's breath quickened, and he raised his light high toward the end of the tunnel. The boneyard stretched lengths beyond our sight, all filled with treasure.

"Vultures of the ocean." Jorai's voice trembled. "These river serpents devoured something bright, couldn't fit into their passages to return to sea, and starved. But where did they get all this wealth? A sunken pirate's plunder?"

I released my breath. Thank goodness for Jorai's theory. Yes, that could make sense. Except if the river serpents couldn't squeeze out of the cave with full bellies, they must have found the treasure here. But Laijon would have discovered any pirates' hoards when they installed the cave gates. And this was so close to the Heart. I reached between bones to grasp a lump of strange, purple-tarnished metal.

No. Something was wrong, or Laijon was living a lie. Our ancient treasure could not have survived.

Jorai hunted among the skeletons, splintered another rib cage, and excavated a dripping gold flagon, embellished with jewels and other discolored precious metals. "I have only seen such finery in my father's apartments. And I had hoped to find a coin."

I straightened. "You should put that back."

"Why?"

"Because gold shouldn't be here. The cave is supposed to be empty."

Jorai's voice pitched. "Are you serious? I'm holding my independence."

"We need to understand why this is here." I stepped backward toward the Heart with a churning stomach. Please, Jorai, come with me. "What if someone found gold like this in your possession? They might think you're a thief." I hated how weak I sounded. "We can't even tell Kiboro. But you and I," I added, "we'll come back."

Jorai sighed. "Do you swear?"

My resolve wavered. "Yes." Anything to make you come and avoid getting into trouble.

He dropped the golden flagon and stalked after me. That was too easy, but judging by his pinched expression, he was also concerned about finding all this.

I clenched my hands at my sides. Treasure couldn't be here. Yet it was. Why? Then I looked at my lantern. The candle had burned past three-quarters. "*Qo'tah*, I'm late." I raced toward the Heart. Jorai fought to keep up.

We burst into the Heart and crossed the stone slab to a narrow passage with a gate so thin, it appeared like a crack. I gestured for the key. "This leads to the Archives."

He blinked, startled, but hurried to free the lock. To my relief, this gate, too, groaned open.

I whirled toward him. "Can you find your own way out?"

"Look for soot." He sounded breathless. But his eyes sparkled. "Seyo, this is the best adventure I've ever had."

"Go straight to the palace." I pushed my lantern into his hands. He couldn't stay with dying candles anyway. "And don't come back without me." I dashed into the narrow passage and glanced once over my shoulder.

Hallowed with candlelight, Jorai shook his head and swept a bow. He shut and locked the gate.

I squeezed through the skinny path I remembered seeing once as a child until reaching a wooden door. I pushed it open against a tall piece of furniture. An empty bookshelf. I squirmed through the tight opening, secured the hidden door, and peeked into the unlit Archives.

No one was there. Good and unsurprising.

I crept across the familiar room, past dusty bookshelves and glass displays, and exited into the temple's sacred hallways. Murmuring came from the sanctuary. I was late, and my chest pounded as I untied my damp skirts to slap around my ankles.

I stole into the sanctum, already filled with priests and priestesses in yellow. After removing my soaked shoes to stand barefoot like everyone else, I slipped toward the other blue-clad temple helpers.

The circular sanctuary stood in dim lighting, for now. Between towering alabaster walls, many bowed in the center of the stone floor before the altar.

We in blue filed into a line to wash our hands at the ceremonial cleansing bowl and bowed before an older priestess. She dipped her thumb into a vial of holy oil to anoint us for prayer. When my turn came, the priestess frowned at my soggy hem, but did not question me because I was Princess Kiboro's attendant. She dipped her thumb in oil and pressed it against my forehead.

I bowed again, and hurried to the far side of the room to retrieve a candle from a pile of lit tapers. I did so, and hid among the helpers again.

Everyone knelt for final confession, then rose off their knees to lift hands in light. The room brightened above the array of giftings, from summer sunshine to average glows.

I raised my candle and pretended its light also filled the sanctuary. Some cast looks toward my blue garments, my wet skirt, my candle. When they clasped their hands against their shoulders and lowered their faces to the ground, I set my candle in front of me, before also touching the floor.

I was supposed to confess my invisible sins, all the rules broken. Instead, I pressed a shaky hand against my overlay pocket. Against the lump of tarnished metal I had taken from the tunnel. The corrosion had given it an odd, purple hue, and tickled my memory. Something I'd read about in the Archives. I forced myself to begin silent confessions and recited all of them over and again. And again.

Midnight passed. The priests and priestesses exited first. The temple helpers left next, until I knelt alone in the sanctuary. Dawn touched the high windows. Soon, those serving during the morning hours would arrive.

I stood on weak legs. Felt the metal in my pocket.

Jorai and Kiboro had joked about finding ghosts. The treasure felt like the mystical trove of a phantom. Of course, I would stumble upon something like that. Bad luck had followed me until I began serving Kiboro. Until now.

I gritted my teeth and tipped the candle into my palm. Flames flickered against my skin. I waited. No pain. No burn. My eyes filled with tears. None had ever guessed that I was half-Vedoan, because our divided nations looked so alike. I couldn't cup light in my hands, but I could withstand fire, an unholy ability that no amount of confessions could cover. Even if I never broke rules, never saw the Heart, never found this disturbing treasure, never planned to break a million more rules to figure its mystery out, my mother's blood would make me unworthy to become a priestess. Unless I kept my secrets hidden. So, I needed to identify this purplish ore and where it came from. I would find a reasonable answer. No more bad luck.

I touched the copper bauble pierced into the corner of my ear, returned the candle stub, and left the sanctuary.

2

KIBORO RETURNED FROM THE
palace that morning, quieter than normal. By the time we
breakfasted on steamed grain heaped with spicy fish, she told me
her mother felt better. She didn't ask about the excursion Jorai and
I had taken to the Heart.

I was surprised. I had prepared lies for her questions, although
I hated doing so. At least I didn't have to use them, but what was
bothering Kiboro?

We dressed to attend Laijon's women's university. Kiboro
served the temple, yet she was expected to finish her formal
schooling before coming of age. Once a week, we donned silk
gowns instead of temple overlays and skirts, to look like a princess
and nobleman's daughter again, and took the carriage up the hills
into the walled capital.

As Kiboro's attendant, I gained the privilege of also attending
lectures. But as I sat behind her in an auditorium filled with
Laijon's titled daughters, I couldn't pay attention. The windows
teased glimpses of distant mountains and our glistening harbor, but
I imagined the Heart's graveyard of bones. And the lump of purple-
tarnished metal I had hidden under my pallet. In the Archives,
there was a manuscript that taught how to clean ore. With that, I
could identify the lump as an ordinary metal, like copper or bronze.
Once I identified the treasure as a seafarer's bounty, I could silence
this mystery.

In front of me, Kiboro sat extra straight, and knowing her as I did, I could picture her furrowed brow. I slid my gaze toward the new professor. What were we learning about, again? The women's university held the same classes as those belonging to noble sons, including arithmetic, geometry, astronomy, logic, rhetoric, fencing, which was one of Kiboro's favorites, and light-gifting class, although she had outgrown those teachers last year. Ah, this was geography, and an elementary lesson.

Perspiration trickled down the professor's boyish face. So, he had noticed Kiboro's excessive attentiveness. He raised his volume, as if this would make his review sound important. "Our continent encompasses the three civilized nations. We are Laijon, who hold the light of the sun. There is our esteemed ally, the islands of Ai'Biro, who are gifted to grasp water, but also skilled in invention. Lastly, there is Pirthyia to the south."

Pirthyia, whose loans had kept Laijon alive after the Occupation. Centuries later, their powerful foot still rested upon our indebted necks.

Kiboro raised her palm.

The professor cleared his throat. "Princess?"

"Srolo," she addressed him respectfully, and her voice carried like a bell, "you neglect Nazak. Do you consider them uncivilized?"

The professor shifted his weight. "Wild Nazak has fallen into internal disputes and divisions, and is closer to several nations than one. Nazak also lost her gifting."

"Can Pirthyia be considered civilized if she never possessed a gifting?" Kiboro leaned forward. "Lastly, what of Vedoa, who warped her gifting."

At the mention of Vedoa, the professor, students, and even Kiboro's bodyguard standing behind her, stilled. I couldn't believe she had spoken our estranged sister nation's name aloud. Vedoa's volcanoes, soothsayers, and human sacrifices traipsed through my mind, and I cringed. There was a reason our nation had split in two. Vedoa had left the path of light and twisted their gifting into an illicit power, the ability to wield fire. Or, in my half-blooded case, to withstand flame. I resisted touching my copper earring and squeezed my hands together in my lap. Please let the conversation turn.

"What determines whether a nation is civilized?" Kiboro asked.

The professor twittered. "Princess, such talk must be unpleasant for you."

Pardon? Did he really say that?

But Kiboro held her tongue. She would not show offense or feed nonsense, but I knew I would hear about his rudeness. Thankfully, the lecture ended and everyone spilled from the university to climb into carriages. Barano, Kiboro's monstrous chief bodyguard, assisted us to our seats and drove us toward the temple.

Kiboro chewed her lip. "Egoistic man."

I prepared myself for a justice crusade. "You handled the professor well."

"No. I mean Father." Kiboro jostled against me as the carriage hit a bump. "Last night, Mother told me he is entertaining a marriage proposal from Pirthyia. From one of their lesser kings."

What in the continent? That was a horrifying prospect for Kiboro. And if she went to Pirthyia, so would I. Shivers raced up my back. "The king's heart is soft toward you." Soft, but not loving. King Zaujo spoiled Kiboro, his only daughter, and despised Jorai and his disability. Crown Prince Huari, son of his first wife, was favorite.

"I will not consent to this marriage. If only I were already of age, like you. As soon as I am, I will take my vow as priestess and permanently commit myself to the temple." Kiboro raised her chin. "As royalty, I will also be able to join the council and gain a voice among the Chanji. I will be one of the first priestesses to join the Chanji, and this will put me in the best position to serve my country. Father will be forced to hear intercession for the poor. I will be able to do more for our people than pass out food from the temple, which we missed for this stupid lecture."

I hoped she would be permitted to speak at the Chanji, not be overlooked like Jorai.

"If I married, my bridal payments would be used to finish Father's fleet of outdated ships, import Ai'Biroan steam-powered machines that we can't afford, or build that ridiculous spar extension from Pirthyia's railroad into Laijon. And for what? So Pirthyia can access us more easily? Everyone knows they would love to claim the entire continent. When will someone stand up to that tyrant? No, I will never marry."

Never marry. Jorai's silly objections to my becoming a priestess flitted through my brain. I pushed that thought away, only to remember piles of bones and treasure. How was I going to enter the Archives and grab that book about cleaning metals?

"Seyo, what's wrong?"

I smoothed my expression. "Want to go horseback riding?"

"Where?"

"Circling the temple is always invigorating."

Kiboro laughed. "You only volunteer to go to the temple when you want to visit the Archives. You could have just asked."

Was that the only reason I went to the temple? My stomach squirmed. "We won't have much time before afternoon prayer."

Kiboro's eyes glimmered. "Then it's a race?"

Perfect. Except for one problem.

After a quick lunch and changing into riding clothes, we entered the temple stables. Giant Barano checked our geldings' tack. A frown betrayed his dislike for our spontaneity.

I approached the animal Kiboro lent me and eyed her bodyguard rotation for the first part of the week.

The two soldiers were young, uniformed, and shaved the sides of their heads as was expected, but one was extremely tall and lanky. Despite his bored expression, he readied his mount with fastidious care. My twin brother Roji. He was a faithful soldier, but I suspected that he landed on Kiboro's bodyguard because she had requested him on my behalf. Sometimes I was grateful, other times annoyed, and today I wished she hadn't. He and I had ignored each other all morning, but when I started hunting for books inside the Archives, he would know I was up to something. He always knew when I was keeping a secret.

The six of us jumped astride, leather reins in hand.

Kiboro winked and urged her mount faster down the main temple paths. Soon she, Barano, and the second guard flew several lengths ahead. This left Roji and I alone to chat, a kindness on Kiboro's part. Again, I wish she hadn't.

Speak first. Maybe it will distract his perceptiveness. But what should I say? Uh, hello, dearest, onliest brother. Since you last graced us with your grouchy presence, I have turned to thievery of mysterious, ancient treasure. I thought you might want to know. Mention it to Father, will you, if you two are on speaking terms once more? Instead I said, "May light guide your path. How goes life among the guards?"

Roji offered a respectful nod before shaking his head. "If my life were any better, my superiors would take it from me."

My guffaw was unladylike. "Try again?"

"I could be cleaning mess or digging trenches. I suppose babysitting you and Her Majesty is better." He eyed me. "Are you okay? You're acting strangely."

Qo'tah. He saw through me already? I shot him a look.

We arrived at the temple and dismounted. After passing through its hallways and acknowledging bowing priests and priestesses—it was awkward arriving with a guard, but Kiboro was princess—we reached the door to the Archives. Realizing where we were headed, Roji balked as an elderly priest hurried to unlock the room for us. *Would I, if I became a priestess, gain a set of keys like my father once held?* The door swung open, and the priest bowed and stepped aside.

Barano searched the Archives first, always zealous in caution. His expansive chest swelled as he lifted his hands with sunshine, which brightened everyone's faces and lit the silver medallion hanging from his neck, a soldier's medal of valor. Deeper within the room, spooky shadows danced along dusty, book-lined walls. Old tapestries hung between the shelves, and wooden pedestals displayed crumbling parchments in protective glass boxes.

We entered, and the priest shut the door behind us. Kiboro's second guard raised his hands in light. Roji, too, cupped his palms high, but he glowered at the wall. He hated the Archives that had consumed Father for so many years, and he loathed his weak gifting.

At least he had a gifting. The right one.

Kiboro crossed the room to the agricultural histories. She plucked a book she had studied before about investing in richer harvests, the cornerstone of her plan to improve Laijon. When she carried the book to the reading table, her bodyguard drew near to offer light. She opened the book, and mischief sparkled in her voice. "Seyo, will you find that other manuscript?" That was code for giving me permission to roam.

I inclined my head and tried to walk calmly toward a half-filled shelf along the floor in the far corner, where the bodyguards' light did not reach. I lowered to my knees and turned my body to shield my search. There were manuscripts rebound in leather, annals over a hundred years old, even a codex. As a child under Father's tutelage, when he served the king as historian, I had memorized these books and their scribbled accounts of Laijon's precious metals—their purposes, limited records of what Laijon once produced, and how to clean them. O, wrinkled pages, I need your help. What in the continent did Jorai and I find inside the tunnels? The word *oractalm* snagged my focus.

Long ago, Laijon possessed a rare, red ore, mined from her own mountains. Once cleaned with powdered salt and vinegar, the crimson metal glowed like Laijon's gifting. It was found in every household, shaped into utensils, decorations, bathtubs, and thrones, and was considered the most desirable of metals. Nations had sought this alloy until our enemies seized it all. In their rage of defeat, they destroyed oractalm during the Occupation. The red metal no longer existed.

The tarnished lump I had pocketed from the Heart couldn't be oractalm, but I needed to prove this for myself.

My ears tickled. I looked over my shoulder and caught Roji stifling a yawn. I replaced the book, swiped dust from my skirts, and rose. Wait. I was supposed to bring Kiboro a manuscript. I snatched one off the nearest shelf and returned to her side. Goodness, what had I grabbed?

Kiboro accepted the tome with a nod. She acted unsurprised that I'd handed her a treatise on herbal cures. After a moment of pretend reading, Kiboro whispered, "Prayer."

I replaced her books, then she swept from the room with her bodyguards flanking her. The elderly priest locked the Archives behind us.

After dinner, Kiboro and I dressed for sleep, brewed tea, and opened our copies of the holy Nho. She sprawled on the straw mattress, and I curled into my pallet. Her gifting in one hand provided more than enough light for both of us to study, except I wasn't reviewing our recent memorization.

Once Kiboro was absorbed, I pressed my mug against my middle. What Kiboro didn't know, was that instead of holding tea, my own had a portion of dinner's pickled vegetables and their salted, seasoned vinegar inside. I dropped the purple lump of metal from the Heart into the cup and made myself wait. After a moment, I fished the metal out, scratched the thick, violet tarnish with my fingernail, and ceased to breathe.

The ore was shaped into a tiny, detailed horse. A figurine. First, I noticed letters trailing across its metal hide. I knew six languages, including Laijon's modern tongue and ancient script, thanks to working with Father in the Archives. The symbols were old and named an illustrious king from the fourth century. This horse did not belong to the humble nation of Laijon today.

Second, calling the metal red was a weak description. Its brilliant, scarlet color rivaled rubies. And under the brightness flowing from Kiboro's hands, the figurine emitted a rosy glow.

I stuffed the treasure under my pallet and glanced toward Kiboro. Unaware of my distress, her lips moved in silent recitation.

I sank into my quilt. I trembled.

Oractalm, more valuable than gold, wasn't supposed to still exist. Who had lied to us? And if we had found a handful of wealth in the bellies of river serpents, how much more lay lost in the secret depths of the tunnels?

3

THE ORACTALM CONSUMED ME.
My mind wandered during sunrise prayer and my stomach churned
throughout breakfast. Away from the women's compound, Kiboro
and I fenced under Barano's tutelage. After trouncing me more so
than usual, she called me distracted.

The historian in me was thrilled about finding the precious
artifact. We could fill museums with the treasure from the tunnels.
My practical side demanded that it be used to pay off Laijon's debts
to Pirthyia. Kiboro would agree, if she knew. But my priestess's
training screamed that Jorai and I had broken the king's command
and were rewarded with a sinister discovery. Not one piece of our
ancient treasure remained, if the records were true, so what had we
found? We were trapped in secrecy, though no one would believe
our tale anyway. No one would recognize glowing oractalm after its
disappearance centuries ago. If someone found the horse figurine
under my pallet, with its exotic crimson hue and glow, I would be
named a thief, or even a witch. So what should I do?

After washing and changing into our skirts and overlays, Kiboro
and I walked with the other helpers to the temple. Today, we served
laymen and laywomen who visited the sanctuary for confession.
The sun shone warmly at last, and Barano trailed at a distance. Roji
and the third bodyguard were dismissed until tomorrow.

Upon reaching the temple steps, a priest directed Kiboro and
the other underage helpers to stand outside and greet parishioners.
The handful of us wearing blue were sent to the washroom adjacent

to the temple's entry. Inside the washroom, wooden bowls, pitchers of water, and hand towels rested atop pedestals for ceremonial hand cleansing. We each claimed a pedestal and bowl. I ended up at the front with a good view through the doorway into the entry, where a yellow-robed priest and priestess stood ready with anointing oil. They would press a thumbprint of oil against each visitor's forehead and pronounce them clean and able to enter the sanctuary.

Would I someday announce someone as cleansed? I couldn't imagine that, when my soul felt so filthy. Perhaps I belonged in the washroom.

Greetings chorused from the helpers outside. The priest and priestess bowed, and I hid surprise when I recognized our first visitor.

Srolo Faru, wearing wide-shouldered plate armor and with his silver beard braided, strode into the washroom. Though slight of build, the captain of the bodyguard was an honored soldier, second to the king, and carried himself as such. Under Faru's command of the army, Laijon's border skirmishes with the mountain tribes had ceased. Kiboro, Jorai, and I spoke fondly of his kindness toward us when we were children, especially Jorai. Faru, unlike the rest of Laijon's high nobility, respected the second prince and never spoke against him. Sometimes I wondered if he knew that Jorai snuck out to visit me and Kiboro, as it was Faru's business to know everything, and turned a blind eye to his antics. Srolo Faru even remembered my name when I became Kiboro's attendant, but right now, he did not notice me and looked stern.

A murmur rippled through those outdoors. Inside, we in blue craned our necks to see who was coming, and then I wished I hadn't.

Crown Prince Huari, dressed in brightly dyed brocade worthy of the king's firstborn and favored son, stalked past the bowing priest and priestess into the washroom. Angry.

We helpers in blue dropped into a deep bow. I gritted my teeth. Why was Huari here? Certainly not to pray. It wasn't even a holy day, when he could flaunt pretend confessions in front of a crowd.

Ah, it was Faru's day to educate Huari. Faru visited the temple on a scheduled, complete-as-necessary basis, and must have forced Huari to attend too. But Huari's plumage was too ruffled for an inconvenience like that. Had they been quarrelling? It was common gossip that the two didn't get along.

Following like a dog, Huari's sharp-faced valet also sauntered into the room, as if he were more than a servant. The valet prowled past me to wash his hands at a bowl manned by one of the prettier helpers.

Faru and Huari advanced in my direction.

Wonderful. I trained my gaze below theirs, as befitted my rank, and emptied the pitcher into the washbowl. Hopefully they—or really Huari—wouldn't recognize me. I'd stomached the prince's mockery as a child, and Kiboro wasn't beside me to glare him into civility.

But Srolo Faru inclined his head. "Good morning, Srawa Seyo."

Oh well. I bowed again. "May the light shine upon your esteemed paths." Unless the Father of Light deemed that our crown prince should trip into a muddy pothole and learn humility. *Qo'tah*, that wish warranted confession.

Huari's gaze flicked over me before ignoring my presence— he would have omitted the respectful srawa title for nobleman's daughter anyway—and tapped his fancy leather boot.

Faru didn't acknowledge his cue. As elder, he dipped his hands into the bowl first.

Huari leaned toward Faru and deepened his voice. "Srolo Faru, I swear that Jorai is a thief."

My pulse jumped. When Faru dried his hands on the towel, I crept forward to change the water. What was Huari doing?

Faru's tone remained neutral. "I will tell King Zaujo that your manservant found Prince Jorai walking through the palace last night. I'm sure the king will dismiss the prince from the upcoming meeting of the Chanji, if that satisfies you."

I blinked at Faru's barb, then caught the valet perking up,

hearing himself mentioned. What was Jorai doing, sneaking around last night? And why had Huari's valet been watching him?

If Huari noticed Faru's sarcasm, he didn't let on. "Excellent srolo, I am asking you not to tell my father about my half brother's indiscretions until I can prove that he is stealing. He was not embarking on another jaunt to play with Kiboro and his girlfriend." Huari jabbed a finger in my direction.

I almost dropped the pitcher. How did Huari know about our meetings? Why did he call me Jorai's girlfriend? Did he know about our trip to the Heart? No. That would be stronger evidence against Jorai than stealing. I bit my tongue and poured fresh water into the bowl. I would have rather dumped the pitcher's contents upon Huari's feet, but held my breath for Faru's response.

Faru's eyes narrowed, and he smoothed his silver beard. "I am tasked with protecting the king and his family, not looking to cause the crown embarrassment."

Huari's face flushed, and he spat a foul word. In the holy temple. "Do you forget that I am next to be king, Faru?"

The two men stared at one another. At last, Faru bent his head, but he did not answer.

Huari sniffed and plunged his hands into the bowl.

A chill swept through me. Once the crown passed to Huari, maybe Jorai's dream of running away wasn't such a bad idea. Jorai. Why did he sneak around the palace last night, if the valet spoke the truth? Jorai wouldn't. Oh, but I knew him better than that. He would. My chest squeezed. I realized Huari's valet had almost caught Jorai returning to the Heart. To the treasure.

Huari finished washing, as if even temple water would clean him. I lifted the wooden bowl to change the water again, but bumped it and water sloshed across the floor. Droplets landed on Huari's boots.

Huari roared, startling the other helpers, priest and priestess, even his valet. He flung a hand toward me, but couldn't speak, and stormed from the washroom. The priest and priestess hurried to anoint his head with oil, and his valet scampered after him.

Srolo Faru looked at me with both pity and a raised brow. He knew Jorai and I were friends. Did he think I spilled the water on purpose? Would I be punished? But Faru exited, knelt for anointing, and followed Huari into the sanctuary.

Just before curfew, Kiboro gave me permission to walk around the women's compound for fresh air. It was our midweek routine. My true mission was to tie our freshly written letter to Jorai among the branches of a certain flowering bush. This was how the three of us scheduled our late-night meetings.

I remembered my decision to quit breaking curfew and sighed. Not only had we scheduled another rendezvous, but I also carried my own, private note for Jorai, one Kiboro didn't know about. In my note, I told Jorai that I had another midnight vigil in two days and asked him to meet me beforehand. Without Kiboro. The vigil was a lie, which tied my stomach in knots. But I needed to tell Jorai that Huari was watching him, my terrible suspicions about the treasure's origin, and plead with him to never return to the Heart. Abandoning the mystery pained me. But perhaps as a priestess I could research further, and maybe even confide in Father. But not now, when Jorai was under Huari's suspicion.

Thankfully, few temple helpers milled about. I exchanged bows with those returning inside and stole along the low, night-covered walls encircling the women's compound. From the forest canopy, a bird chirped to its mate. I reached the bush, and its blooming scent draped over me as I buried the oractalm horse figurine at its roots, tied both letters to leaves with twine, and then stopped.

A thick envelope sagged from one of the branches. I seized it and read *To the historian* in Jorai's scrawl. He meant me, and it was heavy. I tore the seal and tipped the contents out. A thick bracelet dropped into my palm and shimmered in the moonlight. It was made with ancient gold coins threaded into a circle with silk ribbon. No, not gold. The coins were scarlet oractalm.

I groaned. Jorai had not only returned to the Heart, but he had the gall to make me this? It was far too dangerous to wear. Was he out of his mind?

I stuffed the bangle into the envelope, the envelope into my pocket, and spun in retreat to the women's compound. What was I going to do with this? Kiboro couldn't see it. I should bury it with the horse—

Footsteps rustled.

My heart leapt into my throat. I spied a figure vanishing into the thickening darkness. But not before seeing his gaudy clothing and foxlike face.

Huari's valet. He'd been waiting and had seen everything. Jorai dropping the envelope off, me opening it to shimmering coins.

I raced toward the compound.

4

I LIED TO KIBORO ABOUT attending another vigil.

Under the cover of dusk, with nerves coiled so tight I felt ill, I crept to the Handprint of God and circled the fenced tangle of brush waiting for Jorai. Through the tree line, final rays of sunset gleamed against the white-stone temple, its tiered roofing, and commoner's balcony, always empty. Would I be forced to confess from the balcony if Huari proclaimed Jorai and me thieves and we were cut off from the sanctuary?

Uneven footsteps shuffled near.

I turned. Even though I expected him, my stomach caught.

Jorai wore a cloak and carried his cane. Hair tied in that Nazakian knot. His golden eyes brightened seeing me, and he closed the length between us to catch my hands. "May light guide your path. I have so much to tell you. I am glad we are alone again."

I wanted to slap him. How could he have returned to the Heart? How was I going to tell him about Huari?

Jorai carried on, oblivious that I hadn't returned his greeting. "But first, the weather has warmed up. Would you mind me swimming?"

Was it warmer? I supposed so, and the lake underneath the cliffs was far from listening ears. "Go ahead."

The moon rose one fingerlength by the time we reached the cliffs. At their base, a small lake lay caught between the arms of two bluffs.

Jorai stabbed his cane into the base of the taller ridge and climbed. I slowed down to match his pace until we reached the crest. With heaving breaths, he removed his cloak, lowered himself to the ground, and sprawled his legs over the edge. "Sit with me?"

I obeyed and gazed into the watery mirror far below. The lake held stardust, tossed against a spill of midnight paint. I glanced to the heavens. Could the Father of Light, who formed this, help us out of our mess? I took a breath to tell him—

"Seyo?" Jorai also watched the sky. "Do you ever pretend that your mother watches you from up there?"

I closed my mouth. Did he forget that mine still lived? But culturally, after Father was dismissed as royal historian and she abandoned our family, Mother did die. Her desertion shamed us, and I lived trapped by this until Kiboro requested me as her maiden attendant and raised me into honor again. I caught myself fingering my copper earring and dropped my hand. "No."

"I wonder if my mother entered Heaven."

I suppressed a gasp. "Don't say that."

"You know what she did."

Yes, and I tried to put it from my mind. The second queen had committed suicide. It was as unthinkable and dishonorable as abandonment. And she had not been a faithful visitor of the temple. Neither was Jorai.

His shoulders rose. "She hated me first, and then she ruined me with her death. With my twisted foot and lack of gifting, she once called me cursed."

I ached for him. Her cruel words weren't true, as I had told him countless times before. "Jorai—"

"But now I have a way to disprove her." He scooted closer and lowered his voice. "I returned to the Heart. Please don't be angry. I had to see it again, and there is so much gold. More than I've ever seen in one place besides the treasury. And then some of the metal, if you scrape the tarnish off, glows."

If I had been in my room, I would have shouted into my quilt.

"Can you believe it? I may or may not know some bootleg buyers who would be willing keep this bizarre, glowing metal a secret, if I sold them smaller, affordable pieces. This treasure must have come from far-traveling pirates, since I've never heard of a such a thing, even perhaps from across the sea. I also explored some of the other passages and found a store of ancient boats, but they're decrepit and useless. Down the third tunnel."

How many times did he go back? And boats? I pushed my historian's intrigue away and interrupted. "I need to tell you something."

He pointed to my wrist, and hurt filled his eyes. "You're not wearing it."

The bracelet. Oh, I really wanted to scream. "Of course not. It's hidden under my bed because it's priceless, not from across the sea, and should not exist. And you can't sell this treasure and roam the continent like a wild Nazakian because Huari's valet saw me open your envelope."

Jorai's jaw dropped. "He sent his valet to spy on you?"

I massaged my forehead. "Huari visited the temple with Srolo Faru two days ago. He knows we and Kiboro meet together, and he told Faru that you're sneaking around the palace. Huari believes you're stealing—which seemed crazy, until I opened that envelope! That's why I asked you to meet with me. Then the valet saw me with the bracelet. The oractalm coins probably looked like gold to him in the dark."

"Oract-what?" Jorai shoved himself to his feet. "If Huari dares to apply his malice upon you on my account—"

"I serve Kiboro, and King Zaujo favors her. Huari won't touch me."

Jorai stalked the cliff's edge, dragging his foot, and sliced the sparkling sky with his hand. "I won't let him harm you. Whatever Huari says, I will protect you."

Sudden tears sprang to my eyes. I believed him, but I didn't fear for myself. I feared for him. I stood. "Jorai, you need to tell your father about the treasure first. Before Huari does. And you must give up everything you've taken from the Heart." Because there could be so much more down there, and Huari would claim that Jorai looted the entire trove.

He froze. "Tell Father I entered the tunnels. Surrender the treasure. Seyo, are you serious? Do you know what he will do to me?"

I remembered Jorai's previous conflicts with the king and cringed. But it would be worse if Huari spoke first, and he knew it. "Expose the treasure in front of the Chanji."

Jorai scowled. "You want me to incriminate myself before the royal council and watch my father explode in front of all high nobility?"

"His wrath will be held accountable in public. And Srolo Faru will be there. When Huari told him he wanted to catch you stealing, Srolo Faru covered for you. I know he will do it again. He has always helped you."

Jorai heaved a sigh but did not contradict me.

I hesitated over what I wanted to say next, and remembered that I belonged to Kiboro. My voice wobbled, and an invisible dagger impaled my soul. "You should tell the Chanji that I convinced you to enter the tunnels."

"No. I am leaving you out of this." Jorai waved me into silence and muttered, "Perhaps the discovery of treasure will be shocking enough to protect me. I can tell them I found it in the ocean."

Would lying protect either of us?

Jorai decided. "I will do it. But you must promise to attend the Chanji too."

My heart lifted and dropped. "Impossible. I'm not invited to attend."

"The palace holds secret passages and listening holes."

"Are you joking?"

He ran fingers through his hair and mussed the knot. "I can't do this alone. I need to know that a true ally is there. Please?"

But Faru would be there. I couldn't. Yet if I hadn't asked to see the Heart, none of this would have happened. Was he not my best friend? I swallowed. "Yes."

"Thank you, Seyo." His posture sagged. "May I swim now?"

I ignored his mockery and turned away as he removed his tunic, shoes, and rolled up his pants.

"I hope the water is freezing," Jorai said, and cast his cane aside to face the cliff edge. He raised his face heavenward and spread his arms like birds' wings.

Though I had seen him dive many times, my heart quickened.

Jorai bent his knees and jumped, keeping feet down and arms at his sides. He fell lengths and lengths and lengths and disappeared with a splash into the lake below.

I peered over the edge.

He surfaced with a shout. "Cold!"

Somehow I laughed, then grabbed his cane and clothes before scrambling down the cliff.

When I reached the bank of the pool, Jorai was cutting through the water in a circle. "Join me, Seyo?"

I hugged his belongings against me. "You said it's cold."

"You should try high diving this season."

I shook my head. "I am not brave enough."

He moaned and swam another skillful lap. "You just have to soften your feet and aim for dark water. Are not all of our old hero tales full of brave men and women who dove off cliffs to begin battle or something?"

"That is Ai'Biro's history."

"Ah, the island people. How I wish I were clothed in their stunning skin. No, I would choose to become Nazakian. I've continued to study their language and could exchange simple conversation if you would let me, mistress of six languages."

"Jorai, I won't encourage you in idolizing wild Nazak. It gets you into trouble."

He winked and threw himself into a series of tricks before climbing out of the lake and shaking off. I offered his belongings, and he dressed.

"This year, Seyo, I promise I will see you dive. There is nothing better than perhaps to fly." He grasped his cane.

We began our slow walk toward the temple, and Jorai cleared his throat. "The Chanji meets in two days."

Turmoil writhed inside me. "And you will surrender the treasure you've taken?"

His expression hardened, but he nodded.

Did he mean that?

"Two days," he repeated. "Now, I'll tell you how to find the best listening hole in the palace."

5

THE DAY OF THE CHANJI'S MEETING

arrived. Leaving Kiboro to sneak to the palace proved easier than I could have imagined.

We visited Queen Umoli for breakfast at her private residence, a quaint building tucked among the royal gardens. After Kiboro was born, the third queen only reentered the nearby palace to attend the Chanji or upon the king's command. Seated on silk cushions before a low, laden table, her servants offered Kiboro and me steaming bowls of grain and honeyed fruit. The queen took tea. Eyes flashing, tongue like a sword, she relayed news and gossip to Kiboro, tidings of promotions, dissent among the army, even border skirmishes, as if they were the enemy's battle plans. Considering her stormy relationship with King Zaujo, were they not her best weapons?

I did not enter the conversation. Jealousy at their mother-daughter relationship bit me. I tried to ignore it and instead wrestled with my promise to watch Jorai speak at the Chanji. How was I supposed to get away? Barano blocked the door with arms crossing his chest, watching Kiboro. The queen's bodyguard rimmed the walls, holding handfuls of light.

In a flurry of skirts, one of the queen's attendants curtsied and announced that her second lady had taken ill with fever. Queen Umoli ordered a bodyguard to fetch medicines. The healthy attendant began brewing medicinal tea. Time came for the queen to depart for the Chanji, and she hesitated before dismissing her first attendant to remain with the second.

Kiboro's eyes widened. "Mother, don't go to the palace unaccompanied. Take Seyo."

I kept my jaw from dropping. Could the Father of Light be smiling upon Jorai's and my plan? Surely not.

But Queen Umoli only frowned slightly, then nodded.

I scurried into place, the bodyguard surrounded us, and we stepped into the bright outdoors.

The journey was short, and the queen chose to go on foot. We left the green gardens and approached royal buildings dripping with sunlight and ponds rippling with rainbow fish. Queen Umoli led us across their decorative bridges. Passing soldiers bowed. Out of the corner of my eye, I searched their faces for Roji's disgruntled grimace, since he wasn't on rotation as Kiboro's bodyguard today. He would definitely see that I was dabbling in trouble if we ran into each other now. This errand was as unthinkable as entering the Heart. Thankfully, we didn't pass him or his contingent.

The queen led us to a broad gravel entry lined with imperial guards. Giant stone statues, looking down on all, rose on the left and right. We walked, and lengths ahead, the palace rose in dazzling tiers of turquoise-colored roofing. A jewel boasting of how she survived the Occupation long ago, when the city was razed. Though overrun, the palace had never fallen.

Standing guards saluted as Queen Umoli climbed the long stone steps and passed the palace threshold.

I looked back. Rolling valleys and mountain to the east, the adjacent capital city and sea to the west. I remembered to breathe and crested the last step into the palace.

Brightly painted red, green, and blue walls joined high rafters and enveloped us. Our shoes clapped against fine stone. Guards converged near the stairs to the king's apartments and great doors leading to the council chamber.

Pedestals framed each doorway. Lightbearers sat upon them cupping brightly lit hands. All were young noble sons and daughters, chosen for their strong giftings. I had craved that desirable position long ago, and watched one lightbearer, a child, rub his eyes before looking ahead.

Queen Umoli approached the council chamber early and first, like Kiboro. Soldiers opened the double doors as she passed through, shut them after her entry, and took their positions again. I was left alone in the painted foyer, expected to wait and attend her when the meeting ended. Which I would.

My pulse quickened. When the second member of the Chanji arrived, a nobleman representing the rural forest, I slipped toward the servants' halls, found the concealed door covered by a potted tree, and disappeared into the secret passage Jorai had described.

The low ceiling forced me to hunch over as I climbed steep stairs into narrow, dusty obscurity. During the Occupation, Laijon's royalty had used these corridors to escape their overpowering enemies, and failed. These secret halls reminded me of the cave tunnels, the whole reason for my sneaking around, and I swallowed unease. How would King Zaujo react to Jorai's news about the treasure? Would Jorai lie about finding it in the ocean? Even though lying was sin, I hoped Jorai would not be truthful about its discovery. King Zaujo might explode if Jorai mentioned breaking into the tunnels, even with the Chanji present. I had never seen the king delve into his madness, as people whispered. Kiboro and Jorai assured me that the rumors were true. They said their father broke chairs, flung himself upon the ground, or shouted until hoarse. I wondered if Jorai would mention the glowing oractalm? My stomach tightened. Would anyone on the council have answers explaining that?

I reached a flat landing. Fifteen paces, like Jorai said. Among the shadows, a pinprick of light glared from the wall.

Guilt begged me to turn back. Loyalty to Jorai and curiosity drove me to crouch beside the tiny light. Father had sat on the Chanji when he was historian, and he told me that the council chamber was the only room left intact after the Occupation. I'd begged him to describe the space over and over, and he'd shrug and say it held some interest, but never elaborated. I closed one eye to peer through the hole and inhaled sharply.

Glassy marble flooring. Life-sized statues with craftsmanship breathtaking even from afar. Did Laijon create such masterpieces? Every load-bearing column was also made of marble, boasting carvings inlaid with gold. Then I gaped higher. The ceiling was painted with gold.

I sat back on my heels. It was astounding. The history represented there was incredible. How could Father say it held little interest? I squinted through the hole again and contrasted what was ancient from new tapestries clothing the walls, depicting sea and countryside, and the Chanji's chairs, built from our finest wood and decorated with semiprecious gems. These contemporary additions paled against the rest of the room.

Heat coursed through my veins. What else did Father omit? A gilded throne? Unfortunately, the listening hole only allowed me to see the gathering Chanji. I firmed my mouth and scanned for Jorai.

The king's Elite soldiers cast light for the meeting. Queen Umoli was already seated. The final councilmen and councilwomen were arriving.

Huari's seat remained empty. He probably planned a stupid, grand appearance.

I swallowed nerves, spied Srolo Faru's silver, braided beard, then found Jorai.

Dressed as prince, Jorai wore his crown and looked handsome in his finest silks. No cane, he hid his limp as best he could, and my heart tightened. I longed to shout encouragement down below. You can do this, Jorai. Tell them about the treasure and free yourself from Huari's schemes. Then I noticed that Jorai's hair was tied in its usual Nazakian knot. Why today? He alternated between interlacing his fingers and stuffing hands in his pockets, his habit when deliberating over something.

Deliberating? He better not.

Jorai looked toward my listening hole.

A jolt ran up my spine. I knew it was impossible for us to make eye contact, but it felt like we did. I expected to see fear or frustration, but his golden eyes filled with sorrow before glancing away.

I knew that look. Was he considering backing out of our plan?

"Imbecile. Of course Jorai sent you here."

6

I WHIRLED AND GAZED INTO

Crown Prince Huari's eyes. Gasped. Looked down.

He curled his fists and stepped closer. "Treasure won't strengthen Jorai's feeble grip on the throne."

Jorai despised the throne—

"Where did he find that gold?" Huari's hot whisper crawled over my skin. "No. I will learn soon enough. Resist me and I tell my father about your eavesdropping. I can't imagine what he will do to you. It will reflect badly on your mistress too. Kiboro acts like she is above the king's wrath. Do you want to test that?" He gripped my arm and dragged me through the cramped passages, down the skinny stairwell, until bursting into the palace foyer.

Soldiers saw us, and Huari plowed past them. One guard gave me a second glance before hurrying to open the double doors to the council chamber. To the Chanji.

I dug my heels.

With a hiss, Huari hauled me into the council chamber and flung me across the marble.

I caught myself on my hands and knees. I felt the stares, the confusion of Laijon's most powerful people. And then I saw marble steps leading to the foot of the throne. Not gilded. The throne looked like solid turquoise. Its sculpted back stretched to the ceiling, and its arms curved into chiseled trees, flowers, birds. Long, thin scars marred the smooth stone.

An older version of Huari sat upon the throne. Brocade robes wrapped around King Zaujo's thick frame. White-knuckled hands gripped a marble staff between leather-shod feet. A dark beard draped over his knees, and a crown rested heavily above frowning eyes directed toward his firstborn son.

I pressed my forehead against the floor and squeezed my eyes shut.

King Zaujo's large voice soared across the room. "Explain this."

Huari's voice turned meek. "Father, this servant is Jorai's plaything."

From the back of the room, Jorai shouted. "Is nothing beneath you, Huari? You dare drag her here—"

The king struck the steps with his staff. "Be silent."

I dared to peek.

King Zaujo looked like he battled to remain seated. He stretched one broad hand toward Jorai, but he watched Huari. "You arrive to this council late to report his dalliances?"

"Of course not, Father. The servant is also a thief." With triumphant flair, Huari lifted a gold flagon, encrusted with jewels, and its base wrapped in oractalm. The vessel from the tunnels. Everyone leaned forward to see better, even the Elite guards circling the chamber with hands full of light.

I glanced toward Jorai. His jaw dropped and his frame trembled, confirming that Huari had broken into his apartments. But Huari blamed me for theft.

Huari sighed. "After Jorai used her, this girl knew she must seek marriage or be ruined. Motivated by terror, she sought to provide a suitable dowry for a second-born prince through stealing. From the treasury, am I right, Father?"

Air whooshed out of me. Idiotic, conniving fabrication—

Huari eyed Jorai. "I demand she receive a traitor's punishment by public beheading."

Jorai's face bloomed scarlet. "She stole nothing." With shuffling steps, he stood between me and the throne and faced his father. "I found it. And not inside the treasury."

I stilled. No. I found it—

A muffled sound came from Huari. He glowed with delight. He had baited Jorai. Using me.

I choked. Jorai, stop talking.

Srolo Faru came forward and bowed. "My Majesty, Keeper of Light, it is I who guard your treasury, and I have no record of theft. Please allow me to take the flagon and investigate this. Even to maintain my own honor." He glanced at Huari. The hateful looks they exchanged startled me.

King Zaujo roared, "Chanji, be dismissed."

Shock rippled across the room before the council rose in a rustle of silks and exited.

Jorai reached out to help me.

Do not give strength to Huari's story. I stood on my own.

King Zaujo waved secondary guards and the royal scribe out, until he, his bodyguard, Huari, Jorai, Faru, and myself remained. The king's eyes darted between us before his voice lowered. "Bring me the flagon."

Huari raced up the stairs to the throne, held out the vessel, and bowed.

King Zaujo turned the flagon over. Weighed it in his palm, then opened his right hand. "I demand darkness."

The Elites closed their fists to extinguish their lights, and everyone lowered their gazes to the ground. I did too. It was said the king's gifting could permanently blind, stronger than Kiboro's—

King Zaujo's hand burst with powerful light. I could feel its brightness race across my skin, turn my eyelids red. After a long, moment, his light dimmed, and we lifted our heads.

The king now stood and held the flagon in front of him. Its oractalm embellishment glowed and washed the room in rosy light. Many gasped with awe, but the king's face twisted. He moaned aloud and gestured to Huari. "You did not recognize this?"

Huari paled. "Father?"

"Fool." King Zaujo spat and focused on Jorai. "By finding this, you have cursed us all."

My heart hitched. What in the continent?

The king's voice rose. "Where did you find this? Where is the rest?"

Jorai's throat convulsed. "I found it in the ocean. I swear there is nothing else."

"Liar. Just like your mother," King Zaujo snapped. "She chased the treasure to find the Eternity Gate, despite its curse. She, too, trespassed within the tunnels against my command, even prayed to spirits for guidance, the same ones who deformed you before birth. Now they led you to the treasure, recognizing your foul likeness."

King Zaujo was slipping into insanity. His eyes had gone wild. I took in a breath, and movement caught my eye.

Faru's hand slid to the hilt of his sword.

Jorai cried aloud and leapt upon the first stair to the throne. "Father, please." Elite guards stormed forward and restrained him.

"You're hiding the rest of the treasure from me!" The king was shrieking now. "You think to make gains for yourself, but you do not know the curse you have awakened. So comes Laijon's destruction." He signaled to the guards. "Imprison him."

Jorai fought as Elites pushed him toward the double door. He tripped and was jerked back to his feet.

I bit back a cry. Just before they reached the doors, Jorai saw me. His golden eyes rounded, and he mouthed something I could not catch. Then the doors shut behind them.

King Zaujo sat again. Shaking.

Huari's cautious voice floated over me. "Father, will you hear me?"

King Zaujo stared at the glowing flagon and did not speak.

Huari swiped hands down his robes. "I remember your stories now. About the glowing metal and the gate. But perhaps this moment is fated? Pirthyia is our enemy. Wouldn't this treasure, even bedeviled, strengthen Laijon to take back her rightful place on the continent? Is this not what we strive for? What of your glorious plans, Father? We could outfit our entire fleet with steam power from Ai'Biro. Perhaps even this curse could be used against Pirthyia—"

"If the treasure survives, the gate survives with it," King Zaujo hissed. "If the destruction failed, it falls upon us now. And you worry

about Pirthyia? You remember nothing I told you." The king glared
at his son. "Leave me. And curse you for bringing knowledge of the
treasure to my ear."

Huari quickly bowed and fled for the double doors.

I stood alone with the king and Srolo Faru. Did they not see me?
Should I go without dismissal? But then I noticed someone in the
ruby-tinted shadows.

Queen Umoli had remained. Silent. Watching.

King Zaujo did not see her and looked ready to tear the room
into shambles. Instead, he sagged, head resting in his hands. Sweat
glistened on his face.

Faru spoke. "I will question Prince Jorai about the treasure and
search the tunnels myself. Perhaps he speaks the truth and this
vessel is an anomaly."

"He hides the treasure. If you cannot find it, I will question
him. If he does not reveal the location, he will suffer the traitor's
sentence."

My knees weakened.

"Word of the treasure cannot spread. My own guard will watch
everyone who was present here. Including Huari," the king stated,
and then his eyes narrowed upon me.

I clasped my hands to my chest and bowed my head. Would
he arrest me, now, too? If Jorai is imprisoned, then take me, too,
because this was my fault—

Absence filled King Zaujo's expression until his eyes trailed
away. As if he forgot me.

Srolo Faru grasped my elbow. Tension rolled off of him in waves.
"I will escort her out, my king."

King Zaujo did not object, but drummed his hands against
his knees as he continued to stare at the flagon. Gaze full of
unruly storms.

Faru gave me a push and we left the council room and king. If
Queen Umoli exited, too, I did not see her. Faru waved the Elites
back inside the chamber and accompanied me out of the palace
onto the gravel entry.

Footsteps crunched behind us. I looked over my shoulder and cringed to see an Elite guard trailing from several lengths. Following me at the king's command. But Faru continued to walk beside me.

He smoothed his beard and said in a low tone, "Is there more treasure, srawa?"

Tears built behind me eyes, and I nodded.

"Then there isn't much time. I must do everything in my power to free Prince Jorai before the king can ruminate further over the old myths and strengthen his anger. I trust your loyalty and need your assistance. Will you help me?"

My throat tightened. "I will do anything."

Faru nodded. "I remember that you trained under your father Daemu in the Archives before becoming the princess's attendant. Can you translate old Laijonese?"

"Yes."

"There is a document among the king's possessions."

My heartrate quickened. What document?

"I fear involving anyone else to read it, including your father. But Jorai's life may depend on its interpretation and finding a loophole in the stories."

The Elite's footsteps drew closer.

"Wait for my word." Faru bowed and then turned for the palace.

I forced myself to keep walking. Beyond the palace grounds and city. Down paths slicing the hills and forest to the temple grounds.

I clung to Faru's revelations and passed within the walls of the women's compound. Only then did the Elite's silent, towering shadow cease. I plastered a serene expression on my face, and prepared to meet Kiboro—and tell her nothing of Jorai's plight.

7

JORAI WAS PUT UNDER HOUSE

arrest. Gossip would have abounded if he were sent to the dungeons. Kiboro remained ignorant of Jorai's arrest, but she would learn about it when she met with the queen again. Thinking about that made me sick. I would need to act as surprised and outraged as Kiboro would feel. Until then, I hid my grief and tried not to imagine Jorai locked in his apartments near the king and Huari. Was he safe? What if King Zaujo fell into one of his rages and Srolo Faru could not stop him?

Lost treasure.

My fault.

Jorai.

The bones in the Heart.

Jorai.

When would Srolo Faru summon me to translate that document?

On the second day, a soldier arrived at the women's compound. He gave Barano a letter addressed to Kiboro and waited outside for her reply. Kiboro opened the letter and announced that it was from a noblewoman requesting my services as translator. The lady wanted to draft a sale agreement between herself and an Ai'Biroan merchant. I had received interpretation requests like this before, and Kiboro dismissed me to meet the woman.

I followed the guard through woods toward the cliffs and city. Just beyond the temple, I caught the Elite trailing me. *Qo'tah.* I was glad Kiboro and Barano were not with me to notice him, and fixed my gaze on the path.

We reached the royal grounds and passed through its mighty walls. Sight of the palace chilled me. But Jorai was there. When the guard and I entered, I glanced between the colored walls and kept my back to the shut council chamber. I couldn't bear to look at it. The pedestals were empty of lightbearers, since no important function was in session, but there was no noblewoman.

Instead, Srolo Faru stood with hands behind his back, in full uniform.

My mustered strength wobbled with relief.

Faru dismissed the messenger soldier and faced me. "Hello, Srawa Seyo. Come." And he strode into the council chamber. Without the king's presence. No guard dared to question him.

I followed between those terrible double doors.

The room was dark, and our forms reflected against the marble floor. Columns and statues stood in ancient silence. We passed the turquoise throne and its crisscrossing scars. How was it scratched? From Shadows who haunted the palace during the Occupation?

Booted steps clipped behind me.

My heart jumped, but Srolo Faru ignored the Elite's presence and swept aside a wall tapestry depicting the sea to reveal a door. Faru unlocked the door and gestured me within. The tapestry swished into place as he bolted us inside.

The Elite's footsteps halted on the other side of the wall.

Pale blue illumination showered across the room. I spun to stare at Srolo Faru's hand full of sapphire light. Instead of a golden, glowing sphere, twin flashes of brightness, almost like flames, danced from his palm.

Faru crossed an ornate rug, past bookshelves and paintings, to a heavy desk. "Five guards keep Prince Jorai in his room. He is fed twice daily. The king has not summoned me to question him yet."

My heart twisted. "Does the king visit him?"

"No." Faru reached into his robes and laid a thin, leather book atop the desk. "Are you prepared, Seyo?"

"Yes." I had to be, but questions swirled through my mind. What was this book? I had never seen it before. Why wasn't it kept in the Archives with the other manuscript copies and surviving fragments? "What should I look for?"

"The location of the treasure." Faru paused. "Did Jorai tell you where he found the flagon in the tunnels?"

I struggled to speak. How much should I divulge? "In the bones of a river serpent. In a passage near the Heart."

Faru tugged on his beard. "River serpents breed in the depths. The treasure must be there, as the ancients thought."

I couldn't believe he was saying this. "Srolo Faru, Laijon's wealth was destroyed. Our history books tell us this, so do the schools and the older generations. The flagon must belong to some other trove." Except who else besides ancient Laijon possessed oractalm? Ignoring impropriety, I went on. "And the king fears the treasure. How will finding more help Jorai?" I dropped my gaze.

"Lift your eyes, Seyo. Your own doubts and fears are safe here, even shared." He spoke quietly and placed one hand behind his back. "I will talk freely. King Zaujo has knowledge passed on by his fathers, stories concealed for generations. It seems impossible now, but Laijon possesses an illustrious history. She was filled with great riches. The glowing red metal was a key export for many years, the harbor was an intercontinental hub for trade, and the finest youths of every nation trained at our universities. Laijon was famous for wisdom and wealth. It is said great Pirthyia's present might cannot compare. Then the Occupation came and Laijon fell. Enemies gathered Laijon's unfathomable riches with the wealth of every other conquered nation. When the enemy faced defeat, they tried to destroy it all." He looked at me. "But you already know this. Yet tales spread that the treasure survived. For a century after the Occupation, royal historians pored over manuscripts looking for it. Kings sent armies into the tunnels, countryside, and city to search. Finally, they gave up." Faru tapped the book. "Many believed that these pages contained the location to the treasure, but the search was given up two centuries ago, when the gates were installed to seal the tunnels. This book has been hidden in the palace ever since. I doubt even your father has seen it."

I struggled to keep my breathing even. Kings searched for the treasure for a hundred years, after so many agreed that our wealth was lost? Yet Srolo Faru expected me to interpret this book and succeed in finding the location of the treasure where so many failed. For what purpose? I bit my lip. Faru had proven himself loyal to Jorai. I needed to trust and try.

Faru beckoned me to the desk. "Come."

I obeyed and studied the book cover. The leather was plain and modern. Rebound. I turned to the first page and stilled.

The manuscript was made of yellow, folded linen, darkened with age. No one wrote on such material since the sixth century. This was a surviving original. Its beauty stole my breath.

"I need not instruct you to treat the pages with care."

"No, srolo."

Faru lowered his handful of sapphire light closer to me. A little embarrassed he remembered my lack of gifting, I murmured thanks.

Against the linen, ink faded and swam in an accomplished, feminine hand. Ancient Laijonese. I sought familiar shapes and root words then tasted the first line. *To my unknown son.* "Srolo Faru, what is this?"

He bent close. "It is my understanding that it is a bimil, a diary, of one of Laijon's princesses, who was a prisoner during the Occupation."

Nothing could have surprised me more. The royal family perished by sword during the Occupation. How had a princess survived, let alone this document?

I turned soft, fragile pages. The letters and conjugations were informal, confirming that it was a personal bimil. Any other time, I would have been thrilled to hold this in my hands. The thickness of the old words would need to be searched thoroughly, but they were not impossible to translate. There were so many passages within the folded material. I skimmed as best I could. I cringed as she described her capture. "Interpretation will require time."

Faru grunted over my shoulder. "There is only one portion useful to us." He reached and flipped to the last quarter of the manuscript. His fingers were better accustomed to handling weaponry. I tried not to avert my eyes from his rough touch.

He pointed. "What does this say?"

I peered at the page. Except for a handful of lines, it lay blank. It was an expensive waste of parchment in those days, especially for a prisoner of war. These lines would be important. The wording was different and formal, as if the princess quoted someone else.

"Seyo?"

I whispered the words to myself, and then out loud, "After the unfaithful era, a second generation will find the Gate to Eternity and bow before the power of the Father of Light. Destruction will be allotted with fire and water. An evil one will arise. The one chosen to open the gate, of royal blood and disfigured, will welcome judgment from Heaven, and the one born of legend will slay her own soul to finish the age." Shivers raced across my skin.

"Read it again."

I did, and a third time, finally a fourth. One line cut deeper and deeper into my mind. *The one chosen to open the gate, of royal blood and disfigured.* Like Jorai.

"The Eternity Gate," Faru murmured. "If only I could read it myself." His voice tightened. "Are you sure this interpretation is correct?"

"Yes. What is this, srolo?"

"It is believed to be a prophecy. Whispered by memory from king to king, it contains the curse that King Zaujo fears."

I tried to sift through a connection. "Was this Eternity Gate gathered with the treasure?"

"Yes."

But there was no gate in the Heart. "What is it? The Eternity Gate?"

Faru shook his head. "I don't know."

"Srolo Faru, the king must be told that this prophecy is fulfilled. Laijon was already destroyed and judged during the Occupation." I ignored the last part about the slain soul. It sounded like the ravings of a lunatic, and I couldn't stand anymore of that.

"The king believes that the Eternity Gate was never opened."

As I tried to make sense of his words, pieces started to fit. Our mad king feared the curse of judgment from the Eternity Gate, which was supposed to be hoarded among the treasure. Jorai found treasure and matched the description of the chosen gate opener in the prophecy. So King Zaujo imprisoned his second son.

Srolo Faru's expression pinched. He was nonreligious, and wary of prophecy and judgment, yet we had to be thinking the same thing. I was terrified for Jorai. We must keep looking. I turned the parchment.

"Seyo—"

The page fell, and I blinked. This passage was brief and badly scrawled, as if by a child's clumsy fist. But the letters, or glyphs, really, were too small for a child. The symbols showed a rhythm, if unfamiliar. I had never seen this language or such terrible handwriting before. What a ruin of torturous shapes. Then one symbol leapt out, or rather, the marking above it. I had seen this before in a religious context. It was a version of the personal name of God. Every language possessed a symbol similar to this, and it was always ascribed to deity.

I felt Srolo Faru's stare.

"Seyo, can you read this?"

"I recognize one symbol." I looked up. Faru's fierce expression alarmed me. "What is it?"

He straightened, and blue light lessened upon the page. "You don't want to know."

My heartbeat quickened. "Srolo?"

"It is the Shadows' language."

My stomach turned over. I remembered the shrieking statue Jorai and I had found at the Heart. Images of leathery wings filled my mind, monsters devouring Laijon's children, filling the palace. Fisted claws gripping a quill, standing over the princess's body, clutching this book, a creature doomed to eternal agony—

I drew back.

Faru grimaced. "I apologize, Seyo. I should have stopped you from reading."

I shook my head and pressed damp palms down my overlay. But a dirty feeling seeped into my bones.

Faru closed the bimil. "It is time you returned to the temple. I must think and plan." His gaze pierced me. "Seyo, no one can learn about our meeting today. And no one can know anything about this book. Not Kiboro. Not your father."

No. I had to stay until I found the location of the treasure. I couldn't fail. "Yes, srolo. But—"

His gaze softened. "Keep hope. We will meet again." He closed his fist and darkness enveloped the room. Like Shadows.

I swallowed and followed him out. My mind swirled, and I barely noticed the Elite as we passed him or the throne, with its long, haunting scars.

When I returned to Kiboro's apartments, exhausted, she met me with blazing eyes. "Guards say Jorai is under house arrest. Temple helpers are whispering about lost treasure."

I stilled. How had word gotten out?

"Mother visited while you were away." Kiboro's mouth tightened. "Why didn't you tell me, Seyo?"

Had Queen Umoli shared everything? Joari's face flashed through my mind. It all became too much. I dropped my face into my hands and began to weep.

Kiboro sat me on her bed and gently held my head against her shoulder. My height made my neck ache, but I accepted her comfort. I told her about the Heart, finding the treasure, Huari, the Chanji, Jorai's horrible arrest, the Elite that now followed me. Everything except meeting with Faru and reading the bimil.

Kiboro trembled, but stroked my head, as her mother must

do for her. Fresh tears fell, and I clung to the closeness of our friendship.

Then she straightened. "We must pray for Jorai's release at the Handprint of God."

The most holy site. Everything within me balked. How could I go there, steeped in so many secrets and lies? But when she grabbed her cape and summoned Barano, I followed.

We entered the temple, washed our hands in the bowls of cleansing water, accepted a priest's anointing, and exited through a back door into adjacent gardens. Down a lonely path, a tangle of bushes and trees stood hemmed by a rustic fence. Among these brambles and weeds, the Father of Light shaped the world and commanded Laijon to dig a well. The grounds were left wild in the belief that no garden could do the site justice. Once a year, the high priest or priestess drew well water for sacred cleansing. Sometimes I dreamed of joining those who served them in this holy task, even though I wasn't gifted. Even though I was only half-Laijonese. How many times had I stood here and wondered why the Father of Light entrusted small Laijon with light, the first of the giftings, and placed us in this corner of the continent? The holy Nho said that at the beginning of the end of days, Heaven's Doorway would open here at the Handprint of God.

Kiboro knelt in the undergrowth and filled her hands with light.

I realized I forgot my candle. Horrified, I lifted my empty hands and quickly bowed. Kiboro whispered the first adulation fervently, and I joined her, "Holy, holy Father of Light, ruler of every continent and the heavens, you, who visit your creation, are one and unlike other gods. Thank you for watching over Laijon, your humble nation. Thank you for seeing us. Forgive our sins. Forgive . . ."

I tried to recount my sins, but the list was endless. Tunnels. Treasure. Shadows. Curses. Jorai. Lies. I felt filthy and craved to wash my hands again. And again. Also my face. Every part of me. I groaned, and petition escaped my lips. "Please protect Jorai. Please help me." Then I cringed. I was unworthy to ask the Father of Light for anything, especially now. But no lightning struck. Rather, a gentle breeze swept over my bowed form.

Kiboro began the traditional closing prayer. "Laijon waits upon the day you rescue us from our oppressors . . ."

Rescue—Father's face invaded my mind, and I startled. He might have answers about the bimil's prophecy, yet something inside me recoiled. Srolo Faru said not to tell anyone about the bimil. How could I get around that? How could I ask Father for help when he offered me half-truths over and over?

For Jorai, I must try.

8

THE NEXT MORNING, A LETTER

lay tucked into our laundry basket. With my name scribbled across the top. What in the continent? While Kiboro bathed, I opened the note.

> *Jorai gave you something that belongs to the king. My servant will retrieve it. Meet him outside tonight, or else.*

This was a child's tantrum and unsigned, but the expensive stationery gave Huari away. I could have spit. Huari had never tried to contact me before, and the only thing Jorai had given me was the oractalm bracelet, hidden away. Huari couldn't mean that, so what did he want? More treasure? I wouldn't meet his nasty valet.

I shredded the letter into the chamber pot, disposed of its contents, and prepared to meet with my father. I had asked Kiboro's permission to meet Father at the temple. When I told her I hoped to find a way to free Jorai, she had gripped my hands and wished me Heaven's success.

After dressing Kiboro, I left the women's compound. Within moments, the Elite followed me. Barano noticed him the first day, and, of course, I told Kiboro that I was being watched. Today, the Elite was staying closer than ever. I couldn't prevent him from observing my conversation with Father, but I would stop him from eavesdropping. So, which language should Father and I speak? The international trade language was too common and soldiers were required to know it. Ai'Biroan was flowery, and time was precious. Speaking Pirthyian was akin to chewing with an open mouth.

The sun-drenched temple loomed ahead. I paced the grounds as I waited and inspected each approaching visitor. Then I saw a middle-aged man wearing a belted tunic and trousers in rough cloth, common dress for those living in the city. Father's shoulders hunched, graying hair tousled as always. His dark, expressive eyes, like Roji's, swept back and forth until he saw me, then he smiled and waved.

I made myself wave back. I wanted both to fall into his embrace and cry, but also cross my arms and frown.

He approached with a bow, and I returned the gesture. As elder, Father should initiate conversation, but we couldn't speak Laijonese in front of the Elite. I thought of Jorai and opened my mouth with Nazakian, curt and bold. "Good morning, Father. May light guide your path."

Father raised an eyebrow, but replied likewise in Nazakian. "Daughter, may the morning sun warm every day of your life. And to see you in blue." Then his gaze wandered to the Elite and froze. His happiness in seeing me fled, and he spoke faster. "Why are you being guarded? Is the princess in danger?"

The Elite's brow knit. Thank the Father of Light, he didn't understand us.

"No," I said. "Please, let's walk."

We circled the temple, and the Elite stalked after us.

My breath quickened. "Continue to speak Nazakian. Pretend we are practicing. Offer me a correction every so often in Laijonese."

"Seyo, what is going on?"

I had prepared to give my rehearsed speech. Calmly. Self-controlled. Instead, I blurted, "What is the Eternity Gate? Is it real? Do you know about its prophecy? If you do, why did you hide it from me?"

Father's pace slowed. He pondered the passing gardens, just

starting to bloom. "Knowledge of our past is dangerous. I wanted to protect you."

Ignorance safeguarded no one.

"Why is the Elite here?"

I bristled. Why should I answer when he did not? "I am sworn to secrecy, but I need help." An edge crept into my voice. "Will you?"

"Always, Seyo."

Shame crept over me. "You have heard of Prince Jorai's house arrest."

Distaste flickered in his gaze. "Yes."

Why did he look that way? Was it because of Jorai's arrest, or because he disliked Jorai? "He entered the tunnels and discovered a flagon." Except whose fault was that? "It was made of gold, jewels—and oractalm." I hesitated and assessed Father's reaction. He stood erect, seemingly attentive on the gardens. I continued, "The king found out. He believes this flagon is part of Laijon's lost treasure and is terrified of an Eternity Gate that could bring judgment to all. The king thinks the prince hides the rest of the treasure and had him imprisoned. You know Jorai is my friend. I fear for him. I need to learn the truth about the Eternity Gate and where it last stood, to free Jorai." That was Srolo Faru's plan, wasn't it? My brain felt so scrambled. "Can you help me?"

Father began to walk again. "How did you learn about the treasure? And the Eternity Gate?"

I could not tell him about the tunnels, the Chanji, or Srolo Faru. "I am Princess Kiboro's attendant and hear many things."

His expression was still slightly puzzled, but he nodded. "Then the Elite follows you because of the princess's knowledge, which she learned from the king or her brothers."

I let silence be my answer. Even if it counted as another lie?

"Seyo, you must promise not to tell anyone what I am about to say."

The intensity in his gaze surprised me. "I promise, Father. I only want to find or disprove the treasure."

Father discreetly looked back at the Elite and lengthened his stride. "Laijon has sought this treasure for generations, despite the razing. Do you know why our enemies tried to destroy it?"

"No."

Father passed a hand over his chin. "It is said the enemy received a sign that the Eternity Gate held divine power. They wanted to take this for themselves and traveled across the sea to Laijon. When they conquered our people, they found the Eternity Gate and tried to open it, but failed. When the battle turned against them, they blamed it on the Eternity Gate. They ordered their monsters to carry it and all of the treasure away—many believe to the tunnels— and lit it with an unnatural fire they bartered from Vedoa."

Vedoa. As soon as Laijon fell, the fire wielders left their deserts to pick our remains.

"After Pirthyia came to our aid and beat the enemy back into the sea, Vedoa retreated, Laijon's remnant rejoined the war, but no one could find the treasure or the gate."

I knew all of this. "What is the Eternity Gate?" Maybe this time I'd get an answer.

"Do you remember stories of Laijon's mines?"

"Yes."

"Do you remember where the mines came from?"

"They were a gift from the Father of Light. At the beginning of time, he gave the first nations doorways that opened to gifts, such as Nazak's great river."

"The Eternity Gate is Laijon's second gift."

I blinked. "None of the first nations received two doorways."

"Laijon did. The Eternity Gate was a final doorway, and it was never opened. Rumors spread that it was filled with divine treasure to make Laijon the greatest nation in the world. Laijon was already wealthy, and when the enemy king from across the sea, dressed in rags, bartered for the gate, Laijon's king at that time gave it to him. I think Laijon trusted the gold of a stranger more than the Father of Light's promise. This betrayal was the start of the Occupation and Laijon's fall."

I was aghast. "I cannot believe this."

"Greed is dangerous. When the enemy could not open the Eternity Gate, they declared that it was cursed and tried to destroy it. It was believed they succeeded, until a prophecy arose." Then Father opened his mouth and recited it.

My heart beat against my ribs. Some words were different, especially translated into the Nazak language, but it was the same prophecy written in the bimil. An unfaithful era. A second generation to find the Eternity Gate and bow before the Father of Light. Destruction with fire and water. An evil one. The person chosen to open the gate, of royal blood and disfigured. Judgment from Heaven. That strange slain soul again.

"How do you know this?" I asked.

"The prophecy has been passed down through my family. Now, I give it to you. I cannot pretend to understand it, but this is why the king fears the treasure. A belief was coupled with the prophecy, that if the treasure was found again, the omen was near fulfillment. It has long been held that both treasure and the Eternity Gate survived together, or nothing did at all."

I summoned my voice. "What is the evil one?"

Father's expression grew more somber. "Those who first listened to the prophecy feared it meant that Shadows would return."

I inhaled sharply. "Shadows were destroyed in the last battles. And you taught me that the last Shadow was cornered in the northern mountains, slain, chained, and thrown in a lake of ice. You said every document describing the plans for building Shadows from human bodies, along with the accompanying spells, were burned." How anyone consented to the transformation, I couldn't guess. The Shadow form promised power and near indestructability and seduced many into undergoing the vile surgery. It was a piece of our enemy's history all strove to forget.

"Yes, and some have theorized that the evil one could be more enemies from across the sea, or perhaps an organized attack by the mountain tribes. Even Pirthyia."

I felt betrayed. I had spent years studying Laijon's past. How could he keep all of this from me?

His voice broke my thoughts. "The oractalm flagon was found in the tunnels?"

I did not want to answer. "Inside the bones of a river serpent."

"Who else knows of this?"

"Very few." I felt the Elite's glare upon my back.

"Good. If word spreads, every nation will come looking for the treasure."

"Wouldn't everyone fear the Eternity Gate?"

"Every country has their records of the Occupation and the Eternity Gate. Some, like King Zaujo, will fear the prophecy and its promise of judgment. Others will believe that the gate holds divine power, even immortality."

I shook my head. I could not accept this. It was too much—

"There is one more thing." Father's voice gained energy, like when we would work in the Archives and he would pause over a tome before excitedly sharing a new fact. "There are some who call themselves *i Bodask*." He emphasized the Nazakian phrase.

"The Brotherhood?"

Father nodded. "This Brotherhood has devoted their lives, even generations, to opening the Eternity Gate. They believe Laijon remains shackled by her sin of bartering the gate away to her enemies, and that opening the gate will free her."

"You mean there is a group of Nazakians looking to open the gate and unleash judgment on Laijon?" I imagined a handful of ragtag, wild-eyed people waiting to destroy Laijon. Frankly, the Brotherhood was the least of my worries. "Father, what do you believe?"

He paused. "If the Eternity Gate still stands, no one will know until it is opened."

A vague answer. Of course.

"But no one walked away from the Occupation rich. Going back to your first question, Seyo, I do not know where the treasure and Eternity Gate could be hidden. Even our kings do not know. But some believe the answer lies within a book."

My attention perked.

He sighed. "I have longed to see this book. It was written by a prisoner during the Occupation, and many believe it contains the location of the treasure in code. But it is kept in the palace, and none but the king may see it. Once, when I served on the Chanji, Srolo Faru asked if I could read it to him. That might surprise you, but Faru has a strong interest in our history. I told him it was not kept in the Archives. Now that I remember this, my grandfather told me that a key was kept in the book. Naturally, some wonder if this key could unlock the Eternity Gate."

My head swam. Srolo Faru had brought me the book, and there was no key inside its pages. I must read the entire bimil or drain the tunnels and search for the treasure myself.

"Seyo, Prince Jorai will be best helped by time. If more treasure isn't found and word does not spread, King Zaujo will calm and release him." He frowned. "Do you know if there is more treasure?"

Just then the Elite grunted loudly. Father bristled, but I smiled and switched to Laijonese. "Thank you for practicing with me today."

Something flickered in Father's eyes. He wanted my answer, but instead bowed over my hand. "Your skill with language grows every day, daughter." He said it loudly for the sake of the Elite, then cleared his throat. "How is Roji?"

My heart tightened. How I missed when the two of them could talk civilly. "He is well."

"Good." Father's gaze drifted until I squeezed his hand.

We shared farewells and I hurried to the women's compound. The Elite followed, and I could sense his frustration. I ignored him and tried to think how to ask Srolo Faru to let me read the bimil again. Could I send him a note? How?

I entered the compound, escaping the Elite's presence, and found temple helpers clustered in the hallway, even some in blue. Earlier, all they could talk about were predictions concerning the coming monsoon season. Whether the city would be ready for street flooding where their parents lived, or how many vendors' carts would be damaged or overturned this year. I cut around them and their chatter until—

"The second prince was sent to the dungeons."

I stopped. My heart leapt into my throat.

"I heard that he stole something. Did he already have a trial?"

"It was called off," a third voice almost whispered. "A guard told me that the king has fallen into a terrible state. But can you guess which cell they put the prince in?"

The first girl answered in a low tone. "He's in the second queen's old cell. The one where she killed herself."

9

IF THE ELITE REPORTED MY
meeting with Father, nothing came of it.

King Zaujo forbade anyone from visiting Jorai in jail. Even
Kiboro was turned away.

The treasure remained a secret.

Kiboro and I spent hours praying. When I ran out of confessions,
I recited them again. But it felt empty. Meaningless. As if the Father
of Light had shut Heaven's door.

At last, another soldier brought a letter requesting my services as
interpreter, this time to decipher a nobleman's will in old Laijonese.

Inside the palace, Srolo Faru led me into the council chamber,
pushed the tapestry aside, and beckoned me into the cool darkness
of the secret room. The Elite's footsteps stopped on the other side
of the closed door. Again, I marveled that Srolo Faru didn't worry
about his presence. Blue light filled the room and Faru lifted the
brightness high as he pressed his free hand against the desk.

I waited for him to pull the bimil from his belt. Readied my
mind to attack its language and find Jorai's freedom. Even if I
had to read—

"The king remembered that the monsoon rains start soon.
When the rains fall, the tunnels will flood and make it almost
impossible to search for treasure until the end of summer. Soldiers
began exploring the Heart three days ago and found a mass grave
of river serpent bones filled with treasure."

I tensed.

Srolo Faru leaned into the desk and spoke with difficulty. "Early this morning, a soldier brought me two river serpents in a bag. Alive. Both were slain, and it was discovered they had recently swallowed a handful of jewelry, including some made of the glowing metal." He lifted his head to me. "I am required to report this to the king during our daily assembly. This will not ease Prince Jorai's treatment." His gaze searched mine. "Seyo, how strong is your loyalty to Prince Jorai?"

The question twisted around my mind. I imagined facing Jorai, looking into his golden eyes, knowing I had thrown him into this mess. "I would do anything to free him," I said, and meant it with all my heart.

Faru nodded. "Then I ask you to make a difficult choice, though the question shames me. Since seeing the treasure, rage has consumed King Zaujo. He refuses to sleep or eat. He speaks to himself and cannot be swayed from believing that Prince Jorai has brought a curse upon Laijon. At best, I fear Jorai will face a difficult exile. At best." Faru pushed away from the desk. "I would like to send him away before that order is given, or one that is worse. If travel is necessary, he must begin before the rains."

Jorai exiled? For how long? My throat thickened.

"I can remove him from the dungeons and hide him in the temple," Faru continued, "where he will be able to enter and leave with less suspicion. I will supply you with provisions and commoner's clothing before you meet him. Both of you must travel northwest by foot to the borders of the desert. It will be a long journey with his limp, but this path will be harder for the king's search party to follow. You, as a woman, will help disguise Jorai during his journey. You can pretend to be married, or brother and sister. A contact will meet you and take Jorai into hiding. After this, you can return to Laijon. Hopefully, your journey will last less than ten days." He began to pace. "After Jorai is safely away, I plan to take Princess Kiboro into my confidence. She will help spread the belief that you have taken ill. Ah, if only I could send soldiers too. I would go myself, if I did not believe my presence in Laijon will ultimately help Jorai more." He stopped before me. "If you agree to this, you must keep this plan a secret and depart as soon as possible. If you do not agree, I believe you will remain trustworthy and forget this conversation. If I did not believe that, I would never have asked you to undergo this. I will try to find another way to bring Jorai to safety."

My heart pounded. This plan bordered on traitorous, and yet he offered me a choice. What if something went wrong? Traveling the remote north was perilous. Too close to Vedoa. But Jorai was in far greater danger right now. And when he told the king he found treasure, he lied and left me out of it to protect me.

I drew a shaky breath. "How do I meet Jorai?"

Relief flooded Faru's gaze. "Enter the temple before dawn. Can you manage this without telling Princess Kiboro?"

Tonight. My heart now thundered. "Yes."

"Dress in your simplest, warmest clothing. Bring nothing extra. Tell no one what you are doing. You will find supplies and a map left on the temple balcony. Take these and wait. Prince Jorai will arrive after dawn breaks, after the prison guard rotates. When you find him, flee north immediately."

"What of my Elite?"

"I will take care of him." He inclined his head to me. "Thank you, Srawa Seyo. Now, you must return to your quarters and prepare."

I returned to the women's compound. Kiboro and Barano were not yet back from university.

I tidied our room in an attempt to distract myself, then paused before a vase of flowers. The resident priestess must have received the vase and brought it here. A tiny note was tucked among the blooms.

Don't toy with me. Hand it over tonight.

- H

Huari, again? I was too frustrated to be afraid. What in the continent did he want, besides the bracelet? Thankfully, Jorai would no longer need to be concerned about his elder half brother after tonight. So the bracelet stayed under my bed, and Huari's second note also went into the chamber pot.

When Kiboro returned, she had a sour expression, and immediately began dressing herself for bed. I hurried to assist.

Kiboro glared at the paper window. "I want to skip evening meal to pray for Jorai."

I nodded, but could not reply. My voice would wobble and I would break down and tell her everything. But I couldn't.

Oh, Jorai. Will you be safe in exile? Once I leave you there, when will I see you again?

10

KIBORO WAS SO DISTRAUGHT
over Jorai's imprisonment, I convinced her to spend the night with
her mother. I assured her that I would be fine alone at the women's
compound. The whole plan was far too simple.

After she and Barano left, I lit a candle and made confessions.
Prayer felt systematic. I finished and changed into plain, warm
clothing, like Srolo Faru had instructed me, garments I wore before
becoming Kiboro's attendant and began serving at the temple. I
covered my hair, wrapped everything else into my blanket, and
swung the small bundle over my shoulder. Jorai's bracelet went into
my skirt pocket.

I blew out the candle and waited. The resident priestess
approached our door, paused to check that lights were out, and
then padded down the hall to the other temple helpers' rooms. I
kept listening.

Srolo Faru said to leave near dawn, but I knew the temple better
than he did. It was wiser to leave now. The temple doors would
remain open for another fingerlength of the moon to accommodate
late-night workers coming from the city. I would pretend to be one
of them, sneak up to the balcony, spend the night there, and wait
until Jorai arrived after sunrise. I longed to leave a note for Kiboro,
Roji, and Father. I didn't want them to worry. But Faru had forbid
telling anyone.

The priestess's footsteps disappeared around the hallway corner.

I stepped out the door and left the women's compound.

Wind disturbed the now-leafy treetops as I hurried along the paths, listening. I whirled once to peer into the darkness behind me. The Elite was not there, as Faru promised. I continued on and reached the temple. Stairs to the balcony climbed the outside walls, where the outliers of society would not need to wash their hands or be anointed by a priest to enter the sacred sanctuary. I followed the curving steps to the top.

The warm breezes whipped across the landing and spilled evening mist over the painted wood railing. The temple gardens sprawled below. Overhead, sloped roofing protected from the elements. Beyond, moonlight vanished behind angry clouds. Would the first seasonal storm strike tonight? There couldn't be worse timing.

Thick columns supported the roofing and served to divide the balcony into private segments. I circled one pillar and peeked beyond the gloom of the second. As usual, the balcony lay vacant. Small windows were cut into the temple wall and covered with murky glass that allowed one to perceive lightbearing ceremonies below. But no one would spot me up here. Then I saw a burlap sack. Had the supplies for Jorai and me already been delivered? I carried the heavy sack past two more columns and crouched to look inside. Skins of water, dried food, and a dagger hilt.

The lights inside the temple went out. Only one priest or priestess would stay overnight, and the doors would remain locked until sunrise.

My stomach rumbled, but I didn't touch the food. I would wait to eat with Jorai, after we began traveling north. Tears pricked my eyes, and I brushed them away. I should sleep or confess again.

Movement rustled by the stairs.

My nerves jumped. Why hadn't I heard the worshipper climbing the stairs? A whisper rode the mist. I froze, then heard it again.

. . . *Seyo* . . .

Who was it? I peeked around the pillar, but saw no one. Someone had said my name. What if it was the Elite? The wind carried a low, pained sound. Someone stood behind the first pillar.

I swallowed, and then the person dashed through the darkness and hid behind the second column. A bent-over form in a hooded cloak, perhaps hunchbacked. There was a whimper.

I dared to speak. "Who are you?"

Something scraped against the column. White, piercing eyes glinted in the moonlight. Heavy arms hung toward the ground, dangling from a terrible, arched back.

I clapped my hands over my mouth.

The monster sped toward me. I lurched for the sack, but was shoved against the ground. I tried to scream, but an arm covered my mouth and I was dragged toward the fourth pillar.

I struggled against the thin, wiry body and my vision blurred. I was rolled onto my stomach and pressed into the ground. I reached for the bag again, and my fingers closed around the knife hilt. The beast's muscles loosened, and I wrenched away and held the dagger in front of me.

It glared from under a hooded cloak, then cried my name. The face hidden with human hands.

I almost retched, and the dagger wobbled in my hands. "Jorai?"

He curled forward, emphasizing the grotesque curve of his back, a bundle under his cloak.

"Jorai. I did not know you—"

His moan terrified me. I shushed him, dropped the dagger, and held out my hands. He did not take them. Then I saw the cuts and bruises on his face and arms. The crusts of blood. I gasped.

He backed away. "Don't look at me."

"They tortured you."

"Two guards jumped me in jail . . . blindfolded me . . . they took me apart and put me back together . . . rods and hooks. So much chanting . . . I couldn't understand a word of it. I fought them." His voice sped. "I did something terrible, Seyo. It was an accident. I swear. They would have killed me if I hadn't."

My tongue stuck. "What—"

"I swear." I'd never heard him so broken. Quiet sobbing wracked his frame. "Forgive me."

I pressed my hands together and quieted my inner horror. I didn't know what to do. Should we stick to the plan, or go to Srolo Faru and hide him in Laijon, where we could tend to his wounds? Then I realized the time. He'd arrived so early.

Do not hesitate to flee, Srolo Faru had said.

I drew closer and whispered, "Remember the plan to free you. Srolo Faru has gone to great lengths to save you, even given supplies. We must go now."

He looked at me like a child. "What are you talking about?"

"Didn't Srolo Faru explain this before you were released?"

Jorai turned his head. Filtered moonlight illuminated damaged skin stretched over his pronounced cheekbones. "I freed myself."

Hair rose on the back of my neck. "How?"

This new version of Jorai whimpered once again. "I'm . . . I'm so sorry, Seyo."

I felt helpless. I gently took his hands in mine. It was forward, but—

Jorai clutched my hands, then winced, as he straightened his back. What had they done to him? I looked over his shoulder and again noticed the lump under his cloak.

He held onto me, rocking us back and forth. "I promise I will make myself right."

"You will rest and heal when we reach safety."

"You are so faithful." He made a choking sound, then released me to rummage within his cloak. "I need you to keep something for me."

What in the continent? "I will, if you promise that we will leave. Immediately."

He uttered an undecipherable sound. "Yes. We will leave." He pressed closed fingers against my palm, and then opened them to reveal something hard, rough, and cold. He grabbed my other hand and placed it over the object.

"I want you to keep this," he said urgently. "I found it with the key to the Heart, wasting away in my father's apartments. I think I know what it is, and it should protect you. I want you to keep it hidden. Keep it a secret until I return, from everyone, even Faru."

He shuffled back. "When the country believes I am murdered, pretend to mourn me. Do not tell anyone that you have seen me. No one."

My heart galloped. I ignored the gift. "You promised to go with me."

He would not meet my gaze. "I said that we would both leave. In three days, I will come back for you. First, I must flee to the mountains and hide from those who attacked me. They'll be searching for me to finish what they started."

Qo'tah. He wasn't making any sense. "Faru will stop those guards. The mountains are far and dangerous—"

"If I don't return, then I am destroyed and you must forget me." He pushed me back. "Don't look at me. Don't remember me this way."

I gritted my teeth. This was madness. Like the king—

The object he gave me bit my palm. I glanced into my hand. A skeleton key lay against my fingers. Tarnished to the color of charcoal, jagged, chipped, ancient. My memory fought me, then I remembered seeing Jorai holding it while opening the door to the tunnel gate, one of two keys he'd found in a book. This was the one that hadn't fit. How would it protect me? My heart froze. The key that Father said was supposed to be tucked within the pages of the bimil.

Jorai had given me the key to the Eternity Gate.

He hoisted the sack of supplies into his arms, effortlessly despite exhaustion, then scaled the railing and crouched, overlooking the edge. His cloak swung behind him. His back bent.

He wouldn't jump. He couldn't.

Jorai twisted his arm to reach under his cloak, and something like poles and sheets of leather unfolded from one shoulder blade and then the other. He hissed with agony, then the wind tossed his cloak. The back of his shirt was torn. Fresh blood glistened across long, brown wounds and metal hooks embedded into the muscles of his back. Using his hands, he extended the poles, and the material unfolded into something like wings.

I stared, speechless. Unmoving.

Jorai bent his knees and cast himself off the railing. A howl rent the night, and I dashed to the edge. And saw mists.

Silence.

I shrieked and tore around the pillars, down the stairs, and fled into the forest. I circled the premises, but Jorai had disappeared.

I collapsed to the ground and wept.

Kiboro returned midmorning. She remained agitated, and did not notice my distress. When we left the women's compound for prayer, my Elite followed again.

That afternoon, news spread that a bloody body, battered beyond recognition, was found in Prince Jorai's cell, with the keys hanging from the door lock. But I knew the corpse was not his.

The first day passed. I fasted. I confessed.

Kiboro mourned and refused to leave her room.

Barano draped cloth dyed in somber colors over our doorframe.

Jorai's death was whispered to be suicide, like his mother's.

Lies.

I traded my blue overlays for gray and smudged ash onto my face and the backs of my hands.

Lies.

While Kiboro slept, I tied a ribbon around the key and wore it like a necklace under my clothing. It lay across my sternum. Cold. Heavy. At last, I knew what Huari wanted.

The second day passed. Prince Jorai's funeral would be held on the fourth day. I promised myself that the ceremony would be called off when he returned. Until then, I continued to fast and confess.

No word came from Srolo Faru.

Rumors spread that the king did not don mourning clothes.

The first monsoon rains fell.

The third day, I awoke before dawn. Jorai said he would return today.

Kiboro tossed in her sleep and slept late. I would have to make do with sunrise prayer in our room again, and bowed from my pallet. The weighty key dragged my neck toward the ground under my clothing.

Who had hurt Jorai? Whose mind was so twisted as to try to make him in the image of . . . a Shadow? If only I had told the king that I'd found the treasure. Something rational whispered that it wouldn't have helped Jorai. But I suppressed a moan and prayed with silent lips. *I am not good enough, but I have nothing more I can give. I do not bother you with petitions, Holy One. But please, let my mistakes not be used against Jorai any longer.* Tears rolled down my cheeks. *Please, please, let Jorai be kept safe.*

A whisper of peace danced over my soul, followed by despair. What did it mean?

That third night, I snuck out of Kiboro's room.

Barano, standing guard in the hallway, saw me. We maintained eye contact until he touched his chest, where the medal of valor hung, and looked aside. He would keep his silence.

I bowed and left.

The Handprint of God stood in full growth under another cloudy evening. Somehow, seeing the holy site filled me with a glimmer of courage.

Jorai said he would return tonight. But what if he couldn't? What if the hooks and the terrible mockery of wings—

I pushed such imaginings from my mind and waited.

And waited.

Weariness hounded me. The key lay so heavy against me.

Keep it secret until I return, he had said.

And waited.

At last, ghostly fingers of pale orange brushed the horizon.

Jorai did not come.

11

IN THREE DAYS, I WILL COME BACK

for you . . . when the country believes I am murdered, pretend to mourn me . . . if I don't return, then I am destroyed and you must forget me.

Jorai's funeral arrived. The rains continued.

I woke early, dressed in mourning colors, and paused to collect myself. Jorai would come back. He was alive. I wouldn't accept anything else. I slipped the key under my collar when Kiboro stirred.

After we picked at our morning meal, sunrise prayer skipped again, I dressed Kiboro in a sea of midnight. Matching ribbons melted into her smooth hair. Her eyes were hard. Swollen. I allowed her to suffer when I knew the truth, but Jorai told me to pretend to mourn. I applied ash to her pallid cheeks, smudged soot over her hands and face, then did the same for myself. When I saw my reflection in the copper mirror, I was stunned. I looked like a ghoul. We draped veils over our faces.

Barano met us at the door. Ash marked his features also. Two bodyguards joined us outside the women's compound. Kiboro had refused a carriage, so they carried a long, silken sheet to protect us from the rain. Kiboro and I stood between the guards under the canopy, and Barano led our escort from the temple grounds west of the palace and city, to the hills of the dead.

My Elite emerged from the forest and followed.

When we reached the hills, the rain weakened to a pattering drizzle. Fog curled across the ground and cloaked the distant, jagged mountains. We took a timeworn path, strewn with dried brush and flowers to cover the mud, and descended into the valleys.

Soon the hillsides bore marble gravestones at attention in ranks. We reached the tallest mount. Soldiers waited at the top and bowed. Kiboro tucked her arm into mine, a gesture between friends.

Lightbearers formed a human corridor down the spine of the hill, with hands lifted in light. The scent of loam filled my nostrils as I took in the countless grave markers encircling us. We were moving far from the tombs of the kings, but of course they would bury Jorai somewhere else. Then we saw the yawning hole across a modest clearing.

Kiboro held my arm tighter.

We paused near a low, empty table, where gifts would be left for the family of the deceased. I had forgotten to bring a present because this wasn't supposed to happen.

Fresh winds whipped around us.

A multitude of voices neared. The nation arrived and divided into their places. Only the titled would stand near us. I could feel how they pretended respect, holding elaborate umbrellas while their true thoughts dripped between hushed lips. Except for one.

Srolo Faru stood on the far right. Alert, shabbily dressed, eyes filled with grief.

He, too, did not know the truth.

A hush fell as Elites stepped into their formation. I was glad to see mine join them.

In great pomp before the bowing multitude, King Zaujo, Queen Umoli, and Prince Huari stepped beside us, also covered with canopies held aloft by their guards.

King Zaujo wore mourning clothes, but his gaze was emotionless.

I accidently made eye contact with Prince Huari. He glared at me. I startled and trained my eyes ahead. My heart pounded, and I felt the rise and fall of the cool, chipped key against my chest. Of course Huari had known about the key, and he rightfully guessed that Jorai had taken it. How was I going to keep it from him? Could the crown prince have an apprentice priestess's quarters searched? Kiboro would never allow it, but Huari was more powerful than her. I tried to control my breathing as the crowd parted again before the leading temple priest. Elder priests and priestesses laid rugs before the king, queen, Huari, then Kiboro, who requested one for me as well.

The priest lifted hands of light and prayer to Heaven, and Jorai's funeral began.

King Zaujo removed his weaponry first, lowered himself to one knee then the other on his rug, and with great rustling, the rest of us also bowed for confession.

The priest beseeched Heaven's kindness upon Jorai, when none was offered him in life.

Solid footsteps sounded a tattoo up the hill. Rows of servants passed, carrying the coffin. It was made of Laijon's finest wood and covered with intricate carving. They lowered it into the grave and pushed a marble slab over the top. No visitation, to cover the brutal killing. Except the person inside the coffin was not Jorai.

Kiboro wept.

I gritted my teeth. Jorai, please come. Now.

Nobility rose, placed gifts on the table, then visited the grave. A masquerade.

Faru approached the gravesite, bowed deeply, and left.

Finally, royalty arose. King Zaujo went first. Queen Umoli followed. When she reclaimed her place, her gaze flitted over me. I wanted to scream. She understood my relationship with Jorai and had seen everything at the Chanji as she hid in the shadows. But her expression remained blank, and she did not glance at me again.

Kiboro released my arm. She held up a hand to signal that the canopy and guards not follow her, and stepped into the gentle rain. Under her veil, tears marred the ash on her face. Her mouth trembled, and she approached the grave.

I felt sick, and then Huari's stare slid over me again. I didn't know how long I could continue to ignore him. How long I could keep this key hanging around my neck. Why hadn't Jorai come?

The breeze shifted and an acrid taste like smoke filled my nostrils and mouth.

Three shouts rent the air. Srolo Faru cupped hands around his mouth and yelled toward the crest, where a company of mounted soldiers appeared. Our war horns sounded.

Laijon was under attack.

The crowd panicked and time slowed as Elites surrounded the king and Faru continued to shout orders.

"Inside the walls! Protect your king!"

Kiboro called my name as the crowd separated us.

I tried to maneuver through to reach her, but guards cut through, followed by nobility and those of the temple, and I was swept aside. When a lesser nobleman stumbled, I slipped in front of him and ripped the veil from my face. Then I pushed my way through the ring of Elites to Kiboro. She gripped her skirts and scanned the hills.

The wind carried the stench of burning.

We reached the lower palace wall. Haze obscured the sky, and orange streaks reflected against the clouds. Someone shouted that the western wall was aflame.

We poured through the gates and everyone scattered. Guards ran past with bags of water. Battle sounds came from the south and north.

Two points of attack. Who?

King Zaujo roared. Srolo Faru, Barano, and over half of the Elites raced with the king toward the southern skirmish. The rest of us continued toward the upper palace wall—soon to be consumed with fire. Guards worked to put the flames out.

Prince Huari led the rest of the Elites, Kiboro, and me to barrel past the wall into safety. Behind us, a desperate crowd followed and cried out in alarm when fire devoured the open gate.

Kiboro stopped.

Huari didn't, and the Elites followed him.

Kiboro ordered her guards to assist in fighting the flames, but the wind was too strong. The crowd was sent to seek refuge in the city and soldiers encircled Kiboro to usher her toward the palace.

A noble family was calling out a name. Someone screamed behind the fire.

I turned and saw a boy on the opposite side of the gate. One of the lightbearers I had seen at the Chanji, separated from his family and chasing the fire's edge. The boy wouldn't flee. If whoever fought us crossed the lower walls and found him . . . I sucked in a breath as heat and smoke rolled over me, and passed into the flames through the gate. Fire crawled up my arms and bloomed over my face as I grabbed the boy's hand. He looked at me in shock and didn't resist as I pulled him through the blaze to the other side. The boy gasped fresh air. He brushed his clothes, but found them clean, and his brown eyes widened with confusion.

His family called again. He glanced toward them.

I released his hand and raced toward the palace.

Guards were shutting the doors as I tore through the entry and halted before a congestion of soldiers and various other people. Elites led Kiboro into the council chamber. I followed, and the heavy, double doors shut behind me as I took my place at her side, trembling.

Kiboro stood rigid as stone. Half the Chanji, without Queen Umoli, who perhaps had fled to her residence, also entered.

Before the empty turquoise throne, Prince Huari paced like a caged tiger.

Kiboro leaned toward me and lowered her voice. "I hear that the mountain people are attacking. Three tribes are working together to separate our soldiers and spread fire to the walls."

The mountain people never attacked this season, and never in a combined effort. My throat constricted. Where was Roji? Was Father safe?

The mountains. Jorai had fled to the mountains and would have crossed the warriors' path.

Kiboro's soft voice reached me again. ". . . the palace and city are to be secured to keep them out."

Jorai wouldn't be able to get inside Laijon. He would remain trapped outside the walls.

A frozen knife twisted deep within me.

Commotion erupted outside the doors, and then the rest of the Elites marched into the council chamber. King Zaujo had come, but Srolo Faru entered first.

I inhaled sharply in relief to see Roji among an accompanying knot of guards, intense, all stained in sweat. Then I saw the pallor on Srolo Faru's face.

The Elites lowered a litter to the ground. They carried King Zaujo, who lay still with an arrow shaft protruding from his chest.

I stared. Disbelieving.

Huari lurched forward, eyes bulging. His jaw worked and then he fell across his father's body. The Elites surrounded the prince in a circle and faced out. One carried the king's bloodstained crown.

Huari's wails filled the room.

Kiboro's mouth tightened, but she did not look at the king. She studied the prince.

A jolt raced through me.

Huari was king.

Srolo Faru ordered the Elites to take Huari and the litter to the king's apartments, then sent the Chanji out of the council chamber.

Kiboro did not leave with the others, but followed Faru as he yanked the tapestry away from the secret door, and we disappeared after him into the darkened room.

Faru spun toward us, his hand filled with blue light, pain and surprise covering his face. The bimil peeked from his belt.

Kiboro stood before him, face splotched with ash. Fury flashing from her eyes. "Is it true that the mountain tribes are united, bring stores, and set fires to divide our forces and burn the planted fields?"

The lines in Srolo Faru's face deepened. "Yes. You and His Young Majesty—"

Huari.

"—must seek shelter. The Chanji will gather and give counsel."

Kiboro interrupted. "I know what the Chanji will advise. They will want us to wait the mountain people out, as normal. But the tribes never attack until harvest. They are never united, and winter will not chase them away as it normally does." Her voice faltered. "They burn our fields and murder our king. Next, they go after the walls around the city. The mountain people do not come to steal our food this time." And she waited for him to confirm this.

Faru's gaze moved to me—as if to discern how much I had told her—then returned to Kiboro. "You know of the treasure."

She nodded.

Faru hesitated and glanced at me again. "Indeed, the mountain tribes must be seeking the treasure."

"Then we act now." Kiboro drew a breath. "I will seek help from our allies. If I leave now, I can reach Ai'Biro in two days."

My heart crashed against my chest.

Faru's expression tightened. "The mountain tribes are moving across the north and will block your path."

"What about Nazak?"

"You know they will never come to Laijon's aid."

Her brow pinched, then she pulled herself taller. "Then I will go to Pirthyia."

No. I looked to Srolo Faru, and his fierce expression arrested me.

"I cannot send you to them."

"Our alliance with Pirthyia includes their protection of us. They must honor their word."

"You are princess and far too valuable to send to such a dangerous place. Perhaps one of the Chanji or myself . . ."

Kiboro's voice was authoritative, firm. "You are needed here. Today, I am Laijon's crown heir. This is now my role to play in times of war."

I stilled. It was true.

Kiboro raised her chin. "Srolo Faru, send me."

This was insanity—but was this the only way to stop the united tribes? What of Jorai locked outside our walls? If he had survived the mountain people sweeping toward us.

I swallowed. "I will go to Pirthyia and act as Princess Kiboro. She can train me in what to say, and she will remain safe."

Kiboro blinked.

Faru's brow raised. "Will you, too, barter your life, srawa?"

No. My life was already dashed to pieces. "For Laijon."

He watched me a moment, then addressed Kiboro. "I will accept this and speak for the Chanji. You will go, but your attendant will protect you. Teach her what to say. Let us hope that Pirthyia's current Imperati continues to be a gentler ruler than most of their high kings. Regardless, the danger will be grave. Do you understand?"

Kiboro looked ready to reject my offer, but didn't. "I agree."

"We must make preparations and gather your guard before the gates close." Srolo Faru strode to the door.

We followed as he quickly entered the council chamber into the palace common and began assembling soldiers. Guards came in every rank except for the Elites, who now remained with Huari.

Srolo Faru picked nine soldiers, a generous number for an ambassador, including the three Pre-Elites present, who stood broader and a head taller than almost everyone else.

I desperately wished Barano was with us and not fighting—and then I saw Roji handpicked and included with the nine. Srolo Faru glanced toward me, and responsibility lodged deep inside me.

Supplies were gathered, then Faru led Kiboro, myself, and Kiboro's soldiers outside the palace to a wall gate untouched by fire. Horses waited, fully tacked.

The battle was a distant roar. Wooded groves stretched before us beyond the valley.

The nine guards, including Roji, mounted.

Srolo Faru held Kiboro's reins as she jumped astride, then gave quiet, clipped instructions. ". . . will send Barano to you within three days . . . goodspeed, Princess." Then Faru made his way to me.

I mounted my gelding and watched his approach.

Faru tucked a gold statue into my saddlebag, surely from the king's rooms. "Present this to the Imperati when you see him face-to-face. Goodspeed, Srawa Seyo." His sad gaze tore at me, then he saluted the soldiers.

The leading Pre-Elite cried aloud and led the ensemble cantering down the hills.

I hesitated. I couldn't hide the truth from Faru after what he'd done for us. Forgive me, Jorai. I reached and touched Faru's shoulder.

"Jorai is alive," I said.

Faru stiffened, then stepped so close his shoulder brushed my arm. "Again."

I leaned down and whispered, "Jorai lives and will return." I pulled the bimil from Faru's belt—he did not feel it go—and slipped the small, thin book into my skirt pocket, and urged my horse to join the others. When I caught up with Kiboro, I dared to look over my shoulder.

Faru's eyes glistened as he raised a hand. Then he and Laijon faded behind the hills as we made our descent.

The key thumped against my chest.

The bimil lay heavy within the folds of my skirts.

To Pirthyia.

12

THE JOURNEY WAS HARD.

The first day, we examined the supplies Srolo Faru had packed for us. There hadn't been time to retrieve our things from the women's compound, so he had taken Kiboro's old gowns from her rooms in the palace, along with some servants' dresses. For now, she and I wore rough travelers' robes and skirts.

On the second day, we accepted the things missing from our satchels that we would need to live without. Somehow, Kiboro had snatched a copy of the Nho—Faru wouldn't have thought to pack that—but a common copy, not hers.

When we rested the horses, I was too exhausted to speak. Kiboro remained quiet, too, surveying our surroundings.

Roji and I made frequent eye contact over meals around our campfires. He often seemed like he wanted to say something, but would then look aside in dumbfounded wariness, like he couldn't believe what had happened. Perhaps I looked the same.

What would Roji do when I wore the princess's silks?

After soldiers prepared our tent each night, Kiboro opened the Nho and led us in confession and prayer by the light from her hand, no matter how much we wanted to collapse onto our pallets. Twice, I thought she might cry, but she never did.

As I fell asleep, I promised myself that Jorai was alive. Over and over. He said to pretend to mourn. That was easy when my fears were so strong. Why did he fail to return? Jorai was alive . . . was alive . . . alive . . . why hadn't he come?

On the sixth evening of this, my resolve weakened. As the moon arched over a sky divided between Laijon and Pirthyia, while Kiboro and Roji and the rest of the guard slept before another strenuous day, I opened my hands and released this burden of hope. Jorai said that if he did not return, he was destroyed. But he must live. My tears dried against my cheeks like flames surrendering to ash, and my heart grew cold.

On the seventh day, we emerged from Laijon's thinning woods and crossed Pirthyia's border into a flat, dusty expanse of red dirt. Midday, we circled the first outpost hosting the farthest reaches of Pirthyia's infamous railroad. The metal tracks cut across the land and glittered under sunlight like a great extravagance to our Laijonese eyes. The leading Pre-Elite, our captain, gave a command, and we followed the railroad into endless cultivated grain fields, Pirthyia's agricultural wonder. Only faraway forested bluffs, the eastern border, broke the skyline.

After three days of farmland, interrupted by small towns that we avoided, our scouting guards reported that we were two and a half days from Pirthyia's capital.

Purpose untangled itself from the emptiness inside me. I thought of Father again and worried for him and Laijon's siege. During nightly camp, when Kiboro and I sought refuge in our tent, I began opening my ears to the guards' gossip outside.

They shared rumors of the lost Laijonese treasure and the curse it held. I cringed hearing them speak of the discovery as common knowledge. They argued over King Zaujo's death, wondered how an arrow had zipped past his bodyguard, rued over missing the battles, complained about Pirthyia's heat and choking dust, then threw dice to draw lots. Apparently, Srolo Faru had instructed three of them to act as the princess's advisors, a role none of them wanted. After the captain volunteered for one of the slots, lots were drawn for the other two. The dice chose another Pre-Elite and Roji.

Under different circumstances, I would have laughed at his bad luck. I peeked over my quilt at Kiboro.

She lay too still. Definitely listening too.

The soldiers grumbled about Pirthyia. Didn't these people perform bloody, superstitious rituals? Barbarians. Hadn't they ravaged Nazak long ago and perhaps stolen their gifting over the earth? Didn't monsters still roam these lands?

My ears pricked when Roji muttered a reminder that they had already seen Pirthyian dignitaries visiting Laijon's courts.

Then they whispered that every Imperati was known for unspeakable cruelty. To become the high king, you must be willing to murder rival kings from every province of the country.

I turned over and pressed the quilt against my ears.

The next day, sun beat upon the rusty landscape, and the distant railroad tracks shimmered like water. Neither we nor our horses were used to such heat, so we decided to take cover under a clump of trees and travel during the night. One guard was chosen to keep lookout.

Inside our tent, Kiboro and I scrubbed the dust from our nostrils and eyes. The mourning ash had disappeared days before. Then Kiboro opened the Nho for prayer.

I did not want to pray, but bowed beside her anyway and tasted the grime lingering in my mouth.

Her whispered petitions irritated me.

I should pray for our meeting with the Imperati. I should pray for success. I should pray for Jorai. Hope must be kept—but I felt only fury.

Kiboro sat up. "Seyo, we must discuss your role—"

A guard's curse split the air.

We jumped to our feet and exited the tent.

The entire guard gathered around the lookout, a young man I had recognized from Roji's unit. Was it Bo? He was spouting apologies.

Roji's horrified gaze and rigid posture made my heartbeat quicken.

The lookout had fallen asleep.

The captain approached Kiboro with a bow. The two of them convened quietly, and Kiboro's face paled.

As crown princess, it was her responsibility to pronounce the lookout's punishment.

Death.

Kiboro faced us, and the captain grimaced behind her. Her gaze flicked back and forth. "He will be given one hundred lashes, but let it be broken into four days."

So he could live.

The lookout was stretched across the red ground on his stomach and restrained. The captain approached with a whip and glanced toward Kiboro.

She took her place to watch the sentence, as was expected of her, and I stood in my place at her side.

The first blow cracked.

I longed to close my ears. Kiboro's demeanor was stony, but I could sense her trembling beside me.

When the twenty-five lashes were complete, pink touched the bottom of the sky.

The captain wiped sweat from his brow. "Break camp."

Roji lurched forward to cut the lookout's restraints.

I thought I would throw up, but Kiboro hurried into the tent and I followed. Tears dripped down her face as she indicated our meager belongings. "We may reach the capital tonight. Change clothing."

We undressed, and with weak fingers, I put on one of her gowns. It was a garment I had seen so many times. The fabric was too fine for me. Slippery. I slipped the key beneath my underbodice.

Kiboro wore servants' clothing and finished braiding her hair before gesturing that she would do mine. I crouched and allowed her to arrange my hair, and saw that her dress hem dragged and mine was too short. She placed the crown upon my head, a simple metal circlet adorned with small, shimmering blue gems, then applied jewelry to my neck, wrists, ears, frowned, and unclasped my second piercing and handed it to me. I stuck the bauble into my undergarments pocket—with the oractalm bracelet and bimil. When she painted my face, she hid my second piercing. "I worry about your brother standing next to you as an advisor—that you will look too similar. Thankfully, your skin is darker, and your hair curls. I will thicken your makeup just in case. Grab one of the short swords and secure it under your skirt like I do."

When Kiboro and I emerged, the guards' gazes felt sharp as they bowed—to me—before disassembling the tent. The captain, who had changed into a nobleman's long robes and wide-brimmed hat, helped me mount my gelding and, with difficulty, ignored Kiboro.

I resisted squirming under their attention and looked for Roji's comforting presence. Though he and the rest of the guards had been briefed on our masquerade for days now, he appeared shocked at my transformation.

Not helpful, brother. I wanted to tell him how uncomfortable he looked dressed as an advisor. Yet he wore the fancy garb better than the captain and Pre-Elite, whose broader shoulders strained the delicate fabric.

The lookout struggled to sit upside in his saddle.

Kiboro bumped my elbow. "Gaze up."

I obeyed, and we headed into the coming dusk.

Hours passed. The guards reported half a ride tomorrow, and the danger ahead of us swirled in my mind.

Our scouts galloped toward us and reined in near the captain.

"Twenty Pirthyian soldiers advance toward us," one said.

I froze. Twice as many as our company, and early. Were we closer to the capital than we thought?

The captain looked to me for instructions.

"Wait for their approach," Kiboro murmured.

I repeated this, and soon, we saw the Pirthyians coming and felt the ground pound under their hoofbeats. But they did not carry the current Imperati's banner.

Our soldiers lifted their hands in light.

The Pirthyians halted. Their twenty warriors stood in strong but wild formation, compared to Laijon's discipline, and their sand-colored horses were shorter than ours and far stockier. The men wore belted weapons, linen wraps around their hips, and tall leather boots, exposing the ruddy-brown flesh of their legs. Dyed feathers stood from sleek, metal helmets, and shields covered their backs. Strips of fabric crisscrossed their bare chests, and the unwelcome flag drooped in the windless air above them as they gazed at our gifting in open interest.

My stomach plummeted. Kiboro had made me memorize every Pirthyian king's insignia. Instead of a jumping stag, a terrible sky dragon adorned the banner. This was Warlord Emeridus's symbol.

The Pirthyian squadron inclined their heads without dismounting. One spoke in the international trade language with a guttural and harsh accent.

The captain stepped forward to offer me, as princess, a simple translation, even though I didn't need it. He said the squadron came in the name of Warlord Emeridus, the new Imperati.

I fought to keep my expression neutral. Emeridus was known for his ruthlessness, especially against neighboring Nazak. I heard that he fed his opponents' bodies to the wild dogs he tamed and kept for his protection. Srolo Faru would have never sent Kiboro if he had known—

The Pirthyians said they would now escort us to the capital fortress where the Imperati waited.

Be Kiboro.

I raised my hand to signal that we would follow when the Pirthyian demanded that the Laijonese princess ride in their midst.

What in the continent? I looked for Kiboro's guidance and felt her irritation.

The Pirthyians surrounded our company, gave a strange cry, and we had no choice but to ride with them. They urged their horses mercilessly. I wasn't sure ours would make it after already traveling so far.

Faster. Faster.

The moon traveled toward its zenith, and lights appeared in the distance. The outline of a castle stabbed the night sky, with its city behind. It stood alone. Glorious. Afraid of none.

We passed a low stronghold wall and entered lush grounds.

Two stone aqueducts, surely purchased from Ai'Biro, soared on either side of the fortress to water the gardens and feed large, man-made ponds.

My eyes climbed the endless castle walls. They stole my breath.

A second company of soldiers met us on foot. Our Pirthyian escort jumped to the ground and handed off their horses. We dismounted as well, and I watched as our own animals were led away. The sight unnerved me. Kiboro brushed my side, and I tried to grasp her confidence. But I sensed that she, too, was uneasy as we were ushered into the brightness indoors.

An expansive entryway met us, with floors of large, polished stones, and plastered walls inlaid with tiles. Soldiers and servants stood at attention everywhere. How were there so many? Multiple stairways led to upper levels with gilded balustrades. Somewhere deeper inside, I could hear a large gathering. Two huge fireplaces roared with indulgent, sweltering discomfort. Pirthyia did not possess the gifting of light—they did not possess any gifting naturally—and I wondered if they wanted to impress us.

Or make our light useless here.

I swallowed. Yet they welcomed us with such pomp. Would we meet the Imperati now, despite the late hour?

A cluster of noblemen officials approached. They wore shimmering, brightly colored tunics encrusted with a dazzling display of small gemstones. Tight reddish curls, almost matching their skin color, hung close to their faces, and all had dark blue or brown deep-set eyes. We were a fingerlength or two taller than them, except for Kiboro.

The officials lowered themselves into slow bows.

Our soldiers and Kiboro also bowed.

I would only do so for the Imperati.

One elderly man stepped forward and spoke in broken Laijonese. "W-welcome, Lai-Laijon."

We greeted our guests with fluency. I overlooked their offense and focused on his words. The man glanced at my brow and

Kiboro's crown—which now felt plain compared to Pirthyia's embellishment—countless times.

The nobleman smiled widely. "And you are the pr-princess?"

I nodded.

The Pirthyian's eyes sparked before he bowed an unnecessary second time and barked a harsh command that made my heart skip. *Qo'tah—*

Their soldiers took our bags, and the officials motioned for us to follow them up the nearest flight of stairs.

We passed six floors and wove through several hallways until I felt dizzy, and stopped in an endless corridor before two opened doors.

The noblemen gestured my pretend advisors inside one room and Kiboro and me inside the other.

The Pre-Elite still dressed as a soldier checked our premises, like Barano would, and then Kiboro and I passed the threshold. When I glanced back, I saw the Pirthyians arranging our guards into place and closing the doors, leaving Kiboro and me alone.

I stared at the surrounding opulence. Rich carpet. Colored paper covering the walls. A silver statue of an unclothed woman stood in the corner next to a golden, clawed bathtub atop a tile pedestal.

I looked aside to the fireplace dominating the room, thankfully unlit. A wide, low bed claimed the far wall next to a washing basin. Fur blankets and a thick pallet were pulled back from the bed to show that the mattress was made of expensive marble, an exotic finery for the upper class.

This was more overwhelming than anything I had ever seen before. And something was wrong.

I looked around again. "Where are our bags?"

Kiboro's brow knit. "They must be coming."

After they rummaged through them, most likely.

"The Imperati will likely summon you tonight. Prepare for a late evening. Pirthyians do not sleep." She used her thumbs to neaten my face paint. "I have instructed the captain to speak for you, as is customary. I have told him what to say. Only respond directly to the Imperati in greeting. May the Father of Light permit that Pirthyia has not heard rumors of the treasure. That would complicate everything."

My shoulders began to ache with tension.

She retied my sash and murmured, "I know Faru gave you a welcoming gift to present, but I think you should wait."

What if their soldiers stole Faru's golden statue before returning our satchels?

I smoothed my damp palms down my skirts and felt the lump of belongings in an inner pocket and the short sword blade on my right.

Footsteps scuffled outside the door.

Kiboro and I froze until the hallway quieted. Then someone knocked.

My breath quickened. I looked to Kiboro.

She nodded at me. "I will be at your side." Then she strode to open the door with characteristic dignity.

A new group of Pirthyian nobility and soldiers waited outside the door. What were they trying to do? Amaze us with their numbers? All bowed, then stepped backward in an invitation for us to join them.

This was it. I took a breath and entered the long hallway.

One of the Pirthyian soldiers extended his hand to bar Kiboro from exiting.

I looked in surprise and saw the soldier close the door on her and stand in front of the chamber.

Five other Pirthyian guards lined the nearest wall.

Our soldiers and acting advisors—they were moved further down the hall. But three out of nine were missing—the Pre-Elites, including the captain, were gone.

Roji remained in his fine clothing and wide-brimmed hat and kept no secrets with his clenched jaw and darkened eyes.

Energy flooded my veins. Where had they taken our Pre-Elites?

The Pirthyians encircled me and marched down the hall.

My guard did not follow. Apparently, like Kiboro, they were not permitted to.

I choked.

Be the princess.

I stopped and pointed at my guards. I longed to erupt in Pirthyian and demand my entire escort.

A nobleman looked me up and down then gestured that one may join us. He chose Roji.

My brother came to my side, and I inhaled relief. Then we were striding through the castle again at an uncomfortable pace.

I blew out a breath. Don't fight this example of famed Pirthyian rudeness. We were allies, after all. I was Princess Kiboro and Roji stood beside me.

Qo'tah. I needed Kiboro and the captain's instructed words.

I really needed Kiboro.

They were forcing me to bargain with the warlord Imperati alone.

13

I LONGED TO SPEAK WITH ROJI.

He was dressed as an advisor, so we could get away with it, but I resisted. Talking to him would weaken my portrayal of Princess Kiboro further than their amputation of my escort.

But Roji himself moved near and muttered quietly, "They forced them to tend our horses."

I kept myself from reacting. That was boorish treatment of our Pre-Elites and wasn't remotely reassuring.

We wound through this web of a castle by a different route than we had entered. Looming windows betrayed the late hour. When we reached the primary entry again, muffled festivity sounded from within.

Powerful guards stood before ornate doors. The grand hall.

My pulse quickened.

Roji was close behind me as the soldiers opened the doors—to chaos.

The grand hall, comprised of three levels, could swallow Laijon's palace. Roaring fireplaces lined the walls with blinding flames, overheated this arena, gushed smoke, and tossed dancing shadows onto the high ceiling.

The lower bowl held performers fighting for the favor of the crowd.

Laughing nobility and titled military, lounging at low tables and shouting to be heard, congested the floor level. They were adorned with unbelievable finery and immodesty. My eyes went from the men's short, belted tunics to the Pirthyian women. Jewelry, like dust, covered their hair and glittered in the surrounding firelight. Bright paint made their faces unrecognizable. I looked away from their scandalous attire.

The third and highest level, where smoke and servants were thickest, held seven large tables, each heaped with food, filled by the kings of Pirthyia's seven provinces and their immediate courts. A central table set atop a circular, raised landing, was largest of all. Its occupants did not join the clamor. The Imperati's table.

Of the six other tables, how many of their regional kings had the warlord killed, along with the former Imperati, to wave his dragon banner from the castle heights? I wondered how quickly the lesser thrones had been refilled.

Our escort led us to a stairwell built into the side of the room, and we climbed. I let my hand skim the wall, as there was no railing, and smooth, rich wood passed under my fingertips. Laijonese timber. Payment of everlasting debt.

We reached the highest landing and walked toward the Imperati.

Lesser kings watched Roji and me with rapt attention. I sensed that they had anticipated our arrival, and I struggled to keep my gaze straight until our escort climbed the circular pedestal and halted before the high king, who reclined at his low table.

The oppressive presence of bodyguards blended with his accompanying noblemen's open scrutiny. Two lengths aside, the Imperati's queens, older children, and concubines sat at a smaller table.

I looked down and met the dark blue eyes of the Warlord Emeridus, Imperati of Pirthyia.

To my relief, the Imperati stood, and his retinue followed.

He was slightly shorter than me, somewhere within his third decade, young to be high king. His coarsened skin betrayed much time outdoors protecting his southern region. Scars bespoke battles fought, likely against the Nazaks across the border. His tight curls and beard were trimmed, and his heavy crown was of rare, pale metal. He wore Pirthyian ambition like a cloak, and after eyeing me brazenly, he bowed.

I bowed in return and wobbled upon catching him assessing my too-short skirt hem. He gave Roji a casual glance, who earlier had the good sense to pull the brim of his hat low over his eyes.

I struggled to remain calm.

A nobleman gestured for me to join the table.

Roji offered me his hand to help me sit on my knees across from the Imperati, then stood behind me.

The Imperati sat too.

I felt the nearby women's looks and spared them a glance. Two wives. Eight children. Three concubines. I repressed a shudder, then almost jumped when food and drink were placed before me.

The drink was strong and sweet-smelling. Meat stew filled a massive bowl, and I recognized Vedoa's famous spices, for Pirthyia kept open trade with them. I remembered my mother sneaking pinches of spice into her meals, and my heart twisted.

The Impertai's noblemen began conversing in Pirthyian. Their rudeness astounded me. Would they have done this before King Zaujo? I listened while I pretended to watch the performers' frantic display in the lowest level, then studied the ornamentation littering the walls. The animal masks and hides, representation of half-Pirthyian and half-animal gods, were treasures from every nation on the continent. Especially Laijon.

Servants flitted by to refill mugs again. Wait, not servants. Most of these people were slaves from Nazak, with iron bands covering their wrists and second piercings symbolizing their position as servant.

The concubines whispered derogatory comments about me.

I thought of Kiboro and the missing guards and bit my lip.

At that moment, the Imperati's retinue stood and offered me greetings in Pirthyian. I understood, but I was supposed to have an interpreter.

I was surprised when Roji bowed and translated beautifully, even if he stumbled twice. If I had not been so anxious, my jaw might have dropped. For all his complaining about Father's work, he had not forgotten our childhood language lessons in the Archives. One point for Roji presenting Laijon as sophisticated.

Before his retinue could respond, the Imperati raised his hand for silence. He nodded toward me and spoke in passable trade language. "Princess of Laijon, Pirthyia is pleased by your arrival."

Sweat trickled down my spine. He had conversed directly with me. I wished I could launch into Pirthyian, to demonstrate that Laijon was cultured and educated, not poor and weak as they assumed. I pictured Kiboro's strength as I inclined my head and replied in the same trade language with eloquence. "High King, Imperati, much honor has been bestowed on you and your ascension to the highest throne." The compliment was film on my tongue.

He nodded.

Pirthyia was a terse nation, so I would state my plea without Laijonese fanfare. I had to request their aid against the mountain tribe, without begging, to help our people.

Father's face flitted into my mind. Then Jorai's. I spoke. "Esteemed Imperati, I, princess of Laijon, come to you in the need of my country. We are attacked by a confederation of mountainous tribes. We remembered Pirthyia and her valiant strength that rescued us in the past." And buried us in the present. "As allies, we request Pirthyia's help again."

The Imperati's eyes simmered. "The attacks have been reported to us. I am surprised that King Zaujo sent his daughter to me."

Then he did not know of the king's death. Should I tell him, or would that knowledge weaken our image further? I remained silent.

The Imperati watched me for another long moment. "What gift does Laijon offer me in exchange for my protection?"

His frankness was astounding. Was he already agreeing? "High King, no less than the standard payment will be offered to you."

The Imperati's slow smile transformed his face. "Does the standard percentage increase with Laijon's newfound wealth?"

I stiffened, and so did Roji. Pirthyia already knew about the cursed treasure.

He placed a hand on the table. "Your king sends you because you are difficult to refuse."

My face heated. Did he mock me—or Kiboro?

"Rumors of Laijon's newfound, endless riches have reached us also. Tell me, why haven't you brought it to pay your debts, after our decades of patience with you?" He crossed his arms. "Instead, you come to tell me stories. Laijon fights the mountain people every year, and now you are overwhelmed? I am tempted to think you are lazy and trying to bait me with a fabrication of treasure."

Mysteries of the continent—

"I have, in fact, sent my scouts to Laijon this morning. If this treasure is real, the scouts will return with ten percent of your debt payment. If the attacks on your country are true, I will send soldiers to aid you and to collect the rest of the treasure owed." He glared. "May Laijon not spread lies to me."

I fought for breath. This was impossible. Only a portion of the treasure was found.

The Imperati's voice softened, and I strained to hear him above the ruckus.

"But you are only a messenger, Princess. I am inclined to believe you, and cannot send you back into the danger of battle. I offer you sanctuary here in great Pirthyia until my scouts return with the treasure, and then my army can return you to your home. You are a prize to our enemies, and I can do nothing less."

What in the—

His gaze intensified. Testing. Raking across my soul.

I refused to look away.

The Imperati downed his cup and did not look at me again.

I was dismissed, and yet kept at his table.

My heart raced. He would retain us in Pirthyia. He would punish us when his scouts did not find the treasure. Could this become worse?

Servants shouted over the din, and soldiers began putting out the fires. At this, the crowd hushed and looked toward the ceiling.

Through the smoke, glass balls hung overhead. Something hummed, and then the spheres burst with glowing light.

The crowd uttered cries of awe.

I stared at the artificial lights until my eyes burned. How had they accomplished this? Would they harness the very sun?

"Princess."

I glanced toward the Imperati.

He regarded me with a sardonic smile. "Do you feel at home now?"

One of his noblemen, half-drunk, murmured something in his ear and gestured to me.

My skin prickled.

The Imperati growled his answer in Pirthyian. "We have Laijonese performers." But he studied me again.

Laijonese performers—*qo'tah*. The nobleman wanted to see my light gifting. Panic rushed through me. I—I couldn't.

More announcements rang through the hall and stole their attention.

"Look here! See the spectacle!"

In the performers' bowl below, soldiers lined up and pushed a large box covered with cloth. One guard stepped forward brandishing a strange, old sword over his head.

Whispers slithered over me.

"I have heard of this one. Wasn't it captured in a field?"

"It injured twelve men and has been chained twice."

"But it is human? Perhaps one of Nazak's champions?"

The Imperati refused a servant wishing to refill his cup, and his eyes narrowed at the stage.

I clenched my hands in my lap and braced myself for whoever this Pirthyian captive was. Just let us leave—

A soldier signaled, and the cloth was tugged to uncover a large cage. Inside, a man wearing ragged trousers crouched. Mud splotches covered his incredibly pale skin.

Guards hurled buckets of water over the prisoner. He shuddered. They commanded him to stand, but he did not obey.

The guard approached with the sword and used its point to prick the man's side.

The prisoner cried out and unfolded his body, length by length, until I saw the metal collar around his neck, and his wild, dark hair brushed the cage ceiling.

Dismay hit me. He was two heads too tall to be a man. Water dripped from his bushy hair, limbs, and the bars of the cage. There was no mud on his skin—the markings were a part of him.

Taunting soldiers prodded the man to face the crowd. His giant's body was taut and wrapped in chains. He tucked his chin to his chest and covered his face with large, manacled hands.

I stared at the terrible, unnatural charcoal symbols crisscrossing his long, fair arms, hands, chest, legs. They were not scars. Many nations decorated their skin permanently, but this was something different.

The crowd burst into hisses.

"Monster!"

"Creature of the underworld!"

A soldier shouted that the beast-man had been found trespassing on farmland and had injured over half of the Pirthyian farmers seeking to restrain him—with the power of his eyes.

The Imperati leaned forward.

The first soldier shrieked an unintelligible command. The others fetched ropes, climbed the cage, and slipped a noose around the prisoner's head. As soon as he felt the loop, he fought, keeping his head down, until guards pulled upon the chains around his wrists and stretched his arms at his sides. The noose was tugged tighter around his neck, then another chain, one attached to his collar, was yanked to force his head up.

I stared at his shut eyes and mouth screwed in agony. His ears— so many slave piercings. The man shouted something and startled me. He yelled, "Father," in the Nazak tongue.

A leering soldier reached through the bars to force the man's eyes open. And then the soldier screamed. Screamed and fell writhing upon the ground.

All other sound ceased.

The Imperati hurtled to his feet and shouted.

Guards fell upon the cage and beat back the prisoner, then covered the cage and removed it from the hall.

The screaming soldier was kicked until he wept, then dragged out of sight by his companions.

Palpable uneasiness gripped the room.

Nausea rose inside me, and Roji murmured an oath. What had we just seen?

A cautious group of acrobats filled the bowl. Servants hurried to pour fresh drinks. Murmuring ensued, then laughter, then the clamor returned. But quieter. Restrained.

Even Pirthyia was afraid.

The Imperati's noblemen talked over one another in hushed tones. Would the beast be executed? Sacrificed? The gods would be pleased.

The Imperati said nothing, but sipped from his cup with a thoughtful look.

The guards who escorted us returned to take us back to the rooms. No formal farewell was offered, so I stood quickly and followed the soldiers back across the landing.

I felt the Imperati's gaze follow me until we reached the bottom of the stairs.

Roji's agitated breath tickled the back of my neck as we left the great hall and were led through the castle's labyrinth again at an outrageous clip.

Roji and I needed to talk—now. I clasped my hands in front of my chest and inclined my head toward him, as Kiboro would a nobleman, and spoke in ancient Laijonese—hoping Roji remembered all of his lessons. "Find escape."

Several guards eyed me.

Roji made eye contact with me and nodded.

I did not speak again, but memorized the path we took. It was a different one again. They were trying to confuse us.

When we arrived at our guest apartments, the Pre-Elites still had not rejoined the others, and Pirthyian guards opened the door for me.

I walked in alone, shut the door, and listened for Roji's entrance to the neighboring room to make sure no one followed him, then froze. My gaze swept the room.

Kiboro was gone.

Nausea overwhelmed me as I scanned the room again. There was no sign of a struggle. The window had a hinge and could swing open, but the latch was in place. Kiboro couldn't have secured the window from the outside. I peered through the glass, down lengths and lengths of smooth-stoned wall to a lake below.

Would even Jorai dare to jump that far?

I pressed my hands against my face.

Where had they taken Kiboro?

Helpless, I crawled onto the bed, wrapped my arms around my knees, and felt the sword hilt under my skirts. I reassured myself that Kiboro was also armed and well trained with the sword. Surely, she would be returned soon? Why did they take her? Skipping confession, I breathed a prayer for Kiboro's safety, but my body shook.

All of this was wrong.

The wild, fiery court swirled through my mind. The Imperati's conflicting words and glances. Bright, fake lights wreathed in smoke.

The monstrous, marked slave imprisoned and tortured in his cage. Forced against his will to harm his enemy—but how? With the power of his eyes?

Nausea rose inside me again.

Find escape.

14

THE FIREPLACE CRACKLED WHEN
I awoke.

Our bags sat on the foot of the bed, opened.

I lurched upright—in my gown from last night—and saw a slight girl with round eyes and dark, curly hair wrapped in a scarf. My awakening didn't surprise her. She fingered Kiboro's crown and offered a smile.

Qo'tah. I summoned a stern look and stretched out my hand.

The girl considered me before surrendering the crown with a dismissive sniff. "It is clean now," she said in the trade language, weighted with a rural accent. She pressed hands to heart in a foreign curtsy.

She was not cleaning anything, and she spoke without permission. I assessed her pale skin. Southern Nazak. Bands covered her wrists, and she wore the second piercing. A slave.

I gathered myself. "Who are you?"

"I am Cira, and I am sent to serve you." That said, she waltzed around the room and pretended to be busy.

Pirthyia sent this girl—likely commanded to spy on me—to replace Kiboro? I was frustrated and embarrassed that I had slept through her arrival.

Knocking pounded on the doors, and they opened for two Pirthyian soldiers hauling pails of steaming water.

I stared at their unannounced entry then caught Cira's coquettish glances. The soldiers ignored her as they filled the golden bathtub in the corner and left.

She spun toward me. "I shall assist your bath."

Never. "I bathe alone."

She murmured something under her breath and sprinkled scented oils into the hot water.

Did she just call Laijon backward?

Cira looked me up and down. "You're darker skinned than I heard. And taller."

My jaw fell open.

"I'll return." She skipped to the door and knocked a strange rhythm. Someone opened the door to her, and she went out. The lock clicked.

Qo'tah.

I pressed my palms against my temples.

Stay calm. Inspect the bags.

I did and found our clothing rumpled. The weapons had been removed from their oilskin coverings. The saddlebags, including Faru's golden statue, were not included. The Nho lay at the bottom of the satchel.

I bit back a curse and sat on the edge of the bed.

And now?

I must speak with Roji and the remaining guards. We needed a plan to find Kiboro and the Pre-Elites.

Perhaps I could request to walk the grounds, to understand the castle better. But I couldn't walk unattended without Kiboro.

I frowned. Perhaps Cira could be useful in this way. I could walk with her. She should know the castle well and I might learn something from her. I just needed to demand Roji's presence.

The bathwater's fragrance was overpowering, so I quickly washed my face and hands and changed into a fresh gown. Then I folded my nervous hands and waited. And waited.

Perhaps I should've read the Nho and practiced memorization, but my mind was too scrambled. But I should confess, make petitions for Kiboro and the guards, for Laijon. For Jorai.

A sudden realization made me gasp. I couldn't pray from Pirthyia. The Father of Light would not hear me from this horrible place. Yet I needed to do something.

My mind went to the bimil from my underskirt pocket. I drew a breath and, with tentative fingers, removed it. If the treasure really existed, its location was said to be written within the bimil's pages. What if it was written in the Shadow's indecipherable passage?

I opened to the ancient princess's script and crept through her words. She told of her capture, the enemies from across the sea, and their created Shadows. Monsters once human, who surrendered their bodies and souls for unholy power. One particular Shadow was sent to watch over her. He followed her everywhere except near the Handprint of God, where she would seek refuge to pray.

Chills swept up my spine, but I continued my pursuit and came to an entire page describing the treasure.

My breath caught. Was this it?

I combed the writing twice, three times to be sure. The princess told how the enemy gathered the first pile of wealth, artifacts taken from Ai'Biro, Nazak, the mountain tribes, and Laijon. Our red, glowing ore was deemed most valuable. Weaponry was listed next. And gilt-bound scrolls—an entire library of ancient writings—were locked in sealed chests.

Impossible.

Excitement welled within me. If this Laijonese library survived, we would know our past. And the remaining treasure could pay our debts to Pirthyia. We would finally be rid of their threats.

But then my hope faded. The Eternity Gate would still stand.

And the parchment did not offer the location of the treasure.

Defeated, I turned another page, and paused.

. . . *the Brotherhood* . . .

Father had said the Brotherhood were zealots from Nazak determined to open the gate. Why did the princess mention them?

As I continued to read, gooseflesh pricked my skin.

I couldn't believe this.

Laijon's first Elite soldiers were legendary. All were royalty, the second and third and fourth sons of our kings. It was said there have never been men as mighty and courageous as they, and that one fought like a thousand. But the bimil revealed they did not protect the king, as was assumed in our history. They protected the Eternity Gate. And when the disguised enemies from across the sea bartered for the gate, this said that the Elites agreed to the payment. They failed to safeguard the Eternity Gate, the Father of Light's gift to Laijon, and then Laijon fell. Filled with shame, these Elites fought hardest during the Occupation, and only a few survived. After Laijon was recovered, the Elites who remained removed their legendary swords, carved with the symbol of the blazing sun, and dispersed in self-exile all over the continent. But some hid in Nazak, as far from Laijon as possible. The Brotherhood was descended from these disgraced Elites.

I sat, stunned, staring at the page, grasping the implications. Did the Brotherhood seek to open the Eternity Gate to judgment, and so clear the centuries-old stain on their honor? Were all their famous swords destroyed too?

I pressed my hand against my chest, against the key, as Cira returned with much noise and a tray of food. I slipped the manuscript back into my pocket and stood.

"I saw that Pirthyian food didn't agree with you, so I brought something bland."

I flushed. So forward—

"But you need Pirthyian dress."

Never in the continent would I wear their scandalous clothes. "I will wear my own clothing."

"That is not what I was instructed."

So outspoken. "And you will escort me in a walk."

Her eyes flashed. "You can't do that."

Because she didn't want to or because the Pirthyians wouldn't let me? I stuffed uncertainty down. "I am princess of Laijon. We will take fresh air—"

Cira opened her mouth to object again.

"—then I will assess your Pirthyian garments." If they could be called such. But I would use this as my bargaining chip.

She hesitated before nodding curtly and knocked rhythmically upon the door. When it opened, she huffed to the Pirthyian guard. "The princess wants air."

The guards stood aside.

I took the hallway and rapped on Roji's door. He poked his head out, still in the same noblemen's clothing, startled to see me, but quickly took my side.

The Pirthyian soldiers glanced at Roji, but did not stop him.

Cira studied him with suspicion.

Then I noticed that my guards, driven farther down the hall, had been reduced by two.

"Come this way," Cira called.

I glanced again at the remaining three guards and then our outing began.

Cira led us up countless flights of stairs, with the Pirthyians following, until we stepped onto a wide balcony. Hot air assaulted us. The sun glared from above, and an army of white clouds gathered on the horizon. The walkway hugged the highest reaches of the castle, and short, stone railing offered dizzying sights into Pirthyia's flat, red land and fields. Guards on duty shouted to each other from the levels above and below.

Roji whispered in Laijonese, "They're in the prisons."

My stomach tightened. "Kiboro?"

"Yes." Pent-up energy rolled from him. "They're picking us off. I'm just waiting for my turn."

Cira tossed us an annoyed glance.

I ignored her and fought down panic. "Don't say that. Have you heard anything else?"

"It's hard to learn anything trapped in that room. I did learn the way to the prisons."

"Where?"

"Next to the grand hall. We walked right past it last night. Also, the soldiers guarding your room rotate at evening meal. They drink a lot." He grimaced. "Coming here was a mistake. The Imperati will not release us. What will he do once we're all imprisoned? Release the tattooed giant from its cage to finish us off? That—whatever it is—is more dangerous than the Pirthyians."

"They forced him to open his eyes. He resisted, even though he is their prisoner." He could have overpowered every soldier, even all of us, and yet did not.

Roji shook his head. "We just need to run."

Suddenly, my arm was gripped by Cira, who bore a strained smile. "Princess, how do you find great Pirthyia's landscape?"

Roji shot her a look as we rounded a bend. The resulting view seized my breath.

The castle entrance and man-made lakes lay far below. Beyond the lush grounds, red dirt stretched north, east, and south, broken to the west by the forested backbone of bluffs that would eventually mature into Laijon's mountains. The road that led us to Pirthyia stretched into the distance.

A jolt ran through me. Barano was supposed to come. I had forgotten. Faru was sending him to us. Did Roji know?

Our Pirthyian guards halted to hail soldiers standing on the lookout parapet above us.

Cira still clung to my arm. Even if she was a spy, it didn't matter if she heard me if she couldn't understand. I lowered my voice in old Laijonese and spoke to Roji again. "Barano is coming."

His eyes widened. "They could be a day from us now."

Cira tried to interrupt our conversation. "Princess—"

Roji shushed her before I could, earning her glare. "Seyo, Pirthyia will detain Barano too. We must meet them before they are sighted. Today."

I forced my voice to remain serene. "Yes. But how can we escape? We'll have to go on foot."

"Or steal their horses. Crawl. Saddle their soldiers. I don't care."

"Calm your tone."

Roji rolled his eyes. "They know we distrust them. We should quit acting like unthinking idiots."

"We'll give ourselves away."

Two younger guards, sweating under the sun, shouted from their posts ahead.

Cira's frustration disappeared as she released my arm. She called out flirtatiously in accented Pirthyian, speaking loudly and sounding silly. The soldiers guffawed at her antics then eyed me. Cira noticed their waning attention and her tone became desperate as she drew closer to them. "Do you toy with me?" she whined. "Do you care about me at all?"

Goodness, were her eyes filling with tears?

The shorter guard reminded her that she was beneath them. She crossed her arms and twirled away, but the taller guard laid a hand on her shoulder. "Cira," he soothed, "I will show you something interesting, yes?"

She shrugged, then snapped toward me in the trade language, "Come."

I nudged Roji, who glowered, but followed her too.

The soldiers led us around a second bend in the parapet, then gestured over the railing. We beheld a shocking display of supplies piled across the western grounds. Heaps of food and trinkets sat between wooden stakes driven into the ground, all connected by rope. Among this mess, soldiers prepared mounds of stone, kindling, and logs for bonfires.

The taller guard spoke. "The sacrifice begins tonight. The guard is to be quadrupled." His chest puffed. "I will be among them."

Cira was breathless. "The second army is arriving?"

I avoided glancing at Roji.

"Yes. The sacrifice will please the spirits and keep us safe."

"What is the sacrifice?"

"You'll find out eventually."

She gushed. "Is it the famous man-beast? The one with death in his eyes? I wanted to see it first."

I stilled.

"Not that Nazakian monster. The Imperati wants it and keeps it inside his quarters."

He did?

The soldier continued, "Everyone will stay inside if they know what's good for them. Doors shut after the moon rises, so be inside before then." He ruffled her scarf.

Cira batted his hands away and simpered. "Do you pretend to care for me?"

He bent and snatched a kiss from her.

I blushed as Cira giggled and kissed the second guard, also, before flouncing farther down the balcony. Sacrifices, food piles, and the castle locked up. Why did Pirthyia welcome the second army this way? And where was the second army coming from, and why?

Roji's jaw tightened. Helplessness swept over me. Thankfully, Cira was too far to hear now. "We must go before the doors close," I said. "I will find a way to escape during dinner, when the guards rotate." And drink. "Tell the others to meet me . . ." Where? Then I remembered that I promised Cira could dress me in Pirthyian garments. I realized what I needed to do, and I swallowed. "No. We will go together. All eleven of us. I will get Kiboro and the others."

His eyebrows shot up.

"Just wait for me."

He nodded. "I will."

I wanted to tell him how much I wished he wasn't here, but how glad I was to have him beside me when we entered the cool silence of the castle. I went over my crazy plan again and again and studied every passage we crossed.

Cira preceded me into the room, and we left Roji and the guard behind. The door locked. "Now, I dress you like a glorious Pirthyian." She planted her hands on her hips and awaited my resistance.

I stood before the vanity, and she threw herself into a rough, hurried dressing. My Laijonese gown came off. I refused to don new undergarments, which hid my key and short sword. She cursed softly, pulled something golden and Pirthyian over my head, and had me sit. As her fingers raked through my hair, I knotted my hands in my lap and wondered if these new clothes meant that I was supposed to go to the grand hall again.

We needed to be gone far before that hour.

I reviewed the plan one more time. Sneak out of the room. Somehow free Kiboro and our guards. Go back and get Roji and the others. Flee. If something went wrong, the blame and punishment would fall on me. But if we succeeded, we would be free.

Jorai flitted unbidden through my mind. I gripped his memory tightly.

"Look."

I dared to see her completed work, and closed my mouth.

Fabric like liquid gold covered my body. I felt naked. Gold paint covered my arms and neck, my face was lightened, and makeup made my eyes look round. Kiboro's crown was hidden by a thicket of jewels and strips of gilt fabric braided into my hair.

"Finished." Cira put the face paints away.

I took a deep breath, freed the strips of fabric from my hair, and stood.

Cira turned and looked at me with an appalled expression.

Thank goodness for my height. I grabbed her and tackled her to the ground. As she squeaked and fought, I wrestled her slave's outer clothing off of her, tied her hands and feet with shimmering gold material, and silenced her with cloth torn from her underdress. Guilt coursed through me, but I remembered Kiboro, who taught me such self-defense.

I dressed in her clothes, then wrapped her scarf over Kiboro's crown tangled into my hair. At last, I wiped the gold paint from my skin.

Cira struggled against the floor.

I performed her song-knock upon the door. As soon as it opened, I slipped into the hall away from the Pirthyian guards. They gave me a brief look.

I summoned an image of bossy Cira, kept my Laijonese-shaped eyes down, and glanced at my remaining Laijonese guards.

They were gone.

Roji's door was ajar and his room dark. They'd taken him too. My heart stopped.

A squadron of soldiers marched toward me. The new rotation.

My chest almost burst. I ducked my head and hugged the wall to pass them.

"Ho, Cira." A soldier clutched my wrist, then looked surprised. I wrenched free and ran, but was caught again.

My captor wrapped massive arms around my waist, yanked the scarf off my head, and barked in Pirthyian. "Look here. That slave girl will pay for letting this happen."

I snatched the scarf back.

Another soldier studied me and laughed. "Is that the princess? Well, the Laijonese are crafty, yes?"

The rest sneered, and I was hurried down unknown corridors. Down and down, till I feared we would enter the grand hall. But we continued past that horrific place, and my stomach somersaulted as we entered a long corridor, painted entirely with gold, ending in a marble doorway blocked by bodyguards.

The Imperati's quarters.

15

THE BODYGUARDS PARTED AND
opened the doors to a golden atrium. We stepped onto plush,
foreign rugs. Electric lighting illuminated the ceiling, despite the
three alcoves hosting lit fireplaces. Marble sculptures of lions
glistened near three passages that must lead to the Imperati's
private dwelling places.

In the middle of the room, the Imperati, dressed in a rich tunic,
lounged against the colorful cushions of a tall couch. Behind him,
five bodyguards stood. Before him, a short table held choice food
and drink.

In the left alcove in front of a blazing fireplace, the prisoner's
cage stood covered by cloth and watched by ten soldiers. One guard
wore the key to the cage on his belt.

I heard a growl and froze.

The growl rose from the middle of the room, as two large, wolf-
like creatures skulked from behind the couch. They were easily
three lengths, with long bodies and necks, square faces and small
ears, canine teeth protruding from their jaws. Their spotted coats
were dark across their backs and pale under their bellies. Thick,
gold collars wrapped around their necks, and they sat on their
haunches at the Imperati's feet.

The Imperati noted my slave clothing and motioned to the guard
restraining me. "Release her."

The guard shoved me forward.

The Imperati studied me with disgust, then swept his hands

toward the solemn animals at his feet and spoke in the trade language. "These are my Trackers. I have five, the finest on the continent. If someone passes my dragnets of guards circling the palace—and I have four warriors for every Laijonese soldier—I send my Trackers after him. They hunt to kill and do not fail." Then he motioned toward the couch. He wanted me to sit beside him.

My heart thudded. Would Kiboro obey? I didn't know, so I held my breath and navigated one of the Trackers to lower myself onto the far edge of the couch. My sword hilt bit into my hip under my skirts. I stuffed Cira's scarf into my pocket.

The Imperati regarded me. "You reject my protection, my gift of fine clothing, and attempt to flee. Why?"

A vision of Kiboro, regal and composed, flashed through my mind. I straightened. "I ask that my retinue be returned to me."

His eyebrows lifted. "You dislike my guards and servants too? Is Pirthyia so distasteful?"

Chains clinked from inside the cage.

The Imperati inclined his head toward the sound. "Incredible, isn't it? I have asked my Nazakian slaves about this monster, since it came from their lands, but none have seen anything like it, and fear it. By your reaction, I assume Laijon does not possess more of its kind either. It is a mystery. A powerful one. It refuses to speak, but my guards will break it, and this monster's curse will serve me well."

My breath caught.

"Now, would you like to recant your lies before I list them? King Zaujo is dead. The crown prince sits on the throne. I offer my condolences, Princess."

I flinched. How did he know?

"Your new king does not come and pay his respects to me."

We were at war—

"That was the first insult." The Imperati's voice deepened. "The second is this. When we spoke of the treasure, why didn't you offer me the Eternity Gate?"

His question hung in the air. Threatening.

"Foolish Laijon forgets that long ago three nations searched for the lost treasure and Eternity Gate. Laijon, Ai'Biro, and Pirthyia. Together, we slayed the last Shadow and reclaimed the key to the Eternity Gate, and Laijon's king keeps it."

He knew. The key burned against my chest.

"Finding the Eternity Gate is Laijon's blessing, as it is the only way you can repay your debts to me." His voice turned harsh. "This gate, a source of endless power given by the gods, belongs to Pirthyia. No one else is strong enough to possess it. Who else is worthy? Speak, Princess."

This—this was impossible. "River serpents were found with treasure in their bellies. Nothing more has been discovered for centuries."

"The ancients said everything survived, or nothing." He considered me. "I believe you have told me everything you know."

I resisted squirming.

"So I will share my full plan." The Imperati leaned against the couch. "I know that the mountain peoples attacked Laijon. I know, because I gathered and sent them."

What?

"Laijon could not find the Eternity Gate and open its power first, so I sent the mountain peoples to distract you. I could have sent more powerful allies, but chose to be merciful. Once my second army arrives tonight, I will go to Laijon myself. Then, I will meet your new king."

Laijon, my Laijon. Kiboro, what should I do?

"Bargain with me now, while I listen. I alone can offer hope for your people." He placed his fingertips together. "King Zaujo entertained a marriage proposal between you and a lesser king. I conquered this king and inherited everything belonging to him. When I overtake your country, having the Laijonese princess as wife will allow me to assimilate your people into mine. Regardless, Pirthyia will devour Laijon in life or death."

I couldn't speak. How could I agree to this? Kiboro—

Two high-ranking generals gained entrance to the room. They

offered sweeping bows and gave a report in Pirthyian. "The sacrifice is prepared. Shall we chain the prisoners outside?"

Kiboro, Roji, the guards.

The Imperati responded, but I didn't listen. It didn't matter.

Prisoners were the sacrifice.

I looked toward the cage, to the flames within the fireplace. I longed to hurl myself within the flickering red and orange tongues and disappear. Let them think my life was lost as I saved my friends. A soldier seemed to stand in the fire before I realized he was actually behind the blaze. It was a two-sided fireplace. How . . . useful. A better plan struck me.

The generals bowed again and strode from the room, and the Imperati's fierce gaze went to me.

Placate him. Now.

I gathered bravery like a cloak about my shoulders. Kiboro would not do this, but I wasn't her. I adopted a respectful tone. "High king, Laijon accepts your offer of . . . protection." I could not bear to say the rest.

The Imperati's eyes flickered.

I shivered. What was he thinking?

Then he relaxed and nodded toward my Pirthyian guards.

I was dismissed.

The Trackers' eyes followed me as I rejoined the soldiers.

The Imperati spoke in Pirthyian. "Keep her far from their arrival."

What did that mean? I was swept from his golden atrium back toward my prison. After a long, convoluted walk through the palace, we entered the familiar hallway. Pirthyian guards drank and caroused outside my room.

The soldiers escorting me ignored them as they opened the door, thrust me inside, and turned the lock.

I pulled a deep breath, then faced Cira's terrified eyes.

16

"YOUR STUPID, FOOLISH ESCAPE
failed, Princess, and you've been returned just as I knew you would
be. Now those mongrels drink for battle. Tonight, they might forget
to respect even you." Cira pressed her ear against the door, even
though the Pirthyians' muffled revelry filled the chamber. Her
thick, unbound hair cascaded down her back, and she wore my—
Kiboro's—gown over her undergarments. How quickly had she
untied herself? Given what was occurring outside the door, I was
thankful she was free, for her sake.

Everything within me felt numb. I wrestled the crown from
my hair.

"I will not tend you," Cira declared.

I ignored her and approached the satchel, still atop the bed,
to feel its lining. It was waterproof. I tore the lining out, spread it
across the bed, and poured the contents of my inner pocket into the
middle. Cira's scarf, the bimil, earring, and Jorai's bracelet. It was
silly, but I wore the earring again before gripping Kiboro's crown
and snatching the quilt.

Cira watched me warily.

I wrapped Kiboro's crown in the quilt and gripped the corners.
Forgive me. I swung the makeshift sack over my shoulder and
slammed it against the floor. Again. And again until I heard
a shatter.

There was an exclamation from Cira.

I checked inside the quilt to see a small, sparkling pool of jewels and metal circlet. One larger gem stood out. I scooped this into my palm, poured the rest into the waterproof lining, then secured the lining into a parcel and slipped it into my pocket against the sword. So heavy. I handed Cira her scarf.

She snatched it. "Are you mad?"

Maybe. I climbed onto the bed, unlatched the window, and swung it open to a red sunset stretching across the continent. Muggy air rolled over me.

Fingers dug into my ankles.

I looked down.

Cira clung to me, face white, eyes wide. The scarf restrained her hair again. "If you seek the eternal sleep, you send me there too. The Pirthyians already promise to punish me for your first escape."

Qo'tah. I hesitated, then offered her the larger, single jewel.

She gawked, then grabbed it.

I loosed the cumbersome sword from under my skirts, laid it across the bed, and faced the window.

Jorai spoke from my memories . . . *you just have to soften your feet and aim for dark water. I promise, there is nothing better than perhaps to fly . . .*

Oh, to be with him again.

I planted my hands on the window frame and trembled. "The Father of Light be with you." I leapt onto the sill and Cira cried out.

I jumped.

My stomach flipped as the world flew past, and then I hit lake water. Pain coursed through me, but I swam. Conscious. Unbroken. I surfaced for breath before plunging underwater again, and swam down the canal, past any guards who might have heard my splash.

The water's chill entered my awareness, along with its firm tug against my body. Did Pirthyia have river serpents? I turned over onto my back to float and kicked harder, until reaching an embankment and climbing out.

Bathed in dusk's rosy light, a trio of guards manned secondary gates into the castle, only lengths away. Awaiting orders to lock the doors before the second army's arrival.

They saw me.

Darkness, hide my dripping.

I bobbed Cira's curtsy and spoke Pirthyian. "My mistress needs me."

None moved. "Who—"

I darted past. One bawled an order. Two pairs of feet pounded behind me. I slipped through the gates into the castle and around a sharp, unfamiliar corner. And another. And another.

The soldiers gained. The passage would not end—

A double-sided fireplace on the left.

I threw myself into the flames.

Roaring drowned my hearing. Blinding brightness danced around me. I crouched to hug my knees to my chest and endured the flames licking up my limbs and across my head and back. A terrifying sensation, despite my suddenly fortunate gifting. Steam hissed from my soaked clothes.

Shadowed forms of the soldiers rushed past, not seeing me in the fire.

A sob rose in my throat. Do not stop. I pushed hair from my face and peered into the adjacent room, warmed by the same fire. I had not been here before. This chamber was abandoned and held more fireplaces.

Find the dungeon.

I crept from the fire, and my dried skin chilled in a room that should have felt warm.

Boxes, weights, and walls covered in blades surrounded me. A swordplay arena. I snatched a small dagger to tuck under my skirts and stole across the room to an opposite fireplace. I passed through its curtain of flames into another room and another fireplace. I halted in surprise.

The grand hall lay before me. Empty.

Roji said the dungeons were adjacent to this hall.

I forced myself to cross the room. The lower bowl stretched before me. The Imperati's lonely table reigned high above.

I felt exposed and raced by walls covered with gaudy decorations to hide in the next nearest fireplace. I peered through the licking blaze to see appalling lavishness and a covered cage, surrounded by four guards. The royal quarters, so close to the grand hall.

I tensed.

The Imperati was not present. Nor his Trackers.

I needed to find the prison. Yet I stood unmoving, struggling to breathe through the smoke.

The cage, with its dangerous prisoner, drew me. I thought of the Imperati's plan to enslave him.

My insides twisted. Time was too short, and I could not take on these soldiers. And what if the prisoner looked at me when he was released? Who would free Kiboro and Roji?

Dizziness swept over me, I backed into the grand hall, away from the prisoner, and gulped fresh air.

A decorated bear skull, covered with leather ties and feathers, was mounted on the wall a length away. One of many masks representing their gods.

I knew I could never live with myself if I didn't try to free him.

Without further thought, I snatched the bear skull and reentered the fire. The headdress burst into flames.

I placed the mask atop my head and stalked into the Imperati's apartments.

The guards saw me and cried out and drew swords from their sheaths.

I rushed forward.

Two guards darted into the hallway, shouting. I faced the two who remained. Their weapons glinted above ruddy, uncertain faces. The key to the cage hung from the shortest one's belt.

The other stepped back. "Fire demon."

Of course. I captured flames in my palm, set the rug on fire, and shrieked.

The soldiers stumbled as they ran. I chased the one with the key, seized his arm, and wrenched the key free before he flung me off. They fled into the corridor, and I slammed and bolted the door. I caught my breath and removed the bear skull from my head, tossed it into the fireplace, and stamped out the rug.

The guards would return with reinforcements.

I neared the cage, my heart pounding. I grasped the cover and pulled. It gave way, and I covered my face—my eyes—as the cloth rippled to the floor. I parted my fingers to see.

Iron chains bound the prisoner's legs and wrists, crusted in dark blood, forcing him to stand. My gaze trailed the dark, swirling stains covering his chest, arms, neck, to the burlap sack over his head.

Trembling, I fitted the key into the cage lock.

The prisoner's burlap-covered head turned.

I flinched, then the cage door grated open.

He pulled against his chains with—rage? Fear?

I could not make myself draw any closer, and whispered in Nazakian, "You will not serve the Imperati. Hurry. Open your hand."

He quieted and obeyed.

I dropped the key into his outstretched, mottled fingers, and his fist snapped closed.

I leapt backward, tore through the fireplace, and raced across the grand hall. Into another fireplace. Into the—yes—the stone dungeon.

But it was empty. The prisoners were already removed.

I hurried through the maze of passages. Where were the soldiers?

Drinking inside.

I ran through countless hallways. Fireplaces. Atriums. Fireplaces. Foyers.

All empty.

At last, I came upon a ground-floor window revealing a starless, charcoal sky and flickering bonfires. I used my dagger hilt to break and clear the glass before climbing out.

I dashed between the fires. Mountains of supplies stretched toward thick incoming clouds, and beyond them, several people were tied to stakes and connected by ropes. Their clothes were dirty, faces thin.

Bile rose in my throat. Barbaric Pirthyia would not have her sacrifice.

I ran toward the prisoners. Before the first one, a man, could cry out, I lifted my dagger and sliced his restraints.

Down the line, I slashed rope after rope and searched unfamiliar faces. Where were they? I hastened, my arms grew heavy, and dizziness threatened me again as I reached a broad-shouldered young man.

One of our Pre-Elites.

I groaned and cut his bindings.

When I offered the dagger, he took it and moved down the line of captives to finish my work. Some prisoners fled, some doubled back to help the rest.

I collapsed to my knees in the grass and pulled shallow breaths as a headache pounded. Why was I so exhausted?

A soldier ran past me. I looked up. Another Pre-Elite in battered noblemen's clothing. With Kiboro.

My voice croaked. "Wait."

Kiboro stopped, resisted the Pre-Elite's urging to continue, and ran to my side. Her face swam in front of me. I was crying.

"Carry her," Kiboro said.

I shook my head and struggled to stand, when a ghostly screeching rent the air.

Everyone froze, searching the skies. There was nothing but thick darkness, mist, and the rising wind.

The cries echoed closer.

What animal made that sound?

Kiboro's hand tightened on my arm.

Then I saw a figure. And another. Bodies sliced through the clouds until the heavens writhed.

Mysteries of—

Kiboro inhaled sharply and yanked me toward the bonfires. Prisoners scattered. I tripped, and Kiboro lost her hold on me.

Creatures dove from the sky and landed lengths away with unearthly howls. Pandemonium erupted.

I covered my ears and scrambled closer to the fires. Where was Kiboro? Blankets of mist curled across the ground.

Somewhere, Kiboro called my name.

From the mist, a creature unfurled its enormous, arched back. Firelight flickered over its wings, each the length of a man. Its agonized bellow rippled up my spine before it dropped on all fours.

Impossible. Shadows no longer existed. Their transforming spells were destroyed. Who would be willing to become—

It saw me and screeched.

I raced through swirling mist and jumped into the fires. Charred brush cut my feet. I gasped as claws gripped my arm and hurled me from the flames to cool, hard earth.

Darkness glided over me, then a scuffle exploded. The Shadow fought one of its own.

I gained my feet when I heard one lumbering after me. I ran through the haze, and the belabored gallop ceased before the creature barreled into me from above.

The Shadow flipped me face down and straddled my middle with crushing weight. My nostrils filled with its stench. The Shadow dug his clawed fingers into my clothing and spoke the trade language. "Is it you? He said a Laijonese girl had it. That was with his last breath." The Shadow searched my ankles, my wrists.

When the creature scrabbled with the front of my blouse, I fought. Then, I saw a medal swinging from his wrist. It was Barano's medal, encrusted with blood.

The Shadow cursed, spat, then searched my neck and pulled. The ribbon securing the key to the Eternity Gate bit into my throat and jerked my head off the ground.

It grasped the key and laughed wildly. "The damaged one did not lie before his death."

My heart stopped. The Shadow held the key to the Eternity Gate in its claws. Damaged one. Jorai's limp.

The Shadow wrestled to tear the ribbon off my head, and I screamed.

The monster howled and tumbled off of me. Someone swung me aside into a patch of weeds.

Against fire, the two battled. The Shadow sliced at its opponent and earned a groan from—my eyes flew wide. It fought the Imperati's prisoner.

The Shadow pinned him to the ground, as it had done to me. Its wings beat against earth and air, billowing dirt and fog until I couldn't see. The Shadow struck the prisoner again and again, then screeched. And screeched again. It choked, and then silence fell.

I stared through dust and ash. The Shadow's wings lay motionless, one stretched over the ground and the other fallen across its monstrous body. I waited for it to stir. Barano's medal lay on the ground near its hand. The Shadow was dead.

The Imperati's prisoner recoiled from the Shadow and retched. His back was to me, dressed from toe to wrist and up his neck in coarse fabric and leather, hiding his markings.

What had I freed?

More Shadows would come.

But I crawled to the winged corpse and pulled Barano's medal free. I brushed aside blood with my thumb, dizziness and weakness again gripping me.

The prisoner had turned and was approaching. A sword hung from an old scabbard at his hip—untouched during the battle. Its hilt was engraved with whorls, sea waves, and a shining sun.

Flee.

I couldn't.

I dropped my face to the ground and sensed his nearness. He hesitated, then slid careful hands, covered in leather gloves, under my shoulders and lifted me. I squeezed my eyes shut and bucked.

"You need to run," he said in Nazakian, like an apology.

He held me over his shoulder with one arm, the other wrapped around my left leg to clamp my right arm, and hoisted me into the air.

He ran from the bonfires, from the Shadows, into darkness. I bounced against his shoulder and struggled. He didn't slow, and his engraved sword slapped against his hip. My vision blurred as the headache strengthened.

He was kidnapping me. He was taking me away from Kiboro and Roji. He killed a Shadow.

Barano was dead. And Jorai—

Agony spilled into every corner of my body and mind. Tears came, and I wept until I couldn't breathe. Darkness crowded my vision, and then there was nothing.

17

HIDE.

I awoke to the rustle and twitter of forest. A blanket lay across my shoulders. Leafed branches and brush formed a shelter over me.

I tested my limbs. Stiff, but nothing was broken. I wore Pirthyian clothes. The key still hung from my neck, hidden under my clothes. Barano's medal pinched inside my fist.

Nearby movement captured my attention. I peeked through the brush and saw a cliff edge slicing across the dawn sky. The Imperati's prisoner sat lengths away with his back to me.

I suppressed a cry and dropped my gaze to the ground. My mind filled with the image of Shadows stirring Pirthyia's darkness. Comprising the Imperati's second army. Shadows supposedly no longer existed, but I saw them. Who were they, to warp their lives this way? One had climbed over me to steal the key—I looked at the medal in my hand.

Barano was dead.

I reached into my pocket and felt Jorai's bracelet. In my memory, I saw Jorai's smile.

He said you had it. With his last breath. The damaged one did not lie before his death. The words of the Shadow. The monster had encountered Jorai. He learned from Jorai that I held the key. My eyes welled with tears, and I wept. I mourned the torture he'd endured, for everything we had lost. If the Shadow had slain me, would I have crossed the Doorway to Heaven and seen Jorai again?

Kiboro and Roji must believe I was dead. Surely they traveled toward Laijon, looking for Barano and his accompanying soldiers. In vain. They did not know of the Imperati's betrayal against us or that Shadows served him. And these enemies were coming.

I must escape and rejoin them. Until then, I had to believe that Kiboro, Roji, and our guards would reach Laijon. If I doubted that, I would not be able to go on.

Barano's medal and chain went into my pocket. My fingers touched the key, under the Pirthyian bodice. Jorai, what about the key?

I glanced at the prisoner again. He remained seated, angled toward me just enough that I could see the side of his face. Markings swirled across his skin. A bow and quiver were strapped between his shoulder blades, and a huge knife lay sheathed against his lower back. He was covered in leather breeches, a loose, long-sleeved shirt tying up the front, with upturned collar, and boots tucked into his trousers. His wild hair swept across his face as he watched the sun crest Pirthyia's horizon with intense focus.

Shadow killer.

I studied his gloved hands. When he picked me up, he had not actually touched me. Were . . . his markings contagious? An old sword lay across his lap.

The prisoner stirred and wiped what must be an oiled rag across the blade. The unique weapon was engraved with whorls and waves surrounding glorious suns—

Mysteries of the continent.

The emblem of the sun belonged to the first Elite soldiers who handed the Eternity Gate to our enemies before the Occupation, if the bimil was true.

Impossible. He could not be one of the fabled, self-exiled zealots, bent on opening the Eternity Gate to redeem their honor. But if he was, were his markings some sort of curse for their betrayal?

The key burned against my pounding chest. I needed to leave.

A sensation crawled over me. It was heavy and made me feel like cornered prey.

The prisoner watched me from the farthest corner of his eye.

Qo'tah—

He turned his head forward, the strange feeling left—did I imagine it?—and he sheathed the sword, slipped it into a rucksack, and rose to his towering height.

I remembered the abandonment of my own sword.

The prisoner flexed his shoulders and lumbered about camp, packing everything up. Soon, every supply hung from the rucksack against his back, with the bow on top—I supposed he had reclaimed these things from the Imperati's quarters after I freed him—and he scattered his own shelter of brush before facing the rising sun, like the suns on his blade. He waited for me.

What should I do? Fighting him was a ridiculous thought, and the landscape was too open to run.

I could pretend meekness and find the right moment for escape, but what if he made eye contact with me?

I braced myself and exited the shelter.

He stiffened, which made me tense, but did not turn toward me, and kept his head bent toward the earth.

I tentatively prepared to scatter my shelter as he had done when I saw roasted meat wrapped in a large, charred green leaf lying on a nearby stone. I blinked. I did not dare eat it, but hid the meal under the brush and picked up the blanket. Why had he given these to me?

His head barely turned, and the awful sensation crept up my spine again. He looked at me, but yet he didn't, as if he studied my shoes. His gloved hands rubbed one wrist, then the other, before he spoke in a soft, rusty voice. "The Shadows are behind us." He nodded in an awkward manner. "Geras." He extended one gloved hand, palm down.

I didn't know that word, unless Geras was his name? An involuntary greeting in Nazakian tangled my tongue, but I didn't speak. Was he wanting the blanket?

After a terrifying moment where neither of us moved, he dropped his hand and strode into Pirthyia's forested bluffs, but hesitated when I didn't follow.

Go after him. Before he looks your way again.

I did, and he continued. I kept a careful distance as we headed up a rugged incline and wrapped the blanket around my shoulders. His pace was quick. Just when a cliff's crest looked near, I saw a higher mount behind. I fought against nausea and hunger pains. My throat was dry. I willed my body to be strong, and jumped every time he cocked his head to the side. But he only scanned our surroundings, again and again.

After the sun achieved its zenith, we reached towers of warm-colored rocks creating high-walled corridors. Clumps of vegetation and spindly trees clung to the stones and crevices. He picked thicker passages when possible and squeezed through the rest.

A feeling of entrapment increased until we reached a circular clearing with a small stream.

He—Geras—pointed to a flat rock.

I sat and watched him gather brush, again taking great pains to face away from me. A small pan emerged from his rucksack. When he stooped to spark the fire, hair fell back from the side of his face, and I saw the swirling stains trailing across his cheek.

I resisted recoiling.

He proceeded to purify stream water by boiling.

I crossed my arms against my middle. The sun had tipped just enough to discern that he'd traveled west. That took me away from Pirthyia's red earth and Kiboro and Roji. Panic rose before I noticed a skinny path twisting through the rock behind me.

Geras watched steam waft from the pan. He held a drinking tin. No, two tins.

I rose slowly, inhaled, and then fled down the thin path as he turned.

Rock walls soared above me, and the passage narrowed just when I heard his pursuit. I jumped over a stone, ran harder, and wriggled past the narrowest arms of the passage.

His pursuit halted, but I heard rocks crumbling and chanced a glance backward.

He climbed the walls.

I sucked in a breath and drove myself down the corridor, crawling through a tunnel and over gravel just before the passage widened.

Geras raced across the plateau above and gained.

No.

The waterproof bag in my underskirt pocket bounced against my thigh. My breaths became shorter, and dizziness befriended me again. Then I saw trees at the end of the tunnel.

I burst into a wide decline down the side of the cliffs, but Geras was right behind me. The sensation of his gaze strengthened.

I dashed for the forest. But he neared, closer—and grasped my arm. I screamed.

He covered my mouth with a gloved hand, crushed me against his chest with his free arm, and pushed me back toward the tower of rocks at an alarming pace.

He would hurt me. He would kill—

His terse whisper stopped my squirming. "Pirthyia tracks us. We will not lose them until we cross the border."

Pirthyia—of course the Imperati would send someone to pursue Geras. And me, for my illicit knowledge of the high king's dealings and as a bargaining chip. Did his bodyguards seek us? Or his Shadows?

Geras released me while continuing to push us through the rocks, via a wider passage, back to the clearing. When his gaze abated, he offered me water and hardtack. I made myself take it. He drained his tin in one mouthful, took my now empty cup, and stamped out the fire.

How was I going to escape?

Why did he keep me here?

I felt for the key. Nothing. Panic thundered through me as I reached around my neck for the ribbon.

"It is safe. Forgive me."

I froze.

Geras stood with his profile to me, palm open.

The key, dull and jagged, lay within his glove.

My chest rose and fell. He had taken it. A likely member of the fanatical Brotherhood held the key to the Eternity Gate. I imagined him touching the back of my neck to retrieve the ribbon.

Nazakian words flew from my tongue before I could think. "It is trash."

He stilled, likely shocked that I spoke his language, before his expression hardened. "The Shadow attacked you for this." He knew I lied. "When we arrive, and are safe from them, I will return it to you." When I did not respond, he slipped the key into his boot and shouldered his sack, ready to move on.

I didn't dare vex him further and kept pace when he moved into the wider passages cut from the rock. I had never felt so helpless.

A zealot wouldn't return the key to the Eternity Gate. Yet he'd revealed where he'd hidden it and had allowed me to live. Why? Was he so confident in his own strength? He acted like he kept it for my protection—unless he didn't know what the key was? Ridiculous. But he treated it so casually.

Hope flickered. He didn't recognize the key. Yet. I had to get it back so I could escape him. I found my voice. "Arrive where?"

I feared his anger, but his voice sounded surprised. "Laijon."

I startled. When he strode forward, I struggled to keep up.

Laijon. He traveled to Laijon. Why? Did he keep me with him as a guide? Me leading his power into my country—never.

I would deal with that later.

I tightened my resolve and trailed him at three lengths. Soon weariness invaded my bones, and I gritted my teeth every time he checked our perimeter and I felt the hint of his gaze. He was checking on me too.

The passages widened further, and I spied the sun's arc. We headed north and emerged in rising forest. He left me once to disappear into the woods and returned with a wild fowl over his shoulder. I took the opportunity of his absence to take care of personal needs, then we continued.

At evening, we stopped and made camp. First a small fire, two new shelters of branches, then the prepared pheasant began roasting.

I kept him in my peripheral vision. When he approached, I flinched. He bowed his head and placed a sharpened stick laden with meat on another stone before returning to the opposite side of the fire. He faced north, crouched as he ate, and then pulled the dagger free from the sheath across his lower back to whittle at a branch.

After I downed my meal, I hid the pointed stick in my skirt and retreated to the closest shelter. I found the quilt inside and arranged myself into a comfortable position.

He neared again.

I snatched my stick—

But he only laid a spear outside my shelter. The whittled branch was sharpened to an arrow's point. Then he stamped out the fire.

I pulled the blunt end of the staff inside with me and lay back down. After he retired, I pressed my face into the blanket and screamed.

He was not making any sense. I didn't know what to do.

I wished I was in my corner in Kiboro's chambers.

I curled into a ball and wept, not caring if he heard.

18

TREASURE SPILLED BEFORE ME
as jars of anointing oil burst into dancing flames. My skin charred.
Humans became Shadows, stirred the fires, and remained
unburned. Screaming. Seeking me.

I lurched upright.

Night paled. Across camp, Geras stood with arms crossed and
faced the heavens, looking like he was studying the fading stars.

Did he never sleep?

When he began preparing leftover pheasant for breakfast, I
crawled from my shelter, wary of his oppressive gaze. But he did not
look at me and stayed away, head down, as usual. We broke camp,
and I gripped the spear at my side as we headed north.

The sky pinked. I realized my strength had recovered and was
more aware of my filthy clothing and the grime on my skin. After
a while, he paused, removed his bow, and rubbed one thumb
over the string in what looked like indecision. Without looking
in my direction, he motioned for me to stay and disappeared into
the forest.

I felt the urge to run, but I needed the key first.

He returned empty-handed and we started again.

Midday, we paused for refreshment and tin cups filled with
water. I found a vine climbing a nearby tree, and as I busied myself
plucking and braiding the vine to tie my staff around my waist,
I had the strangest sensation that someone, other than Geras,
watched me.

Something shot through the treetops with a cry.

Shadow.

I recoiled, then saw a large, pale-colored bird catch the wind down the mountain. Geras had not been startled by the sound.

Our incline increased, and mist began curling among the treetops. My legs grew weary, and every time he checked on me, my frustration grew.

The earth dove into a narrow ravine with a stream far below. We leapt across. Soon, a mountain cap rose on our left, and a deep, rushing sound disturbed the wilderness. We reached a shallow canyon slicing across our path and discovered a river of frigid ice melt. The river was wide, deep, and quick, with banks covered in gnarled trees. It would be suicidal to swim.

Geras prowled the bank. He searched for an alternative path. That would cost us days. Days with Pirthyians following us. Days with him.

My stomach tightened, and I, too, began searching the bank, until spying a log fallen on the outskirts of the forest.

I ran toward the tree trunk and pushed. Then he was beside me, and together we dragged the log over the riverbank. It rolled two lengths downriver before its top crashed into the opposing bank and the opposite end caught in a thick tangle of bushes. But it held.

This was so dangerous.

Geras watched the churning waters. "This will be dangerous."

I startled at his echo of my thoughts. What did he know about water, coming from Nazak's dry wilderness? If he fell in, his abundant clothing would drag him to the bottom, and I avoided considering the weight of my skirts, which I also wouldn't dare remove.

Geras slung the rucksack off his shoulder and removed a rope to create two loops around the tree for our security as we clambered across.

My heartrate increased when he clenched the first loop of rope and crawled first. I lowered my stomach against the trunk and grasped my circle of rope.

A guttural howl rent the air, followed by echoed chittering.

I froze.

Shadows.

"Go," Geras said, and quickened his awkward pace.

I did, but looked back.

One of the Imperati's Tracker dogs emerged from the edge of the forest, lifted its snout skyward, and gave an eerie cry.

I willed myself to breathe.

From the forest, four individual cries coiled the air.

Five total.

The Tracker lunged forward to claw the bank and snarl, its long teeth gleaming. I bit back a shriek. The beast shook its bearlike coat, its gold collar flashing, as baying increased from the woods.

The log quivered as Geras paused and looked back.

We weren't going to make it—

The Tracker leapt atop the trunk and stumbled when it moved. Something snapped upon the bank. Our world jerked forward, and I toppled into the river. Freezing water gripped my entire body before my hold on the rope jerked me. I kicked, burst my head above surface, then sputtered against a large splash.

Geras dropped into the river and hugged his buoyant rucksack in front of him.

The Tracker mounted the tree again.

Geras reached for me with a gloved hand.

It was the only way. I stretched my free hand and grasped his with numb fingers, then released the rope. I swung close enough to grab hold of his bag, saw the strain in his free arm as he held to his loop of rope, then let go.

The river battled us downhill. Water rushed over my head and into my mouth. I resurfaced choking, and the howls of the Trackers filled my ears. Geras fought to steer us with his staff until it snapped, and we plunged into the mercy of the current.

Waves battered us faster and faster down the mountain, and I choked for breath as we plunged into rapids. I found myself facing backward. I turned to look ahead when my hold on the bag slipped.

He reached for me, faltered, and disappeared underwater.

I cried out, scrambled for a better hold on the sack, and then the river dragged me under and spit me out again. The bag sagged toward the riverbed—Geras held on and clawed for the surface. The river's roar grew. I flailed, but couldn't feel my limbs anymore.

The severed horizon promised a drop-off, just lengths ahead.

I kicked with strength I didn't possess. The opposite bank rolled into my vision, and an odd wave pattern splashed in a nook among a blur of dirt and gravel. Sandbar.

My body strained against the river, against the tug of Geras's weight and the sack.

The spear.

I freed the stave, drove it toward the riverbed, and my arm jarred with impact. I threw my body toward the wayward current. The river fought, but so did the weak tug toward the bank. My toes touched bottom. The grip of the river released, and a wave lashed us into shallow water.

I gasped and dragged myself onto dry ground, and Geras struggled after me. My muscles trembled beyond my control.

Praise be to the Father of Light. We should have drowned.

Something massive crashed past us, and I swung my gaze to see the log dive over the waterfall.

The Trackers. They stood on the opposite bank, watching us. It would take time, but they would catch up.

My satchel. I checked my pocket and teared up. Everything remained.

Geras rose from all fours and checked his zealot's sword inside the sack. Panting and dripping, he touched his boot. The key also survived the river. Then his gaze slid toward me. "Do you need a fire to dry your clothes?"

I paled. The thought of undressing in front of him . . . I preferred hypothermia. I shook my head. "We need to create distance."

He nodded and lifted his gaze north. "There are no more steep grades to help us lose them. We must push hard to reach the border."

Steep grades. He had known about the Trackers this entire time. I stood, and Geras took the lead.

We crested ridges and dove into valleys at a brutal pace. Breathing hard and listening. Desperation spurred us on until nightfall. At last, I dared to hope that we had lost the Trackers.

But Geras did not start a fire. Our clothes had dried, and the warm season was in our favor. He scaled a nearby tree with startling ease and arranged two sleeping spaces by looping more rope around branches and brush. After descending, he rummaged through his sack and took every effect out.

I observed from a distance with both hunger and strengthening anxiety. Why didn't he abandon me to the Trackers? I slowed him down. I cost him food. He wasted energy keeping an eye—sort of— on me constantly. He didn't harm me. What did he want? Why was he traveling to Laijon?

Kiboro and Roji crept into my mind. Were they close to reaching Laijon? Kiboro—

I stilled.

Did Geras think I was Laijon's princess? He hadn't seen me in Kiboro's finery, but he heard me in the Imperati's apartments, even if he did not understand the language. I sucked in a breath. *Qo'tah.* Did he keep me for ransom? Did he want me as security for the treasure, like the Imperati? Or worse, for the Eternity Gate, as a member of the Brotherhood?

I bit my lip. This ruse would not last once we reached Laijon, and I could never escort him into my country. Unless I misdirected or lost him somewhere like the tunnels. Him and the horrid key.

Bile rose in my throat. Could I do something so wrong?

Geras tugged a waterproof bag, not unlike mine, from his sack and checked the contents. A scroll and a thick book. He inspected the scroll, but the tome captured my curiosity.

Was it the rites of the dread Brotherhood? Superstitions of the faithless Nazak? Incantations to fuel his power?

I squinted in the dark and gasped.

It was a very old copy of the holy Nho in Laijonese. How had he acquired this? Terrible possibilities flooded my mind just as Geras's gaze swept over me. Though his face was down, looking at my shoes again, I knew he had seen my reaction.

"Can you read it?" he said.

The question took me aback, and I nodded.

He hesitated, then tucked the Nho under his arm, shouldered the rest of his belongings, and climbed the tree.

I forced myself to follow and scrambled up the first branch. He left me the highest shelter, and I climbed to it, then stopped, seeing a lump on the latched bed of branches.

His Nho.

Why did he put that here? It was a strange gesture, but I did not dare approach him to give it back.

Geras slipped under protective loops of rope on his "bed," and I did the same, tucked the Nho beside me, and breathed once the branches stopped undulating.

What was I to do? What was I to do?

He believed I was Kiboro.

I needed the key.

He gave me this Nho.

I remembered the Nho I had left in Pirthyia. I had not even missed it until now, the only instrument of faith we—Kiboro—had brought from Laijon.

Tears filled my eyes. I was among the worst—

Branches creaked.

I swiped my eyes and looked down. A pocket of moonlight washed over Geras's form climbing down the tree. After pulling the dagger free from his belt, he reached for the lowest branch, severed and dropped it into the brush below, then returned to his shelter.

19

I AWOKE TO MIST AND GLOOM, stiffness, and Geras scouting from our swaying treetop. No early morning reverie for him today.

The ropes restraining me helped me shimmy down the trunk to the forest floor. I readjusted the staff at my waist and laid his Nho in the open.

Breakfast consisted of berries and water before Geras tore down camp. I helped and worried. How far could the Trackers travel while we slept?

Geras passed me, and my shoulders tightened, remembering he thought I was Princess Kiboro. I needed to stop him from entering Laijon.

His terrible gaze swept over me, waiting. I locked my jaw and forced my feet to follow him down the zenith of Pirthyia's foothills.

Geras's pace was quick. I slipped twice striving to keep up, but otherwise ignored his broad back and gloved hands in front of me. As the sun arced, we sped on. Geras believing safety lay beyond the border.

The feeling of being watched touched my awareness again. I lifted my eyes skyward, saw nothing but blue, and rubbed my arms.

The forest thinned, and my eyes filled with a sea of tallgrass. We were so close to the end of Pirthyia. Geras's posture relaxed as we parted the grass and kept the falling sun on our left.

Fortune offered a hare in our path, and exhaustion forced us to stop and light a fire. Geras poured water into our tins and crouched over the roasting meat. I reserved my last swallow to moisten my face and hands, then I stared into the fire. The strangest desire to dance my fingers across the flame struck me. Better yet, to throw my whole being into it, pretend to be a fire demon again, and frighten Geras into letting me go.

Wait. Would that work? Or could anything frighten someone like him?

I chided myself and took out my Pirthyian braids, struggling to comb my fingers through the matted curls. With the extracted pins, I restrained my hair at the back of my head, then my stomach clenched as Geras's look rolled over me like a storm.

I frowned and thought of Kiboro. I straightened my spine and snapped my eyes up toward him, trained to his shoulder. Geras's entire body lurched, and his gaze slammed into the ground between his feet.

I breathed surprise. I had startled him.

I asked for more water. His eyes widened before he complied. That evening, I requested a larger shelter. He nodded. The following morning, after wading through endless savanna, I demanded an extra break, and we sat, and after a moment, when I stood, he stood as well.

I wondered if he would pluck leafy branches and carry them over my head as shade if I asked. His obedience wearied me, and I allowed my carriage to droop as he parted tallgrass lengths ahead of me.

Except I was catching up.

I slowed down, and the gap shrank again. He was doing that. He turned slightly and his scanning look brushed over me. "How long have you been away from your homeland?"

I stiffened and did not answer.

He tried again. "I hear that Laijon holds mountains and ocean."

His painstaking way of speaking was irritating. And he dared converse with the princess. Had our river escape made us too familiar?

"Do you remember your homeland?"

I interlaced my fingers in front of me and forced myself to remain calm, as Kiboro would. "Of course."

"My da told me about Laijon."

I swallowed as the Imperati's haunting question returned to me. Were there more of him?

Geras swiped a gloved hand against the back of his collared neck. "He is ill, so he gave me his sword and task."

The ancient, sun-engraved sword he kept in his rucksack. Then his da was the true zealot.

Answering him marred my pretend position, but I could not stop myself. "What is the task?"

Geras stood taller, if that were possible, and spoke faster. "I will meet with his liaison in Laijon and then join the rest of the Brotherhood in the mountains."

He actually said it. Geras was part of the Brotherhood, and they had a sympathizer in Laijon. Now he traveled to meet this blasted traitor.

I had to stop him. But how?

He brushed another swathe of grass aside and looked like he was stumbling over a question. "What is your name?" He sounded hesitant, not rude. Like he did not know how to phrase that question.

Howls tore the air.

We broke into a run. Surely our feet gained wings, but their cries gathered and neared. A squeal caused me to stumble. Behind us, a squabble followed a terrible yelp.

Geras slowed and I almost ran into him. We faced a narrow clearing with a quiet stream and its banks. He stepped into the stream and movement caught my eye.

A Tracker emerged several lengths away.

Geras froze, but it was too late.

The Tracker lifted its muzzle in a piercing cry and charged past him. For me.

Geras reached out and tackled the Tracker. Both careened into the water. The Tracker reared, then lurched aside, unmoving.

Geras rose to his feet and wiped his bloody dagger against the ground, breathing hard.

My chest rose and fell, and I pulled my staff free.

One Tracker out of five.

Geras jogged to me, slipped his rucksack to the ground, reached inside, and pressed a second, smaller dagger into my hands. Then, he pushed me to my knees in a clump of grass and covered me with an armful of dead brush.

I realized what he was intending, but they would still find my scent.

Geras removed his gloves and shirt, stepped back into the stream, and waited. Knife in hand.

Through sticks and leaves, I stared between the markings swirling across his torso and the abandoned rucksack.

Two more Tracker cries filled the air.

Geras's posture tensed, and the animals materialized from the grasses to circle him. He eyed both, and the Trackers jumped. Geras stabbed the first and flung the second aside.

My eyes widened upon the fourth animal sneaking through the grasses past me. It limped and blustered before lowering its sniffing nose and creeping toward me.

I held my breath.

Geras shouted.

The limping dog jumped onto my hiding spot. Its weight sank on top of me with a flurry of clawing paws.

I jabbed my dagger upward twice. It yelped and wrenched away, taking my knife with it. I scrambled from under its body and braced myself with my staff, but the Tracker collapsed with the dagger hilt in its ribs. Barely breathing.

Geras struck at his Tracker, missed, and the creature pounced.

The sword.

I lunged to Geras's rucksack to grasp the sword with both hands and whirled to meet a hurtling mass. Teeth sank into my leg. I shrieked and sliced downward, making contact, but was dragged to the ground. I turned onto my back and lifted the sword for the awaited impact. Instead, Geras grabbed the Tracker around its middle and hauled it backward.

I stood and clutched the sword tighter.

The dog was on top of him. Geras roared, flipped the dog, raised his knife—

I averted my eyes as he struck and heard the animal's dying cry. I ran a hand over my face, then looked down. Red trickled down my leg, but I felt nothing. My gaze shot to Geras.

Bloody, clawed wounds covered his chest and back, his markings.

"We must continue." Geras stumbled toward his sack, fell to his knees, and rose again.

I scanned the stream, then the four Tracker bodies. The embedded dagger.

I approached the formerly limping Tracker. It no longer breathed. I tensed, then pulled the dagger free and jumped away. Then I saw the deep, thin slashes across its hide. More than my one or two strikes. Something else had attacked it first.

Geras groaned as he pulled his shirt and gloves on, and glanced back and forth before finding the sword in my hand. I gave it and the dagger back to him, then tore strips of my underskirt for his wounds and mine. We bound ourselves, he cleaned and stowed the blades, and we ran the best we could. I threw countless glances backward as tallgrass whipped our sides.

Where was the fifth Tracker?

Just before night fell, we reached a hill of rocks. They seemed stable and formed a cavity with just enough headspace to sit upright.

We crawled inside the cave, and Geras covered the opening with brush. We made no fire and sat catching our breath. At last, he reached into his sack and pulled the stopper out of a jar. The reek of animal fat and herbs swirled into our cramped space. A poultice?

Geras ducked his head and gestured for me to open my hands. "For your wounds."

I shook my head. "You first."

But he insisted, and I used my thumb to scrape a little into my palm. When Geras turned and reached under his shirt, I turned to face the opposite direction. A metallic scent filled my nostrils. So much blood lost, especially his. The poultice stung the cuts on my calf, but when Geras groaned, I swallowed.

The first Tracker racing past him repeated in my mind. They had wanted me, not him. He could have escaped, but he'd fought. His power hadn't worked on the Trackers, but he had seemed to expect that. He'd protected me and the lie I lived. Even if he planned to gain a ransom for a princess, let alone destroy Laijon by opening the Eternity Gate's judgment, I couldn't bear my guilt. And what paltry ransom of Laijon's, even if I were Kiboro, would be worth him risking his life for mine twice?

Geras grunted as he rebound his gashes with the same bloody rags. I heard the jar go back into his sack. Then he settled himself to guard the entrance, the dagger across his lap. He pressed his gloved palm against his damp forehead.

My insides twisted, but I had to speak. "I am not who you think I am. I am just a handmaiden." You gamble your life for nothing.

He went still. "The Pirthyians did not enslave you?"

Enslave—I looked down at Cira's ruined clothes and touched my piercing. Something crashed inside of me.

He didn't think I was Kiboro.

My heartrate sped, and I blurted, "My name is Seyo, and I serve Laijon's princess." Wait, that made me sound important.

His chest heaved as he struggled to straighten. Panic hurried his words. "Forgive me. I did not know."

No—don't treat me differently.

Then he slumped, and I realized how pale he was. "I must rest." And then he closed his eyes. His breathing evened out. Asleep.

I pressed my back against the opposite wall and covered my face.

He hadn't thought I was Kiboro. He had believed I was a slave. Yet he'd allowed me to order him around and had risked his life for me. Was this part of the Brotherhood code, or was he repaying me for freeing him from the Imperati's cage?

A shuddering sob rose in my chest, and then my eyes strayed

to his boots. The key. But I reached out for his sword inside the rucksack.

He did not stir.

I shifted to the front of the cave and sat with the blade held in front of me, as he had meant to do. Endless tears slipped down, and I remained on guard until dawn, when I fell asleep and he awakened.

The fifth Tracker never arrived.

20

MY ILLNESS CAME WITH EXHAUSTION
and chills. Geras noticed immediately, despite my efforts, and we
remained in the cave. He only abandoned the cave entrance to hunt.
We never spoke of the missing Tracker, and fever scrambled my
thoughts anyway. Even after the fever broke, I inhabited dreams and
snatches of consciousness that I was too weak to fight.

Through this, Geras spoke. "I became ill after Da took me in . . .
he read to me," he said. Shifted. "It strengthened my fight, like yours,
Seyo . . ."

His words slipped in and out of my mind like an anchor to reality.
He spoke of Nazak, her remaining gardens of renown and uncharted
wastelands. His halting murmur strengthened. He spoke of his
adoptive da, descended from the Elite soldiers of Laijon, who served
as a skilled warrior in his youth . . . my repetitive thoughts took over.

The Brotherhood made their tarnished honor more important
than Laijon in their pursuit to open the Eternity Gate . . . without the
key or location of the gate, they remained a small threat compared
to Pirthyia and her Shadows . . . would it be any worse if Vedoa rose
from their flaming deserts to devour us, too . . . was Geras's skin
contagious . . . ?

Geras's voice grasped my wandering mind. He spoke of his first
slave master . . . and my consciousness slipped . . . he spoke of his
third master at the age of eleven, and then Da adopted him as his
son, despite Geras's curse to hurt, even kill, through eye contact.

Now he cared for his aging da, and he swore before the Father of Light to never use his curse again.

Somehow, my desperate mind wrought one answer from this.

Geras, in his markings and power, was alone . . . how did he gain a curse?

My disorientation passed. I focused on a tin of water, drank, and struggled to raise myself on my elbows.

Geras sat in the cave entrance with the Nho open across his knee. But he stared at one page and never turned it.

For the first time, I wondered how old he was. If one removed the unseen burden that aged him, and occasional childlike ignorance, he seemed like he would fit in with Roji and his soldier friends.

Geras's gaze seared across me, though his eyes never traveled higher than my feet. He expelled a breath. "How do you feel?"

My voice scraped. "Better." I paused. "Thank you."

The tension in his brow eased.

After another day, my strength returned. When I gathered my things and exited the cave, he did too.

We dove into more tallgrass. He slowed the pace for me. We stopped at the first stream to wash our arms, necks, and faces, and blood stained the water. Rain fell, and the wet grasses surrendered to wilderness. The border.

I held my breath as we crossed into southwest Laijon, and tears stung my eyes.

I would find Kiboro. Roji. My father.

But Huari now sat on the throne as king, and his threats resounded in my mind. He knew I held the key, and it could not fall into his hands—after I liberated it from Geras, somehow. But the key was now safe outside Pirthyia and far from the Imperati.

Yet it neared the Eternity Gate.

We camped on the outskirts of the desert. The rain eased enough to start a fire and build shelters. But I could not stomach food and was uneasy under Geras's gaze from across the flames. At last, I retired to a sleep invaded by nightmares.

We were in the smaller house in Laijon's inner quarter,

purchased after Father lost his position as royal historian. Mother gripped my wrist and plunged my hand into our lit fireplace, and then she ran away from us again and again. A Shadow set ravenous fire to the house's creaking frame, but Barano slayed the monster. When Kiboro's bodyguard turned toward me, his face hardened, his body morphed, and wings burst from his back.

I shrieked, and a young man called my name from the burning doorway. It was Jorai, shining like a heavenly messenger. His limp was gone.

I wept and ran toward him, but the first Shadow snatched me. I fought, then saw that the Shadow was Roji. I screamed—

—and roused with a gasp.

The desert whispered night sounds, but the position of the moon promised morning's near arrival. Something shifted outside my shelter. Geras, standing guard.

I exited my shelter, breathed fresh, cool air, and seated myself a little distance away. Of course, he watched me, but with hesitation, as if he was about to say something. "You grieve."

Surprise and embarrassment flooded me. Had I cried out in my dream?

Geras sat with his elbows on his knees. "I cannot fight your grief."

I stiffened. I needed to be strong for myself. Don't try to commiserate with me. Please, just leave me alone. I drew my legs into my chest. My heart had given up. Emptiness crowded everything else away.

Geras shielded the side of his face with his hand and lifted his eyes to the starry heavens. I still looked away, just in case.

He spoke slowly. "When I was young, and the terrors came, my da took me to the forest and told me to find strength in the skies."

Did he mean star worship? Perhaps this was a ritual to strengthen his awful power.

"The sun surrenders to night. Sometimes the moon disappears. Yet through the stars, the Father of Light still shines, and the greatest darkness cannot defeat them."

Not idolatry. He quoted the Nho in Nazakian. For some reason, his faith in the Father of Light didn't surprise me, and yet I swallowed uneasiness. It seemed impossible that we could share the same faith.

He rubbed his wrists—why did he keep doing that? "Da says there are times to groan and wrestle with grief, to lament, and there are times to remain silent and know that you are small."

He began to murmur. Under his mess of hair, a blush crept across his coal-stained neck and ears at my notice, but he continued. Once I understood his words, my blood chilled.

He prayed the first adulation from the Nho.

My jaw fell. He petitioned without anointing oil, without the holy text, without kneeling. It wasn't right.

I pressed my face against my knees and waited for his display to end. Surely he was innocent in his ignorance. The Father of Light could forgive this if someone taught him how to confess correctly. Someone trained at the temple. Like me.

No. I was steeped in lies and secrets and mistakes, and wore prayer like a ragged blanket. I couldn't even dream of donning priestess's robes anymore. The broken places inside of me became unbearably sharp. Would nothing heal me?

A sob rose in my throat, and I begged for this torture to end. But I knew it couldn't. Why?

Because Jorai was gone.

I squeezed my eyes closed and rocked back and forth.

Why had the Father of Light allowed this?

I found the treasure in the tunnels, and Huari condemned Jorai, King Zaujo imprisoned him, strangers tortured and warped his form into the sick likeness of a Shadow, and Shadows killed Jorai for the key he didn't have. Because he had given it to me.

I should have suffered, but Jorai stole my fate and died for it. And perhaps that was better than for him to be reshaped into a Shadow and doomed to eternal separation from Heaven's gate.

The gaping hole inside me widened, and I forgot about the night sky and Geras. A moan escaped me.

I, and perhaps all of Laijon, was abandoned.

The petition escaped my lips as my breath hiccupped. "Please. Oh, please. Let me see him beyond Heaven's Doorway. Protect Laijon. Let me bear the consequences. Please . . ."

Something touched the inside of my heart.

Peace, like what I felt at the Handprint of God, held me still. Stayed my tears. I did not see it. I did not hear it. The warm, invisible companionship lasted forever, yet it passed in a moment. And everything settled.

This was not Geras's gaze. I moistened my lips. *Who are you?* my mind cried.

I didn't receive an answer, but the incomprehensible peace drew closer. My eyes widened. I heard without sound.

I would see Jorai again, and evil would not be victorious.

I drew a long breath and the presence released me, but left something within my heart. A sureness . . . freedom. I tasted this and felt ordinary, desert air waft over me. The presence had been untouchable, indescribable, unbelievable. Yet it was more real than anything else I had known.

My grief was for what was lost, but lost temporarily, I knew now. And the Father of Light, through this invisible messenger he sent, seemed to promise that he did not abandon what was his.

Didn't the Nho say that too?

The wilderness brushed and skittered and sang with distant night birds. I listened with fresh awareness and suddenly realized I missed my father. Father of Light willing, I would see him again soon. And Kiboro and Roji.

I scrubbed my eyes and looked toward Geras, wondering if he had witnessed my experience—but he stood. And the world glowed.

I looked around and stared.

A carpet of pink, orange, and yellow blanketed the desert and illuminated the night. Large flowers erupted from every bush and cactus like a fantasy world. Heady fragrance filled my senses. Was this from the rain? I had read that rain could cause even the desert to bloom. It was so bright, I could hardly see the stars. Almost as if the Father of Light transported his brilliance from the skies to our feet. So glorious.

A night bird swept past Geras, and he smiled. I had never seen him smile.

For the first time, I did not fear or hate seeing Geras, even with the key tucked in his boot. I could almost believe that he would return the key to me soon. And then—

The answer became clear, and I missed a breath.

The key must be destroyed to protect Laijon before Huari seized it, Pirthyia arrived, or the Eternity Gate was found. Was the key destructible? Could I melt it, or break it, or feed it to the tunnel flooding to be swept to the depths of the ocean? I would send the bimil with it, which somewhere kept the secret of the gate's location.

But what of Geras? Didn't I now owe him a life debt?

I bit my lip and squirmed considering that. I would keep him from harm. I would help him find his liaison. Geras seemed like the kind of person who would be impossible to move once his mind was set. And without the key, it would not matter if the Brotherhood reunited.

I looked at the sea of flowers. Bright, yellow blooms rose nearby, and I stooped to cup a bud in my hand. It gleamed against my palm, like Laijon's gifting. I released the flower and climbed back into my shelter.

With the quilt rearranged, I could fall asleep watching the glowing desert and hold on to the peace I'd felt moments ago. I untwisted my skirt from my legs and wished I could wear something else into Laijon, not that anyone would notice me next to Geras. But we couldn't let anyone see us, anyway.

Then Geras and I would part ways. Part of me felt remorseful. He was kind, and the mystery behind his curse would tug at my curiosity for the rest of my life.

What did one see within his eyes?

Qo'tah. I banished the wild thought and rolled over. For the first time in so long, I fell into a deep and quiet sleep.

21

I CHOSE TO BELIEVE THAT ROJI, Kiboro, and the guards had already arrived in Laijon by following Pirthyia's train tracks and avoiding the strenuous foothills. I could not consider anything else.

We neared populated areas, and Geras decided to travel during late hours. As we navigated Laijon's thick, southwest forest, now in full bloom even after dusk, I completed my plan. After Geras met his liaison and handed me the key, I would destroy it—but not in the tunnels. That would put the key too near the bellies of river serpents and Huari's soldiers, and the tunnels reminded me of Jorai. Instead, I would go to the Handprint of God and drop the key into the covered well. No one would search there, and it felt right, like I was returning the key to the Father of Light.

But I needed to part with Geras first. Secrecy was crucial, and I could not bear to see him pray incorrectly at the holy site.

The forest thinned, dawn neared, and Geras asked if we would see Laijon's mountains soon. My heart galloped at the thought—of home, despite everything—and I said yes.

Geras nodded, but his pace did not quicken. His heavy gaze swept over me twice. "Seyo." He still hesitated pronouncing my Laijonese name. "Have you traveled into the mountains?"

My shoulders hitched. The mountain people controlled that region and only abandoned it for war, such as now. "No."

"The Brotherhood meets there, Seyo."

He had already told me that, and I was starting to wonder if he wanted to say something more, but kept cutting himself off. For the past two days, he said my name in every other sentence. It was considered rude. I wondered if he wasn't used to talking to anyone besides his da. The thought saddened me, and I did not correct him. Perhaps I should ask some of my questions, too, before we parted.

I clasped my hands behind my back. "Who is your liaison?"

"My da was friends with his father. That is all I know."

So, it was a man, and someone with Nazakian connections. The son of a merchant? Soldier? "What will you do after journeying to the mountains?"

"The Brotherhood will make plans to find the Eternity Gate and open it. But I must prove that I come in place of my da." He frowned.

"Geras, the Eternity Gate is prophesied to hold terrible judgment. Is the Brotherhood's lost honor worth this?" I wanted to clap my hand over my mouth. So forthright, and should I have given my knowledge away? But with pieces of the treasure found, every nation was digging into their texts and finding remembrance of the Eternity Gate, as Pirthyia had done.

Geras held his gloved hands behind his back as well and supported his rucksack with his wrists. "It is not about honor. The Father of Light gave the Eternity Gate and commanded it to be opened."

That was it? What of Laijon's wrongs? The Eternity Gate could not be a gift to our nation anymore. And soon the key would be gone. "Why do you need to prove you come in your da's place?"

"He is a great leader among the Brotherhood, and I can only add his sword to the soldiers' ranks, if I am accepted." Geras rubbed the back of his neck. "They will not expect me."

I winced under his double meaning. The Brotherhood would not expect a man standing a head taller than them, covered in strange markings, able to kill without touch.

There were so many questions I was afraid to ask. I chose two and asked the easier one first. "How old are you?"

His ears pinked. "I think I am twenty winters."

He *thought*. I had embarrassed him, and my heart ached as I reached to touch my copper earring. Neither Kiboro nor Jorai knew it was a slave piercing because forced labor was illegal in Laijon. Tol, who had been like a sister to me during our childhood, was smuggled into our country by my mother, who lied and called her an orphan and housemaid. Vedoa kept slaves, and Tol had been enslaved too young to know when she was born. I remembered when Tol told me, when I first saw her second earring. We had wept together, and I had sworn to always protect her and help her gain her freedom. Tol and I had chosen her birthday, too, the same as mine. If Geras was right about his birthday, that put all three of us close in age, if Tol still lived. When Mother left, she took Tol, and I couldn't stop her.

I pushed those awful memories away, ignored the familiar churning in my stomach, and focused on my last question—because I needed to escape its torment. "You said you swore to never use your power again. Why?"

Geras stiffened, and so did I. I shouldn't have asked that. Had I angered him? But he spoke mechanically. "It is not from the Father of Light."

Ice trickled into my veins. Then where did his power come from? He had broken his vow to kill the Shadow who'd attacked me.

I swallowed. That was why I would help him find his liaison, and refrain from spitting on the traitor's shoes.

Geras halted. I looked past him and shouldn't have been surprised by the sight, but I was.

Bathed in pale sunrise, Laijon's distant mountains rose, but the fields between us stretched in charred ruins. Tree trunks stood riddled with arrows, surrounding an abandoned camp belonging to the mountain tribes. Hastily dug graves lay beside mounds of dirt to shield against Laijonese artillery. Smoke stretched across the horizon far away.

The Imperati said he had paid the mountain peoples to attack us.

I narrowed my gaze. "Hopefully they moved west. Let's continue before making camp."

At dusk, after awakening and eating early fruit for a meal, we reached a rural town. Ransacked. I explained that the people had fled to the capital within the castle walls. Geras nodded and, his map memorized, turned east.

Slowly, the way became familiar. My chest throbbed, and then the walls and gates surrounding the temple grounds appeared, washed in sunset. Why was he taking us here?

Geras reached the nearest gate and swung it open.

I held my breath—but the grounds were intact, unsullied by enemies, but deserted. All priestesses, priests, and temple helpers must have sought refuge within the walls too. The emptiness felt wrong.

Geras continued.

I followed and moistened my lips. "Where are we going?"

He didn't pause. "I look for a well called the Handprint of God. Do you know it, Seyo?"

Speechlessness robbed my reply, and he was too focused to notice as he searched for unspoken landmarks. The pebble path crunched underfoot past silent housing, the temple, surely locked up, and then the fence hugging the Handprint of God's untamed brush.

But Geras did not approach the covered well. He found a skinny path that led to one place. The temple drenched in moonlight.

My pulse quickened.

Geras approached the heavy doors.

The priests would have secured—

But he pushed it open, stopped me with an extended, gloved hand, and patrolled the darkened interior first. Like Barano would. Then he waved me in and closed the door.

We entered empty, holy chambers littered with the remains of meals, unfolded bedrolls, and muddy footprints. *Qo'tah*, Laijonese soldiers must have used this as an outpost. Geras led us through hallways to a plain, wooden door, and I stared. It was the Archives. He was meeting his liaison here, of all places? Geras entered, and I made myself follow.

Trash filled this room, including bottles of hard drink, though the scent of parchment remained. I stepped over half-used candles and a tinderbox, a dangerous item to place among precious manuscripts, before inhaling sharply. Between dusty tapestries, some wall-to-ceiling bookshelves lay bare. Then I recognized the deliberate order of removal. Important copies and the few surviving originals were missing. The priests and priestesses must have transported these precious documents within the city walls when they left.

I swept my gaze to the corner with the king's laws, which were also removed, and to the back wall, where another empty bookshelf hid the secret door leading to the tunnels—and saw Jorai leaning on his cane.

I blinked, and the illusion vanished.

Geras lowered his rucksack and bow to the dusty, wooden floorboards, knelt, and removed a strip of crimson fabric from the bag. He left the Archives and returned moments later, empty-handed. Surely, the scarlet flag was tied to some tree to signal his liaison.

I cleared a spot on the floor, sat with my tattered skirt spread past my ankles, and waited. Geras faced the empty bookshelves.

It was beyond strange seeing him here. The Archives were the hallowed ground of my past, and here was Geras, a piece of the scary, new world that I hoped to escape as soon as possible. And yet, Geras didn't seem out of place.

The empty shelves taunted me, and my throat constricted. The bimil said that the lost treasure included the gilt-bound books that our historians had desperately copied from memory following the Occupation. Was it true?

Qo'tah. I wished Geras would give me the key and release me, but I had to make sure he met his liaison.

I could hide nearby until this person came—I wanted to see who it was too. Then I would return to the Handprint of God, perform my deed, and find a way inside the castle walls.

And then what?

I would reunite with Kiboro and Roji.

And then what?

I squirmed. I must tell them of the Imperati's betrayal, that he stirred the mountain peoples against us and commanded the Shadows. We would need to tell Prince—King—Huari, who would search me for the key, but it would be gone.

And then Laijon would fight. Even if Pirthyia found the Eternity Gate, they couldn't open it. Maybe the gate had always held judgment, and that was why our ancestors had sold it.

The thought surprised me. I supposed no one but the Father of Light remembered the truth.

The Father of Light gave the gate and commanded it to be opened.

I winced. Geras could not fully understand what he'd said. But what would have happened if the Eternity Gate had not been sold, but swung wide? Would it have stopped the enemies from across the sea? Could it have prevented the Occupation? Would Laijon still remain in debt to Pirthyia? Would Jorai have lived?

I shook myself, then saw Geras crouching to pull the ribbon and key free from his boot. What was he doing?

"Are you safe here? Are you near your home?" he said.

My heart skipped a beat. "Yes." Was he changing his mind about giving it to me?

Floorboards creaked as he neared and lowered his gloved hand within reach, gaze aside.

The key was so jagged.

I stood, gripped the ribbon—goodness, the key's weight—and turned to tuck it into my skirt pocket. Geras had kept his word. "Thank you," I whispered.

His gaze brushed me. "Why did the Shadow want that?"

I forced my voice to sound calm. "I am not sure." That wasn't a lie. "It belongs to someone else." But it would drown in the Handprint of God forever.

Geras nodded—though clearly unconvinced by my vague answer—and crossed his arms. He worried for me.

I should leave. But where was the liaison? I realized that their rendezvous was possibly delayed due to Geras's capture in Pirthyia. And my sickness had slowed him down too. What if the liaison hid within the castle walls and couldn't leave the city?

Slow footsteps sounded against stone in the hallways.

Geras cracked the door to look, and I joined him. An elder priest rounded the path toward the Archives with a burlap sack over his shoulder.

I couldn't believe it. He was the liaison?

A small contingent of Laijonese soldiers appeared behind the priest as escort. They carried the burlap for books.

I leapt backward and reached to shut the door, but a soldier had spotted me.

Geras heaved two bookshelves and the reading table against the door.

Hurried bootsteps stomped near. The priest's keys jingled. The door struggled against the bookshelf, and a fist fell upon the door. "Open up, vagabond."

First the Laijonese language washed over me, then their irritation. No fear or horror. They hadn't fully seen Geras. Yet.

The banging increased by several fists then paused. A sudden, great boom rocked the walls. Dust motes flew.

Geras strapped his rucksack and bow across his back again and said, "Seyo, show yourself to them. Your people will protect you."

"They'll see you." His markings—

"Do not defend me or they will think I cursed you."

What in the continent? But he was right. And as I was helped to safety, the soldiers would attack him. He knew this, but did not reach for his bow, knife, or sword. He said he had vowed never to use his power, and with no one beside himself to protect—

I choked. "Will you defend yourself?"

He heaved a breath and shook his head. "They don't know any better."

No! He would be killed. My mind raced. What if we disappeared in the tunnels? Soldiers would follow and seal the exits. Vanishing was impossible.

The door heaved with another blow and soldiers shouted.

Sweat dripped off Geras's face. "Go now, Seyo."

And abandon him here? I couldn't. The only way to save him was to . . . pretend he died.

I darted across a mess of glass bottles to grab a filthy bedroll, then budged the far, empty bookshelf aside to reveal the hidden door. "It leads to a tunnel. Follow it." My voice caught. "I'll distract the guards and then follow."

Geras's wide shoulders bunched. "I will stay with you."

Qo'tah. "Then wait here. Do not intervene." I gripped the bedroll in my fist and hurried to toss it against the threshold of the main door just as the soldiers rammed against the other side again.

I dashed to the nearest filled bookshelf, tugged a handful of tomes to the floor, and ripped their pages free. Without hesitating or allowing myself to think, I pushed the small pile of parchment atop the bedroll and felt backward for the tinderbox. I gripped the metal case in my shaking hands and struck twice to light the dry fibers inside.

I couldn't think of any other way. Forgive me.

I scattered the ignited kindling against the door, then the bedrolls, until I ran out. This was going to take too long.

Across the room, Geras watched. Shocked.

I lifted a burning paper, carefully so he would not see me touch fire, and lit the tapestries. I looked back.

Flames crawled and smoke rose from the door to the nearest bookshelf. Book covers slowly caught fire, then wrinkled and shriveled as the inferno grew and spread across their spines. A plume of boiling air swept across the room.

Tears filled my eyes.

Outside, the soldiers cried out as blazes climbed the door.

Something monstrous groaned. Wind gusted as the nearest bookshelf buckled, and Geras and I scrambled aside as the shelves toppled and spilled their blazing contents across the floor.

He slapped ash from his clothes and sack and shouted. "Stay down."

Smoke rolled across the ceiling. *Qo'tah.*

I grabbed Geras's gloved forearm and spoke above the roar. "Hold my hand and do not let go. The fire will not harm you. I promise." I crawled around the bookshelf, toward the tunnel door, dragging him with me. Smoke swirled above, and flames devoured portions of the floor.

Father of Light, please—

The Archives burst into flames.

The fire consumed us. Geras's hand clenched my wrist. Heat raked over me, but without pain. It would be the same for him if he held on.

I felt along the floor, found the open doorway, and plunged into the sudden cool of the tunnels, still gripping Geras's arm. Flickering firelight danced behind us, and Geras slammed the door closed.

I released his forearm, and we ran across wet ground until we reached the locked gate. I gasped. We didn't have the key. But the gate's rusting bottom half had been knocked out. It hadn't been like that before. We crawled under and through toward the Heart.

Something crashed above and the earth trembled. Flashover exploding in the Archives fire.

I folded over my knees. My breath hiccupped, and my vision swam. I couldn't think about what I had just done. But days would pass before the soldiers could search for our scorched corpses and realize our trick.

Geras swatted his clothes before finding no fire. He stilled. "I don't understand. Something protected us . . . the Father of Light?"

Would the Father of Light protect us using my twisted Vedoan gifting? I could not consider that blasphemy right now. "These underground tunnels will lead to escape." Unless the seasonal rains or stronger gates cut us off.

The rush of water sounded through the darkness. Monsoon flooding was already high. We needed light.

From my pocket, I pulled out the oractalm bracelet, which glowed from being in the fire. I took a breath and forged ahead. Geras's footsteps remained close behind, and I sensed his gaze alternating between me and the bracelet. But he didn't ask any questions.

Our tunnel intersected with a crossway surging with water. I paused. Anything deeper than knee-high would be dangerous. What was I doing?

My hand went to my pounding chest. Where was the key? Oh yes. In my pocket—

Finish it. I startled at the thought. I could release the key to the water. I didn't have to return to the Handprint of God. Geras wouldn't see. And it would be finished.

My veins pumped with energy, and I slipped the key from my pocket.

But if a river serpent swallowed it, like the treasure—then fate had decided. But hadn't fate chosen enough?

If Geras was right, what did Laijon lose when she failed to open the Eternity Gate?

No matter what happened, Laijon would fight her enemies. We could face them as we had for centuries, weak and alone, or we could battle possessing the key to the lost Eternity Gate, even though it held judgment. Was this what the Father of Light wanted? Would he find our tardy obedience worthy—worthy of what?

I remembered the messenger in the desert. I wanted to be worthy.

"Seyo?"

The glow of the bracelet was almost gone.

I trembled as I slipped the key and ribbon around my neck and under my bodice. I blew on the stone to illuminate the tunnel again.

Geras stood beside me, looking ill with concern and suspicious of our surroundings.

My voice quivered. "Geras, I will show you the way out of here closest to the mountains, and then I must enter Laijon and give them a warning. I will share this warning with you, too, to report to the Brotherhood. Tell your leaders that I am maiden attendant to Princess Kiboro, daughter to the late King Zaujo." I could not bear to mention Huari. "Tell the Brotherhood that our plan was that I pretended to be the princess while in Pirthyia. There, I learned that they stirred the mountain tribes against us and command Shadows as their army—" I paused to regain my slipping composure. "Pirthyia will attack Laijon for the treasure and Eternity Gate. On behalf of the princess, I ask the Brotherhood to join us in arms and fight them." But what about the key? I pushed the thought aside. "Will you tell the Brotherhood this?"

Geras opened his mouth, shut it, pulled the dagger from behind his back, and stepped in front of me.

Beyond the water barrier, someone stood in the darkness with one hand filled with soft light.

My breath caught. A soldier?

The person raised a fist and shouted something I could barely understand over the water—in Nazakian. "Who trespasses in Laijon?"

Geras stood tall and returned the gesture. "May the Father of Light gain all glory across every nation."

Mysterious continent. His liaison?

The man lowered his fist and struggled across the intersecting tunnel.

The glow of my bracelet faded again, and Geras ducked his head before stepping back out of the stranger's light.

The liaison huffed. "Good. I have rotted weeks here waiting for you, then I saw the red fabric and soldiers surrounding our meeting place." His gaze narrowed to perceive Geras through the shadows, his own light illuminating his face, and ignored me. "You are not Ortos."

I gaped at the man. Recognizing him in disbelief.

"I come in Ortos's place. He wrote one letter for you and one for the leaders." Geras removed two rolled parchments from his rucksack and offered one.

The liaison unrolled the document, read, and returned it. "Geras, is it? Keep both to show the leaders. Ortos's absence will be felt keenly."

I cried out in Laijonese. "Father!"

Geras jolted, and his gaze swept over me.

Father froze, stared, then with an exclamation, drew me to him to kiss me on the head and search my face.

My throat tightened. I could speak my native tongue, make eye contact.

Father spoke in a torrent. "Seyo, you should be inside the walls with the royal family. With Roji."

Had he seen Roji and Kiboro return? "Have you seen Roji?"

"No," he replied. "I have been hiding here, waiting for this meeting."

They must have arrived. They had to.

Father spoke in Nazakian again. "We will flee to the mountains. The tribes have regrouped and will attack any day."

I shook my head. "I must return to the palace."

"The walls no longer open to anyone without papers from the king."

But Roji and Kiboro didn't have papers.

"The mountain tribes are catching those outside the walls for impossible ransoms and public executions. Seyo, you must come or risk capture." Father gave me a pained look. "How did you know the way down here? Never mind." He took my arm and hurried us through the labyrinth into water that reached our shins.

Geras remained close behind.

My heart thudded. I could not comprehend this. I would not travel to the Brotherhood with the key. But how could Father be Laijon's traitor?

The tunnel narrowed, the flooding receded, and we emerged through another broken gate from a pile of boulders into the western forest, heavy with shadows and moonlight. Father concealed the tunnel entrance again with rocks. Behind us, the foothills rose and held the palace high.

Geras held back. But not enough.

Father looked for him, and then his eyes widened. He took in Geras's size, bowed head, and markings, and his expression hardened into stone. Fear.

The moment stretched, and my stomach twisted. I opened my mouth to speak when the scent of smoke wafted over us.

Father's eyes swung toward the hills, the Archives, then Geras. Then, with pinched brow, he cupped my elbow and, saying nothing, led us under the cover of forest.

We reached a copse and found hidden bags of supplies. Father hesitated before slinging both across his back. "We can procure mules further out." He avoided glancing toward Geras and picked up our pace until I felt like we were fleeing the Trackers again. Geras remained a length behind us, shouldering his own rucksack and bow. I did not feel his gaze once.

Father drew me close and whispered, "Are you hurt? Should I—"

I shook my head and tears unexpectedly gathered in my eyes again. "Geras is safe."

Father grunted, and we moved faster. Away from Laijon. Away from the burning Archives.

Toward the Brotherhood gathering in the mountains.

22

AN ABANDONED LAIJONESE township guarded the tributary winding between us and the mountains. The warring tribes had passed through and seized most supplies, but left the buildings and dirt street intact.

An empty wattle-and-daub home, complete with two rooms, rush-covered floors, and a stone fireplace, became our camp alternative. After fleeing through Pirthyia, it seemed like a palace. Father spoke with me in Laijonese. I almost cried.

Geras did not enter, but removed his rucksack and disappeared with his bow and quiver into the waning afternoon light.

From the first room, Father watched him go, before pulling rolled quilts from his supplies and arranging one pallet on the bed and one on the floor. "Seyo, may I be direct?"

After all these years, it took war and finding me with colossal, mysterious Geras for him to speak openly with me. I crossed my arms. "Yes?"

Father pressed his palms against an emptied chest of drawers. "What is Geras?"

Who, not what. But I remembered my own first impression and swallowed. "You read his introduction letter. Beyond that . . ." How much should I tell him? "We traveled together. From Pirthyia." Oh, dear, Father, be calm—

He jerked. "You left Laijon's walls? For Pirthyia? Who sent you?"

"Srolo Faru." And how I wished we had his strength and wisdom with us now. "Princess Kiboro, myself, and a bodyguard traveled to Pirthyia to request the Imperati's aid in repelling the mountain tribes. However, I acted as princess for Kiboro's protection and she pretended to be my attendant, but the previous high king had been replaced by Warlord Emeridus."

"Emeridus." Father frowned. "That is not in our favor. Did he admit to knowing of the treasure?"

I paused. "Yes."

"You returned without escort. After dismissing you, the Imperati should have sent soldiers to accompany you to Laijon." I could see his thoughts churning. "Where is Princess Kiboro? Did Geras kidnap you?"

What in the continent? I shook my head. "The Imperati did not dismiss us." And Geras kidnapped me out of necessity because I had passed out from smoke inhalation. "When we arrived in Pirthyia, we were patronized and then sabotaged. I was left in my room alone." And given haughty Cira as maid to spy on me. "The Imperati met with me." The image of Geras, blindfolded and caged as a spectacle, made me shudder. "Father, this is difficult, but the Imperati sent the mountain people against us, to weaken us. He does not only want the treasure with interest, but the Eternity Gate. Kiboro was taken away from me, then the guards, to intimidate me." And lastly Roji. "I had to escape and search for them." I thought of the plunge into the lake. Passing through fireplaces. Freeing Geras. Looking for and finding Kiboro and Roji, then losing them again. "But the Imperati possesses—" and commands an army of Shadows who attacked me for the key to the Eternity Gate. Who killed Jorai. The words would not come. I gasped and doubled over.

"Seyo."

Father took my elbow, but I wrenched away. "I'm fine." I stumbled to the nearest pallet and sat. But my heart beat too quickly.

He knelt in front of me and sought my eye contact.

I flinched. My new habit.

"Seyo, did the Imperati harm you?"

"Not in that way." I struggled to speak. "He will not coerce Laijon this time. He wants to crush us once and for all and seize the Eternity Gate. He commands Shadows. I don't know how. I still cannot believe it, but I swear I tell the truth. He will send them after us too."

Father's expression tightened.

"Do you believe me?"

"I never doubt you. Members of the Brotherhood have sent word of Pirthyia's secret war and army of Shadows—may the Father of Light deal with those mighty tyrants. I thought we had more time before the Shadows assembled. Laijon must be warned. The Brotherhood could send a runner, but a bird would do better passing the walls. We must reach their encampment quickly."

My thoughts tripped at how much he knew. How did the Brotherhood learn of this?

"Seyo, can you tell me what the Shadows looked like? Is it too difficult for you?"

I shook my head. "No." I paused. "It was night and misty. I was running away. They looked damaged. They hunch over with claws for hands, yet they speak like and resemble humans. Their wings are so large that some cannot stand, and yet they possess more strength than they deserve. They scream." I clasped my shaking hands in my lap. "I saw one die."

Father's jaw set. "Then it is true that these are copies of the original Shadows, the ones brought from across the sea," he continued, repeating what we had discussed before. As if I could have forgotten. "Those were written to be monsters three times larger than a man, to wear power as flesh, and unable to die by natural means. When Laijon fell, men and women surrendered their bodies to surgery and spells to gain the strength, power, and appearance of those first Shadows. These were the first copies. After we three nations, Laijon, Ai'Biro, and Pirthyia, finished off these imitations, we chained and drowned the last true Shadow in a freezing mountain lake before winter, for he survived every stabbing. The spellcasting books used to create copies of Shadows were burned. But now Pirthyia somehow hosts a Shadow army."

And someone had tried to make Jorai into a Shadow too.

Father gestured to the door where Geras had disappeared. "Are the Shadows like him?"

"No!" I reacted before I could stop myself. "Geras killed the Shadow that attacked me." *Qo'tah*, think before speaking—

"What?" Father exclaimed. His face grew somber. "To that I owe Geras many thanks." He frowned. "Is this why you remain with him?"

I stiffened. "Any life debt is paid."

He exhaled. Relieved. "How did he kill the Shadow?"

My blood iced. Not by natural means. I deflected the question. "First, I would like to know how long you have been a part of the Brotherhood and for how long you intended to keep this secret?"

"Your safety prompted me to hide this from you. I could never tell Roji."

Because he and Roji always argued.

"The Brotherhood's aims are dangerous and controversial. My father was a soldier, as you know, and he became close friends with a Nazakian soldier-for-hire who confessed his affiliation with the Brotherhood. My father agreed to help their cause and passed this pledge on to me."

Surely there was a better reason for his involvement? Was this why he left his position as historian, or part of why King Zaujo released him? "The Brotherhood share our nationality, even if it's mixed with Nazak blood and culture. Do you hope to convince them to join Laijon in arms?"

"Of course I long for that, but I cannot ask on behalf of our king and Chanji, even if I still served on the council. And I am not a full member of the Brotherhood. Just a contact."

"We must speak with . . . the king."

"King Huari," Father said with little pleasure. "Would he accept the Brotherhood?"

I caught his meaning and pressed my lips together. Huari wanted the Eternity Gate for himself and would despise the Brotherhood's plans to seize it. "No."

Father steepled his hands together. "Even if the king reached out to the Brotherhood, today they are a nation unto themselves, despite their Laijonese heritage, and loyal to the Father of Light and his command to open the Eternity Gate. This has been their purpose since self-exile after the Occupation. They would choose that at the cost of their lives, and their forces are not large. I do not know if an agreement could be reached."

That was far from encouraging. "What will you do if Laijon finds out about your association? You could be seen as a traitor."

"I will not hide anything."

If Father didn't believe the Brotherhood would fight for Laijon, he must be genuinely dedicated to their mission. Including opening the Eternity Gate. I found myself unsurprised—it was Father's way to join the lost, if noble, cause. And it frustrated me. As for me, Laijon must be protected.

"What if King Huari finds out?" I pressed.

"I will speak the truth even then. I would have requested to speak with him about the Brotherhood if I had not been waiting outside the walls for Ortos. And instead, I received this Geras stand-in." Father's brow furrowed. "Seyo, how did Geras kill the Shadow? It is written that blades are useless against their thick hides. This knowledge could aid us in battle."

I had to tell him. "Geras has a power to kill upon eye contact."

Silence.

"He has been enslaved for this," I explained. "The Imperati had imprisoned him for use as a weapon. But Geras hates this curse. After I stopped fearing him, I learned that he had sworn never to use it again. This is why he keeps his gaze down."

Father's mouth opened and closed. "Has he tried to look at you?"

"Of course not." I straightened. "Since our escape from Pirthyia, he has been nothing but gentle and humble." Please accept him.

"In all my study, I have never heard of such a thing. He will need to tell the Brotherhood leadership this." Father lowered himself beside me on the pallet. "*Qo'tah*, Seyo."

Indeed. Thank goodness he didn't ask why Geras broke his vow in Pirthyia. "Father, Geras and I were separated from Princess

Kiboro and her retinue. We traveled the foothills. She followed level ground." My chest tightened. "Do you know if she arrived?"

Father expelled a breath. "May the Father of Light have permitted her safe entry inside the walls."

Tell him. I moistened my lips. "Roji was part of her guard."

Father tensed. "Alive?"

"Yes." My eyes burned. "He is with her."

Father seemed to hold his breath. "Roji is well trained. Determined." He stood and slapped dirt off his trouser legs, any emotion barricaded away. "We must pray for their safety."

I swallowed. "Yes."

"Mountain tribes. Pirthyia. Shadows. Will Vedoa rise up against us next?" Father shook his head. "I will look in the house next door for firewood." And he left.

I stared long after he exited.

Father never mentioned Vedoa. It always led to one-sided conversations about why he didn't stop Mother from leaving, and why he never admitted to us that she was Vedoan.

He did not believe Kiboro and Roji had made it to Laijon.

The Brotherhood wouldn't fight with us.

Father of Light, what do we do? I dropped my face into my hands. We could only wait. Cling to hope.

By sundown, Father returned and started a fire on the hearth. We did not speak of Roji again. Through the open door, I spotted Geras arriving with a small deer slung over his shoulder. He remained outside and laid the animal out to skin and quarter.

I hesitated. I hadn't spoken with him since the tunnels.

Father pressed hands to knees to rise off the floor and spoke to him. "A successful hunt?"

I stared at him in surprise.

Geras murmured something I couldn't hear, then Father passed through the door and assisted with the cleaning.

Something in my heart eased.

Before dawn the following day, Father returned from exploring the town with a bundle of clothing. I accepted two skirts, blouses, sashes, overlays—a cake of soap—and looked up in question.

"I left coin for the villagers' return," Father said. "I cannot bear to see you dressed as a Pirthyian any longer."

One at a time, we washed in a secluded finger of the tributary. As the sun rose, I bathed first, as Father stood guard out of sight, but within earshot. Afterward, I shivered as I changed into the new clothing. The rough fabric felt glorious, and I hid my Pirthyian rags in the woods.

I combed my fingers through my wet curls and opened the supply bag Father had given me. Inside went the extra clothing and the waterproof sack with the bimil, bracelet, Barano's medal, and the jewels from Kiboro's crown. How had I lugged all of this in my skirt pocket for so long? The staff Geras had carved hung snug against my hip under my overlay sash, and I touched the key under my bodice, then the bauble in my ear.

Father washed, and I returned to our shelter. We passed Geras sitting outside cleaning his da's sword, and his gaze rested on me, flicked aside, returned, then he shifted his weight and studied the blade.

I had been filthy for so long, he probably did not recognize the clean me. "The mountain water is colder than the river we crossed."

He gave a half smile. "But without the chase?"

He made me laugh for the first time in forever, even as something inside me pinched, remembering the Trackers. My eyes strayed to the sword, and the pinch increased. I wanted to tell Geras that Father would help the Brotherhood leadership accept him, but my tongue tangled. What if the leaders rejected Geras? Or worse? How powerful was his da Ortos among the Brotherhood?

We ate a midday meal and prepared to continue our journey. Father left payment in the house for our stay and also on the dock where we borrowed a boat to cross the tributary. Once we landed on the opposite bank and the boat was secured, I lifted my eyes to the approaching mountains and swallowed. They were part of Laijon, but an untamed land haunted by the ghosts of explorers, hunters, soldiers, and the mountain tribes, who now camped around Laijon's walls. Would the Brotherhood be any safer than these?

Father found an overgrown path that parted the forest and circled the roots of the mountains. Once he discovered that Geras only understood Nazakian—not even the trade language—Father spoke it for Geras's benefit, but sometimes slipped into Laijonese with me. Every time I responded in my native tongue, I felt Geras's gaze. Once, I glanced toward him, and he ducked his head to rub his reddening neck. Why was he embarrassed? I switched to Nazakian.

We made camp at the base of the first mountain just before nightfall. Father had brought two tents, another welcome delight, but Geras insisted that he preferred to make his own shelter in the forest. As we roasted leftover meat from Geras's hunt, Father removed a copy of the Nho from his bag and offered to read aloud in Nazakian.

Under a canopy of twinkling stars, his clear voice washed over me in memories of nightly childhood readings with Roji before bed. Mother had complained that we were too loud, but reading was one area where Father never budged for her.

He handed me the Nho, and I continued the translation where he'd left off.

Geras sat at attention and seemed familiar with the passage. Had his da read to him too? Then Geras abruptly stood and faced the woods, hand on his knife. Father also rose.

Footsteps crunched in the undergrowth. Someone attempting stealth.

Father raised a hard voice in the trade language. "Who are you?"

The steps hesitated. A response wandered through the trees. "We will work for food, srolo." A young man stepped into our flickering firelight. His face was smudged with dirt, and he wore a rumpled and torn Laijonese soldier's uniform that reeked from a distance.

A jolt ran through me. It was the lookout who fell asleep, from Roji's unit, Bo. He looked so dirty, hungry. Beaten.

Father's gaze narrowed as he spoke in Laijonese. "Where is your squadron, soldier?"

Bo blanched. "Srolo—"

I jumped to my feet and lifted my palm toward Geras, who looked ready to defend us. "I know him. He's not a deserter." I turned to Bo. "Where are Roji and Princess Kiboro?"

23

HESITANT, GERAS RETREATED
into the forest as footsteps crashed near and a second, very
tall soldier burst into our camp. Under the grime and beard I
recognized his eyes.

My heart leapt. "Roji!"

His fierce expression melted. "Seyo? You're alive." His
disbelieving stare swerved, and he stiffened. "Father?"

Father advanced, hands lifting as if to embrace the prodigal son,
but halted when two more guards emerged. With Bo, they took
their places behind Roji.

Roji had become captain of Kiboro's guard since Pirthyia?
Where were the Pre-Elites? Where was Kiboro? I met the gaze of
the fourth soldier.

His uniform was baggy, trousers cuffed, sword sagging from
his belt, but he wore Kiboro's delicate, dirtied face, and dark hair
chopped short.

I shook my head, aghast.

She stepped forward. Roji lifted an arm to restrain her, to keep
her hidden, but she shook her head with dignity that could not be
concealed. Her voice was a whisper. "Seyo?"

Tears filled my eyes, and I knelt on the ground. I saw Father do
the same.

Boots entered my vision, and Kiboro bent to wrap her arms
around me. It was too informal—but we held onto each other tightly

and together we stood. For a brief moment, her teary eyes revealed panic and loss before her expression masked.

I choked back sobs of relief at seeing both of them, bowed again, and counted six guards missing, including the Pre-Elites. What had happened? Then I noticed Geras's disappearance.

Kiboro inclined her graceful head toward Father. "Historian Daemu."

"Princess Kiboro, may light guide your path." Father's eyes sought my brother. "Please, will you share our humble meal?"

Father and I laid quilts before the fire. First Kiboro, then Bo and the other guard sat across from us as Roji continued to stand. Bo pulled a corner of the blanket around his shoulders. Kiboro did not speak. All looked starved.

What had happened to them since Pirthyia? I wouldn't ask until they were fed and rested, but dread would devour me until then. What were we going to do with Geras? And why in the continent was Roji standing? He looked exhausted.

At last, Roji moved forward, leg stiff, and with a pained expression eased himself to the ground.

My heart hitched. He was injured.

Roji's mouth firmed. "Permission to speak?"

Kiboro hesitated before nodding.

Roji leveled his gaze at me. "We saw the monster attack you. How did you survive? Why didn't you follow us?"

So, the interrogation would start now, after all. Why didn't I follow them? Why didn't he check to see if I was dead, I wanted to demand. But he wasn't really angry, he was afraid and shocked. I seemed like a ghost to him. I could hardly say that Geras killed the Shadow, carried me into the foothills, and that we fled all the way to the temple, reunited with Father, and were going to find the Brotherhood.

Wait. Roji had said *monster*, not *Shadow*—

He persisted. "Seyo?"

"Captain," Bo said. "Forgive me, but there was one more here with them when we arrived."

My insides constricted. Oh, please, no. "I can explain."

Father, still watching Roji, spoke too quickly. "Yes. Geras, the prisoner you know from Pirthyia, is with us."

No, Father, you don't understand—

Roji's mouth flattened. "Who?"

"Wait," I intervened. Only Roji and I had seen Geras's terrible power. I needed to speak with Roji about this alone. "We should eat first." I looked to Kiboro for help. Please see my distress and intervene. But she was looking away, like her thoughts had wandered.

"Hardly." Roji grimaced as he stood. "Bring this person to me. I must assess him for the safety of the princess, even if he is a victim of Pirthyia too."

I scrambled to my feet. "I need to tell you something first."

Roji's eyes narrowed. Now, he was angry. "Seyo, you are not in charge."

I sucked in a breath, then felt Geras's gaze from behind me. Oh no. He knew we spoke about him. Or worried that I was in harm's way.

Roji stumbled backward and tore his sword from its sheath as Geras stepped out of the forest. Shoulders hunched, gaze down.

Roji trembled. "Seyo. Come."

Please, brother, be calm. I faced him and spoke in Laijonese. "Geras is not as we first understood."

Father interrupted. "He saved your sister's life."

I wanted to melt. Not helpful.

Roji pointed at Father. "You weren't in Pirthyia. I was in the Imperati's hall and saw this creature attack a soldier until he writhed on the floor screaming. This is the monster that murdered Seyo when the Shadows descended."

"Do I look dead?" I steadied my voice. "Geras helped me. He follows the Father of Light."

"It is cursed and lies," Roji hissed. "It has bewitched you. Both of you."

I flinched, and Geras moved forward—not understanding, but thinking I was threatened.

Roji yelled and advanced two painful steps.

Qo'tah.

I freed my spear and jumped between them. Both startled.

"This is my stupid brother," I said to Geras in Nazakian, not caring if Roji remembered this language, too, then leveled my staff and a glare at Roji and switched to Laijonese. "The night we escaped Pirthyia, I freed Geras from his cage. Later, a Shadow attacked me, and Geras rescued me."

Roji choked. "You did what?"

"We traveled through the foothills and fled to Laijon." My voice faltered. "My heart wept for you every day, and I made myself believe that you had found safety within Laijon's walls."

Kiboro stood. She looked pale as she studied Geras. "Seyo, may I question you?"

I could not refuse her, and bowed my head.

"Who created the world?"

I blinked, and the memorized response rolled off my tongue. "The Father of Light, when he touched the Handprint of God."

"How does the Father of Light care for his creation?"

"He visits it, waters it, shines the sun upon it."

"How does a follower seek the Father of Light?"

Tears stung my eyes. She asked me the first calls and answers we learned from the Nho as temple helpers. She doubted me. "By humility, confession, petition, and worship."

Kiboro nodded and raised her voice. "It is written that light is greatest, and that one bound to falsehood or sorcery cannot speak truth. Seyo has spoken truth and is not cursed." Then she glanced toward Geras again.

He kept his head down.

"Do you know who I am?" she said in Laijonese.

I came up beside her and translated into Nazakian. "Geras, this is Princess Kiboro of Laijon."

Geras stilled before bowing.

Kiboro hesitated. "Please rise."

I interpreted, and Geras obeyed, but took a step back. He rubbed his wrists over and over and flicked his gaze toward me.

Roji forced respect into his tone. "Princess, forgive me, but you did not see what I saw in Pirthyia."

"You told me what you witnessed." Her voice was so quiet I barely heard. "And I have seen enough. No more death."

We all stood there awkwardly until Father spoke. "Please sit and eat." Everyone obeyed, if with greater wariness than before.

Geras remained lengths away.

Kiboro ate slowly, before speaking to Father, the highest in authority besides herself. "Historian Daemu, did you leave Laijon's walls to meet Seyo, and now seek shelter with the militia gathering in the mountains?"

Father appeared as flabbergasted as I felt. Did she mean the Brotherhood?

Roji coughed and gave her a look.

She ignored him. "While in Pirthyia, Soldier Roji overheard much from their guards. They spoke about this militia who is sympathetic to Laijon's cause."

Sympathetic? As if sympathy was the Brotherhood seizing the Eternity Gate before Pirthyia did and opening it to judgment, not caring about Laijon's fate one whit. How much did she truly understand? Did she know about the Eternity Gate?

Roji spoke up. "We found Laijon's walls controlled by the mountain tribes. We thought we had no other choice than to request shelter among this rogue army."

And that was because Kiboro did not possess keys to the underground tunnels and their escape routes into the palace, and had not learned, like Father, that the gates were crumbling. What a difficult decision she had been forced to make.

"Now we don't need the militia because we found you." But Roji said this toward Kiboro, not us.

"We need a doctor. There is injury among us," Kiboro said, and I glanced toward Roji's leg. He looked ready to explode.

"There is more," Kiboro continued. "Perhaps you already know or guessed, but Pirthyia plans to attack Laijon for her treasure." A painted expression crossed her face. "I know my brother Huari's pride and fear. He will avoid seeking help, so I have decided to petition this militia, whoever they are, to become our ally."

I kept my jaw from dropping.

She raised her chin. "Perhaps you are scandalized. But if necessary, I will reveal myself to convince them to join us."

"No." Roji spoke quickly. "Can I defend you against an army?"

Father broke in. "I must disclose something as well."

I tensed. Would he tell them everything—

"The militia calls themselves the Brotherhood. I am their friend and travel to bring them news. Princess Kiboro, I, too, hope that the Brotherhood will fight with Laijon. If you permit me, I will request their help so your presence may be kept secret."

Roji gaped at Father.

"Yes. I accept this." Kiboro inclined her head. "Seyo, do you have any of my belongings from Pirthyia to prove what we have learned?"

A broken crown. "Yes," I managed.

She nodded. "Then it is decided."

Roji gestured toward Geras. "What of him?"

"He, too, carries a message for the Brotherhood," Father said firmly. Entertaining no argument.

"But Seyo needs to be disguised."

Father's voice deepened. "I will tell the Brotherhood that she is my daughter, for they are honorable. I would never endanger her."

This time, Roji shut his mouth.

We decided to travel at dawn. All the men but Geras, who remained in the woods, took one tent, and Kiboro and I claimed the other. In the morning, after a hasty breakfast, everyone gathered their supplies. By habit, I stepped to Kiboro's side. Though she was dressed as a soldier, not a princess, Roji and the guards still surrounded her.

Father stood in front as if he were the one being escorted, but Geras fell several lengths behind. Having him far away felt odd, and

Roji shot him a dark glance before giving the command to renew our journey. At least we were all together.

Our path began a steady climb into the mountains. Wind rustled in the trees as clouds thickened overhead and hid the sun's journey.

The tension enveloping us was nearly unbearable.

When Kiboro raised her hand, we took a break among the boulders studding our path. I sat on her left, and Father on her right. After hours of hiking, Roji favored his good leg but refused to sit and stood behind Kiboro with an icy expression. I heard her murmur that he should rest, but his jaw tightened and he shook his head. Geras remained out of sight.

Weakening sunlight glowed upon rising cliff faces of sheer rock. The remains of a crumbling stairwell was a welcome sight, but promised a difficult climb. Even as the air cooled, sweat poured down our faces.

Kiboro's slight frame labored under her baggy clothing as she set one resolute foot in front of the other, and Roji's face paled with pain. Father noticed, but wisely did not comment.

We slowed until, at last, we reached an even greater cliff, split by a thin, winding crevice, almost like the rock formations in Pirthyia's foothills. If there was ever an ideal place for ambush, this was it. And now night was falling.

My nerves tightened with every length we advanced. How much longer could we continue? Could we defend ourselves if needed? I hoped bringing Kiboro dressed as a guard was not a mistake, and wondered if we would be the only women present. Were the Brotherhood as honorable as Father believed?

I swiped a hand across my forehead and peeked at Geras still climbing below, who struggled the least even under his rucksack and bow strapped to his back.

A guttural cry in Nazakian interrupted our labored breaths.

The Brotherhood.

Roji and the guards bristled with swords, and I held my breath, hand on my staff. Geras caught up and stood behind me.

Atop the cliff, a scout shouted again as twenty men jogged

through the stone path and made a defensive formation in front of us.

My eyes widened. Geras boasted a collection of weaponry, but he had nothing on the Brotherhood. Knives, swords, clubs, slings, spears, bows, and some firearms lay strapped, sheathed, or tucked into their boots, against their ankles, thighs, backs, chests, wrists. Their clothing was an array of garments from every nation on the continent. Some looked like warriors, others like hunters. Each man wore an ancient, sun-engraved sword against his hip. The blades of the traitorous first Elites, their tainted heritage.

None shared Geras's size, markings, or bowed head.

Was this the entire Brotherhood?

Father stepped forward, bowed, and spoke in the trade language. "We seek the *i Bodask*. I am Daemu, your friend from Laijon, and expected."

One of the warriors nodded. "Please come."

The scout disappeared, and rock walls swallowed us as we followed, but this time Geras did not fall behind. The path opened and we faced the sudden Brotherhood camp.

At least two hundred tents with campfires sprawled across a broad, rock ledge, hemmed in by cliffs and a drop-off into the forested ravines below and the mountain chain beyond. At the scout's third yell, the small army gathered and neared without ranks. They, too, boasted diverse garb, but the majority appeared Nazakian. All appraised us with suspicion.

Roji's fingers whitened against his sword hilt. I could sense Father steadying his breath.

My throat dried. Zealots, indeed. What had we done?

Geras came beside me. I glanced toward him out of the corner of my eye and felt his anxiety.

Young men carrying torches advanced, and three warriors lined up between them. Surely these were the leaders, and they represented almost every nation.

The first was an older gentleman from Ai'Biro, Laijon's island allies, with graying hair and flowing robes trimmed with rare shells.

A middle-aged woman from southern Nazak—praise be. And yet her severity did little to comfort me. Metal rings circled her neck, stones rippled through her hair, and her skin looked cracked from sunshine.

Beside her was a gap. For Geras's da, Ortos? To represent northern Nazak?

A young man, short in stature, observed us with curiosity. He wore hunting clothes and tight copper curls—my stomach dropped. Mysteries of the continent, he represented Pirthyia. Did this man somehow carry Laijonese blood?

No one stood in for Laijon, and, of course, there was no representative for Vedoa. All of them wanted to open the Eternity Gate.

The key weighed against my chest.

Father bowed low. "Leaders of the Brotherhood, I am Daemu, a friend and sympathizer from Laijon."

The Ai'Biroan gentleman responded. "Daemu, we have awaited your arrival. Where is our compatriot Ortos, who planned to travel with you?"

Geras moved into the torchlight. He spoke slowly, as if doing everything possible not to stumble in his speech. "I come in Ortos's place."

He spoke Nazakian. Should I translate?

The grim woman from southern Nazak looked at Geras from his boots to his bowed head and interpreted into the trade language with a surprisingly gentle voice.

When the man from Ai'Biro, as eldest, spoke, she translated for him as well. "How do you prove yourself?"

Geras removed his rucksack, drew the ancient sword free, and presented it with a bow.

The Ai'Biroan took it and examined the engravings. "This sword is Ortos's. Who are you?"

Geras fumbled for the two rolled parchments, handed these over, and stepped back to rub his wrists.

The three leaders drew close to read. Each, in turn, stole glances at Geras.

My nails bit my palms. Did they see the stains on his skin? His strength and height?

The Ai'Biroan jerked and his eyebrows lifted.

Qo'tah—did the letter explain Geras's power?

The young Pirthyian murmured with a heavy accent, "My father fought beside Ortos. I knew him as a boy. I promise this is Ortos's hand."

The woman nodded, and the Ai'Biroan gestured to the letter. "Geras, adopted son of Ortos, I have never seen or heard of such a thing that is written here."

So the letter did reveal everything.

"Ortos leads the largest portion of our forces and is honored with great respect. We will remember his sickness in our prayers daily. To replace him is both painful and difficult, and whoever is chosen must come from those who share the bloodline and are proven trustworthy. You may stay tonight, and tomorrow we will decide if you have a place among us."

I warred between thankfulness for Ortos's influence, because that could have gone much worse, and feeling like Geras was slapped in the face. But he bowed again before receiving back the sword and letters and securing them within his rucksack. He took a large step back to my side, his breathing uneven.

The leaders declared that we would meet in the morning for formal introductions and offered us a corner of their cliff-top camp, near the night watchmen and on the highest point of the bluff.

Roji, Father, the two guards, and Geras set up our tents and a fire.

The Brotherhood watched us, but did not approach. When they finally returned to their meals and conversation, I tied the remains of Kiboro's crown into a cloth. Apologies about that were for later. I slipped the bundle to her and hoped it would strengthen Father's negotiations.

As soon as we ate, the men, except Geras, took one tent and I entered the other alone. Kiboro, dressed as she was, could not be seen entering my tent.

I lay on the hard ground, kept the spear close, and blocked my ears from the talking, laughter, and song coming from the Brotherhood. Thankfully, it was not drunken carousing like the Pirthyian soldiers.

Someone crept nearby. I tensed, but it was Geras unrolling his quilt a length away, to stretch out under the stars. Having him between me and the noise brought a sense of comfort, strange as that was. I rolled over, but sleep refused to come.

My ruthless mind imagined scenario after scenario of what could happen tomorrow. For Father's mission. For Geras.

Would the Brotherhood accept or reject us?

24

THE CHANGING OF THE BROTHERHOOD

guard awoke me. Through the leather tent flap, pink mists peeked over cliff edges. The ground breathed cold into my bones.

After breakfast, one of the Brotherhood gathered Father and Geras. Roji accompanied them as Father's guard. It distressed him to leave Kiboro and me behind, but as captain, it was necessary to maintain our charade. The rest of the soldiers, including Kiboro, were left to protect me, Daemu's daughter, and stay out of sight.

I folded my quilts and fought anxiety. Kiboro's slight frame and distressing moments of distraction would give her away. How long could this continue? Even now, Geras and Father were approaching the Brotherhood, seeking acceptance and an alliance in war.

The tent opening fluttered as Kiboro slipped inside, checked over her shoulder, and faced me with intense eyes. "I will not pretend to be a soldier any longer. It will not work here."

I blinked and remembered to bow. "But—"

She interrupted. "Historian Daemu agrees and said you have extra clothing. I will play your maid again, and we must begin now, before it is too late, and while Roji is away. Where is the clothing?"

I pulled the skirt, bodice, and overlay from my bag and removed her stiff, reeking uniform. Dressed, she sat on her heels on my quilt as I appraised the challenge of her hair.

"Seyo, can you pull it close against my head to hide its length?"

I did, and she wet her underskirt to wipe her face and hands before sitting tall and lifting her head high.

Too high. She'd played a better attendant in Pirthyia. Yet her restless gaze wandered around the tent, something she never used to do. It reminded me of King Zaujo. My stomach tightened. No. Kiboro was not mad like her father. But something had happened after Pirthyia.

She drew a deep breath. "I will wait at the Brotherhood leaders' tent."

Why?

"I will order the guards to escort me." Her voice wobbled. "Will you come?"

What was she thinking? Perhaps we would be safer close to Father, Roji, and Geras. And we could eavesdrop, which must be her plan.

We exited the tent. Kiboro spoke to her two guards, who glanced at each other before bowing at her request. Our destination was a large, leather shelter standing in the center rear of the encampment, where the cliff ended in sweeping views of valleys and mountain spines. All stopped their tasks to watch us pass. We ignored them.

When we approached the tent, the Brotherhood soldiers on guard offered us questioning looks. We stood away from the entrance and attempted to look official. It was awkward, but the conversation inside drifted to us.

Father was giving a summary of Laijon's search for the treasure in the trade language. He and the leaders murmured over the possibility of hidden chambers within the tunnels, then moved to Laijon's defenses against the mountain tribes. A voice I did not recognize mentioned Pirthyia and spat, then others thanked Father for his information.

The Ai'Biroan leader spoke, and Father translated into Nazakian. "Let us discuss Ortos's absence. Ortos's place is now filled, and we have read the introduction and recommendation of his adopted son Geras, that he be allowed to serve among us. Vispirios confirmed Ortos's handwriting and we have seen his sword." The leader's voice deepened. "The treasure is found. We near the destination of a holy path that cannot be tainted by evil.

We bear the shame of our fathers, whose wrongdoing made our journey necessary, and walk a strict code of conduct, that we, too, may not be led astray."

The Ai'Biroan sat and another stood. The woman. "Geras, we will read aloud Ortos's description of your curse so that a decision can be made. Do you object?"

I held my breath.

Geras's voice came steady but strained. "I do not."

She continued, "Ortos wrote that you served a master of foul magic as a life-bought slave and escaped after contributing to your master's death. Ortos brought you into his household marked on the skin and carrying a dangerous curse held since birth. This curse has given you power to see things that should remain unseen and to harm, even to kill. With Ortos as witness, you surrendered this power to the Father of Light and vowed to never look another in the eye."

Her proclamation sent chills racing down my spine. He couldn't have helped to kill his master. Geras was good. I wanted to burst inside the tent and demand that he recite the verses he had spoken in the desert to prove he was not bound by sorcery, as Kiboro had tested me.

"Yet Ortos recommends your service to us, and Daemu agrees, after traveling with you."

My heart gladdened at that.

"We have considered this matter long into the night. If you remain, your power cannot be used in any capacity, even toward an enemy. If you break your vow, grave punishment will be administered, as it is for anyone who breaches our code of conduct."

Geras spoke again. "I agree."

The Pirthyian raised a voice of affirmation, and the others followed. And so Geras was welcomed into the Brotherhood. They discussed preparations to leave the mountains in the coming weeks, and then welcomed Father to speak for Laijon.

Something shiny caught my eye.

Kiboro clutched a circle of braided reeds. Jewels from her crown lay tucked into the twisted folds.

I stared. Father was supposed to use her gems to bolster his position. Did she forget?

Kiboro whispered, "I cannot hide any longer."

As understanding hit me, my heart dropped into my stomach.

She met my gaze and I saw the zeal and strength that was my friend Princess Kiboro. "Seyo, will you translate for me?"

I nodded, and she gave me the makeshift crown. I set it atop her shorn hair. The two guards pursed their lips, likely imagining their captain's displeasure. But Kiboro held final authority, not Roji or Father.

Inside the tent, Father's voice rose. "Brethren, may I speak?"

Kiboro strode to the tent entrance. The guards and I fell into position.

The Brotherhood soldiers jerked with surprise. Kiboro looked each in the eye, and, silently, they pulled the tent flaps open.

We passed the threshold, and all talking ceased.

Dirt floor cradled a stone firepit that breathed smoke up the folded ceiling chimney. The Ai'Biroan, the woman, the young Pirthyian, and a fur-covered individual, who must be Ortos's northern Nazak replacement, rose from woven mats and animal skins.

Across the fire, Father stood with Geras and Roji. All stared. Even Geras, with his face toward the ground, watched from the corner of his eye.

Qo'tah, what we were we doing?

But Kiboro, despite her petite form and peasant's clothing, wore confidence and dignity. She dipped her head in respect and spoke with a clear voice that rang like Heaven's bells. "I am Crown Princess Kiboro of Laijon, daughter of King Zaujo."

I remembered myself and translated her Laijonese into the Nazakian, Ai'Biroan, and Pirthyian. Everyone appeared stunned.

Kiboro smiled as she spread her arms open. "Welcome to Laijon's mountains."

Would they believe her? But when Father confirmed her identity, the leaders bowed low to the ground and repeated their introductions from the previous night. Father took over translating the second two languages, while I kept with Nazakian.

The Ai'Biroan, our closest allied country, seemed glad, but concerned. The woman's ferocity did not shift. The fur-covered northern Nazakian looked awed. And the Pirthyian—Vispirios— seemed delighted by this turn of events. More mats were brought, including a wolf pelt for Kiboro, and we sat.

I studied blade after blade strapped to the sides of the Brotherhood leaders and soldiers. All engraved with blazing suns.

Kiboro inclined her head again. "I believe Historian Daemu has shared of the mountain people's attack on Laijon, along with Pirthyia's recent hostility. I visited Pirthyia to confirm their support and was imprisoned. They have severed their alliance with my country. I escaped to warn my people and was attacked by an army of Shadows."

At the translation, the leaders' expressions turned grim, but not surprised, and they nodded.

Kiboro's eyes flashed, and her urgency boiled over in a spoken rush I struggled to follow. "Pirthyia seeks to destroy Laijon and seize an ancient treasure, a legend I do not know, a hoard I cannot promise exists. A portion of my country has always survived capture, and it will not fall now. My retinue and I overheard Pirthyia speak of the Brotherhood's army and your sympathy to Laijon's cause." She held out her hands. "Because of this, I ask your aid now. We can help one another, as Pirthyia will not spare anyone who aligns with us. If you seek the treasure, I promise a generous payment, up to my entire portion of what is recovered."

I felt uncomfortable as Father and I interpreted. She understood so little, but there hadn't been time to explain.

The Ai'Biroan's answer came slowly. "Princess, you misunderstand us. We have no interest in the treasure, and our history will not please you. Our fathers stood before your ancient kings to guard the lost treasure and open the Eternity

Gate it surrounded, as the Father of Light commanded them in prophecy. They failed in their responsibility, and so, we believe, the Occupation began. We return to complete our fathers' task."

The woman spoke up with a gritty voice. "In my clan, our fathers, husbands, brothers, and sons dedicated their lives to fulfilling the prophecy of the Eternity Gate. All were killed in battle, leaving us, mothers and wives, sisters and daughters, to carry the sacred blades. We fight for something much greater than wealth."

"Yes." The Ai'Biroan's expression saddened. "Our path is not as hired soldiers."

Kiboro offered the woman a deferential nod, but her brow furrowed. "I do not know the Eternity Gate."

The Ai'Biroan's expression softened. "Too long has Laijon's history been hidden from her people. The Eternity Gate is a heavenly gift given to Laijon and believed to hold many things, from eternal life to retribution of past sins. We carry the command to open the Eternity Gate, regardless of what it holds. We are loyal to Laijon, but swear allegiance to the Father of Light. We expect your resistance, Princess, and will not fight you. You are welcome to stay or leave, and we will not hinder you."

I sucked in a breath before translating. We needed the Brotherhood.

Kiboro bowed her head in thought. "The Father of Light grants salvation, but Laijon looks to the hands of my brother and myself to deliver it." She lifted her gaze. "Brotherhood, if Laijon is consumed, there is nothing left for you to seek. I, too, am dedicated to the Father of Light and have made my own vows before Heaven. I am not my brother, but by the light in me, I promise that if you join arms with Laijon, I will offer you the Eternity Gate."

My heart stopped as silence fell. I forced myself to translate. *Qo'tah.* She didn't know what she was doing.

The leaders glanced at one another. As if some unspoken word was given, the four stood. The Ai'Biroan, as eldest, bowed first. "We accept your agreement, Princess Kiboro."

Kiboro, too, bowed, lifted her hands, and filled the tent with the most radiant outpouring of dazzling light. Our way of signaling international agreement.

The Brotherhood stared in amazement. The Ai'Biroan, familiar with agreements between his and our countries, smiled and unsheathed his sword to the sky with a shout to seal the agreement. The rest followed. So, after years in exile, they no longer possessed their giftings.

Everyone was smiling but me. Roji suddenly gripped his leg. Father reached to support him. "Is there a doctor?"

Vispirios bolstered my brother from the other side. "I am here, friend." He pulled Roji's pant leg up to reveal an ugly wound. I gasped. Roji was helped to lie down, and Vispirios shouted to the entrance guards to retrieve his medical supplies and for onlookers to leave.

Bo and the second guard escorted Kiboro and me to our camp. I wanted to stay with Roji, and tried to be thankful that he was receiving help. Even from a Pirthyian. Once we reentered our tent, Kiboro took the makeshift crown out of her hair, murmured something to me, and lay down in exhaustion.

I knew better than to talk now, yet I couldn't rest. I exited the tent and gazed over the cliff as my mind spun.

By Kiboro's word, the Brotherhood possessed the Eternity Gate. But I had the key.

I sensed movement and turned to find Geras beside me. He deserved congratulations for his acceptance into the Brotherhood, but I couldn't. They controlled everything.

"The doctor says that your brother's wound will heal," he said.

Something crumbled inside me, then I felt ashamed of my previous thoughts. "Thank you."

"The Brotherhood prepares a dinner to welcome the princess. Your father asked me to bring all of you."

Dinner? I glanced at the waning sun, then roused Kiboro. I stood beside her as the guards and Geras took their places. We wove through the encampment and heard a crowd murmuring. My jaw dropped. The Brotherhood stood in rows, framing woven mats spread in a long line, covered in steaming dishes, cutlery, and wooden trenchers. When they spotted us, they lifted a mighty shout. The leadership and every soldier welcomed Kiboro with bows. She and I were ushered to the center of the mats and seated between Father and Roji.

A blessing was given, and dishes were passed, platters emptied, and mugs filled. Before we newcomers could help ourselves, others were reaching to fill our trenchers. I realized this was their show of hospitality. After Father filled my mug, I took a sip to ease my dry throat and tasted something fermented, diluted and sweet, but not unpleasant.

Kiboro remained poised, though I sensed her exhaustion. Past her, Roji stretched his bandaged leg to the side and, for once, didn't scowl, but watched the surrounding activity with bewilderment. I longed to catch his gaze, but he seemed to be avoiding mine.

I looked for Geras.

Even seated, with shoulders hunched with self-consciousness, his monstrous height was easy to pick out at the far end of the table. Why was he separated from us? Even our guards were nearby. I noticed that Geras was being given wide berth, and I fisted my hands in my lap. But then, the leader Vispirios sat beside him. Did that Pirthyian dare interrogate Geras again? But Vispirios only grinned and chatted, and I recalled him saying his father and Geras's da were friends. When Geras relaxed, I did, too, and focused on my meal again.

Torches were lit, and the night filled with the Brotherhood's noisy camaraderie. So many Nazakians. The majority of the ancient Elites must have exiled themselves there. While friendly Ai'Biro's deep-colored skin comforted me, I struggled seeing the few Pirthyians. Yet most were of mixed blood, and there was no hierarchy in seating, just pockets of regional dialects. Weapons were worn even at dinner, even more so among the handful of southern Nazakian women. Everyone strapped an ancient, sun-engraved sword to their side—except for we who did not possess one, and Geras, who kept his in his rucksack.

Countless eyes flitted to Kiboro and me before platters were passed again. Father alone served her, but a bolder youth stretched to offer me a ladle. *Qo'tah*. To avoid offense, I accepted and caught Father chuckling and nodding toward the Brotherhood soldier seated across from him.

When was the last time I had seen Father laugh?

Finally, eating slowed, a second blessing was given, and the Brotherhood soldiers were dismissed to clean up.

We were offered better tents, and placement near the leaders' quarters and the cliff's edge. After accepting, we set up our new camp and retired.

Kiboro and I lay down on new pallets of pelts. Father, Roji, and the guards moved into their tent, and Geras stretched a bedroll nearby under the stars.

Questions haunted me, but I waited to ask. Tomorrow.

Lingering smoke and song kept me awake. Most sang Nazakian ballads about fertile fields that once covered their wilderness. Perhaps they wished the opened Eternity Gate would revive their starved lands.

I placed a hand over the jagged piece of metal lying against my chest.

But they didn't have the key.

25

THE BROTHERHOOD LAUNCHED

into preparations to leave the mountains for Laijon.

We accepted tasks among their ranks, even Kiboro, to everyone's distress. Father continued to advise the Brotherhood. Somehow, Roji earned a position as scout. Armed ankle to wrist, he left with the lookouts to keep watch on neighboring ridges.

Kiboro and I helped prepare meals for the small army, and the leaders sent their personal soldiers to support her bodyguard. They joined us in seasoning, roasting, and drying countless roots, vegetables, and meats, while warning us that remnants of the mountain tribes had attacked camp twice. No one—especially us—were permitted to descend the cliff without permission. I worried for Roji.

Geras performed odd jobs around camp. As usual, I felt his gaze before seeing him, and held back surprise when Vispirios appeared, clapped Geras on the back, and launched into animated conversation. And Geras paused to smile, duck his head, and respond.

Daily, Kiboro consumed her midday meal in our tent and rested. As she did, I took my satchel and sat outside the shelter facing the cliff edge. Fog gathered in the valleys, and I brought my knees up as a shield and opened the bimil's ancient pages across my lap.

I untangled translation of the princess's Shadow sentinel. She retreated to the Handprint of God countless times. The invading king from across the seas summoned her to Laijon's captured throne room, but I could find no mention of the treasure's location or description of the Eternity Gate. Did it stand tall and golden with Heaven's blinding splendor? Or would it be barred with iron and chains to mirror its judgment? Was this why the first Elites dared not open it, unlike their descendants?

Speaking of our new, unlikely allies, I didn't know how I was going to protect the key from the Brotherhood or Huari or Pirthyia and her Shadows. Who was strong and wise enough to keep the key? Not I. Maybe Kiboro.

I hid the bimil inside my satchel and reentered the tent to find Kiboro sitting on her knees, dress and hair rumpled. The twining of reeds and jewels lay across her lap, and her gaze seemed lost.

How could I consider giving her the burden of the key? I chastised my wild thoughts and knelt beside her.

She drew a breath and turned to me. "How did you escape Pirthyia?"

I startled at her direct question. "I jumped from the window into a lake."

"Impressive." Kiboro gave a small smile before sobering. "Your brother told me about his experiences with you before he was imprisoned." She paused.

It was an invitation to speak, so I did. I told her of the grand hall, meeting the Imperati, and Cira. I avoided describing my terror as everyone disappeared and hesitated while mentioning Geras. She did not comment. I skipped sneaking through the fireplaces and the Shadow's attack to traveling the foothills and reaching Laijon. When I came to burning the Archives, I stopped.

"Seyo?"

I smoothed my voice. "I found my father and then you."

Silence fell between us. Then Kiboro spoke. "The guards and I slept on uncovered floor, in their prisons. Every day, another joined us." She folded her hands. "Our rations did not increase, and I knew you were alone. The Pirthyians challenged us to dice, but seized our belongings whether they won or lost. They drank and quarreled. Our captain sought to take advantage of this." Her voice trailed.

Was that when the others were lost?

"You were not killed by Shadows," she said flatly.

I stiffened. "You cannot accept responsibility for leaving without me."

"Your brother does. When he saw you, I feared he would come apart."

Was that because he saw me or Geras?

"After we escaped Pirthyia, Soldier Roji rejected rations and demanded more than his share of night watches. He became weak. Pirthyian patrols chased us to the border, and he was wounded in their last attack." Her eyes drifted. "He killed one of them in duty, to protect me. The new captain of my guard fell, and as highest in rank, your brother took his place."

My heart constricted. I couldn't process what Roji was enduring. I knew I needed to speak with him.

"Perhaps we are all altered." She fingered the edge of her quilt. "You, too, carry a burden."

Yes. Several. Jorai wearing wings paraded through my mind, and I blinked against unbidden tears. I would spare her this knowledge.

She did not notice my distress. "I feel as though I have been kept in the dark my whole life. Historian Daemu—your father—has explained to me the Eternity Gates's prophecy of judgment. True or not, you must think me a fool for promising the gate to the Brotherhood." Her voice lowered. "But certain danger marches toward us, even now. Pirthyia advances, and Huari sits on our father's throne. The leaders here told me they have already sent messengers to Laijon to offer help. My half brother refused them."

Of course. Huari lived bound by pride and fear.

"Seyo, your father said Laijon remembers their sins of the past, and now, fearing war, they make confessions in droves. Huari refuses outside help and the people hate him for it. They may lead a coup against him. As weak and dangerous as Huari's rule is, revolution would destroy our country. Unity must be upheld somehow." She set her jaw. "Once we return to Laijon, I will not speak until I stand before the Chanji and Huari. I will advocate for the Brotherhood, and my agreement with them made upon this cliff will be upheld. But now that Huari is king, he possesses the key. Father's precious key, hidden inside that old book, must unlock the gate. Huari will never give it to me willingly."

I almost choked. Of course she knew about the key, through her mother, Jorai, or her own means. And she understood Huari's hunger for it. He would covet anything that someone else wanted. But Huari didn't have the key.

I never kept secrets from Kiboro, but everything was falling apart. A sudden thought struck me.

Faru could take the key. It did not belong to him, but who else could I trust? Yet weeks would pass until we reentered Laijon. Weeks surrounded by enemies stronger than us—

"Seyo?"

My thoughts were wandering, and my reply followed their track. "Srolo Faru will support your alliance." Perhaps more so if he held the key.

"Yes. Thanks be to the Father of Light." Kiboro paused. "I need to ask you one more thing."

I bit my lip, uncertain what that might be. "Of course."

"Did you learn anything about Barano's arrival in Pirthyia?"

My stomach pitched.

She tapped nervous fingers against her knees. "Barano is capable and would not want me to be concerned, but when I imagine him in Pirthyia's dungeons, I cannot rest."

Oh, Father of Light. I steadied myself and slowly pulled his medal from around my neck. I handed it to her. "I found this during the . . . attack." I could not make myself say Shadow.

She gave a sharp gasp and clutched the chain. "He was coming for me."

I bowed my head. "Barano would not entertain any regrets."

"I have lost all but three guards." Her face crumpled, and I held her as she wept and allowed my own tears to fall.

The next day, Kiboro and I took Barano's medal as far from the Brotherhood's camp as her bodyguard would allow, to the highest point on our cliff. There, among flowering brush and rocks, we buried the medal.

Should I leave Jorai's bracelet here, too, in remembrance? I pushed the thought aside as we knelt in the dirt.

Our escort remained standing, heads bowed in respect as Kiboro murmured prayers for the dead.

At last, we stood, brushed dust from our skirts, and returned to the encampment.

After dinner, as songs filled the night, Kiboro and I braided each other's hair and retired early.

I rolled over and loosened the ribbon around my neck, like I did every night before battling Shadows and Pirthyians in my sleep. But tonight I thought of the Brotherhood preparing for our near departure while their scouts, including Roji, watched for mountain tribes and Shadows. Over dinner, I had heard whispers that we might see the flying monsters before reaching Laijon's gates, if Pirthyia sent them ahead.

And then there was Huari.

Movement stirred outside. Geras.

Wait. Geras. What if he kept the key until we passed Laijon's walls? He did not know what it was and was always eager to help. Who would be a better protector, even if he promised not to look at his enemies again? Then I would not have the key when Huari demanded it from me.

But Geras stood among the Brotherhood now. What if he discovered the key's significance?

Kiboro whispered, "He stares at the ground because of his curse, doesn't he?"

I startled. Had she read my thoughts? "I think so."

"Did he ever look at you?" She sounded merely curious, if cautious. But she had not seen Geras's power as Roji and I had.

"No."

She fell quiet.

A question nibbled at the back of my mind. "Have you felt his gaze?"

"Twice." She scooted closer and propped her head on her hand. "It is a strange sensation."

Relief flooded me. So, it wasn't just me. "Yes."

"But he does not watch me nearly as much as he watches you. You must feel it constantly."

She had noticed that?

"His constant observation would be alarming if I did not know that you had freed him from captivity. He must feel indebted to you. At least once we return to Laijon, we will go our separate ways." She sighed and rolled over.

But sleep eluded me deep into the night.

26

BEFORE SUNRISE, RESTLESS AND
exhausted, I knelt twice to pray while Kiboro slept. When no
answers came, I fisted the key. Was there no better way to safeguard
this than to give it to Geras? There was no air in this tent. I reached
for the entrance flap and paused.

On the edge of the drop-off a towering figure faced an expanse
of mountain and fading stars. His da's sword lay strapped across
his back, passive placement that Kiboro would frown upon, and
his hands hung at his sides. His broad shoulders were pulled back,
not hunched forward, and his head was up. Eyes upon the heavens.

Geras finding strength in the skies by remembering that he
was small.

Kiboro's comments from last night flashed through my mind.
Would Geras carry the key for me? Without a doubt. I could give
it to him now.

A watchman called the hour. Geras brought his head down.
Kiboro stirred, and I retreated into the tent.

During morning meal, I sat with Kiboro and her guard, but
watched Roji settle several lengths away among a pocket of
Ai'Biroan Brotherhood. He consumed his rations with a customary
scowl. At least his limp seemed healed.

He caught my gaze and raised an eyebrow. Good. I nodded, our
signal that we needed to talk. Even if the timing was horrible.

The meal completed, and I held back from the crowd as he
marched to my side and tapped his boot. "What is it?"

I reviewed what I wanted—must—say. Thank him for serving Kiboro and Laijon, encourage—

Geras's gaze touched me as he passed.

Roji watched him go and spat before lowering his voice. "Beware of that monster. Wolf on a leash."

My rehearsed speech turned to mush. That was uncalled for. I was about to snap a response when he rolled his eyes.

"Now to dress in ridiculous getup and sit on a rock for another endless day of scouting." He pivoted and disappeared into the throng.

Midday, Kiboro skipped her afternoon rest to meet with leadership. Father arrived to escort her and whispered to me, "We leave within a week."

My heart flipped as they departed. I needed to seek Geras now.

Cutting across camp by myself earned curious glances from the Brotherhood, but no one hindered me. They assumed that I, "the one who speaks a thousand languages," ran errands for Kiboro.

Today, Geras tended livestock. I had seen him lead animals through camp with an ease that suggested experience.

Vispirios passed me on his way to the meeting and waved.

I startled and hurried on. What was I supposed to make of this young, curly-haired Pirthyian? I appreciated his courage in befriending Geras, and he was friends with Ortos. But Vispirios was also Pirthyian, like the Imperati, who caged Geras to exploit his power.

The animal pens lay beyond natural stairs of rock below camp. Descending the clifftop unaccompanied without permission defied the Brotherhood's warnings. I reminded myself that the scouts, including Roji, would give warning if danger neared. And I would be with Geras.

I glanced backward twice, saw everyone focused on their work, and hastened down the steps. Geras wouldn't be alone, and I couldn't imagine creeping past the Brotherhood with him. How could we talk privately?

Bleating cajoled me forward, and I found animal pens

interrupting the forested hillside. A handful of men ate lunch under a shady tree, but Geras sat lengths away, sword across his back. His sleeves were rolled down, but he wore no gloves. Marks swirled over his hands, and his weighty gaze found me.

You must feel it constantly, Kiboro had said.

He stiffened, stuffed his hands into his pockets, and stood. Looming. Troubled that I came alone.

The others also rose, wondering why I was here. Sun-carved swords hung from their hips, and many of their leather smocks held blood.

I adopted a self-possessed mask. Would my coming here become the Brotherhood's gossip tonight? Did they notice how much Geras watched me?

I inclined my head and offered a greeting in Nazakian, as all hailed from that region. As usual, their stony facades softened when I spoke their mother tongue. Then I trained my gaze to Geras's elbow, regretting my commanding tone. "There is need of you."

His mouth flattened before he came beside me.

The others' frowns betrayed questions, but I dipped my head again and rounded the curving cliff. To escape their sight.

The ground sloped past large boulders, trees, and bushes. Songbirds chortled among leafy branches swaying against the sapphire sky.

When we were beyond anyone's hearing. I stopped.

Geras halted too. A tower of anxiety. "What's wrong?"

"Nothing." My thoughts tangled. Would he take the key? He had kept it for my protection before and was always quick to offer aid. I pulled a breath. "I came to ask for your help."

His gaze strengthened. "Yes."

"I hear we will leave the mountains soon. Danger lies between us and Laijon." I hesitated. "You remember the valuable thing I possess. Could you . . . carry it?"

He stood erect. "Of course. I will carry it for you."

For you. "It must be kept secret upon penalty of death." Death by judgment. I suppressed a shiver.

He nodded, and I believed him. "Thank you." I reached for the
back of my neck, my fingers trembling.

Watchmen yelled from the cliff.

We froze, and then I understood their cries. The scouts were
sighted returning early. Something was wrong.

The surrounding thicket rustled. I glanced toward the forest. A
tribesman glowered three lengths away.

Qo'tah.

The tribesman charged. I spun, but dirty fingers grazed
my elbow.

Geras slammed between us, caught me by the waist, and swung
me behind him. He pulled a dagger from his belt.

The tribesman shouted, "Release her." Laijonese.

My heart stopped. It was Roji.

My brother lunged with his own sword.

"Stop!" I cried. Roji was better trained, but Geras was strong.

Roji feigned a strike. Geras fell for it. They scrambled, slipped,
and Roji's scream ripped through the air. He collapsed and flailed
in the dirt, his sword abandoned.

I stared at my brother, but my mind saw the Pirthyian soldier
writhing in the Imperati's hall and heard the Shadow's final shrieks.
My knees buckled. Roji was dying.

I threw myself beside him and swept his sword out of reach. I
could not control his thrashing and earned several bruises.

The men from the animal pens surrounded us and restrained
Roji's limbs. Soldiers from camp arrived with more scouts disguised
as tribesmen. Then Vispirios knelt beside my brother, forced a
liquid between his clenched lips, and searched for invisible wounds.

Geras wrapped both arms over his head and crouched.
Trembling. When seven guards approached, he did not move.

The soldiers tackled him.

27

THE SCOUTS REPORTED THAT

Pirthyia, in full might, stalked Laijon's southern border by foot and train. Shadows were not yet sighted.

The Brotherhood prepared to leave.

Tasks stopped only for a hurried dinner. Torches were lit at sundown. Kiboro joined Father and the leaders for conferences, and I worked alone. I forbid myself to think or feel until a soldier brought me a message from Father. He turned away as I read, and my self-control disintegrated.

Roji had recovered. Thanks be to the Father of Light. I blinked back tears.

Then the guard announced I was summoned as witness for Geras's trial, and he was ordered to escort me to the leaders' tent immediately.

I sat between Kiboro and Father on a fur rug. Father looked exhausted. Kiboro gazed into the cold firepit before us, her thoughts wandering again.

I noticed a huddled form in the far corner and jerked. It was Roji. He appeared lucid but extremely pale, and he ignored us.

The leaders, the elderly Ai'Biroan, the Nazakian woman with eyes like lightning, the fur-clothed man, and a frowning Vispirios sat facing us. Surplus guards stood behind them, a backdrop of swords and grim concern.

The leaders cast lots and determined that the Nazakian would preside as judge.

The Ai'Biroan turned to the guards. "Bring him."

The soldiers exited and returned with Geras. Unarmed, hands bound behind his back. Blindfolded with leather. The guards prodded Geras to his knees and surrounded him.

He remained silent. Taut.

I looked away.

The Nazakian spoke in her gentle tone, and Father's translation followed. Geras was accused of breaking his oath and using his curse to hurt another.

Roji stood to give testimony and favored his uninjured leg. His hollow response was a thousand arrows piercing my soul. He had seen me with Geras and believed I was being attacked. He struggled to describe fighting Geras and stopped.

The woman asked if he believed the eye contact was intentional.

Roji hesitated. "No."

"How did the curse affect you?"

"I prefer not to say."

She frowned and repeated the question.

He spoke as if strangled. "I saw death."

I inhaled. He saw his own death?

The woman gave Roji permission to sit, then her demeaner hardened. "Geras, please stand."

The soldiers shuffled positions as Geras obeyed. His shoulders hunched, his face turned to the ground.

The questions came. "Do you contest Soldier Roji's account?"

Geras's chest rose and fell. "No."

"Was your eye contact intentional?"

"No."

"Do you wish to defend yourself?"

"No."

He was ordered to sit, and the soldiers converged around him again.

Why didn't he defend himself? He didn't do so here, before the Imperati, nor when meeting the Brotherhood leaders, or at the Archives. Didn't he understand the punishment?

The Nazakian's gaze pierced me. "Seyo, please stand."

Father touched my hand. I fought my nerves and rose to endure the same interrogation. But my voice stuck in my throat. If I told the truth, I could not protect both Roji and Geras.

"Did Geras attack you?"

I shook my head. "No."

"Did you think your brother was an enemy?"

"Yes. I tried to stop their fight."

"Was Geras's eye contact intentional?"

I remembered Roji thrashing on the ground and whispered, "No."

"You may sit."

Sit? Why didn't she ask why I stood alone with Geras in the first place?

Because I served Kiboro.

I lowered myself to the rug on shaky legs and glimpsed Roji. I expected his wrath and hurt for my weak, if honest, response to what Geras did. But Roji was holding his head in his hands. I realized that he hadn't condemned Geras either.

The leaders convened and gave their decision, a lashing by whip followed by the night in the stocks. Geras was stripped of the honor to fight alongside the Brotherhood and could choose to remain and carry supplies or return to Nazak, for Ortos's sake.

Geras was escorted to the stocks, on the far corner of camp where evening's arms stretched the farthest near the drop-off. The entire Brotherhood paused their work to hold torches and watch.

Soldiers removed Geras's gloves and shirt at sword point, and most stepped back at the sight. Not I. Torchlight shimmered across his rigid, sweat-stained body and the twisted markings marring his torso. Underneath the healing wounds from the Tracker dogs, he bore a maze of old scars I hadn't seen from the Imperati's table.

The guards forced Geras onto his stomach. He resisted only once when his wrists were secured to the ground. After his ankles were tied, the guards stepped back and kept their swords unsheathed.

A large soldier, one fingerlength shorter than Geras, lifted a single-tailed whip.

My stomach churned. Experience told me I would be sick. This was my fault.

The whipping began, and I made myself watch the punishment I should receive. Wave after wave of nausea swept over me and tears dripped off my cheeks. Geras did not cry out until the end, and then his limbs were unbound and he was secured into the stocks.

The rest of us dispersed to continue preparations deep into the early hours. At last, all retired. No songs enlivened that night.

I asked Kiboro's permission to leave the tent and relieve myself, but instead rushed far from the watchmen and threw up.

Roji was alive, but Geras had lost everything. Geras, who rushed to defend another and never himself. It had been an accident, but the Brotherhood knew this, and it was why Geras wasn't executed. But I found no thankfulness, only shame.

I had to do something, and remembered Geras's vial of ointment. He kept it in his rucksack, which he left near our tent with his quilt.

If I wasn't caught, would helping Geras betray Roji? Would Geras accept my aid? He must despise me. Would he wish to harm me? I deserved it.

Shaking, I returned to the tent and peered inside. Kiboro slept. I picked up Geras's rucksack, found the ointment and other supplies, and crept under the longest shadows to the corner guarding the stocks. Lookouts focused their attention outside camp and did not spot me. The leaders' tent held dim lighting, and heated conversation sounded from within.

Without torchlight, the stocks stood in a thicket of gloom. Geras sagged against the wooden structure, and his usually restless hands hung limp until he heard me and recoiled.

My heart twisted at the tangle of welts across his back. The blindfold remained, so his gaze did not touch me. Yet everything in me demanded that I turn back.

I whispered tentatively, "Geras."

His hands closed into fists. "Leave me."

I forced myself to crouch beside him and wet a generous strip of my petticoat with the flask of water from his rucksack. My hands shook.

He gasped as I brushed the cloth against his lacerations. Dizziness swept over me, but I did not brush my hand against his skin and used another strip of fabric to apply the ointment.

Geras hissed with every breath, straining the silence. "You cannot be here."

I winced and did not reply.

"They cannot see you." He groaned, and I faltered. Stunned as his meaning became clear. He still protected me. He didn't hate me. How was that possible? I covered burning tears with my hand.

"I hurt your brother."

"It was an accident." I thought my heart would break. "I descended the cliff."

He shook his head. Why wouldn't he stand up for himself?

"What did Roji see?" *Qo'tah.* What was I asking him? I longed to take the question back.

But he answered. "When I look at someone, I see their evil. Acts completed or considered. The longer I see, more is revealed to me. Even unto—" he clenched his jaw. "They see what I see."

I stared at him. That was why his gaze did not affect Trackers, who did not sin. Just humans. And Shadows. After speaking with Kiboro, I knew what Geras had seen in my brother. The Pirthyian soldier's death.

He could know the truth about me.

I wanted to throw myself from him. Who had cursed him from birth? Why had Ortos adopted him? Had he been cast aside by his parents?

Geras spoke. "I've tried staining my skin. I've prepared to pluck out my eyes—" Geras ground his teeth.

I choked back a sob and clasped my palms. Palms pulsing with half-Vedoan blood. Wearing the stolen key to the Eternity Gate around my neck.

My scars and stains were better hidden than Geras's.

Years of temple training screamed at me, reminding that

my own confessions were countless, and something inside me crumbled. The invisible yoke strangling me remained, yet I found the strength to rise and to say what was needed. "I forgive you, for my brother's sake."

His upper body tensed then collapsed. He tried to respond and failed.

"Peace, Geras," I whispered. I looked at him one more time, then slipped through camp. Replaced the ointment. Crept into my blanket beside sleeping Kiboro.

We might leave tomorrow. So be it. I should sew the key into my shift for safekeeping.

How long would it take to reach Laijon? Would Geras go with us or leave?

The blind survived without looking another in the eye, but Geras lived in perpetual exile, never trusted, and alone. Couldn't others see that he would give anything to shed his power?

I curled against grief.

This was Geras's true curse.

The Brotherhood broke camp, and we descended the cliffs. Thunderclouds mingled in the distance. The first seasonal storms brewed. Kiboro said nothing about Geras and his punishment.

After reaching the plains, we regrouped. One of the Brotherhood's few horses was tied to a cart filled with quilts for Kiboro and me. We were to travel in the center of the convoy. Father would ride alongside us with Roji and our Laijonese guards, who wore their washed and mended uniforms again. The leaders' personal soldiers also joined us in their wild clothing. It felt extravagant and desperate.

Shouts rang among the Brotherhood's divisions. Roji assisted Kiboro into the cart, though she did not need help, and his gaze collided with mine.

I expected anger, not the haunted fear scribbled across his face. He wanted to say something, but didn't, and mounted his horse.

The trade language, spoken energetically with a Pirthyian accent, accosted my ears. "May I offer you a hand?"

I faced Vispirios's wild, copper curls with surprise. For the first time, I noticed the wedding band around his wrist, a southern custom, and imagined him with family. I gave a nod. "Thank you."

Vispirios swung me into the cart beside Kiboro and waited.

Did he want permission to speak? "Yes?"

He inclined his head. "I will watch over your protector, my lady."

Geras.

Vispirios saluted before leaping onto his mount and charging down the assembled procession.

My monster, my protector—did Kiboro hear? No, she concentrated on the horizon with a look I knew well, an expression she wore before sparring with Barano. Before challenging her father.

I twisted to look behind at the rows of Brotherhood soldiers.

At the rear of the supply train, Geras pulled carts, as horses and oxen were scarce. When I spied him earlier, I was relieved to find his arms unbound and his da's sword strapped across his chest to avoid agitating his wounds.

Our cart lurched forward, and Kiboro brushed against me.

I fixed my posture and thoughts forward. Toward the spring rain gathering on the far horizon.

Toward Laijon.

28

ON THE SIXTH DAY, WE SPOTTED smoke rising from Laijon's charred fields. Rain extinguished the last of the mountain tribes' fires.

We avoided flooded plains. Vispirios told me that those tending the supply train toiled faithfully. Including Geras.

On the eighth day, we sighted the castle. My heart tore when we retreated out of sight and awaited further information from the scouts. They reported that the wall gates remained shut. No welcome fires glittered from the ramparts, so Laijon remained unaware of Pirthyia's advance. A second band of lookouts estimated that the Imperati's army marched two days away.

My chest squeezed. We were so close. I could taste ocean on the summersaulting winds.

But Laijon's closed walls stood before us like giants.

The spring rains lessened. Thick fog fell.

29

KIBORO MET WITH FATHER AND
the leaders to determine our entry into Laijon. Before she left, she
ordered me to pray.

For centuries, no one had succeeded in breaching Laijon's walls.
They did not expect us, and stormy mists blanketed everything.
If the unknown, uninvited Brotherhood materialized in the fog,
Laijon would see them as an enemy. Sending a messenger under the
arrows of our desperate countrymen was deemed too dangerous.
Kiboro, without her usual retinue, might not be recognized.

The tunnels were the only way, even considering monsoon
flooding. Imagining reentering that lightless labyrinth made me ill.
Yet, could I remain skewered between Huari and Pirthyia with the
key to the Eternity Gate sewn into my shift?

Hours later, the leaders, Father, and Kiboro emerged from the
meeting tent with sober expressions.

The rest of us gathered and waited.

I dared to hope Father and Kiboro had found another plan,
but they announced that we would travel the tunnels and enter the
palace from underground.

Qo'tah. So be it. But how would we access the locked royal
passages?

That night, Kiboro opened her hand to reveal a familiar metal
object. "Mother gave it to me."

My throat thickened. The last time I saw the key to the tunnels,
it had rested in Jorai's elegant fingers. Below his playful gaze, before

he pleaded that I go exploring—I pressed the memories away. Only Srolo Faru and the king possessed keys to the tunnels. Jorai had "borrowed" his father's a million times. I wondered if Queen Umoli had taken her husband's key after he'd passed, or if it was stolen from Huari when he'd inherited it with the crown. After all, the queen had been present when Huari exposed the treasure before the king and Chanji.

"If I lead," Kiboro told me, "we will not be harmed for using the royal passages. Your father and I are working on a map, but neither of us are very familiar with the tunnels."

I was, but remained silent.

30

COBWEBS OF LIGHTNING

skittered across the clouded sky. Booming flashes brightened our tents for half moments, and a drizzle tapped against the leather walls. No fires were lit.

We waited, knowing we would hear Pirthyia's marching the following day, leaving a sliver of time to reach the protection of the castle and join Laijon. With Kiboro in our midst, Huari would let us in.

At last, night fell.

The Brotherhood broke into small groups to sneak to the nearest tunnel entry. Father had chosen the opening buried at the foot of the hills, the one he, Geras, and I had taken to escape Laijon.

Kiboro and I joined Roji, Father, our Laijonese guards, the Ai'Biroan leader, and a slew of soldiers to form the vanguard. We stole through the misty forest to the roots of the outer castle walls, a pile of mossy boulders.

I imagined Pirthyia pitching their camp here and lifted my gaze. Wind stirred the fog and unveiled the palace towers far above. There, we would be safe.

Father found the entrance covered with stones, how we left it, and Roji helped him clear the rocks from the broken gate.

I shivered. The abyss was a gaping mouth. I swear it taunted me, gloating that all of Laijon's gifting couldn't illuminate its depths. I removed the oractalm bracelet from my supply bag and held it close.

We lit sputtering torches and passed into the damp, gloomy

corridor. My bracelet began to glow, but none noticed. I remained close to Kiboro. Father opened one hand in light, but closed it again when Roji muttered that he should wait until a torch failed, to not waste his gifting.

Kiboro approached Father with fragments of directions she must have heard from the king. Father pointed to the soot stains on the ceiling.

The second group of Brotherhood arrived with the Nazakian leader. We needed to continue on to make room for the rest, so we wound into the heart of the hills. Water trickled everywhere, up to our knees in places. Some soldiers held back to act as a bridge between trailing groups. All of us kept our weapons ready, and my mind strayed to river serpents. The burnt Archives. Jorai.

We reached several cavernous intersections. Twice, we made wrong turns, but Father redirected us and we climbed dry ground uphill.

Aged stones gave way to newer passages, only a century or two old, and the way widened. By now, the entire Brotherhood should have gained the tunnels and sealed the entrance.

We were close, but then Roji's torchlight splashed across a dead end. Father passed him and grasped the handle to a metal trapdoor in the ceiling, an archaic escape path that would lead us out of the hills and to the castle grounds above. Kiboro handed Father the key, and the trapdoor groaned open.

Roji and the Laijonese guards went first. Once they faced the royal guard, it was better that our countrymen saw them before they saw the Brotherhood. They assisted Kiboro through the hole, then me, into a musty cellar, and torchlight flickered against bare walls. We had entered a portion of the castle barracks, and no one spoke.

When our group filled the room, Roji stepped to the cellar door, peeked out, then turned back with a confused expression. "It's empty."

Kiboro frowned, and Roji crept into the hallway. The rest of us followed. My chest pounded as we passed quiet rooms filled with bunks and exited onto the royal grounds. Those in front paused. We couldn't stop now. I peered over the others' shoulders.

A powerful wind stirred the empty, battle-scarred green, and the palace silhouette stood tall against the swirling sky. There were no guards. Wheel tracks and footprints crisscrossed the grounds. Roji scouted the ramparts, looking for Laijonese watchmen.

I spied someone seeming to slouch atop the wall. Before I could speak, lightning flashed with a rumble and illuminated the hulking, motionless body, tied to a stake and sagging under heavy wings.

I covered my gasp. Some of our men ran to investigate and declared that the executed Shadow's corpse was days old. Killed by a violent blow to its heart.

"Check the storehouses."

My head jerked at Kiboro's firm command, which my brother obeyed. What was she doing?

Roji came back stricken. "Emptied."

My mind raced. The siege hadn't lasted long enough to exhaust our reserves. Why would Laijon remove them? There should be watchmen. The ramparts were littered with unmanned cannons.

Father and the Ai'Biroan approached Kiboro, but she gestured them away and faced the darkened palace. It stood silent as death.

I stared. It couldn't be. Even in the Occupation, Laijon did not evacuate—

Kiboro whirled toward the barracks, and we ran to catch up. Inside, the walls were stripped of swords, the bunks lacking bedrolls. Everything was missing.

She retreated to the trapdoor and collided with the last group of Brotherhood climbing out of the tunnels. Confusion ensued before they backed up and she could push herself into the dark underground passages again. We followed blindly. Soldiers held their torches high and barked demands for space. Roji squeezed past and pressed me between Kiboro and Father.

Father spoke with bewilderment. "Huari must have learned

about Pirthyia's coming. But the Brotherhood's scouts would have seen Laijon's evacuation."

"Abandonment." Kiboro's voice was taut. "Huari would flee by sea."

Neither said where, but I knew. Laijon would seek Ai'Biro, our nearest and strongest ally.

"Are we strong enough to claim the castle?"

"The supplies will not last."

A cry rang through the multitude, and the Nazakian woman shoved between a knot of soldiers. "Princess, the scouts have sighted Pirthyia."

A stunned hush fell. It was too soon. We were trapped.

I looked to Kiboro. All the others did the same.

She looked ready to crumple from the pressure, but then she drew her shoulders back. "Alone, we perish. We follow Huari. What vessels remain in the harbor?"

"There weren't enough boats for all of Laijon," Roji said.

My chest hammered. That meant Huari had left others behind. How many? The Father of Light wouldn't bring us this far to abandon us—

A memory came to me. After we'd discovered the treasure, Jorai had returned to the Heart, and he said he'd found a store of ancient boats. Down the third tunnel.

I sucked in a breath. "There are more boats." Without waiting for a reply, I ran down a narrow intersecting hallway and thrust the glowing oractalm bracelet aloft.

Torches licked the walls as soldiers hurried after me. Behind them, someone cried out.

Just remember the way.

Water gathered into pools up to our waists. I slipped going uphill. We needed to continue east, toward the harbor and higher ground that never experienced flooding. I reached a fork and chose right.

Remember.

A turn and a twist. The corridor widened into a massive

chamber. The Heart. We scattered across the carved, stone slab covering the ground into the tunnel Jorai had told me about. After walking a long distance, I reached a small cavern filled with mountains of darkness. The boats were real.

Praise the Father of Light. I stopped to catch my breath.

Roji and others gained the atrium and flooded the space with light. Father, his wet robes flapping, began pulling leather coverings off the vessels. More joined him.

These were not steel-reinforced, modern watercraft. The wooden hulls peeled with bright paint and boasted carved and weathered masts, outdated weaponry.

Many of the larger boats had unrepairable damage and were thrust aside. Everyone swiftly worked on patching the smaller holes, and these were lifted by six guards for transport as we hunted for missing oars. When the final boat was readied, Kiboro helped carry it, and I joined her.

Father kicked a covert door open, and we emerged onto the head of a modest peninsula washed by moonlight. In the distance, Laijon's ebony castle dominated the twisting skies, and wind carried sounds of marching, rolling weaponry, shouting. Pirthyia battled the castle walls.

Let them remain distracted as we fled unseen.

Our company quieted and advanced across the beach. Thick mist swirled over the water, and through it, the harbor lay empty, just as Kiboro had predicted. Huari had taken everything.

The Brotherhood heaved the archaic boats to the lapping sea's edge. Others moved supplies and formed a defensive border. All cringed at every splash, creak, and groan that was made.

I stayed close to Kiboro and looked for those I knew. Father, Roji, the leaders, Vispirios. Perhaps several of us could board the same boat? Then I spied Geras towering among the supplies.

Father returned. Kiboro's gaze flicked between the ships. "There aren't enough."

Father's voice lowered. "We must destroy the supplies."

A hum swept through the scouts and soldiers. Kiboro glanced toward the city and froze, and the rest of us did the same.

A bonfire danced from the castle pinnacles. Now two. Three.

Pirthyia gained the palace. The castle should have stood secure for days, even under their powerful weaponry. Huari could not have been so stupid as to leave the gates unsecured.

The Brotherhood unsheathed their swords and looked up. Pirthyian trumpets blared, and a far, ghostly screaming answered. Living darkness, warped and winged, tore across the heavens then veered toward the castle. To their Pirthyian masters.

Kiboro squeezed my arm. "Go."

Roji jumped beside us, and the army parted to usher her to the first readied ship, a two-masted vessel.

My heart raced, and I looked back to see Father giving orders to pitch the supplies into the ocean, where Pirthyia could not retrieve them. My boots slapped against the wooden, moaning deck, and Roji claimed the helm. Suddenly, my toes were soaked.

With a muted cry, our accompanying soldiers tried to coax our sinking craft back to shore, but it wouldn't move.

"Leave it," Kiboro commanded. When the guards continued to struggle, she freed her skirt to stand in her shift and dove into the water. I ignored the Brotherhood's shocked expression and followed her to the beach.

All around us, boats were dragged to shore and given frenzied repairs. Two vessels that did not sink filled with Brotherhood soldiers and scudded across the water into the mists.

Vispirios appeared and, in rapid Pirthyian, motioned Kiboro toward a new ship.

Something massive crashed near the beach and several of us stumbled. I caught my balance and looked toward the castle.

Shadows shrieked and crowded atop the towers, far from the multiplying bonfires. By the blazing glare, Pirthyians prepared catapults on the ramparts and heaps of boulders.

They saw us.

The beach erupted in chaos. Someone knocked me to the

ground. I scrambled to my feet and searched for Kiboro. She cried my name, then I spotted her boarding a ship with the Brotherhood. My heart dropped, then I saw Roji climbing into a different, closer boat.

I chased him into knee-deep water, but was too late. He didn't see me as he scoured the coast and shouted my name and Kiboro's. More boats shoved off. A hand clasped my shoulder, and I whirled to face the Ai'Biroan leader's deep-creased eyes.

"Come," he said.

I raced alongside him to the last two vessels. The rest already passed into the fog. Kiboro and Roji were gone. Father—

Something howled across the sky. Shadow.

I ducked, and a massive splash shot water high and raining upon us. A second flaming boulder plunged into the ocean lengths away, and oil and fire flickered in its rolling wake.

Soldiers steadied our boat. The Ai'Biroan swung me aboard before joining two Nazakians, claiming a pair of oars, and motioning me to the prow. I obeyed as discarded supplies bobbed against our hull. We needed the cover of the mist, but it seemed too thin.

Shouts rang from the beach. A handful of Brotherhood dove from the final, failed boat. Some swam for the fur-clad leader's vessel, and two headed toward us.

One was Geras.

He and the other man reached our boat, and the Nazakians helped them climb in. Geras lowered himself onto the bench, dripping and breath heaving, and began to row. He cautiously scanned the beach, those seated beside him, then his eyes shifted to me. He ducked his head and increased his rowing.

Huge stones splashed several lengths away.

"Follow the West Star to Ai'Biro," the leader said.

But the heavens were covered with clouds. A wail burst in my ears, and a rock crashed into the sea a length away. Its impact rocked our vessel, then a second fell even nearer.

I was thrown sideways, then the vessel slammed back into the water and flung me aside again. Something tumbled overboard and someone cried out. I reached toward the Ai'Biroan, but he had vanished.

Geras was searching the water, and I realized a Nazakian was also missing. I gasped. The second soldier remained seated with a wooden shaft through his chest. The third's lifeless body hung halfway in the water, facedown, he and the boat riddled with arrows.

My vision blurred. Sounds popped in my ears. Then I saw the crack in our stern and flinched as water pooled around my shoes.

Geras reached overboard for a floating oar, claimed the middle of the bench, and rowed.

I couldn't find a paddle for myself, so I cupped my hands to sweep water out of the boat. All the other vessels had disappeared. Were they hit? How far had we spun off course?

Geras grunted and nudged the direction of the boat. Above, mist and clouds parted to show the West Star. Huge splashes resounded nearby. Nothing reached us, and they eventually stopped. Were we out of range?

Bright lights winked across the sky and lit the mist. A shrill singing assaulted my ears before the first flaming arrows zipped into the waves.

I ground my jaw and paddled water with my hands uselessly when a second volley hissed into the sea just behind us. Stray arrows thudded into the seated soldier and struck the side of the boat. Geras paused to heave the burning corpse overboard.

"Row!" I shouted, and wrenched one fiery shaft free from the hull, tossed it into the ocean, and did the same with the second. I couldn't stop shaking. Then I noticed that the guard hanging over the side of the boat wore a shield.

I crawled past Geras to the stern and grabbed the armor, but it slipped and toppled into the sea. I pounded my fist.

Fresh arrows whined overhead.

Geras grabbed me around the middle and pinned me under his weight as the arrows thudded against the deck.

Geras convulsed once. Twice. Then lurched upright. Two arrow shafts bristled from his back.

I couldn't think or process. Should I pull—no, the shafts must stay or he would bleed out.

Geras groaned and lifted the oars. Water soaked his trouser legs and my skirts.

I used both hands to splash sea from the boat as more arrows splashed far away. I had the feeling that the current moved us in a circle. I glanced at Geras.

Wild hair hung from his bowed head. He drew deep breaths at each stroke, but we were slowing. He murmured to himself.

The words disentangled themselves and I realized he chanted the first adulation.

I fought the water leaking into our boat and whispered with him, "Holy, holy Father of Light, ruler of every continent and the heavens, you, who visit your creation, are one and unlike other gods." I swallowed and continued, "Your powers are displayed in the makings of the world. You caused the ocean to fold back as cloth and granted your people safe passage from their enemies." Father of Light, help us.

Geras's rowing grew weaker.

I moved to take the oars from him. We must—

Something twinkled in the haze. A lantern. Another boat.

I shouted, and Geras heaved a shuddering breath and pulled the oars with fresh fervor.

An ancient boat materialized like a specter.

I yelled again, and Geras collapsed. I cried out his name, then seized his oars and strained to dip and lift them.

The larger vessel spotted us and slowly came alongside. Brotherhood crowded the railing and lowered a rope. Two soldiers quickly descended.

My voice cracked. "Him first."

They hesitated, then a familiar voice hollered from above, and Roji climbed down and took Geras's arm. The other two helped hoist Geras up.

I stretched for their hands next and was hauled onto deck. One soldier did not release me, and I met Roji's ashen face.

"Seyo." He crushed me in his arms.

I rested my chin on his shoulder and squeezed my eyes shut.

The Brotherhood roared orders and left our crippled vessel to sink.

Geras, now blindfolded, was carried to the lower level.

I followed into the cramped darkness and watched the guards clear rotting barrels and carefully lay Geras on his side. They cut his blood-soaked shirt away. Geras's exposed chest barely rose and fell.

We needed Vispirios.

A soldier with doctoring experience appeared with a torch and bag. He glanced at the arrows protruding from Geras's back—and the maze of markings. Scowling, he refused to intervene.

My face heated. I was about to demand treatment in Kiboro's name when Roji stepped forward. He crossed his arms over his Laijonese uniform, drawing attention to his position as captain of the princess's bodyguard, and glowered.

The soldier thinned his lips but readied his instruments and donned thick gloves with exasperating care. At his curt nod, the others returned to deck.

I would not leave Geras alone with him and was relieved when Roji also remained.

After surgery, the soldier declared that Geras would die overnight. He tossed his soiled gloves to the floor, thrust the torch toward Roji, and exited.

Fury. Horror. I could barely breathe. With unsteady hands, I tested a barrel for soundness and sat. To my surprise, Roji did the same and held the torch in front of him. We did not speak until evening fell, when he said that it was his shift to keep watch and rose.

I did not stand. I would stay, and braced myself for an argument.

But my brother only sighed, set the torch in a wall sconce, and headed up the stairs.

Geras's breaths were shallow. Erratic. Under his blindfold, his face twisted in sleep, so pale and shining with sweat.

I covered my face with my hands.

Why? my soul cried. I dared to offer petition for Geras and hoped for a washing of peace like in the desert, but felt nothing.

After his shift, Roji rejoined me to sleep in the hold. When we awakened the next day, I scrambled to Geras's side. He still breathed. I asked Roji for any clean material soaked in saltwater. He promised to try and brought back a dripping shirt before returning to his tasks.

I cleansed Geras's wounds, careful not to touch his skin. His panting intensified with nightmares and pain.

My focus went from his covered eyes and pinched features to his restless hands. Somewhere along our escape, he'd lost his gloves. His fingers twitched, opened, and closed, straining for something. Exposed marks swirled down his arms to his clenched fingertips.

He needed to calm. My heart pounded. *Qo'tah,* what should I do? I pushed fear aside and grabbed his hand.

Geras gripped back painfully.

I did not let go, even when he relaxed.

We remained so for hours. Weariness accosted me, and I nodded off. When I awakened, Geras slept quietly, my hand still in his.

I quickly glanced at the skin on my arm. Its color had not changed.

Shouting erupted on board. "Ai'Biro sighted!"

I straightened. Implications of our arrival, without warning or supplies, struck me. And then there was facing our new king.

Someone thundered into the hold, and Geras stirred. I pulled my fingers free from his just before my brother appeared.

Roji's eyes were dark. "We see the Laijonese fleet."

But we'd expected them. We wanted to reunite. I opened my mouth, but he stopped me.

"All ships carry distress flags."

Stunned, I asked him to repeat himself. My gut twisted. Impossible. The king—Huari—was mortally wounded.

31

AI'BIRO'S ISLANDS SPARKLED LIKE emeralds against rising sun and silver ocean. Seasonal storm damage revealed itself in bent trees and tossed charcoal beaches. Pale-rock lookout towers, gigantic water wheels, and the famed aqueducts, bridging jungles to transport water between villages, were eye-catching. In the harbor, Laijon's modern and ancient boats stood surrounded by Ai'Biroan steel-clad, steam-powered warships.

A parade of identical, lonely days began. By the time I rose from our bamboo bed and crossed the smooth-wood floors to the row of windows, Ai'Biroan warriors in traditional armor and a Laijonese bodyguard of Pre-Elites escorted Kiboro to the royal infirmary. Roji had returned to his squadron and no longer served as her bodyguard. At the infirmary, she joined her mother and an army of healers to watch over her half brother Huari and the arrow that had almost pierced his lung. Rumors whispered that the shot had come out of nowhere, at close range. None dared come forward, and it was declared an accident.

Despite Huari's cruelty and my fear, I prayed for healing. Laijon could not lose her king now. If his decision to surrender our castle was idiotic, finding refuge in powerful Ai'Biro could be providential. Were we not centuries-old allies? Once Huari healed—Father of Light, let it be so—he could ask them to join us in war to reclaim Laijon. Ai'Biro was small, but what other nation was powerful enough to drive off Pirthyia? With Ai'Biro's strength on our side, perhaps Laijon would not need the key to the Eternity Gate as a weapon.

What about the Shadows and Laijon's impenetrable castle?

An uneasy hush gripped this foreign place, likely due to our arrival and everything it meant. I needed air and sifted through a pile of temple overlays and split skirts delivered by Laijonese servants the day before. The familiar clothing felt both soothing and yet strange. I swiftly donned them and fled to the outdoors.

The royal courtyards, including the palace and guest houses where we stayed, were part of a sprawling complex of creamy stone buildings and gardens hemmed by high walls. As I wandered the gravel of columned walkways, overhung with awnings for the frequent rain, I met Ai'Biroan servants and guards who stopped to offer me respectful greetings. All wore sleeveless tops, both for the tropical weather and, I thought, to boast their proud, beautiful skin, a hue deeper than even mine. I craved to ask if they would join Laijon in arms, but I bowed instead.

I passed lecture halls, imperial guards' quarters, training facilities, and a library. The latter tempted me, as did the amphitheater. Inside, Ai'Biroan performers sometimes stood before crowds of people in shallow, man-made pools and wove water through the air like streamers, their national gifting. Their creation of shapes and stories pleased their audience and me. But I wandered on aimlessly. How I longed to beg Kiboro's permission to leave the courtyards—until discovering a startling place. A large building stood dedicated to guest accommodations, except the vacant rooms currently housed emergency food supplies and looked like they had been forgotten for some time. But at its center, there was a modest temple, neglected in silence, and it was extraordinary. I called it the Mirror Garden.

Stepping inside the holy place, my boots crunched against pebbles covering the floor. Exotic flowers bloomed without a gardener's help in marble jars. From skylights of thick glass, rainbow sunbeams poured upon countless tall, standing mirrors. Despite dust, they reflected each others' images on and on, but in perfect clarity, without a bronze tint. If this Mirror Garden was a small gift for guests, I could not imagine how stunning a full scale, maintained equivalent would be within the palace. It was like standing inside a faceted diamond. I remembered reading that this Ai'Biroan art form was an attempt to replicate the seas and sky and what it might be like to ascend to Heaven's Doorway.

But despite the wonder, all I saw was my own despair captured in countless reflections. I looked down to my fingers. My skin remained unstained from touching Geras's marked hand.

I shivered, pressed deeper into the room, then looked around and panicked. Could I find my way out of here, surrounded by images of myself? But when I turned, I found all the mirrors were backed with silver, and the entrance easy to locate.

I exhaled and went outside. I needed normalcy or a familiar face. If these days stretched any longer, I would go mad.

Someone called out across the courtyard. "Seyo!"

My heart soared as Roji appeared through the columned walkways. His strides were strong, without sign of injury, and he halted before me. Frowning once again.

I wanted to throw my arms around him. "I'm so glad you're here."

"What are you still doing alone over here?"

"Excuse me?"

"It's said the princess spends day and night in the infirmary. I expected you to visit the Laijonese camp by now and began to worry."

I blinked. "I haven't been able to ask permission. I'm glad your commanding officer is so lenient to let you come—"

"Permission." Roji sighed. "Allow me to catch you up. Laijon doesn't know left from right. According to records, I apparently haven't returned from Pirthyia yet, and those in authority over me—whom I have spoken to—don't care about updates. Usual procedures are tossed. No wonder you're still stuck here."

I stared. "What is happening?"

"Everything to be expected, given our circumstances." He

looked at me. "I'm going to visit Father. You should come with me. Kiboro wouldn't want you trapped here like this."

Father. I willed my racing heart to calm. "Please."

We hurried past the arching, white walls of the palace grounds, beyond the sharp eyes of the Ai'Biroan guard, and down dirt pathways winding into the jungle. Lush greenery surrounded us, and exotic birdsong and animal calls filled my ears. A thought struck me. "You're visiting Father? He's not staying in camp with you?"

Roji thumbed over his shoulder. "Laijon is near the palace. All are dressed in mourning colors, if they can get them. There is so much prayer and confession."

"Where is Father?" I interrupted.

"He chose to stay with the Brotherhood."

"Then where are they?"

"The Brotherhood was ordered to camp on the opposite side of the island." He scowled. "Come on, Seyo. You were much more dedicated to Father's history books than me. The majority of the Brotherhood are Nazakian, and Ai'Biro and Nazak still hate each other after the ancient wars. Ai'Biro treats Laijon like respected refugees and the Brotherhood as scum. If either of our nations were to be sent back to sea, the Brotherhood would go first."

I did not reply. He was being dramatic. Ai'Biro wouldn't fully reject either of us. They couldn't.

The trail rounded without end, and after passing two villages, we came to a clearing framed by towering trees. The space was covered with makeshift lean-tos, as the Brotherhood's tents now lay on the ocean floor. The Brotherhood, in their wild array of clothing, milled between smoking fires.

Roji had not exaggerated their poor treatment.

They saw us and gathered, many hailing Roji. I searched faces, and when I spied my father, I lunged forward, and he caught me in his arms. Tears stung my eyes. Father eventually released me and clapped Roji on the shoulder, then turned me to face the Brotherhood, who had divided into squadrons. In a burst of noise, the Brotherhood cheered and clapped.

I stared, confused, until Father spoke quietly in my ear. "They wish to honor you for leading them to the ancient boatyard."

I glanced between his shining eyes and Roji's rare grin before being led to sit on a nearby rock, and the first group of Brotherhood soldiers approached. One at a time, they made brief eye contact with me as they knelt, murmured a word of thanks in their native tongue, then rose and formed ranks to my left. Then the second group came.

The procession overwhelmed me. Did no one question how I had known about the boatyard's location? Others, like Kiboro, had done much more. I had just been—a gateway.

Roji, mischief sparking in his eyes, bowed with the scouts and stepped aside. Several leaders came, including Vispirios, whose curls bounced with his sharp salute. I could not deny that I was relieved to see the good Pirthyian.

By now, over half the company had greeted me. Then I felt a gentle heaviness and held my breath. Geras stood behind a fresh handful of guards with his gaze skewered to the ground. The only one who did not look me in the face. He remained thin and weak, but he should not be alive. Death cheater. Reckless protector.

Dear Father of Light, thank you. But Geras, perhaps least of all, should kneel before me.

I longed to say something, but did not, and a new group of soldiers stood before me. Geras stepped aside near Roji. Mysterious continent, did my brother offer him a nod in greeting?

At last, Father and the leaders presented me with a ceremonial dagger. I accepted the weapon, full of craftsmanship and carving, and bit my lip. I did not deserve this. But I felt their expectation, so I raised the knife toward Heaven before sliding it into my overlay belt, like they did.

Fresh cheers filled the clearing. I felt my cheeks heat before Father took my elbow and escorted me to a long table of mats and blankets, laden with the midday meal.

The leaders prayed, and we passed the food. It was simple fare, but somehow still boasted the known world's offering of spices.

Afterward, warm drinks were poured, despite the island's heat, and laughter and conversation grew as several strummed instruments and sang.

The leaders congregated beside Father on my right. To my left, Roji chatted with the lookouts, and I tried not to stare. When had he made friends among them? I wondered how often he had visited the Brotherhood since landing in Ai'Biro.

A warm sensation washed over me, and I glanced lengths down the table.

Geras sat between several soldiers. They gave him space, but showed no visible discomfort at his proximity. Perhaps these desperate times dulled fear of him.

Geras caught my observation and dropped his gaze. The sensation left me.

I squeezed my steaming cup. Did he know I had stayed with him in the hold of the boat? Kiboro's comments about him feeling indebted and Vispirios calling him "my protector" waltzed uncomfortably through my mind. Yes, we helped each other, and I befriended Geras when few others did. It would be natural for him to form an attachment. But how strong of an attachment?

Stop. This was ridiculous.

I studied my hands. He did not know that I had touched him, did he? I had been so afraid. How much more reckless could I get, besides daring to look into his eyes?

I choked on my drink and met my own haunted gaze in the dregs of the cup. He'd risked his life for me again, and I now owed him another life debt. He would never demand that I pay it back. Such a thing was impossible, but the burden was unbearable.

Hunched over, he also stared into his mug.

I startled. *Qo'tah*. Studying his own reflection didn't harm him?

Father's voice rolled over me. "King Huari's life dangles by a strand."

I snapped my attention toward him and the leaders.

They grimaced. Vispirios spoke with his Pirthyian accent. "Will this affect Ai'Biro's decision to join our fight?"

"I don't know. There aren't provisions for us or Laijon on the islands, even with the calculated fourth of our nation left on the mainland," Father said. "Shadows have not yet crossed the ocean, so Ai'Biro believes they enjoy special protection from the Father of Light. They fear that our presence will harm that. Their piousness blinds them, even after learning that the Shadows attacking Laijon wear Pirthyian uniforms. And then there are evil rumors circulating Laijon." Father gestured toward Roji. "You heard my son's report."

The Nazakian woman spoke. "Yes, but I do not accept that your people speak of surrendering to Pirthyia."

My stomach dropped. What? Laijon considered giving in to Pirthyia? Father caught my gaze, and I froze. He watched me hard. He would send me away.

But Father returned his attention to the leaders. "I do not doubt my son. A deceiver breathes defeat within Laijon."

I could not feel. Could not think. It would be better to remain refugees forever than surrender to Pirthyia. They offered nothing but enslavement. I could attest to that after meeting the Imperati. What Laijonese traitor would suggest such a thing? Someone compelling enough to move Huari to squander the castle, our best stronghold? We needed Ai'Biro's support. We needed—

I thought of the key sewn into my shift and stiffened. Never. The key was anything but a harbinger of hope.

Roji scooted beside me. So, he had been listening too.

"We should go," he muttered.

I noticed dusk falling across the forest. When we rose, Father stood to embrace us. Roji and I dipped our heads toward leadership and followed the winding trail back to Ai'Biro's capital. Once, Roji glanced back toward the Brotherhood, and I swear I caught longing in his eyes.

He returned to Laijon's camp, and I to Kiboro's guest room within the palace. Of course, I found myself alone and fiddled with my new dagger before securing it against my thigh under my skirts. Then, I sat on the bamboo bed and felt my skirts for the hidden key.

Kiboro. I could hand her the key to the Eternity Gate. What

else could give Laijon the upper hand in this battle? I massaged my temples. The key would endanger Kiboro. I would never do that to her. The vile instrument belonged to King Huari, but he could not be trusted with it—if he lived. Neither could the Chanji. What if the traitor whispering our surrender to Pirthyia stood among them? There was Father, but he would give the key to the Brotherhood. So again, that left Srolo Faru.

I straightened.

For decades, humble Faru had given his life in service to his country. His fear of the Eternity Gate's judgment would overpower any greed for divine treasure. Roji said that Laijon made confessions, but it could not be enough to face supernatural wrath. Could Laijon make amends for all of her failings?

I paused. Yet, if Laijon could cleanse herself, the judgment might act as a sort of fiery healing. Would Laijon return to continental prominence? And the sick be healed, as in stories of old? Would we be able to claim the fabled treasure? I wondered if my gifting could be removed, even replaced with the gifting of light. And if Geras's curse could be lifted. Would Jorai's limp have been mended?

I shut my eyes tight. What if Ai'Biro did not ally with us? What if they did? The islands were strong, but second in might to Pirthyia. Either way, Pirthyia and her Shadows could chase us here. So much for Ai'Biro's assumed protection.

If I gave Srolo Faru the key, he might be able to convince Ai'Biro to join our war. We would possess Pirthyia's lust for heavenly power in the palms of our hands.

I drew a shuddering breath.

So be it.

32

RAIN PATTERED UPON THE WINDOWS
when I awoke to Kiboro sitting on the edge of our bed, dressed in
yesterday's clothing.

I bolted upright. "Kiboro?"

She looked exhausted. "He mends."

Breath left my chest in a whoosh. I felt dread, not relief, even if
this was best for Laijon. "Can you rest now?"

Kiboro's lips pursed. "No. Once he is well enough, our king,"
she spat the word, "will answer why he gave up our castle and . . ."
her voice trailed.

Why he had also abandoned her when he fled.

She stood, and I hurried to dress her. Once finished, she
returned to the infirmary, and I again received our breakfast
delivery alone.

I stared at honeyed fruit in linen-lined baskets. What could we
do about Huari? Nothing. He was king, and we were powerless
against him, much worse than when he was crown prince. But
Laijon needed a leader. Huari could approach Ai'Biro about an
alliance. But if he hadn't survived, who would have taken his place?

Kiboro. She was the last of King Zaujo's bloodline. But she was
dedicated to the temple and its service to the poor, a more noble
aim than my own reasons for becoming a temple helper. Yet, had
Huari succumbed, she would have been made queen. Dignified,
strong, and compassionate, but young and inexperienced. Would
she have wanted that?

It didn't matter. Huari healed. Soon he would remember and search for the key. More than ever, the key must go to Srolo Faru. Today. But I needed to do something first.

I pulled the bimil from my satchel and cradled the manuscript in my lap. This ancient chronicle belonged with the key, and I would finish its translation before delivering both.

I turned to the pages describing chests of gilt-bound scrolls. Could our lost history really have survived? I shook my head and moved to the unread parchments.

The princess was taken to the treasure hoard again. Her Shadow followed like a ghost. The invading king—the deceiver from across the mysterious seas—sat on Laijon's throne.

I read quickly, as if the words might writhe off the paper. Pages dwindled at an alarming rate. Centuries of historians believed this record told the location of the treasure. Where was it? Or a description of the Eternity Gate. Majestic and golden, encrusted with jewels beyond price, pulsing with terrifying power? On the second-to-last page, I found something and stared.

The deceiver king summoned his Shadows and ordered the Eternity Gate to be chopped down.

I reread the passage twice. What in the continent? After the Eternity Gate was destroyed, the princess returned to the Handprint of God. A Shadow stalked nearby. She mentioned a light.

I turned the page, the very last one, and it lay blank. The records ended.

I felt as though I had been punched in the stomach. Historians and kings had searched this manuscript. They would have read that the Eternity Gate was cut down. Why did we still fight this battle? All because a prophecy promised that the Eternity Gate somehow survived. What happened to the princess?

I turned to the pages with the Shadow's scratching handwriting, but attempting to translate that was useless.

I skipped breakfast—I couldn't have eaten if I wanted to—wrapped the bimil in clean linen from the breakfast baskets, and tucked the book under my arm.

Mist and rain filled the royal courtyard. Walkway awnings kept all but my skirt hem dry as I rounded white-stone buildings in search of the towering, spired palace. A long, neighboring edifice stood guarded by Laijonese soldiers. The Chanji, including Srolo Faru, as captain of the bodyguard, and Queen Umoli, leading in King Huari's absence, would be there.

A marble colonnade led to massive wooden doors framed by Elites and Pre-Elites. I spotted the guard King Zaujo had assigned to me long ago and stiffened. But he showed no recognition in his brief glance and ignored me like the rest. After all, I was the princess's attendant. Not a threat.

If they only knew what I carried.

The rain eased, and I retreated into a nearby garden and waited for the council to dismiss. Soon, Srolo Faru would protect the key. I wouldn't bear this secret alone any longer.

What if Faru guessed that Jorai had stolen the key and given it to me? None of that mattered anymore.

The Elites raised their swords together, and the Chanji burst from their meeting like a flood. All wore frowns and pinched expressions. But where was Srolo Faru's commanding presence?

A councilman shouted his name.

I shifted my gaze and found Faru hastening down the covered walkways. He shook his head without pausing and disappeared behind a cluster of buildings.

The councilman threw up his hands.

I gave chase. Faru's hurry was maddening, and the growing fog awful. Were negotiations with Ai'Biro failing? Something was wrong. Where was he going?

I caught sight of him again and raised my voice. "Srolo Faru."

He vanished.

Qo'tah. I lifted my skirts and rounded a corner.

Srolo Faru stood lengths away with his profile to me. I skidded to a stop. His shoulders drooped, chin to chest, his silver, braided beard unkept. I'd never seen him like this. It was as if years had passed between our last meeting, and not a single season.

I crept forward. "Srolo Faru?"

He gripped his sword, saw me, and squinted. As if struggling to recognize me. "Srawa Seyo? Where is the princess?"

No greeting. Did he not know that Kiboro basically lived at the infirmary?

"I must speak with you. I have learned something—"

His features twisted. "No."

I froze at his interruption.

"Return to your rooms." He grabbed my arm and dragged me toward the guest buildings.

What was going on? "Srolo Faru, you must hear me."

"No, Seyo—"

I thrust the bimil in front of him.

Faru halted, stunned. "You took it? It doesn't matter anymore." He snatched the bound manuscript before opening the door—we had already reached Kiboro's room—and pushing me across the threshold. "Remain inside."

But the key.

I caught the closing door. "Srolo Faru, I have something of upmost importance. Laijon needs—"

Faru cut me off. "Seyo, I don't have time."

Screams rose from beyond the walls, from Laijon's camp. Srolo Faru slammed the door and ran. I heard his hurried steps fade away.

What was happening?

I burst outdoors. Srolo Faru had disappeared. I raced along a covered walkway toward the walls. The cries increased. Rain fell again.

Something thumped against the awning above, and I crouched. Heavy hands and feet scurried, then the creature jumped—and did not land. A screech rent the air, and a length away, the overhead awning bulged and tore.

I reached for my Brotherhood dagger and hurled myself inside the nearest building. A skirmish exploded where I had just stood. Two Shadows shrieked.

I barreled into an unlit hallway. Clicking claws scrambled

behind me. I leapt through the nearest doorway into heavy gloom and bumped into barrels and food storage. There was a pile of bags. Spiced, dried seaweed. I lay down and covered myself with the sacks.

The door creaked. A Shadow scuffled across the room, sniffing, growling.

I didn't breathe.

Its claws scratched into the hall and tore into a different chamber. Then, the monster crashed into the room next door. Slashing. Smashing.

I launched from my hiding place, flew past its open door, and faced wrecked chaos in the next room. I jumped inside just as it barged back into the corridor, and pressed myself against the wall beside the open doorframe.

Out of the corner of my eye, I saw it stooping on all fours. Expanding wings close enough to touch. Bent elbows stabbed into the ground. Arched back, too large to be human.

It dashed into the food storage room and I sped down the hall. Would its carnage cover my flight? I reached outdoor access and tripped at its furious scream. It'd found my hiding spot. I needed new cover.

I slipped into the next building. The hallways were familiar.

A clumsy gait lumbered behind me. Two feet—another Shadow.

My chest almost burst before I reached the third door.

Silence engulfed its scampering. A breath of wind—but no. I swung the door shut, and the flying Shadow crashed into it. The impact threw me backward against thick carpeting. Books fell off shelves, and I dodged them and several chairs to a back door.

A door was torn off its hinges and flung.

I zigzagged into new halls. Anything to create distance while exhaustion nipped at my heels. Sounds of warfare grew outside. More Shadows? Shouts from the Brotherhood were so close—

A Shadow slammed across my path.

My heart stopped, and I tripped into the nearest room. Endless, glittering reflections surrounded me. The Mirror Garden.

The monster shrieked.

I ducked behind a silver-backed mirror as a horrific, inhuman cry tore the atmosphere. I fell to my knees and blocked my ears against the squabbling. Two Shadows fighting. One squealed in Nazak's language, the struggle ceased, and claws scratched against the gravel flooring.

I glanced into the nearest mirror.

The victorious Shadow appeared in every reflection. This one was thin and tall, clothed, standing upright on two feet, despite its arched spine, and faced the mirrors with wild disorientation. A heavy, gold collar shimmered around its neck, unlike the others. It wrapped its wings about its body with a glare before bumping backward into another mirror. It hissed and smashed the glass with a clawed fist. Shimmering shards rained upon the ground. The Shadow advanced, focused on its direction and ignoring the broken glass.

I did not tear my gaze from the creature. Then, the reflection of its eyes found the reflection of mine. I jumped back, and it howled and crashed deeper into the room.

I ducked behind mirror after mirror. The Shadow toppled and smashed them in confused pursuit. Destroying hiding places. I must circle to the front.

Cries rang from the doorway, and the mirrors filled with armored soldiers.

The Shadow spun with a growl. Its reflection, mine, and the soldiers' swirled all around the room.

I opened my mouth to shout, but the Shadow was closer than they were.

The monster stretched its wings with a wail and lurched into flight.

I darted toward the back until the mirrors disappeared and I faced white walls. Cornered.

The frantic Shadow circled above, and soldiers yelled orders. One was Vispirios.

I screamed as the Shadow rushed me. Its massive wings and

jerky flight filled my vision, and I raised my dagger as it careened into the nearest mirror. Glittering fragments rained, and I backed into the wall and sank to the floor. Play weak. Then jump for its face.

The Shadow rose to its towering form with something like a laugh—in Nazakian—then lurched and collapsed.

I recoiled, covered my head, then looked. A different dagger protruded from the Shadow's curved back.

Laijonese, Brotherhood, and Ai'Biroan soldiers exploded through the remaining mirrors and tackled the monster. Vispirios's stocky form filled my vision, and he extended a copper-colored hand. "Lady Seyo, can you walk?"

Seeing the Shadow and hearing that accent made me want to shrink back, but I accepted his help.

The others struggled to lift the Shadow's body, now tightly bound. They eyed the golden choker, but did not remove it. Vispirios assisted, glass splintering under his boots, before putting his hand on his sword.

"It still lives," he said in the trade language.

A tall, deep-skinned Ai'Biroan grunted. "We are commanded to capture one alive."

"Foolishness."

One Laijonese guard sneered. "You Brotherhood were ordered to stay back."

Vispirios's eyes flashed. "I fight for innocent life, as I would protect my wife and children."

They ignored him and bore the Shadow's weight through the door. I followed and turned my eyes from their bloodstained hands, cuts crisscrossing their arms and legs, to the creature's leathery flesh, and the weak rise and fall of its chest.

Vispirios was right. The creature should be killed. Then I remembered what the Shadow used to be.

We gained the royal courtyard. First, I saw battle-stained Ai'Biroans and Laijonese, then the Brotherhood standing farther back. The rain was gone, but clouds still hung low and thick.

Slain Shadows claimed the center of the courtyard. Their cursed spirits loosed.

I shuddered. How many people were also lost?

More Ai'Biroan soldiers received our living Shadow, and my rescuers dispersed. I looked around, lost, until Vispirios laid a hand on my shoulder and pointed toward a knot of Elite guards and Kiboro.

I met his gaze. Thank you—but I could not make myself speak.

His eyes crinkled, both sad and compassionate. "Thank the Father of Light for your safety. And may Heaven help your protector when he learns of the danger you were in while he was kept from fighting." Then Vispirios inclined his head and trotted toward the Brotherhood.

I spotted Kiboro and went to her side. She barely acknowledged me as she stared at the winged corpses. Then I noticed Ai'Biro's king and queen standing nearby. Beautiful younger brother and older sister who jointly ruled the islands, dressed like warriors and wearing matching silver crowns. They, too, studied the Shadows with high, creased foreheads. Their assumed mantle of protection was shattered.

The Ai'Biroan king gave a word. The Shadows were to be burned and their ashes poured into the ocean. Immediately.

Soldiers obeyed. It took three men to carry one Shadow. Ten monsters were removed, besides my attacker, which was hurried to the dungeons. How many Shadows had escaped? Or had so few flown across the sea to attack us?

Kiboro swept away from the throng toward our guest room. Her guard was doubled. They checked every part of our accommodations before allowing us to enter and change into dry clothes. Kiboro ordered an Elite to bring a list of the Laijonese and Brotherhood lost in battle today. When he returned with the names and food, I recognized no one. Despite my hunger pains, thinking about eating sickened me.

Had the Shadow that attacked me, the one Ai'Biro kept alive, recognized me, as his brethren had in Pirthyia? The girl who holds the key, the one Jorai described before his death?

Within an hour, soldiers opened the door without warning, and we blinked to see Queen Umoli standing before us, more rigid than usual. She ordered the doors closed and approached Kiboro. "Be strong, daughter. The Chanji are meeting, and it is best for you to join us this time."

My stomach jumped. Another attack?

Kiboro pressed her hands together, voice tight. "Huari?"

"No." The queen's lips tightened. "Srolo Faru is arrested for colluding with Pirthyia."

This was a nightmare. A horrific misunderstanding.

Srolo Faru was no traitor.

Inside the meeting building we borrowed from Ai'Biro, Kiboro and Queen Umoli crowded among the Chanji, and I remained at Kiboro's side. No Brotherhood were present, nor my father. A few Ai'Biroan nobility were in attendance to take a report to their king and queen.

Judges were chosen from Laijon's elders, and Srolo Faru was summoned to stand in the center of the room.

Faru arrived, flanked by two Laijonese guards, previously under his command, and their eyes shifted with discomfort. His arms and legs were free, but he hadn't changed after the battle and rain. He stood pillar straight, unlike earlier that day. Rage glinted in his eyes.

Incriminating letters, discovered among Srolo Faru's belongings, were presented before the judges. All were addressed to and from Pirthyian high command. They contained promises of service in exchange for treasure and position once Pirthyia claimed Laijon's land.

It was a trick. Someone was trying to destroy us from inside. Yet all too soon, they were verified as genuine, and Srolo Faru's handwriting was confirmed.

Soldiers came forward, even Elites, and gave testimony of Faru manipulating trade laws and accepting bribery with border passage. Some said Srolo Faru gave no orders when the Shadows attacked today. Others claimed that when the monsters passed over him, he did not unsheathe his sword.

My heart rammed against my ribs. Why didn't the Chanji stop this madness? Srolo Faru had been acting strangely, but none of this could be true. But the letters.

As judges called for a vote, Kiboro's cheeks paled, and she leaned against me.

The decision was cast. Srolo Faru, captain of Laijon's bodyguard, was stripped of his title and sentenced to the Ai'Biroan dungeon.

Sharp silence fell and the last defenses within me crumbled.

Guards approached with clanking iron chains, restrained Faru, and forced him away.

The Chanji was dismissed.

How long had Faru been Laijon's traitor? I had almost handed him the key to the Eternity Gate.

After a restless night, as breakfast was delivered, a heavy knock made Kiboro and me jump. I rose from sitting cross-legged before our low, Ai'Biroan table and readied myself to meet Queen Umoli's severe frown. When I opened the door, I found Kiboro's bodyguard at attention, which was strange. Yes, the queen stood in the courtyard, but with the whole Chanji, except Huari, of course. What in the continent?

Kiboro stepped past me, searched their faces, and curtsied.

All lowered themselves to their knees to bow. The eldest councilmember spoke.

"Daughter of King Zaujo, Queen Kiboro—"

My insides clenched, and Kiboro's stricken gasp interrupted him.

Huari was dead.

33

INFECTION HAD CLAIMED KING
Huari. Ai'Biro agreed to hold his funeral in three days.

Before sundown, I dressed Kiboro for her coronation. Queen Umoli lent her a gown that was too long, and my fingers trembled with the hooks. Arranging her chopped hair was almost impossible.

Kiboro could not be crowned inside the palace, but the Ai'Biroan king and queen offered her the castle terrace, where she could be publicly seen. Soon, Laijon, Ai'Biro, and the Brotherhood were pressing into the royal courtyard. Our people dressed in what mourning colors they could find. Above, lingering winds dragged clouds across the hard, blue sky.

I stood with the servants, and we watched Laijon's priests and priestesses ascend the terrace to meet Kiboro. She bowed, and the bodyguard of Elites fanned behind her. An elder priest anointed her with oil, placed the king's heavy crown against her brow, and declared her reigning queen of Laijon.

The gathered shouted. Laijon lifted their hands in light. The Brotherhood, many Ai'Biroans, and I, too, lifted empty palms to show her honor.

Kiboro raised open hands, a symbol of prayer, and offered blinding light that snuffed the rest, eliciting cries of astonishment. Perhaps because of that, or our current tribulation, the people knelt when she knelt, and joined her in public confessions. No Laijonese monarch had begun their rule in this way for generations.

My best friend, just come of age, became ruler of a people with no country. She, the third heir, faced Pirthyia and Shadows. In private, she requested that I continue to call her Kiboro and assured me that I retained my position as attendant before disappearing in endless meetings with the Chanji. Two guards stayed with me, a precaution after the Shadow attack. No more exploring without a soldier following. I remained in our room alone with my thoughts.

Srolo Faru was a traitor. Huari was dead. Kiboro was crowned. The key, with its danger and responsibility, belonged to her. If we went to war, and Pirthyia captured Kiboro with the key, there would be no ransom. Could I do that to her? But what would happen if I continued to keep this secret?

Two days before the funeral, Kiboro rose early to join the Chanji. After I readied her in another of her mother's dresses, this one hemmed, she requested my accompaniment.

Images rose of the one other Chanji meeting I had witnessed, against my will, at Huari's hand. The red ore glowing in King Zaujo's hands. Jorai's imprisonment. I steadied myself before inclining my head.

Exiting our guest house, I walked paces behind Kiboro, surrounded by her Elites, toward the long, white-stone building. Guards bowed low as we passed the gardens, marble colonnade, and double wooden doors.

Inside, windows were curtained around an ornate table filled with chairs, too many for us. The Chanji had already arrived, as was expected, and rose at Kiboro's arrival.

She claimed the head of the table. Her bodyguard formed a semicircle behind her, and I pressed myself into the corner to stand.

The Chanji sat again. Queen Mother Umoli lowered herself at Kiboro's left and wore her usual mask. Did she gloat at her daughter's ascension? Mourn? Or wish for the title herself, despite lacking royal blood? I supposed I would never know.

The seat at Kiboro's right, which for decades belonged to Faru, was filled. By my father.

I swallowed surprise. When had Kiboro invited Father to the Chanji? Did he serve as royal historian again? He would not replace the captain of the bodyguard.

Many among the Chanji narrowed their eyes toward him, and I guessed that their thoughts repeated what I heard whispered years ago, *The king tires of looking backward and dismissed his historian. Such disgrace. What will become of the historian's children?* For once, their cruelty met numbness inside me. But when I followed the rest of the Chanji's glances, I stared. Two more newcomers sat at the end of the table, Pirthyian Vispirios and the Nazakian woman, exotic, metal bands covering her neck.

Kiboro looked each person in the face. I did not expect pleasantries, and indeed, she cut to the point. "What will we do for Laijon?"

The Chanji raised their voices together, even stood, to list their needs.

Supplies.

Tend our wounded.

Weaponry.

We wearied Ai'Biro's hospitality. They would probably send us away after King Huari's funeral.

Their demands turned to the Shadow attack. The monsters screamed in Pirthyian, Nazakian, even Laijonese. Two of the slain were females, made by surgery and incantation. If more came, would they drag darkness across the sky, like the ancient legends? Would their greater predecessors from the Occupation, bred beyond the fiery Divide, who traded their souls for uncommon strength, return from the dead?

I clasped my hands in my lap. I knew what the Shadows wanted. The key. Memories came of meeting Father at the temple after Jorai's imprisonment, and hearing his tale of the last Shadow of the Occupation, chained and drowned in an icy lake.

Someone shouted. "What of returning to Laijon? Will we go to war or become Pirthyia's slaves?"

Quarreling exploded across the table. Kiboro studied each person, weighing. When she rose, they silenced.

Kiboro lifted her voice. "Laijon will fight. When did we last ask Ai'Biro to join us? Who has sent messages to Nazak to see if they will bear arms?"

A young man from the Chanji bowed his head. "My queen, King Huari was unable to speak with Ai'Biro." He hesitated. "Why would Nazak join us?"

Her mouth firmed. "I will speak with Ai'Biro. Do not they and Nazak have families to protect?"

"Your Majesty, we are outnumbered and without supplies or weapons," a councilwoman said. "Perhaps Pirthyia will find what she seeks and leave Laijon."

"May Pirthyia seize the cursed treasure and return to their lands," another yelled.

Father swept his robes behind him and bowed toward Kiboro. Face flushed, she nodded permission for him to speak.

Father faced the Chanji. "Pirthyia is glutted with wealth. What use do they or Shadows have for treasure?" His expression clouded. "Pirthyia seeks power from the Eternity Gate."

Some of the Chanji hissed or spat. Most stared.

"Daemu," the councilman offered my father no title, "you speak of a myth."

My blood boiled.

Father's voice remained calm. "Pirthyia does not invade Laijon for fables." When none responded, he reached into his robes and laid a thin, old book on the table.

The bimil.

"This account of the Eternity Gate, written before the Occupation, was found among the captain of the bodyguard's belongings." He avoided saying Faru's name and omitting his Srolo title, giving the condemned more grace than he, himself, was offered. "Her Majesty has asked me to translate this record."

Again, I recalled meeting Father. We had discussed the bimil. He had never seen the manuscript before and said he longed to read it. Now, knowing his connection with the Brotherhood and their determination to open the Eternity Gate, I understood why, and my stomach sickened seeing the book in his possession.

Father bowed again. "May I share my findings?"

Kiboro agreed. Father sat, opened the bimil, and began. His rolling voice transported me to when, as a child, I sat on the Archives floors and listened to his translations, except now my heart climbed into my throat. He explained how the first Elites sold the Eternity Gate to the usurper king from across the seas. Then he described the controversy of what the heavenly gate held. Divine power or judgment? Father read the prophecy.

Hearing it aloud, shivers danced across my skin.

After the unfaithful era, a second generation will find the Gate to Eternity and bow before the power of the Father of Light. Destruction will be allotted with fire and water. An evil one will arise. The one chosen to open the gate, of royal blood and disfigured, will welcome judgment from Heaven, and the one born of legend will slay her own soul to finish the age.

Father closed the bimil. "There are lists of treasure, even weaponry, and that is as far as I have translated. But I think it is clear what Pirthyia seeks."

But what would Father think when he read that the Eternity Gate was chopped down? Did the Chanji know Kiboro had promised the gate to the Brotherhood?

"The prophecy says that only one can open the gate, and tradition dictates that this person will be Laijonese. Not Pirthyian." Father looked at Kiboro. "I once thought it could be your half brother."

He meant Jorai, because of his limp, and my chest squeezed.

"My queen, you alone carry Laijon's royal blood. I wonder if the Father of Light has chosen you."

The room seemed to freeze. Indeed, his words sounded mad.

Kiboro replied, head high. "Historian Daemu, I have lived among the Brotherhood and know they believe if Laijon fails to open the Eternity Gate now, we will be destroyed. I also discern that they believe there will be a reward or protection over us if we obey. That Laijon could be spared and even restored as she once was."

But the Eternity Gate held judgment. Could we expect the Father of Light to stand between us, the fathomless divide, and Heaven's Doorway, as he would at the end of known time?

"Queen Kiboro, there is a second possibility," Vispirios said.

I surfaced from my thoughts, and realized he spoke without permission.

"Our fathers, the first Elites, bartered the Eternity Gate to Laijon's invaders. You know this is why we fight to open it and end our disgrace."

The Chanji's bewildered looks sharpened.

Vispirios ignored them. "Perhaps you do not know that the first Elites were second sons of Laijonese royalty. Though faint, the blood of kings runs through our veins. If it pleases the queen, the Brotherhood would be honored to protect Her Majesty and attempt to open the Eternity Gate."

Kiboro responded with a troubled shake of her head. "I am humbled by your sacrifice, but there is something you should know. The key to the Eternity Gate, which belonged to my father, is lost. It was supposed to be hidden within the pages of the book Historian Daemu holds, and we could not find it among . . . King Huari's belongings."

Father looked unsurprised. She must have already delivered this news to him. He bowed his head. "We cannot lose hope. The key must remain hidden in Laijon."

Guilt squirmed inside of me, and then I noticed Vispirios's confusion.

He spoke. "My queen, what key is this?"

Vispirios didn't know about the key? Apparently neither did the rest of the Brotherhood, who repeated his question. Had so much time passed that they had forgotten?

One of the Chanji raised his voice. "Your Majesty, how can we hope to find this gate that has been lost for centuries without a key?" The chamber erupted in disputes and interruption again.

One day before Huari's funeral, Kiboro met with Ai'Biroan royalty. The king and queen promised to convene with their advisors concerning joining our war against Pirthyia.

And so Laijon waited.

Kiboro assigned two of her Elites to guard her mother and, to the mute horror of everyone, summoned Vispirios and Geras to replace them in protecting her. Selecting Vispirios was a diplomatic move. Choosing Geras was desperate and controversial. Kiboro overrode the Brotherhood's sentence by outfitting him with weaponry—knowing his curse, tolerating his risk. Geras was the most dangerous person among us. Requesting his presence revealed her fear. But he had sworn to never use his curse, not even against an enemy. Did she forget this? Did I forget this, and put too much trust in him?

How many times do you expect him to save you, Seyo? I startled at the thought. But he hadn't rescued me during the last Shadow attack. *May Heaven help your protector when he learns of the danger you were in,* Vispirios had said. *Qo'tah.* That hardly lessened what I owed him. Would my debt be added to my judgment when the Eternity Gate opened? I wished Kiboro hadn't picked him or Vispirios to join her guard. But they had already appeared in the Ai'Biro's courtyard, performed rustic bows by Laijonese standards, and received placement.

Geras stood a head taller than the Elites and earned an enormous amount of attention. Face down, he wore his Brotherhood clothing, but a Laijonese sword hung from his hip. His da's blade lay strapped across his back again, an impossible place to easily unsheathe the blade. He appeared agitated.

Kiboro announced that the Ai'Biroan king and queen had

invited her to join them in questioning the captured, surviving Shadow. She had accepted, and we would depart as soon as our escort arrived.

My blood ran cold. As if the creature would cooperate. This could go nowhere but ill. Judging by Vispirios's fierce expression, he concurred.

Father of Light, don't make me face that monster again.

Royal Ai'Biroan soldiers met us. Together, we started for the towering, slate walls of the dungeons. Rows of soldiers opened the stone doors and ushered us into a maw of darkened passages. Torches were lit and Elites cupped handfuls of light, drawing eyes. We took the center hall and passed barred cells, filled and empty. My pulse raced when I imagined passing Faru, but I dismissed the thought. Decorous Ai'Biro would not subject Kiboro to that.

The corridor turned with solid walls. We passed another cluster of Ai'Biroan guards, a second stone doorway opened, and we filed into a lightless chamber with a single barred cell.

The Shadow scuttled into the corner and wrapped wings around itself. Torchlight and shadows cavorted across the creature's mangled body and torn clothing. It stood upright, and I realized it was smaller than those that crawled on all fours. Darkness clung to the creature, dulling the gold collar it continued to wear.

I stayed as far from the cage as possible.

An Ai'Biroan interpreter barked commands in the trade language, Nazakian, Laijonese, and Pirthyian. I remembered that the Shadow spoke Nazakian.

"Bow to the king and queen, Creature."

The Shadow ignored him, and a guard slipped a spear through the bars. The Shadow cried aloud and flapped its wings until wind filled the chamber. Before the guard prodded it a second time, the Shadow turned, craning its long neck to scrutinize us with slits for eyes, pausing at Kiboro and then fixating upon me.

A burning sensation enveloped my senses. It watched me—like Geras, I could actually feel its eyes, and the feeling was so awful I wanted to fall to the ground and cover my head. The Ai'Biroan interpreter spoke, but the Shadow ignored him and continued to stare, head cocked.

Did it recognize me?

Geras's gaze fell over me like a blanket of iron. Frantic.

Others also noticed the Shadow's attention. The Ai'Biroan king and queen whispered to Kiboro. She said, "My attendant can interpret. Perhaps it will respond to her." Then Kiboro was looking at me. "Seyo?"

I understood what she wanted. But I could not do this. It would expose me.

The Shadow beat its wings, stirring dust and darkness. Its claws shot out to grasp the bars.

I jumped back. Unsheathed swords whispered into the air as the monster straightened to its full height and groaned. Where not covered by a ragged shirt and trousers, patterned burns covered its leathery flesh like branding. Ribs protruded, the thin bones of its wings folded. Its eyes met mine. Great, fathomless orbs. Discerning, gloating. In a tangled, gray voice, each Nazakian word a knife thrown, it declared, "They fought. I fought. I won. I live." Then the Shadow covered its head with its claws, moaned, and folded chin to knees.

A convulsion ripped through my body. I would have fallen if Kiboro had not caught my arm and her guard tightened around us. Kiboro faced the Ai'Biroan royalty and demanded that we leave. The king and queen ordered their soldiers to lead us out.

Hurry. Please. I passed the cage with Kiboro's arm looped within mine.

The Shadow shuffled closer. Its voice seethed. "Run, Laijon." Then it laughed.

Geras lunged out of line between us and the cage. The Shadow flailed against the bars. Vispirios barked something and pushed Geras, whose eyes remained down, ahead, and was last to reenter the darkened hallways. Dungeon guards shut the stone door to the cell, while the creature shrieked an agonizing, muffled scream.

We fled a caged Shadow.

That night, the evening before King Huari's funeral, Kiboro returned from another meeting with the Chanji and woke me. She sounded out of breath.

Ai'Biro would join Laijon as allies in our war against Pirthyia and her Shadows. Perhaps that afternoon's disaster in the dungeons had borne fruit after all.

"Ai'Biro has a plan for infiltration." Kiboro nodded to herself. "We will fight, Seyo. We will pray. Your father searches the bimil for the Eternity Gate."

Had he reached the part where the gate was chopped down? Would he recognize the ghostly, ending script as scrawled by a Shadow?

She left me to change and declined my assistance. I turned over on the bed to face the wall and hugged a corner of our quilt to my chest.

Laijon could not fight Pirthyia without the key. Kiboro must have it. Now.

No. Tomorrow after Huari's funeral.

I squeezed my eyes against tears. I would give the key to my friend and queen, put her in further danger, and if the Eternity Gate opened . . . the responsibility was unbearable. Roji said our people made confessions. Perhaps the Father of Light would spare Laijon, even the Brotherhood, for following Heaven's will.

And I? Perhaps I would join Faru in jail for acting the liar first.

I knew I might lose Kiboro's respect. And that of my father and Roji. The Brotherhood, even Vispirios, could reject me even after honoring me. What of Geras? Would he realize he had tasted death for a thief?

And if judgment fell, what would happen to him?

34

RESTLESSNESS PLAGUED MY SLEEP.
I awoke multiple times to a handful of skirt and key clutched in my fist, feeling its teeth bite my palm.

Today, I would relinquish this burden.

I stared at the darkened ceiling. The funeral would commence in the afternoon. This morning, I would do something for my friends before my secret was exposed. I would return the Brotherhood's engraved dagger, through Vispirios perhaps. I would give Roji something too. Perhaps my glowing oractalm bracelet. For my dear father, I couldn't think of anything.

I owed Geras a life debt. It was impossible to pay that back. The best I could offer him was a warning. That Geras could not approach the Eternity Gate with the Brotherhood. The judgment would destroy him.

Lastly, I would give Kiboro the key.

I tried to remember where I had put the Brotherhood's dagger. Where had I seen it last?

In the Mirror Garden with the Shadow.

There were no meetings with the Chanji today. Instead, after breakfast, Queen Mother Umoli arrived at our guest house for a visit. The older woman sent me a look that communicated she wanted to speak to her daughter alone.

I left willingly. Time to search the Mirror Garden. Kiboro didn't allow me to walk unaccompanied, but I had my pick of escort.

Outside the guest house, surrounded by Ai'Biro's lush courtyard, the Elite bodyguards for the queen and the queen mother spied me and paused their gossip.

In the past, these favored nobility's sons ignored me. Why their sudden notice? Perhaps becoming the queen's attendant made even the disgraced historian's too tall, ungifted daughter valuable. How I wished Roji was still captain of Kiboro's guard.

Vispirios's copper hair and energetic posture caught my attention. I would go to him—then Geras's warm gaze touched my awareness. He stood alone, towering over the rest in his Nazakian leather and gloves, despite the heat. Scorned. Isolated. It didn't matter that Ortos, the most respected leader among the Brotherhood, called him son. Or that Kiboro had handpicked him for her guard.

My shoulders hitched. "I require escort."

All straightened, but I faced Geras. "Will you come with me?"

The Elites startled. Some glared at him—and me—but Vispirios grinned. He must enjoy seeing those peacock soldiers rankled.

Geras stepped behind me. The tension enveloping him since the Shadow attack hit me like a tidal wave.

I chose the nearest walkway, and Geras's heavy presence trailed me. Beyond a customary greeting, he did not speak. I couldn't summon conversation either. When our path rounded another garden, I glanced at him from the corner of my eye.

Head down, of course. The hilt of his da's sword peeked over his shoulder. In all the battles we had experienced together, he'd never wielded it. The blade was passed down for generations, forged to defend the Eternity Gate. Could the weapon serve no lesser purpose? Or did Geras feel unworthy of it?

I gathered myself, rehearsed my warning for the millionth time, then entered the cool interior of a white-stoned building.

Inside, everything remained dusty and quiet as before, but my mind brought back the Shadow chasing me down this hall. My footsteps quickened and the door appeared. I reached for the handle.

Had anyone cleaned up? What if my dagger wasn't here?

Geras stood close behind me as I pressed the door open and briefly closed my eyes against the shimmering mess.

Mirrors lay cracked and smashed across the ground. From the skylights, cloudy sunbeams poured over the carpet of broken reflections. I had hidden behind these mirrors' silver backs. And watched the Shadow shudder from its own appearance.

I walked deeper into the room. Glass snapped under my heels. Everywhere, I saw jagged fragments of my form and face.

Geras paused, looked into the countless mirrors, and followed. He saw himself. Why wasn't he harmed? I averted my gaze with a thudding heart. What was I thinking, bringing him to this place where eye contact was far too easy?

"The Shadow attacked you here."

I startled at his voice. *May Heaven help your protector* . . . "Yes. And I lost my dagger here, I think."

A trio of mirrors remained standing in the corner. Steel glimmered at their feet. My knife.

I rescued the weapon and paused. Brown blood stained everything from where the Shadow had fallen.

Geras's palpable anguish grew. "If I had carried it for you, the Shadow would have attacked me." He meant the key.

Geras, stop. I am already tormented by my debt to you! "After today, I won't carry it anymore." I kept my gaze down, away from his reflection in the mirrors. But that haunting question rose again. What would it be like to see his eyes? "We are headed to war. None but the Father of Light knows what will happen to us. I want to give you something. A warning for your sake." I drew a breath. "When the treasure is found and the Brotherhood claims the Eternity Gate, you must stand back and hide from the judgment. Keep your Nho with you. Perhaps it will add protection." That bordered on superstitious. Tears welled in my eyes. What was wrong with me? "Stay far from the Eternity Gate."

"You think the judgment will consume me because of my curse."

Was he offended? "Yes. And it is the same for me."

"You will shine—"

I spoke before thinking. "My mother was Vedoan."

Silence fell.

My heart pounded. "She abandoned our family when I was a child. In Laijon, that is shameful, and we bore her disgrace." Just as Jorai had carried the scandal of the second queen, his mother. I flexed my hand. The faint burn scars pulled against my palms. "When I was little, Mother plunged my hands into the hearth fire, saw I was unharmed, then tried to force me to carry her own warped gifting of flames. Vedoa's flames are not like natural fire. She burned me, then thrust me aside in disgust." My best friend Tol had fought to help me and was punished for intervening. That night, she'd applied salve to my hands, and I'd pierced my ears like her own slave piercing. We'd promised to always protect one another. "I am tainted. The judgment will consume me too." I fell silent. And waited.

"I do not see you differently."

He did not need to offer such humble acceptance, and I felt exposed. But something deep inside me eased, like that unexpected taste of the peace in the desert. Even though he could not see me face-to-face, he recognized this part of me better than I understood it myself.

"Thank you," I said softly.

"I hate the evil of this war. I fear it will overcome and exploit me again." He groaned. "I don't know what I am, what I am supposed to be. Da said the Father of Light creates everything, but my curse is not from him. I am a monster."

My heart dropped. I stopped myself from reaching out to him. "I have seen monsters in different forms. What lies inside us makes us one or not. You are not a monster, Geras."

"I harmed your brother." He massaged his wrists. "Seyo, I want to be cleansed."

His meaning struck me. He believed the judgment could break his chains. But the holiness of the Eternity Gate could not meet his curse and leave him intact.

But if it could . . . Geras's power, my false gifting, Jorai's limp if he had lived, all could have been made whole. But this was foolishness. "It cannot work that way."

Geras did not answer.

"Please promise you'll hide." I could not bear this guilt if the judgment destroyed him.

"Can I hide from God's eye?" To my surprise, he laughed. "When the judgment has passed over you, and your face shines like the heavenly messengers', will you change your mind?"

So he wouldn't do what I asked, yet I respected him for it, even as my heart chilled. "Let the judgment never pass over either of us." I extended the dagger. "At least go armed. Take this. I want you to have it."

He sobered. "No. I cannot accept that gift, Seyo."

Qo'tah. I fingered the bracelet in my pocket. "Then please have this." I held the oractalm up to the skylight and offered it.

Geras hesitated before accepting, his gloved fingertips careful not to brush mine, and he studied the glistening oractalm coins from every side. Would he reject this too? The gift was so small compared to what he had done for me.

Across the three mirrors, he slipped the bracelet around his wrist, too big for me but fitting him, before bowing his head. Hair spilled over his face.

What was it like to look into his eyes without the curse? Had he ever seen someone without a violent reaction or experiencing their sins? This had to be why he never defended himself from those who hated and feared him. He could claim victory over everyone he faced.

I stared at his bent head in the closest mirror. Why wasn't he hurt by his reflection?

I held my breath. What was I thinking? Was I fool? It was impossible. I stared at the center mirror and began to shake. "Geras?"

He looked up.

I met his gaze.

A cosmos of colors swirled in the depths of his eyes. Eventide and dawn. The glory of the heavens. Sapphire shadows and golden sunbeams, bright and dark.

His eyes widened.

Agony did not surge through me. I did not cry out or fall. How was this possible? The mirror, Ai'Biro's depiction of ocean and sky, was like rain. Pure. Dropping from Heaven and carrying nothing defiled, unlike our hearts.

I gasped a breath. He studied my own eyes, then the rest of my face. Like one who was blind and received his sight.

Swirling charcoal markings bled across his brow, cheekbones, and mouth. I searched his gaze again for the curse. Somewhere, it waited deep within him. But something else was hidden in his eyes, too, something good and noble. Something stronger.

Words jumped from my mind to my lips. "Geras, Ortos and the Father of Light have given you the Brotherhood's sword. You are worthy to use it."

His brow creased. He continued to stare until his glorious eyes reddened and he tore his gaze away with a severing I physically felt, lowered to his knees, and wept.

My heart pounded. After hesitating, I laid my hand on his shoulder and closed my eyes.

If the Father of Light could champion sight, defeat blindness of souls, and overcome curses to allow Geras and me to see each other through a mirror, how could I distrust his plans?

Geras calmed. Glass clinked as he reached for the ground and lifted a shard of mirror.

"Peace, Geras," I whispered, then removed my hand and left the Mirror Garden.

Once I reached Kiboro's empty room, I pressed my back against the door and covered my face.

Make me faithful, like Geras. And if the Eternity Gate can heal, let it burst open.

35

THE HOUR OF HUARI'S FUNERAL ARRIVED.
Once his body entered the earth, I would surrender the Eternity Gate's key to my country. When I imagined pressing its rough, skeletal shape into Kiboro's hand, my stomach twisted, but no longer with fear. Instead, a warning sounded from my heart, as if I was making a mistake.

Why?

Kiboro and I dressed in mourning colors, and her bodyguard stood ready when we entered the courtyard.

Geras loomed beside Vispirios. We had not spoken since the Mirror Garden that morning, and seeing him filled my mind with the myriad colors that stirred in his eyes. Colors that exposed a goodness brighter than his curse. Things I should not have experienced, but had.

The Elites, Vispirios, and Geras took their positions, and we entered the jungle. Green paths noisy with wildlife ushered us toward Ai'Biro's burial site.

Kiboro looped her arm in mine, and my free hand brushed the secret pocket in my skirt. Hesitation struck me again. Giving her the key was right. Why did I doubt this? With the key, Laijon could return home, we might survive Pirthyia and the judgment, all of this would end, and I could peer into Geras's gaze one more time.

That hope startled me, but it was true. I wanted to see him again. Was it improper? Probably. Dangerous? Extremely. Facing him through a mirror may not work twice.

Above the island's rambling forest, thick, gray clouds swelled across the summer sky. Upon the highest hill, stone burial chambers stood tall across grassy banks. An Ai'Biroan had explained that these weathered tempests better than dug graves.

Ai'Biro's king and queen had given Huari a royal tomb. It was an honor we could not pay back, but Kiboro had ordered Huari's body embalmed for future transport to Laijon.

Two rings of guards circled the base of the hill. They parted and bowed as we ascended the incline. Ai'Biro was determined no enemy would surprise the islands again.

An enormous crowd had already gathered. Kiboro's hand tightened on my arm as we passed the Chanji. My father stood among them, and Roji's lanky form was easy to spy among Laijon's soldiers. Ai'Biro claimed the opposite slope of the hill. The Brotherhood stood at a distance. All bowed as Kiboro passed, even Queen Mother Umoli, her features tightened as usual into a perpetual frown.

Would hardship and fear remake Kiboro in the same way?

Our bodyguard halted at a respectful distance, and Kiboro kept me close as she drew within ten lengths of the crypt. No one else joined us, as she alone shared half of Huari's blood.

Servants laid mats on the grass for us. Kiboro held her skirts and lowered to her knees. I did the same.

The stone chamber towered in intricate carvings, its door opened to darkness where the body would be kept. Overhead, clouds rolled and swirled, like legends of mighty dragons' breath.

Another Laijonese prince was to be buried. Even as similarities and disparities between this and Jorai's funeral pained me, foreboding clouded my heart again as I glanced toward Kiboro.

Her back was straight, hands folded. She looked past the grave, beyond the islands and sea, to Laijon. Wearing an iron burden of responsibility that should not belong to her.

Tears glistened on her face, and she whispered, "I mourn, but not for Huari. Seyo, am I heartless?"

I swallowed. "Huari's death symbolizes our loss. You dedicated

yourself to your people through the temple, and now as queen.
There is no heart as strong or compassionate as yours."

She bowed her head and blinked rapidly.

Dear Father of Light, help me give her the key. Should I
do it now?

Horns signaled the beginning of the funeral.

Kiboro stood, and so did I.

Out of reverence, all laid down their weapons, except for
the soldiers guarding the base of the hill. I suspected Kiboro
remained armed, as did I with the Brotherhood's dagger strapped
against my leg.

Geras's gaze brushed against me, and I glanced back to see him
remove his da's sword—now worn at his hip like the rest of the
Brotherhood—and set it aside.

Priests and priestesses crested the hill in postures of prayer.
Behind them, more Elites bore the casket wrapped in bright cloth.
Everyone knelt, and elder priests prayed aloud.

I needed to give Kiboro the key now, and end my rising turmoil.
Why did my soul churn with warning against this decision? The key
belonged to her, as it had to King Zaujo.

Qo'tah. No, it didn't. For centuries, Laijon's rulers hid the key
within the palace, but it was first given to the Elites who guarded
the Eternity Gate. By law and tradition, the key belonged to their
descendants, the Brotherhood. How did I not realize this before?

I drew a ragged breath. If I gave the key to the Brotherhood,
I would betray Kiboro's authority as queen. If the Brotherhood
slipped past Pirthyia and found the Eternity Gate, they would open
it, even to judgment.

What if the Father of Light wanted that?

Darkness shifted in the mouth of the tomb. I startled. Had I
missed a priest or priestess's arrival?

Shadows stretched into long, bony wings.

My heart stopped and I cried out.

The creature tore from the grave and jumped into erratic flight.
Wearing a gold collar.

Guards roared. Kiboro swung a sword from under her skirts. The Shadow sent her tumbling and veered toward me.

I lunged, then gasped when it slammed into me. Claws sank into my middle, and I was lifted off the ground. Flying just above the earth, I fought as we gained distance, and the tree line neared. I fell and rose with the creature's uneven flight.

I wrenched hard, then felt myself slip. The Shadow screamed before I tumbled into underbrush. Uninjured. I scrambled below the cover of broad leaves as the creature crashed nearby. Clutching my skirt, I raced through dense growth, hearing its rage as it tangled in vines and saplings. Lengths away, soldiers shouted.

I ducked under the branches of a short, thick tree. The Shadow stumbled closer, massive and reeking.

The shouts grew louder. If I moved, I would give away my position.

The Shadow seized me.

I couldn't resist or breathe in its powerful grip. The Shadow battled to catch air, burst from the forest, and soared over rough, downhill terrain. Rocky cliffs bordering churning sea filled my vision. But its strength was waning. The Shadow beat its wings, but listed to one side, losing height.

Soldiers raced to cut us off from the coastline. They bore slings, bows, arrows, and nets. Ai'Biroans, Laijonese, the Brotherhood—Geras racing at the front.

I flailed, and my stomach flipped as the Shadow faltered and dropped me. I rolled against dirt and tall grass, scrambled to my feet, but was shoved facedown. Sand filled my lungs as I thrashed, but the monster increased its weight against my upper back. It bound my feet and caught and tied my wrists. I screamed as the Shadow snatched me up and ran cumbrously on two legs. Its breathing rasped, torso quivering with effort. Then it stumbled to a stop. Growling, it reached toward its leg and yanked a bloodied arrow free.

The soldiers were catching up. Geras was only five lengths away, his da's sword gleaming in his hands.

The Shadow saw this, shrieked, and launched us off the cliff edge.

The world spun. The monster's wings stretched, we jerked, then glided against the cliffs into fog. Three lengths from the sea, its claws released me.

But I didn't hit water. My body snapped upon impact on a rough surface. I battled for breath, and found myself in the bed of a single-masted skiff.

The Shadow landed on the prow, sent the vessel cavorting, then severed the rope securing the boat to shore.

Pursuing border guards and soldiers dove into the ocean. But they were too far. I would have to jump with bound hands and feet.

The Shadow shoved me onto my back against the ribs of the boat. The monster pressed one paw against my sternum and its second filthy, leathery palm closed upon my mouth and nose.

I fought. Bit. Its claws pierced my forehead and temples. I would suffocate.

The Shadow's fathomless gaze consumed me. Then nothing.

I awoke to a pounding head, rocking motion, and the Shadow's hunched form facing misty water. Patterned brands laced its back, revealed under tattered clothing. The gold collar.

I bit back a scream and did not move. My hands and legs remained bound. I panicked. The key. But the jagged metal remained sewn into my shift. Relief swept through me. Why hadn't it taken the key? Unless the creature didn't know I held it? And if not, why did it keep me alive?

The Brotherhood dagger remained strapped to my leg too. But could its blade pierce the creature's thick hide?

When the Shadow turned, I pretended to sleep. Its gold choker haunted me. It was the same Shadow that had attacked me in the Mirror Garden and jeered at me from the dungeon. How had it escaped? I had no idea how far we were from Ai'Biro or how much time had passed.

A wave slapped our boat and sprinkled my face with saltwater. The Shadow squawked and jumped into the mist. Gone.

My pulse quickened. I must try to swim.

But the creature landed on the vessel's edge, causing us to spin, and reoriented its balance with agitation. I pretended to sleep.

Sunless time passed. There was no indication of day, night, or direction. The Shadow took to the air for longer periods of time, and I managed to free my hands and feet. After its third disappearance, I forced myself to explore and found a sack half-filled with sailor's crackers. I devoured a handful and lay down just before the Shadow's reeling return.

I remained still as its hulking, stinking body loomed. The creature nudged my side.

An involuntary moan escaped my lips, then I shifted and breathed quietly, pretending to sleep.

The Shadow grunted and scrambled away.

Every time the Shadow fled, I nibbled on crackers and searched the small vessel. I discovered a flask of water and drank survival. Always to lie down again and shut my eyes against tears.

The Shadow never ate or drank.

At last, fog cleared before starry heavens. The Shadow perched on our prow, muttering. It did not leave again for what felt like forever. Finally, I sighted distant land, shrouded in night. A familiar coast and harbor.

It was Laijon.

The Shadow leapt toward me and caught my arms. A dirty cloth silenced my scream. The Shadow swung me onto its back, between its wings, against unnatural flesh and a sharp spine, punched a hole in the bottom of the boat, then jumped to fly. And failed. We collapsed into the water-filled vessel. I grabbed its shoulder blades as the Shadow leapt again and floundered into nauseating flight.

It careened through melting mists past the empty harbor toward

Laijon's palace. Horror filled me. Extravagant fires lit the ramparts and Pirthyians marched the walls.

The Shadow plunged behind the castle. We headed for one of the border watchtowers.

It hurtled through a dark, glassless window. The creature stumbled, claws scratching against stone, before shaking me off its back and forcing me to climb a spiral staircase. Flight after flight. Panting.

Below, more Shadows howled and scuffled.

We reached the highest room. The monster wrenched the door open, pushed me inside, and followed, shutting the door behind.

I stumbled across the lightless floor and grappled with the binding across my mouth. Just as I reached for my dagger, the Shadow knocked me aside.

I landed in a clattering pile. Metal and leather wings, ready to be fitted to new human victims. I choked back a cry. But something glinted.

I lurched for the rusted sword and swiveled the weapon toward the Shadow's middle.

Darkness curled around the Shadow's form. Its chest heaved with breath.

I realized the smallness of the room. No windows. I swallowed bile, tore the binding at my mouth, and stood on wobbling legs.

The Shadow cocked its head. Its voice was garbled, Nazakian, but shocking in its clarity as it recited, "The girl who holds the key is tall. Of Laijonese blood. Wearing a blood-red bracelet."

My heart froze. It knew.

"But you wear no such finery." The Shadow snarled, wrenched the blade from my hands, and reached around my empty neck. Its opaque eyes narrowed as it clawed my shoes off. Rifted through my hair. I fought, then it seized a handful of my skirt. The key sewn inside.

I shoved the Shadow with all my strength, but it tore the pocket free and rose to its full height with the key in its claws.

The Shadow's features twisted with a glare. "Do you think I

would follow you through mountains, battle the Pirthyian beasts chasing you, cross oceans, and not take what I want?"

I stared at the key, then the gold collar around its neck. The Shadow had taken it from the Imperati's fifth Tracker, the one that had never reached Geras and me. This creature had followed me from Pirthyia.

The Shadow's chest expanded. "My kind do not keep prisoners." Then it pivoted toward the door.

I rushed after it.

The monster thrust me away and slammed the door. The old lock clicked, and a shrieking squabble exploded outside. I covered my ears until the fight cooled. The Shadows scrabbled away and everything quieted into ringing silence.

I sank to the filthy ground, choking sobs wracking my body. I crept from the door, the close walls, the pile of wings and rubbish, and curled over my knees. I reached a trembling hand for the corroded sword and held it ready. Waiting for the Shadow's return.

But it would not return. It held the key.

I had failed.

36

SLEEP WROUGHT NIGHTMARES.

The key and Shadow in reeling flight danced with swirling orbs of celestial colors, blues and grays, tainted illumination. The judgment rose like a tidal wave and collapsed. Through its ruins, devouring evil engulfed the continent.

I awoke, curled into myself, and trembled in the blindness of the tight room.

Don't touch the shed wings.

Don't make a sound.

Rising summer heat was oppressive. The tower shook against stormy winds. In the gloom, I thought I saw creatures peeling themselves from the enclosing walls, and my heart raced. But the real monsters screeched on the other side of the door. Some scuffled on two limbs, but most, the larger ones, scraped on winged elbows and clawed feet. Shadows knew this prison was occupied. Bored, they pawed the handle and hissed at the lock.

My gold-collared captor had said Shadows didn't keep prisoners, and it did not return.

Night melted into night. Did I wake or sleep? The emptiness was unbearable. When hunger and thirst pierced my insides, I found the flask of water and sack of crackers from the boat tossed on the floor. It was a miracle that soon ran out.

Chills gripped my overheated body. My head ached, my nose ran. I smothered a cough that would attract Shadows to the door and squeezed my eyes shut. "In the desert, you said evil would not be victorious." A choking sob escaped my chest. "Are you not greater—?" I tensed.

Something brushed against the door. A Shadow tried the handle, beat its wings, and then all was quiet.

Inside my mind, I screamed.

Father of Light, rescue me! Forgive me.

Heaviness gripped my soul, and I closed my eyes again. Waiting for nightmares. Instead, I dreamed of Father and Roji, Kiboro and Tol, then of Geras lifting his cursed gaze toward Heaven.

Destruction will be allotted with fire and water.
Evil will rise.
One will welcome judgment, of royal blood and disfigured.
Not all is lost.

I stirred with a fit of coughing and stared into emptiness. No terrible creatures heard me and fought the door, and the prophecy lingered within my tangled thoughts like a ghost. Fire and water—I was so thirsty. And the one who would open the gate.

I managed to sit up.

Pirthyia's Shadows had seized the key, but they did not possess the Father of Light's chosen opener of the Eternity Gate. Laijon retained an advantage. If Father was right, the opener could be Kiboro. But she was not disfigured.

Laijon needed to be warned about the stolen key, yet I could not escape this place.

I massaged my damp forehead, felt the empty food and drink supplies, and cast them into the clattering hill of refuse. Dehydration would kill me. Realization struck. If my captor Shadow had not slain me after taking the key, and had bothered to leave food and drink, it was keeping me alive for another purpose.

Qo'tah, I had to flee. But the door was locked, and more Shadows lurked on the other side.

I pushed myself to my feet and reached for the wall. I circled the small room, avoiding the wings, fingertips skimming the stone walls encasing me. My thumb caught a splinter. I flinched, then felt the break. Wood filled a glassless window, one of several, all tall and thin, yet wide enough for me to pass through—and fall to my death. I stood in the turret of a watchtower.

But not empty-handed.

I stooped and felt the ground until finding rods of metal. They were warm with the heat. Bile rose, but I hunted until I found wings without gashes tearing the leather. I tugged the appendage toward the window. It scratched the floor. So heavy, how could it be a help? Reaching the window, I fingered the bones of the wings. There was no way to tie them to myself.

The tower remained quiet, empty of pursuers. But if I survived the jump, Pirthyia would capture me before I reached the harbor. Thinking of Kiboro, Roji, and Geras's imprisonment in the Imperati's castle made me queasy. But even if I reached the ocean, all of Laijon's boats were docked in Ai'Biro. I remembered Roji saying there weren't enough vessels for our people, and many were left behind when Huari evacuated.

If I stayed in this tower, I would die by dehydration or worse. If I lived, I would know the Father of Light had not forsaken me.

With shaky hands, I cleared the window of splintery wood and gaped at the night sky. Clouds veiled the moon and stars, yet their light blinded me.

The ground was far. One copse of wide-branched trees stood below, easy to miss.

I dragged the wings onto my back and struggled through the window. Doubt leered, but I imagined the Shadow's return and gripped the bones of the wings with whitening fingers.

For a chance to live, I pled. For Laijon.

Tears slipped down my cheeks, and I jumped.

A breath of wind sent me sailing from the trees, over hard earth, when a second wind burst from the side. Plummeting—

I crashed into greenery. A branch broke my fall, then I tumbled into the fork of a tree trunk, then to the earth, separated from the wings, which had twisted in the canopy. I was aching but breathing. Alive when I shouldn't be.

Run.

I forced myself to hurry down less-traveled paths away from the palace ground, full of trampled bridges and ponds, toward the temple that had lain abandoned when I'd last seen it with Geras. My body screamed with stiffness, my lungs burned, and my legs were weak.

Two Pirthyians appeared in the darkness. They spied me and shouted.

I fled, but their stronger, fed bodies caught up, and they grabbed me. My heart almost exploded from my chest.

One grumbled in his native tongue. Tired. Frustrated. "Another Laijonese. How many more hide in these hills?"

"She was coming from the towers," the one restraining me said.

"From those winged demons' rotting nests?" The grumbler barked a laugh. "Nothing escapes there alive. But maybe this one will tell us where the rest of her kind are." He turned toward the palace.

The second guard forced me to follow.

I obeyed. I must appear weak.

We passed the broad gravel entry of the royal grounds, now rimmed with roaring bonfires planted between Laijon's mighty statues. The turquoise-roofed palace rose before us, and the soldiers climbed the steps and invaded its doors. More Pirthyians, fires, ransacking, and filth filled the grand entry. Smoke thickened the air. Guards sat on the lightbearers' pedestals, tossing dice.

We traveled through halls to stairs that led down and down, to places belonging to Laijon's royal guards. The corridors narrowed, stonework revealed passage into older architecture, and a chilled damp clung to the air. We entered an expansive chamber of brown rock walls, with a high, murky ceiling. A semicircle of fires blazed before stores of weaponry and empty cages. On the left, Pirthyian guards observed our entry.

I heard water rushing. The rough floor ended in a drop-off.

We had descended deep enough to reach the guards' access to the tunnels, and a monsoon-fed river raged in the chasm below.

"We found another," the soldier leading us declared.

Despite the second guard's hand clamped around my arm, I skidded on mildew.

Among the knot of men beside the cages, a stocky officer, with iron-colored hair, sat in a chair of Laijon's finest wood and semiprecious stones, taken from the council room and meant to seat the Chanji. His narrowing gaze made my stomach knot. "She is tall for Laijon," he remarked, then nodded.

The grumbler grabbed me by the nape and dragged me across the slick ground to the edge of the drop-off. My vision filled with the flood below, moving quick enough to kill even an experienced swimmer.

He grunted in Pirthyian. "I have sent several of your kind over the edge. If they do not drown, they scream as they are eaten by your swimming creatures. Where are the rest of your people? Tell me and live."

Several chuckled. "Maybe they do not answer because you forget to speak the trade language," one said.

The soldier hissed and spoke with an accent so rough, I could barely understand. "Where are the rest?"

I faked deafness and gestured.

"Lying tramp." The guard growled and pushed me closer to the edge.

Hands clapped. The captain stood and bellowed. "Enough. You will not waste this one yet." His sharp study of me appeared too interested. "Confine her."

I was yanked through the ring of fires and shoved on my hands and knees into one of the cages. The soldier secured the metal door and joined the others.

I could not stand. Bars made an uncomfortable floor, and everything was covered in slime or rust. The pile of weapons was out of reach. But if I folded over my knees, no one could touch me from any side without opening the door.

But the Pirthyians, even the officer, fell into loud conversation about supplies, dinner, and irritation with being assigned to this sodden hole. They ignored me.

When they did eat, feasting on Laijon's provisions, they gave me nothing. Dizziness and thirst tormented me as their strong drink flowed. They complained about the cursed Shadows seizing their food, mocked the entertaining women's tents, and devolved into illogical laughter and half-hearted brawling. Almost all passed out upon soggy rugs, except for the captain, who slept hunched in the Chanji's chair with his fist pressed into his cheek. Two remained awake to stand guard.

My spirit failed, but I then remembered jumping from the watchtower. I had survived that. I could not die here. I searched my surroundings for a way out.

On the right, a closed door interrupted stone. Quieter than the snoring men, angry water, and crackling fires, the sound of grinding pulsed. Did the door open to one of the pump rooms, used in ancient times to drain the tunnel waters when the flooding was more severe? Was Pirthyia trying to drain the tunnels?

A warped cry echoed around the cavern.

The standing guards brandished their swords as a Shadow swooped, screaming, and vanished into the dark, fathomless ceiling.

Jerky flight. Gold collar.

I shrank back.

Eventually, the guards sheathed their swords and leaned against the wall again, crossing their arms and closing their eyes. Moments later, three new Pirthyian guards emerged from the closed door.

The grinding sound did come from there. This squadron managed the pumps, yet the flooding remained so high. The monsoon rains must have been terrible since we'd left.

The three roused some of their drunken brethren, who groused awake and staggered into the pump room before closing the door. The newcomers bedded down in their places.

Those standing watch slept.

I rested my hand on my thigh, over the dagger. Heart hammering. Waiting—

Gleaming eyes stared through a curtain of smoke and fire. My captor crossed between the fires, flinching as if the heat or light were torture, and circled my cage before lunging to claw through the bars.

I flattened myself.

The Shadow climbed atop the cage, and a whisper of breath tickled my neck as it grabbed from above. The Shadow hissed and dropped to the ground again.

I swallowed bile and shut my eyes. Yet the Shadow's image was burned into my mind. Its collar, wings.

I lifted my gaze.

The Shadow recoiled and drew its wings close. But I saw the small, dark shape dangling from its neck. The key tied to my ribbon.

The weird cadence of its Nazakian speech slithered. "Pirthyia will not have you." It shuffled closer and cocked its head. "Laijon is sighted. They are too late. But I will set you free." Then it threw itself backward, scuttled into the air, and disappeared.

The creature toyed with me. I clenched my hands before spying something leaning against the cage. A bruised, unripe fruit.

Had the Shadow left that? It was probably poisoned.

I snatched the offering through the bars and ate. There was little juice, and I gnawed the seed, but my eyes brightened.

The Shadow had already stolen the key. What in the continent did it want from me now?

I lay down against the cutting metal bars. The river filled my ears. Flood. Shadow. Fire.

A way of escape nibbled the back of my mind. Yes, I must try, but not yet. Not if this Shadow promised to return.

I would steal the key back first.

37

IN THE CHILL DAMP OF MORNING, the Pirthyians broke their fast. All fires were fed, and shifts of men traded places in the pump room.

I listened to the thundering flood in the chasm below. Waiting. Sweat threading down the center of my back.

A soldier advanced, unlocked the cage, and dragged me beyond the ring of fires. I flinched, but did not resist, skidding again on slippery rock, and faced the captain lounging in the Chanji's chair.

His jaded gaze raked over me, then he sighed. Licentious, but disgusted. My people were too lowborn for his taste. The captain spoke in the trade language, more skillfully than most Pirthyians, and too casually. "Laijon, where are your countrymen? We know they hide in the hills, even in the webbed underbelly of this crumbling palace. Tell me where they are, and you will be spared."

I remained silent.

He pursed his lips and flicked his hand toward the drop-off.

The soldier squeezed my upper arm and tugged. To hurl me over the edge.

No. Not until the Shadow returned with the key.

I twisted free, managed one leap before he could seize my wrist, and lunged into the nearest fire. Flames filled my vision, and they shouted. The soldier hauled me from the fire and quickly let go.

I stumbled, but did not fall.

The Pirthyian's stares were blades. They saw my unsinged clothes, that I was unhurt.

The captain pointed to the fires. "Throw her back in."

Guards grasped my left shoulder and elbow. They pushed me toward the closest blaze and thrust only my hand inside. Fire licked across my bare skin. They pulled me back, grabbed my hand, and looked. Several swore. "She is not burned."

The captain jumped from his chair. In Pirthyian, he demanded an iron poker and received one. With decisive steps, he plucked a glowing ember from a fire and ordered the soldiers to open my hands. They did, and he dropped the ember into my palms.

One moment passed. Two.

The captain's twisted fascination melted into horror, and he lurched back.

The soldiers batted the ember out of my hands, then grabbed me and locked me in the cage, gathering with whispers and grim glances. "Fire walker," they said to one another. Two mentioned that a fire walker was sighted in the Imperati's castle months ago. Four suggested that I was a Vedoan spirit spying on Pirthyia.

That was the closest anyone had come to calling me Vedoan. I had expected their superstition, but not that Pirthyia would suspect that Vedoa spied on them.

"Slay it," one demanded.

"Silence." The captain returned to the chair, and his eyes thinned. "Not yet."

The Pirthyians changed guards and ate the midday meal. More soldiers took shifts in the pump room. When they stoked the fires, all cast nervous looks my way. At last, the captain ordered food and drink to be left outside my cage.

Guards brought me mead and a plate of roasted meat. I barely touched the mug, and gagged after my first bite of food. Vedoan spice overpowered all other taste, but I finished the meal and watched the ceiling. Firelight undulated in the gloom above.

When would the creature come?

Hours passed, and dinner arrived with stronger drink. My stomach knotted as the Pirthyian's movements dulled and their emotions soared. They peered my way.

The captain waved a sloshing, refilled cup. "Yes, uncage the fire walker to perform."

I stiffened and glanced up.

Wings stirred the darkness. I spied a golden collar, then the rest of the Shadow clinging to an outcropping near the roof. It scrutinized me.

That blasted monster needed to fly down here. Now.

The soldiers bickered over my performance, offering horrific suggestions in slurred speech.

The captain perched on the edge of the chair. "Oil and light her."

Argument erupted.

"Sir, she will become a danger to us," a guard said.

"Then ready your bows in case she attacks."

An archer balked. "What if she's immortal?"

The captain roared. "Didn't you touch her flesh when you dragged her from the hills? At the least, she will bleed. And the water is near. Bring her to me."

The Pirthyians drew their weapons and reordered themselves for better viewing. Three approached my cage.

I sucked in a breath as they dragged me out and made me stand in their midst. Arrows and swords trained at my heart.

The Shadow stared.

A soldier tipped a jar of glistening oil over my head. Thick, putrid liquid rolled across my head and shoulders, clinging and dripping. I sputtered.

Their hands slipped on my slick skin. Fingers clenched tighter upon me.

The captain lit a torch, and malice filled his eyes.

My heart pounded. This was not working. When I ran, I would be shot—

A strangled cry rent the air. The Shadow. It leapt from its perch, and the soldiers yelled.

I ducked out from the soldiers' clutches, just as the Shadow crashed into them and reeled toward the captain, howling Nazakian curses.

I jumped over the soldiers' bodies sprawled across the ground. I dared not think of their blades and arrows, or river serpents as I raced for the drop-off. Hoping—needing—this last gamble to pay off.

Soft feet. Dark water. Nothing better than to fly.

The Pirthyians shouted. The ground thundered with their pursuit. Fingertips brushed my back.

I pumped my arms and gasped as the stone floor disappeared under me. Replaced by raging currents lengths below.

My stomach rose, and I fell.

Claws pierced my middle. My plummet jerked to a stop, and I screamed. The Shadow shrieked and fought to lift me away from the water. Toward the Pirthyians and their weapons.

Father of Light, this is my last chance!

I grit my teeth and snatched for the key and chain around the Shadow's collared neck. It wasn't there.

"I need the key." The Shadow growled and shook me.

I slipped. The oil coating my skin. The creature flapped harder. Its claws tightened and tore my flesh.

I curled and reached under my skirts, grasped the Brotherhood's dagger with slick hands, and stabbed the Shadow's shoulder. It wailed.

I wrenched away and fell into the roiling flood.

Water filled my mouth and nose and swept me under. I stilled, allowing the current to right me, then battled to the surface and breathed. The water was too powerful, and the Shadow's shrieks pursued me. But the ceiling sloped downward and would cut it off from me. And me from air.

I inhaled and dove just before the tunnel submerged. Noise from the Shadow clawing the wall muffled and faded.

My lungs burned as moments underwater passed.

The ceiling rose and I sputtered to the surface. Others drowned because they did not know the lightless tunnels, but I visualized my position under the palace and swam for the edge. The channel narrowed, slowed, and I reached the opposite wall. I felt the break in the stones forming a narrow path cut from rock. But would this way be flooded too?

Something brushed my foot.

I imagined long teeth sinking into my calf and flailed. Instead, my toes touched gravel, and, relieved, I climbed into the dry passage. Perhaps I owed Pirthyia thanks for working the pumps. I shivered and steadied myself.

If I understood my location, this would lead me to a trapdoor and the royal gardens. It had been a favorite haunt of Jorai's, one he'd coaxed me to explore a handful of times.

I ran uphill for lengths before collapsing to catch my breath. I realized I had lost my dagger. With trembling hands, I felt the stone walls and continued.

I bypassed intersecting tunnels and, after what felt like hours, reached the trapdoor.

What if Pirthyians waited in the royal gardens? The only other exit from here followed another tunnel that opened inside the enemy-infested palace.

I wrestled the trapdoor ajar and peeked through the crack.

Twisting, scarlet clouds darkened with sunset. Blooming bushes lay trampled in heaps. Supplies were stacked in messy piles.

I recoiled.

The Shadow crouched ten lengths away, his back to me. It scratched at its gilded collar and sniffed. How did it follow me here? Where was the key?

Pirthyian horns sounded, and the Shadow grabbed its ears and howled a searing scream. It glared in my direction, but did not see me. Moaning, it took off in spasmodic flight to disappear around the castle. When the horns blared again, more Shadows followed.

Did Pirthyia call the monsters?

I crawled from the trapdoor and crept into the thickest foliage of the garden. Through tall, wild grasses, I saw Pirthyian soldiers overrunning the highway between the harbor and palace. Like the Shadows, they headed to the castle.

I spied tattered flags waving among a tangle of people swallowed by the Pirthyians. Ice filled my veins. These were apprehended Laijonese, those who had not gained passage to Ai'Biro with the rest of us. Finally caught. But why would they come from the sea instead of the hills? I bit back a cry.

Laijon is sighted. The Shadow had not lied. Did these Laijonese prisoners come from Ai'Biro? It could not be.

I returned to the trapdoor and reentered the tunnels. Rushing through the damp passages, splashing in ankle-deep water, feeling walls for direction toward the palace. A lone corridor ended in a wooden door.

I pressed into the basement pantry of the royal servants' kitchens. The place was plundered, but empty. Connecting hallways led me to a potted tree, still standing and obscuring a concealed doorway.

I slipped into the secret, dusty passage.

Low roofing pressed into me, then I reached the landing. Fifteen steps, and I crouched before the fateful pinhole of light in the wall.

The council chamber stretched below. Every wall sconce flamed. The marble floor was covered with Pirthyians shoving and striving to fit, forcing lower ranked comrades back into the grand entry. Some climbed the life-size statuary. Others leaned against the tapestries, soiling them with their labor-stained uniforms. Most gave the gold-painted ceiling suspicious glances, but not because Laijon's lingering splendor tempted them.

Among the rafters, creeping from high, broken windows, Shadows squabbled and eyed those below.

None wore a golden collar.

Those highest in authority possessed the remaining Chanji's chairs. Space was created between them and the Laijonese throne, which had been moved to the center of the room for the foreigner who occupied it.

No.

Imperati Emeridus sat tall on our turquoise throne. He wore a short, lavish tunic that bared his knees. A crown contained tight curls. More gray touched his beard than when I last saw him in his private quarters.

Young Trackers in gilt collars paced by his feet.

The Imperati's dark blue eyes swept across those gathered. His tanned hands traced the thin scars crisscrossing the throne before he raised an arm.

All silenced. Even the Shadows ceased their quarrels. With an echoing command, he ordered the prisoners brought in. The Laijonese were paraded into the council room. Pirthyians jeered and spit as the prisoners filled the space before the throne. Rope bound their feet and hands. Their posture was meek, but not broken.

I scanned the group—so small it did not make sense—and recognized several Brotherhood among the captured, including most of their leaders. My throat thickened. Father and Roji were there. Then I saw a figure larger than the rest, his face and hands covered in rags, like a marauder or the plagued, head bowed. Geras.

Pirthyians tossed the prisoners' weapons into the corner, except for the Brotherhood's swords. The soldiers put those valuable, ancient blades into their belts and then dipped Laijon's flag in a fiery sconce and cast it to the glassy floor to burn.

The Imperati demanded that the mightiest prisoners be restrained with irons. Pirthyian soldiers hurried to fit stronger Laijonese and Brotherhood with manacles and forced them to kneel before the throne, while the rest of the captives stood behind.

My heart sickened. I watched in despair as their vile antics continued.

They wrenched Roji from Father's side. When Vispirios was recognized as a kinsman, the Pirthyians kicked him facedown against the floor. A double portion of soldiers drew swords to prod Geras to his knees. Two gestured to the cloth obscuring the lower half of his face, but did not touch him.

There were so few of them, with a disproportionate number of leadership, and they seemed too meek, especially the Brotherhood. Where was the rest of my country or Ai'Biro, our promised allies? Why had they sailed so soon—they could not have waited three days to leave after the Shadow had abducted me—into the harbor and Pirthyia's hands?

Unless this was part of Laijon's plan.

My breath caught. If this was our plan, where was Kiboro? I searched the prisoners until discovering a petite soldier standing close to Father, wearing short, ragged hair.

Disbelief stabbed me. Kiboro was here.

Qo'tah. But they did not know I had carried the key and now lost it to a Shadow.

A Pirthyian scout rushed into the council chamber. He struggled through the crowd, prostrated himself before the Imperati, and heralded his news. More prisoners were coming.

Soon Pirthyians ushered more Laijonese captives, who carried precious supplies, into the filled room. Faru, his braided, silver beard mussed, trudged with a barrel over his shoulder and murder scrawled across his face.

Surprise rippled through the first group of prisoners. Then this was not part of the plan. But if Faru was here, so the rest of Laijon must be.

Horns sounded again, eliciting shrieks from the Shadow-covered rafters.

Tensed, with hands on hilts, officers yelled commands, and droves of soldiers emptied into the grand entry, leaving muddied floors behind. Those remaining pressed against the walls, making more room.

Pirthyian nobility rose from the Chanji's chairs. The Imperati took one step down from the throne, arms folded. Gaze hard.

My pulse raced. What was happening?

Distant marching grew in strength, followed by eerie chanting too far away to understand.

Shadows beat their wings and screamed.

The rhythmic stamping of feet neared the palace and claimed the grand entry. A foreign people strode inside the council chamber.

I stared at their tall stature, like mine. They wore long, colorful robes, heavy jewelry, exotic weaponry. Overwhelming, spiced perfume wafted to my peephole, and I choked.

Fire-wielding Vedoa, Laijon's desert sister-turned-enemy, had come.

Shock gripped the Laijonese and Brotherhood prisoners as Vedoan soldiers led their train to the turquoise throne. Noble families with their children sauntered inside. Even their slaves, covered in piercings and arm bands, held their heads high. Women slaves carried litters bearing porous rock, volcanic stone to feed their warped gifting.

Robed in saffron-colored cloth, acolytes surrounded wrinkled soothsayers. They carried a covered, majestic sedan by poles, a chariot of great weight, judging by the acolytes' sweat-stained faces. The single door of the wooden sedan was closed and covered in silk, fit for royalty. Surely a high sorcerer sat inside.

The Vedoan ruler's Shields, bodyguards serving the most powerful ruling chief, entered. These mighty men were stripped to the waist, long hair piled atop their heads. Barefoot, they lifted hands with fire, and halted before the throne.

A serpentine charcoal dragon, decorated with royal jewels and bands of gold, lumbered through the doors. Its slender jaw was muzzled with irons, and its wings bound by its flanks. Something I had only seen sketched in books. Astride the beast, a shockingly young woman, less than three decades old, whose head sparkled with a jeweled scarf covering her bound hair, raised a shout. All eyes were drawn to her, like when Kiboro wielded her light. Surely this woman was Vedoa's empress, and her people would call her half-goddess. Warriors trailed her on foot, and the council chamber was filled again.

The dragon stopped before the Imperati with a low, vibrating hiss. The Trackers bristled.

Vedoa prostrated themselves. The empress leapt to the ground, swept her high-slitted skirt behind, and lifted a proud, youthful face. She wore swords over both hips, and a dagger sheathed across her thin chest. Gold painted her muscled legs and sculpted arms.

As tall as her men, she wore ferocity and impatience like a cloak. When the Trackers growled, the woman speared them with a silencing glance, then dared to impale the Imperati with the same look. As if expecting him to bow to her divinity too.

Emeridus hesitated before descending the rest of the throne's turquoise steps. With a careful smile, he clasped her hand in welcome.

38

THE IMPERATI ORDERED TWO OF
the Chanji's chairs placed on the lowest stair to the throne,
and waited for the Vedoan empress to seat herself. Her frown
communicated disdain for his diplomacy, but she sat, with her
Shields surrounding her. Her demanding gaze raked the height of
the throne.

Shadows continued to shriek from the rafters.

Pirthyian and Vedoan translators were summoned. The two
rulers launched into reaffirmation of allied agreements, full of
outbursts and cursing on both sides. Over her interpreter, the
empress loudly declared that Laijon's lands and lost treasure
belonged to Vedoa, and they would claim it. The Imperati, sitting
tall and rigid, affirmed that Vedoa could have everything but the
Eternity Gate, as they promised. He waved soldiers forward, who
bore handfuls of treasure—trinkets of gold, silver, and red ore—
which they gave to the empress's warriors.

"Pirthyia occupies Laijon. Here is our meager fruit from draining
the tunnels." The Imperati crossed his arms as the translator spoke.
"Is Vedoa prepared to fulfill her half of the bargain?"

The empress bared her teeth. "You control Laijon by the help of
Shadows, and you would not have them if we had not shared our
secrets with you. But where is Laijon's king? You said you would
deliver him to me in chains."

A voice rose from the prisoners. It was Faru pleading in passable
Vedoan. "Remember me, Srolo Faru, who has prepared your

rightful homeland for Vedoa's return. These Laijonese prisoners set a trap for you. The remainder of Laijon's and Ai'Biro's armies seek to ambush your highness. Allow me to speak."

I inhaled sharply. How did he know the desert language?

A Vedoan nobleman bowed and spoke in the empress's ear. She hissed, and her bare-chested Shields cut Faru's bindings and pushed him to the foot of the throne. Before Faru could complete a formal bow, a Shield slapped him and another knocked him to his knees.

Faru trembled, enraged. "My magnificent empress, Laijon's king is dead. A princess pretends to be queen. The second prince Jorai is rightfully king, but is hidden. He must lead your supreme nation to rule Laijon, as promised."

I sat back. This had been Faru's plan? But he didn't know that Jorai had died.

Faru's face reddened. "These Pirthyian barbarians swore to protect the second prince and return him to me. Remember that Jorai is destined to open the Eternity Gate and give you its divine power." He knelt before the empress. "I have suffered for your cause, goddess of fire. Make Pirthyia reveal King Jorai."

The empress's gaze sparked, and she shifted in her seat toward the Imperati. "Where is Laijon's queen?"

The Imperati's jaw tightened. He did not answer.

She spoke to Faru. "Where is this queen, fool?"

Kiboro was standing bound at their feet. Did Faru know that? I would burst through this wall before he revealed—

Faru cringed. "Laijon marks me as a traitor. They keep their plans from me."

The empress swore an omen, and her Shields lifted Faru off his feet.

His eyes bulged, and he fought. "Where is Prince Jorai?" He frantically gestured at the prisoners and gasped in Laijonese. "Where are my loyal soldiers? Elites—"

A Shield backhanded him into silence, and Faru was hauled outside the room.

The empress rose from her chair and addressed everyone standing below. "Where is Laijon's queen? I will burn all of you if she is not found." Her translator echoed her words in Pirthyian and the trade language.

None answered, and Vedoan Shields surrounded the prisoners and began to search. The Imperati scowled, but dismissed his own guard to join the hunt, who gave the dragon plenty of room.

No. They could not find her.

I abandoned the pinhole and ran the way I came, ducking through passages and entering the grand entry filled with Pirthyians and Vedoans.

I wove through the crowd until nearby Pirthyian soldiers noticed and seized me. I screamed in the trade language. "I am queen of Laijon!"

Eager to gain the council chamber, whether they understood me or not, the men shoved and bellowed their way into the doorway of the overcrowded room.

I continued to cry out, and the Imperati's search party heard me. They grabbed my arms and shouldered their way to the throne through the knot of prisoners.   .

My father and Roji stared at me. Shocked, they had assumed me dead, and now comprehended my charade. I didn't dare to glance in Kiboro's direction. Vispirios held his side where he was kicked. Geras was harnessed with new chains. His startled gaze hit me, and I lost my step. I felt his wrath. Fear. Bondage.

The Pirthyians brought me past the first row of warriors and around the unblinking dragon, its scaly hide and ornaments glinting with torchlight. They thrust me before the throne.

I raised my hoarse voice. "I am Queen Kiboro of Laijon."

Sight of the Imperati sent shivers down my spine. Within his lean, bearded face, blue eyes narrowed upon my bedraggled, starved appearance.

The empress eyed me like a predator. Yet her Vedoan characteristics reminded me of my mother and Tol. Her Shields tightened around her, fire simmering in their palms. Incense, body heat, and the stench of grease oiling their hands turned my stomach.

A squeal rang through the air. A Shadow flapped its wings from a broken window. Wearing a gold collar.

The empress lifted her chin. "This wretch cannot be a queen."

"She visited Pirthyia. I will know her face." The Imperati took my chin in his hands.

Geras's felt tension tightened.

The Imperati dropped his hand to survey my unkept appearance with elevated brow. "It is she."

The empress stalked to me. Murder crossed her face, hatred for me and my country. Then, she spun toward her nation, who now crowded lengths away. The soothsayers and sedan waited even closer.

She spoke loudly to the soothsayers. "I have caught Laijon's pretend queen, who stole this land from Vedoa. She holds the lost key."

My heart plummeted. *Qo'tah*, no—

The collared Shadow squealed from the rafters.

A translator bent toward the Imperati's ear, and Pirthyia's ruler straightened. "The queen of Laijon belongs to me."

"She will lead me to the gate belonging to Laijon's god," the empress retorted. "Then you may have her." She clapped toward her Shields.

The Vedoans reordered themselves into rows. The dragon was tethered between two columns, and a Shield escorted me to the front of the empress's train. The Shadows' shrieks increased as they wheeled into flight.

Behind, the Imperati roared orders that the power of the pumps be increased and half his men remain to guard the castle. The rest were commanded to gather the prisoners and follow Vedoa.

My mind urged me to flee, but I couldn't.

The empress approached a wall tapestry and flung it aside to uncover the secret door, the room Faru had shown me, and entered. Her Shields pushed me through the doorway after her. Four

Vedoans with axes skirted the desk and shelves and demolished the eastern wall to reveal a gaping hole to the tunnels.

I held my breath. How did they know about this? Because Faru had given Vedoa the king's plans to the castle.

The acolytes, chanting in low tones, heaved the sedan into the room. The empress gave the carriage a strange look before climbing into a second litter, borne by four Shields. The rest of her bodyguard cupped handfuls of flames, except for the one in charge of me. His strong fingers gripped my arm.

Pirthyia neared with lit torches, spearheaded by the glowering Imperati.

My heart caught. Did they assume I could lead them to the Eternity Gate? I didn't know where it was. Would they search me for the key now?

The Imperati spoke to the empress. She ignored him.

A white-haired, yellow-robed soothsayer left the sedan and scuttled to the empress's litter. He whispered and gestured with crazed motions. Pointing straight, right, right again.

Qo'tah. The soothsayer fed her directions.

The empress cried aloud and led our march into the maw of the tunnel.

39

FIRE AND SMOKING TORCHES chased gloom from the smooth, damp walls as Vedoans and Pirthyians tramped through the tunnel, following their empress and Imperati.

The Shield's grip stung my arm. I tried not to inhale the stench of sweat and grease from the enemies encircling me, and looked over my shoulder for the prisoners.

Acolytes entered carrying the sedan, blocking my view, and the carriage roof scraped against rock. The white-haired soothsayer barked a reprimand. Those bearing the carriage poles stooped to accommodate the tunnel's height.

The empress's litter reached an intersection and stopped. Waterworn statuary adorned all four passages glimmering with firelight. The saffron-robed elderly soothsayer hurried to the empress's side and motioned to follow the passages with blackened ceilings. When he retreated to the sedan, we continued.

My heart pounded at the thought that Vedoa knew the location of the Eternity Gate. Did Laijon and the Brotherhood's plan accommodate this? If Vedoa found the Eternity Gate—I couldn't consider it. But no matter what, they could not seize Kiboro. I would play her part until the end.

People began to yell, followed by incoming shrieks and beating wings. Shadows tore over our heads, extinguishing torches, and vanished into the tunnels' depths.

After the commotion, we moved on. Through the stone walls, a monstrous moaning grew, until we walked underneath one of the pumps. Water sprinkled from above where the gigantic, exposed screw turned slowly, uselessly.

Pooled water swished under our boots. It soon rose to our knees, then chest-high and reaching the empress's litter. Alarmed Pirthyians and Vedoans, coming from drier lands, held their fires and swords aloft. Pirthyian soldiers grumbled against their comrades manning the pumps, and the Imperati commanded them to silence. Vedoans swept soaked robes behind them, chins high. Splashes and cursing filled the air as Shields hacked blades through the water. They cast long, lifeless river serpents aside, and blood rippled through the flood.

At last, the tunnel pinched to narrower passage. Infuriated, the empress abandoned her litter. Acolytes struggled to move the cramped sedan. After a quarrel, the carriage base splashed into water, its roof scratching the tunnel ceiling and walls, but miraculously passed through.

Our way climbed, and exhaustion gripped me. How many fingerlengths of the sun—or moon—had passed? Then, firelight from the leading Shields' hands disappeared into fathomless space.

The ceiling soared, and we entered a large, dry chamber connected by several stone corridors. Then I saw the massive, stone slab claiming the center of the cave floor. We had reached the Heart of the tunnels.

The empress, with the Imperati trailing her, marched onto the carved stone.

From high crevices, Shadows' screams echoed across the chamber. The sedan entered the atrium, and weary acolytes set the carriage down. The elderly soothsayer bowed before the sedan and approached the empress's side. He made frantic motions with his hands to the worn stone under her feet.

The empress snapped orders toward the Imperati. Translators hurried to interpret.

Emeridus drew his shoulders back, eyes fiery, but waved Pirthyian soldiers forward, bearing chisels and hammers. Metal struck rock and mingled with the Pirthyians' grunts as they attacked the slab. The stone split. Soldiers lifted heavy, broken pieces as other fragments fell and splashed into deep, lost tunnels below.

The Shadows silenced. I ceased to breathe.

Through the void, exposed rock steps climbed down into darkness. The breath of trapped space and time swept through the Heart like a spirit.

The empress raised a sword and claimed the stairs. Her Shields, the Imperati, and his Pirthyian bodyguard followed. I was pushed after them down the hole. The suffocating space felt like a tomb, except for swishing and dripping water, untouched for centuries, and then we reached a sepulchral hallway. Long, slimy growth covered the walls as we waded into hip-high water.

Crevice-like paths vanished into gloom before we reached a quiet pool. The empress marched across, rippling the water, to a hallway with a destination lost in an upward climb. I strained to see.

The empress and her Shields crested the zenith and reached a plateau. Their firelight illuminated a vast cavern, with a domed ceiling that disappeared into blindness. There was enough dry ground to fit perhaps one hundred people, but beyond that, a subterranean lake surrounded us. A rising hill of rock pierced the far corner of the lake, accessible by a skinny path.

But nothing glittered. No golden Eternity Gate stood. As more Pirthyians arrived with torches, we saw piles of rubble and rusted weaponry strewn across the ground.

Shrieks reverberated through the chamber as the army of Shadows swooped past and climbed the high walls, seeking perches.

The empress appraised the cavern with a cold eye while the Imperati strode to the lake's edge. Debris clinked and scraped under his footsteps. "Garbage," the Imperati cursed. "Vedoa, is this what you promised me?"

The empress hissed and pointed to the water. "Look, fool."

The Imperati stared into the lake, then erupted with a triumphant cry. He knelt, reached into the water, and pulled something out. His bodyguard clustered close with torchlight. The Imperati stood and lifted a heavy, oractalm pitcher glowing scarlet, beads of water running down its gold ornamentation.

Vedoans and Pirthyians gathered around the lake. The Shield dragged me with him to glimpse past the rock landing.

Crystalline water covered mounds of treasure resting in waves of gold, silver, and crimson ore. Sparkling brilliantly. The measureless treasures of nations.

It was real. And, as if by magic, the metal was untouched. Untarnished. I held my breath and took a step back. Something crunched under my boot. Ancient Shadow bones.

The empress commanded her bodyguard to come. My Shield, with me in tow, joined her at the foot of the dry bridge leading up the lone hill of rock. She ordered her Shields to search the slope.

Nearby, Vedoan slaves created piles of lit, volcanic rock, and soon, bonfires cast writhing light against the towering walls. As acolytes heaved the covered sedan into the cavern, the elderly soothsayer directed the carriage to be placed between three fires. Then, he prostrated himself before the carriage again. This time he trembled.

I shifted my gaze to the lake. Below the firelight playing across the stirred surface, the water now glowed blood red with oractalm. But where was the Eternity Gate?

Pirthyians herded the Laijonese and Brotherhood prisoners into the cavern and divided them into groups. Fifteen captives under two Pirthyians. The Pirthyians cut my people's restraints and, at sword point, made them dive into the lake and retrieve treasure.

I watched in dismay. My people retrieved Laijonese jewelry and decorative ornaments of glowing ore. Golden Ai'Biroan mirrors and tall jars. Nazakian weaponry and silver pottery. Piles of treasure were amassed beside the fires, spilling over.

Pirthyians bellowed, but Vedoans sneered, as if the treasure were worthless, yet their greedy expressions betrayed them. Shadows cackled with frenzied excitement.

Our enemies would take everything.

A prisoner flailed in the water under a heavy burden and went under. When Pirthyians dragged the Laijonese guard onto the ground, he didn't move. A new prisoner was cut from his ties to take his place.

Chest pounding, I looked for my family. Father stood in the mouth of the tunnel with the last prisoners, Kiboro remaining near him. Roji and Geras waited in the same group near the water. Geras, stilled wrapped in soggy rags, flexed his chained hands with rising agitation. Cries heralded the discovery of a large chest, and Roji and Geras were prodded to help the straining prisoners lift the trunk onto land. A Pirthyian overseer raised a hatchet and severed the chest's lock, then he and his comrades broke the wax seal and lifted the lid. The chest yawned to waterproof skins covering stacks of gilt-bound books.

The soldiers scowled and shut the lid. Their irritation increased as more drowned chests were recovered, all opening to ancient manuscripts. They looked ready to feed the pages to the fires.

I froze. The fires. How did flames keep burning in this closed space?

The Imperati stormed past me to the empress, who continued to watch the hill and her Shields working on something at the top. I hated standing so close to her.

Fist pressed against his chest, the Imperati snapped in Pirthyian, and interpreters struggled to keep up. "I was promised the Gate of Eternity. Where is it? You said it would remain standing." He waved toward the sedan. "Or has that desert demon nursed you with lies of the gate's existence?"

The empress spun with a snarl. "You ill-bred dog. The gate stands."

Wet, yellow robes flapping, the soothsayer dashed in front of the empress. His eyes rolled back, and we stepped away. His madness even startled the empress. "Goddess, it demands its reward and warns even you, who are divine, not to forget." He extended a grasping hand.

Fear crossed the empress's face. "It is early."

The soothsayer stretched quivering fingers. The empress swore, cast him aside, then her own hands shot out and clutched me around the neck. Her thumbs dug into my throat.

I gasped and reached for her wrists. Shields caught my hands and forced my arms by my sides.

The empress's grip tightened. "Search her for the key. If you do not find it, burn her."

40

THE EMPRESS FLUNG ME AGAINST
a wall of bare-chested Shields. Their hands crawled over me
searching for the key. I resisted.

She ordered the Shields to create a ring. They released me to
obey, folded their arms, and stood feet apart, facing me.

I trembled in the center of their circle. They hadn't checked my
shoes or hair.

The remaining Shields vacated the hill, crossed the bridge, and
strengthened the circle. Vedoans and Pirthyians gathered, while
the prisoners stared from the lake's edge.

The empress faced the sedan, where the white-haired soothsayer
stood, and proclaimed, "This liar queen does not hold the key, so
she will char in Vedoa's fire."

My knees buckled, and I searched for a sympathetic face. An
intercessor. Not the stone-faced Shields. Not the enemy spectators,
Vedoans who understood this ritual and Pirthyians who grimaced
at an interruption to treasure hunting. The Imperati, who eyed the
empress with disgust, did not intervene.

I looked for my father or Kiboro, but they were hidden by the
crowd. Instead, I found Geras looming in the distance. His posture
was tense, confused, and he pulled against his chains. A Pirthyian
soldier waved a knife at him.

I stepped backward and gripped my elbows. There was no one—

A Shadow screamed and dove toward our circle.

The shields lunged with long daggers. The Shadow wheeled

from their blades, its gold collar winking with torchlight, and vanished into darkness. The guards tightened around me.

"Goddess!"

Gazes swung to the prisoner who dared to speak out. It was Faru.

"I gave Prince Jorai the key," Faru cried. "Return him to me."

The empress spat. "First the false queen, then that brazen informer dies next, and every prisoner until the key is found." She clapped.

The Shields cupped their hands in front of their chests, and their palms burst with rippling, unnatural fire. Like my mother's that scarred me. Flames I could not survive.

The Vedoans erupted with cheers. All jostled for a better look, and I met the empress's glare. Saw the strain in her neck, pallor coloring her cheeks. She was afraid. I recalled the Shields' careless search. The empress didn't want to merely find the key. She wanted to destroy it.

With greased hands, the Shields spun wheels of fire. Volcanic heat washed over me.

I stiffened. My spirit weakened. I could not endure this—but didn't I deserve it? For all my lies and sins? And if one must walk this path first, would I survive longer than my brethren, long enough to waste a portion of Vedoa's warped power?

Geras's intensity swept over me. A thousand furies filled his downturned face. He strained against his chains, lifted his face higher—

No. This was my battle.

I opened my mouth to shout at him to stand down in Nazakian, but instead, the adulation escaped my lips. "Holy, holy Father of Light—" Carry my ashes across the Divide.

The gold-collared Shadow swooped above the Shields.

The guards bellowed and pushed their hands toward me in an outpouring of writhing fire.

I screamed. Searing agony licked my skin and raced down my throat. I shut my eyes and sank to the fiery ground. My thoughts careened, and I saw my mother's hatred, her smoldering hands burning me until her weak gifting extinguished.

I convulsed under the wielders' onslaught. They did not yield. I imagined my body melting off of my bones. I wasn't strong enough to last.

I screamed again and felt my spirit loosen.

Palms pressed against my head. Light separated from fire, and the torment lessened. Someone shielded me. Bore the flames. I dared open my eyes.

A fierce young woman in Vedoan clothes stood over me. Blinding light streamed behind her and cast her features into darkness.

Father of Light, is this a heavenly messenger?

I reached for her forearms to will whatever was left of my inverted gifting to protect her, too, but her flesh shimmered like mist between my hands. Tongues of fire only tasted me now, and I stared at the woman.

She wore a slave piercing and spoke in a familiar voice. "Friend like a sister, your purpose is not finished."

I gasped. She looked and sounded like Tol, but I could not touch her. Did I cross the Divide?

"The One who makes ways in the desert, who gives nations their power for a time, is not finished. There is greater evil to battle."

I choked. "What could be greater?"

"Will you obey and follow despite the sacrifice?"

"I gave my life."

Sorrow crept into her voice. "You will see greater redemption, though it will not look like it. Hold on." A smile touched her lips. "I've missed you. But we will see each other again soon."

How was that possible? Would we see each other in death? I longed to speak her name, but overwhelming light snared my attention. No. It was a shining man. Light brighter than Kiboro's emanated from him, brighter than the heavenly messenger who appeared to me as Tol. He exuded strength and gentleness as the fire dwindled. Then his light dimmed.

The woman pulled away. I reached for her in vain. The fires roared, claimed my vision, and I collapsed. Fire devoured my flesh again, and then the flames ceased. I knelt over my knees on hot, rough stone. Conscious. Alive.

A hush filled my ringing ears. My throat cracked. Water. I blinked to see again. Gray film covered my skin and clothes. I brushed a hand across my arms and saw delicate burns covering my skin. Like my hands.

The vision of Tol and the shining man were gone.

Shields studied me. Stunned. Through swirling smoke, Pirthyia gawked and the empress stammered an order. Vedoan noblemen forced the Shields to their knees, lifted swords, and slaughtered her bodyguard. Then, the empress crept toward me with death in her eyes, pressing a naked dagger against her hip.

With a deafening screech, the gold-collared Shadow pounced on the empress. She fell on her back and stabbed at the monster's deformed body until he screamed and writhed away. But her leg bent unnaturally. She wailed and Vedoan soldiers rushed to her. The Shadow arched its contorted, bleeding back and fluttered away. The key hung exposed from its neck.

The sedan groaned from the inside, and its frame creaked. Prostrated acolytes and soothsayers raised their heads. The elderly one gasped.

"The pretender queen is mine." The Shadow shrieked and lurched toward me.

I collapsed to my knees, reached for the knife I had lost. The Shadow scooped me into its arms and flew across the thin stone bridge up the abandoned hill.

It hissed in Nazakian. "How did you withstand their fire? Why didn't you tell me you could?" It released me.

I landed atop the hill into refuse. Forgotten armor, a tangle of ancient Shadow bones.

The Shadow flung trash down the hill to block the bridge. It rubbed its shoulder, the one I had pierced, and turned. Its wing brushed my back.

I scooted into deeper debris and looked up. My heart stilled.

Baptized in firelight, a stone pedestal supported a cracked doorframe. The wooden door, on rickety hinges, showed the scars of being broken into pieces and fitted back together. Preserved by water, the wood was unadorned. An empty hole betrayed the missing doorknob, the Shields' unfinished work before they were called to execute me.

It couldn't be. I pulled a breath. And the key—

Vedoans and Pirthyians marched across the bridge toward us.

The Shadow's voice scraped. "I will open the gate. To die. Will you stop me?"

I shrank back.

"Shadows don't keep captives. Am I already beyond your memory?" Claws gripped my arms and forced me to look up.

I saw the monster's warped face and cringed. Metal lay embedded against its brow like a thorny crown. Long, limp hair knotted. Tortured eyes, a last vestige of humanity. The dead Tracker's collar, its gold scratched.

Pirthyians and Vedoans reached the base of the hill and battled through debris.

"No?" The Shadow tossed me back into garbage and shuffled toward the pedestal. Clutched the key against its sinewy chest. Dragged its foot. Limping.

I gasped.

The Shadow paused, arched under the weight of its wings. Rusty Laijonese words grated. "Now you know me." It turned. "Tell them who I am."

I bit back a cry. Father of Light—

The Shadow rose and shouted to all within hearing. "I am Jorai, second son of the dead king of Laijon!"

All went quiet except for the murmurings of interpreters.

Faru howled, and Kiboro, small against the lake's edge below, crumpled.

The Imperati and his bodyguard converged upon the bridge, and he commanded those clearing debris to hasten.

Jorai—Shadow—lowered to all fours and laughed.

I stared. Tears streamed down my cheeks.

"Did you mourn me?" Jorai slithered closer. "Would you show such kindness to a Shadow? Shall I skin my scales, tear off my wings? Denounce me, Seyo." He growled. "I am of royal blood and disfigured beyond imagination. Yes, the prophecy is known even by Shadows. But we know we cannot claim the gate's power. We know its opening will destroy our kind, and so Shadows search for the chosen one to end his line. But I have survived in this disguise. The rest of the monsters will die in their freakish forms and be consumed by the Abyss. I will perish by the opened gate and seek redemption, and you will live to remember it." He swept me to the edge of the hill. To throw me down the side.

Vedoans and Pirthyians climbed the hill, halted, and began yelling.

Jorai ignored them, and his mangled body swelled with breath. "Do you bless my crusade with tears, priestess? Condemn me. Say I am a monster."

"No," I whispered. "It is what lies inside us, not outside, that makes us a monster or not." My voice shook. "Jorai, I cannot condemn you."

Anguish crossed his gaze like lightning, then he screamed and tossed me over the hill's edge.

I tumbled down the slope. Scrapes, bumps—handhold. I caught an outcropping of rock and found a place for my toes. I gasped for breath. The lake glowed scarlet with oractalm below.

Jorai shrieked at the top, slammed himself against the ground, then stalked toward the Eternity Gate. He brushed Vedoan hand tools from the pedestal, faced the wooden door, and jammed the missing knob into place. Gripping the jagged key between shaking claws, he searched the doorknob. Felt all around it. Frantic. Made a strangled sound.

A chill rushed through my veins. Jorai couldn't find the keyhole.

Fresh cries came from Pirthyians and Vedoans. Laijonese and Brotherhood prisoners had attacked their enemies, pressing them toward the tunnel in chaos.

Shadows shrieked above, fighting for the exit or disappearing into the darkness of the ceiling. Among the bonfires, acolytes abandoned the sedan, now lying on its side, door removed. The elderly soothsayer lay on the ground, dead.

I looked around wildly. What was happening? I had to get to Kiboro, but then we would abandon the gate to Jorai.

Palpable evil swept over me. Scented like decay and oppression. My chest squeezed. I found my thoughts scattering, as if chasing an unseen magnet. Then I caught movement at the base of the hill.

It was power. A being? Spirit? The terrible form dragged countless, rusted chains binding its arms, legs, neck, middle, and wings.

Wings.

Already it crested the hill and stopped behind Jorai, twice as large as him. It raised its hulking, chained body with effort, the largest flying creature I had ever seen. Its ghostly form, swirling and sharpening, was hairless. It cast its humanlike head about with barren orbs for eyes.

Oblivious, Jorai screeched and reached for the wooden doorknob. Twisted it without the key. He swung the door open and tripped through.

No!

Jorai stumbled through the open door to the opposite side of the pedestal then caught his balance.

It didn't work. The gate was empty.

The phantom snatched Jorai, reached for his wing, and tore. Jorai screamed. The creature released him to the ground with the key in its own hand, and applied the jagged metal to its chains. Clanking metal fell. The phantom's stance lengthened, and it expanded endless wings.

Jorai fluttered over the opposite side of the hill.

A shudder rocked the chamber.

Below, everyone fled. Pirthyians abandoned the battle. Vedoans scooped handfuls of treasure, only to discard them. The prisoners cried out as water pooled at their feet, rising to cover the platform and cut everyone off from the tunnels. A second shudder gripped the room, and the water receded again, as if the pumps had stopped and restarted.

The monster roared and leapt into graceful, silent flight. It seized fleeing bodies and broke them, favoring Vedoans.

My heart pounded. Go.

I released my hold and plummeted into the lake, swimming for the bank and climbing onto dry ground. But a herd of Pirthyian soldiers raced around me. I tumbled before their trampling—

But someone lifted me to my feet, and together we ran. Geras. I caught his gloved hand, felt the manacles circling his wrists, the snapped chain stinging my arm. He shouldered through the melee and pulled me after.

An otherworldly war cry ripped through the air. The phantom.

Geras heaved me aside just as the hurricane of winged blindness swirled through our midst and snatched another body.

I was pressed by others into the cool mouth of the tunnel. I searched for Geras as the phantom dove over the bonfires and extinguished every one. As the last soldiers gained the exit tunnel, the glowing lake illuminated the winged monster's form as it soared up the hill, to the Eternity Gate, and perched atop the frame.

We all splashed deeper across the lake toward the Heart.

Where were Laijon and the Brotherhood? I screamed for Geras, but could not be heard over the drowning panic. And Jorai. I wept and lost my footing only to be swept along. We reached the first intersection and everyone continued for the stairs.

A hand clenched my wrist.

Geras—no. The person's fingers tightened painfully, and we made eye contact.

Faru glowered and yanked me into a crack in the wall. We squeezed past rock, and water lapped at our ankles. I struggled and yelled. Then, the natural corridor widened.

Faru swung me against his chest, where I faced out into blindness. He wrapped one arm across my middle and smothered a wet palm against my mouth.

"Jorai will come for you," Faru said into my ear, then pushed me ahead of him deeper into the passage.

41

WATER HAD RISEN TO OUR KNEES,

and we struggled in sightlessness. Still holding my waist, Faru released my mouth to lift a hand bursting with two-tongued, sapphire light. The brightness bounced across the end of our narrow tunnel, and we crept into a generous cavity split by fractures leading in all directions. Towers of stone interrupted the natural space.

I wrenched away from Faru and backed up. I was unarmed and slowed by water.

He studied me with furrowed brow. "I did not know there were firewalkers such as you."

I fisted my hands. "Let me go."

"After I reason with Jorai, you may join Laijon's defeat."

The world shook. I fell with a splash onto my knees. Faru caught his balance and grimaced. "Pirthyia pounds the earth."

Impossible. After Pirthyia subjugated Nazak, rumors sped that they would twist Nazak's gifting into something like earth-pounding, but I had thought it was a myth. Right?

"War begins aboveground, and Laijon will not last. Time is short, but a Shadow's hearing is excellent, like a bat." Faru lifted his blue light and his voice. "Jorai, I have Seyo. Listen to me, and I will not harm her."

I stiffened. I would not be a traitor's pawn—

Scales skimmed against my legs.

I gasped.

Faru spun toward me. He raised his knife and eyed the spines rippling the water around me.

A shriek cut the air. The river serpent disappeared.

Darkness stirred, and Jorai swooped overhead, skidded across a wall, and clawed to perch atop one of the rock towers, far from Faru's blue light. His torn wing drooped, yet he remained strong enough to fly.

My heart seized. "Jorai, don't trust him—"

Faru grabbed me and covered my mouth again. "Be still." His arms tightened around me, and his voice thickened. "Jorai. Oh, my prince and son."

"Silence." Jorai's chest heaved. Every muscle in his warped frame rippled as his gaze narrowed upon Faru. "They say you invited Vedoans to enter Laijon. They sealed hostages into this bedeviled form with surgery and incantation. Shadows cannot cross the Divide, and we are too strong for easy death. The Eternity Gate should have ended my life. My sacrifice would have spared my soul, but the gate did not open to me. Now an evil greater than us, that Vedoa thought they could leash, is freed. What else do you want, old man? You delay my flight from this cursed place."

Faru's weight pushed against me. "Vedoa will pay for what they have done to you. May their treachery be cursed. My loyalty belongs only to you and myself." He adopted a pleading tone. "Once Vedoa claimed Laijon and the Eternity Gate, you were supposed to rule as a bridge between the two peoples. You were to be king, never Huari. I killed that overindulged swine to prepare your reign."

Faru killed Huari. In shock, I stilled and noticed his arms relax. Another moment, and I would twist and kick so hard—

Faru cursed. "We are betrayed, and I cannot save you from your form."

Jorai spat and spread his wings. "Traitor."

The earth quaked again. Faru gripped me tighter while Jorai squawked and scampered for balance atop the stone tower.

Faru's gaze roamed the cave. "When the water rose over the treasure, Ai'Biro must have defeated the Pirthyians manning the pumps before managing the floods themselves. As long as the water level is stable, Laijon and her allies remain standing. But the battle will end soon, and these tunnels will flood. Laijon is outnumbered by Pirthyia and Vedoa. Laijon will sacrifice her army on the castle grounds to give Kiboro the chance to open the Eternity Gate. According to their beliefs, there is no other path to victory for them. But she will not survive Second. From ancient times, the monster was bound by darkness to destroy the gate opener. It will kill Kiboro for her royal blood. Then Second will seek your life."

Second—was that the phantom? My pulse pounded in my ears. I needed to escape.

Jorai swore. "I will fly faster and hide."

"Second lived hundreds of years, frozen in a foreign lake, chained and stabbed, before Vedoa found it. They made empty promises of unlocking it in exchange for the path to the Eternity Gate. Now, it has overcome and hunts that backstabbing nation. May Second finish them all. No one evades Second, for it cannot die." Faru's heavy breaths tickled my neck, and his tone grew in strength. "My son, I have dedicated my life to seating you on the throne, to give you everything you deserve. Now our world lies in shambles, and I have one last offering. I will save you from death by making you the most powerful being alive. Second is immortal, but you will be invincible and able to withstand it and live forever. Protected from eternal damnation."

I was being held by a madman.

"Live forever?" Jorai bristled and screeched. "Like this? My life is damnation. Give me freedom in death."

Faru shifted. His blade pricked below my ribs.

I inhaled sharply. Warm blood trickled down my skin.

Faru's voice strained. "Accept my gift before she dies."

Jorai screamed and dove toward us.

Faru raised his head. "Forgive me, my son!" He lifted his dagger and stabbed himself in the chest.

I pulled from his grasp.

Jorai reeled to avoid crashing into the older man. But Faru

managed to grab Jorai's claws, and so was dragged across the chamber by the momentum. He convulsed. Jorai cried out, wrenched his limb free, and clambered atop another rock tower. He held the claw to his chest, then opened his leathery palm to two-tongued, blue light. Faru's gifting. His eyes widened with panic, and he flinched in the brightness. "This is not light!"

Faru lay sprawled in the water, clutching his gushing wound. He choked, then slipped under.

Involuntarily, I splashed beside him, but was too late. Through blood swirling in the water, I saw Faru's stricken face. Dead. Yet, for a second, he resembled Jorai. I staggered back.

Perched atop the rock, Jorai fought to extinguish the blue flame in his hand. His face contorted, as if it burned him, and he flung the light against the chamber. A ball of fiery, sapphire brightness smashed against the wall and smoldered in sickly, blue glow.

I froze. *Qo'tah*, what power did Faru give him?

Jorai stared between the wall and his hand. Then he looked at me, eyes wild. Desperate with hatred. "Run."

I stepped backward.

He showed his teeth and wheeled into the air. Extended his hand in blue flames.

I fled for the passage. Tripped at his scream and ducked inside the narrow fissure just before he rammed and skittered against the wall.

I pressed through the tight passage. Cringed as blue flashes illuminated behind me, mingled with shrieks and thrashing water. *Jorai, Jorai*, my heart cried with grief and horror.

I felt the watery walls and struggled through blindness as I made my way to the end of the tunnel and emerged into open space. Was this the intersection? Which way led to the Heart, and which way led to the phantom Second?

I swiped the heels of my hands against tears and looked around. Father of Light, show me the way.

Illumination flickered across the atrium. There were people marching.

I hid. Vedoans? No. A stocky Pirthyian, bearing a torch, was in the lead. His curled hair bounced with his energetic strides through water. Vispirios.

My heart pounded. It was the entire Brotherhood and its leaders, with their ancient swords reclaimed and carrying torches. They formed a wall around a knot of Laijonese Elites and soldiers, ones decorated as strong bearers of light, but their hands were empty. Father walked with them, carrying a torch. I didn't see Roji, but the center of the contingent belonged to Kiboro. Delicate head held high. Spine rigid. Geras walked beside her, along with other members of her bodyguard. They neared the intersection.

I splashed forward.

Vispirios startled, then he whooped and waded forward to clasp my arm. "I could not think of a better harbinger of hope than finding you alive." He turned me toward the group. "Behold, our diversion-maker!"

Father swept me against his chest. "I sent my son to fight aboveground, to escape this place of death, and find you still here?"

I pressed my forehead into his shoulder, then sought Kiboro. She and I made eye contact, but in her deep focus, I swore she saw past me.

I needed to tell her about the key. No, she had seen Second use it to unlock his chains. She must learn about Jorai, then I realized what they were doing. They were attempting to gain the Eternity Gate, just as Faru had predicted. So Kiboro could open the door—at the likely cost of her life. For Laijon.

Father's voice broke as he spoke to me. "The tunnels crawl with Shadows. Any moment, Ai'Biro could lose control of the pumps or the monster could destroy the gate. It would have been better for you to face war."

But the Eternity Gate was not there. I shook my head. "I will see this through."

Something strengthened in Father's gaze, and he inclined his head. Respect given to me.

The Brotherhood's Nazakian leader lifted her voice with final instructions. "When we enter the cavern, you, of Laijon, hold your gifting high. Like all Shadows, even this creature will fear light. It is our strongest weapon now."

All nodded. Some saluted or bowed.

Her eyes flicked between us, and her voice deepened. "May the Father of Light's strength follow us. Move out."

Father pressed his torch into my hands. "Stay near Geras. Keep this lit. May the Father of Light grant survivors, and may you guide them out."

My chest squeezed, but I nodded and hurried beside Geras's hulking form, near Kiboro, holding the torch close. Then we marched into the intersection.

Geras's heavy gaze draped over me. His quiet determination faltered. He stretched a gloved hand, still bound with manacles and broken chains like many of the others, to push me behind his towering frame, then pulled his shoulders back and kept his head down. Gripped his own torch and da's sword tight.

We crossed the first, swollen pool and climbed the uphill tunnel to the mouth of the treasure chamber. Toward the monster.

To live in victory or die in defeat.

42

THE BROTHERHOOD LEADERS raised their torches and advanced into the chamber. Through thick gloom, the lake still glowed with oractalm. Faint crimson glimmer illuminated the dry landing, its piles of treasure and extinguished volcanic bonfires, and the bridge leading to the hill. Quiet evil reigned.

We stepped over fallen enemies.

A low sound curled through the ancient air. A silent shape swooped overhead and stirred the lake, torchlight glinting across enormous, spread wings. Second.

The monster snatched one of the Brotherhood protecting the rear. The soldier screamed before the sickening snap of his body. His torch sailed into the lake and sizzled out.

The Laijonese threw a shower of brightness into the advancing monster's face. The beast barred its fangs, veered violently, and circled the hill. It tucked its wings and barreled toward us again.

The Brotherhood raised a battle cry. Those of us holding torches thrust firelight above our heads. The Laijonese released another volley of light, and Father added his own gifting to the blaze. As the beast swerved, we raced Kiboro toward the hill. Some fell back to relight bonfires, but the monster smothered their efforts, dove toward water, and sprayed us. We protected our torches as the beast beat its wings into the air, clutching another body.

"Advance!" Vispirios yelled and crossed the bridge. Our contingent obeyed and was forced to thin ranks on the narrow walkway.

Kiboro strode forward with Elites flanking her. Why didn't she use her gifting?

Geras moved me in front of him to take the bridge first, near Kiboro's lightbearers. Laijonese and Brotherhood fell into the lake and clambered back out. Drenched torches were abandoned.

My heart rammed against my ribs. We were too exposed.

Second struck another man off the edge, then flung itself from the light. The being eclipsed with darkness, vanished, and lunged again.

One of the Brotherhood jumped to meet Second's claws and jabbed his sword into the monster's heart. Second crushed the soldier against its chest and plummeted into piled treasure. Gold and glowing ore spilled across the landing and into the lake.

"Go!" The Nazakian woman shouted, and we raced up the hill.

Second shook itself and climbed the air with renewed rage. Another soldier struck. And another.

Vispirios cried out and led another charge against the monster. But the giftings of the Laijonese soldiers weakened. Their reserve of light was failing.

The monster circled the Eternity Gate and plowed through a fourth of our ranks, cutting off those protecting Kiboro's front. Dozens of torches quenched. I moved closer to her with my torch. Kiboro looked between her divided army and then raced for the hilltop. Alone.

I fought to keep up, but Vispirios and his group saw her flight and converged in front of me.

Second spied Kiboro's advance and sprang.

Kiboro skidded to a stop lengths from the Eternity Gate and whirled her hands toward the monster in blinding, blazing light.

Deafening noise seared our hearing as Second screamed, pivoted, and leapt between Kiboro and the gate. Recovered, the creature studied her with empty eyes as it morphed in and out of darkness. So close one could see vile symbols painted onto its muscled hide.

Its voice slithered in a language I did not know, but somehow understood. I covered my ears and resisted falling to my knees.

I was not made aware that wielding as great as yours existed in this new age. What is your lineage, small one?

She answered, "I am queen of Laijon."

It left the Eternity Gate and stalked her. *I knew a princess once.* Second's frame rippled. *Are you the gate opener I search for?*

The Laijonese threw a volley of light. Second hissed and whirled toward them.

Kiboro leapt onto the stone platform and grasped the doorknob. Second pounced upon her, then hurtled backward from her second explosion of light. The monster screamed and clawed its eyes.

With a cry, Kiboro opened the Eternity Gate. I crumpled to the ground and covered my head. One moment. Two.

Kiboro stood by the empty doorframe, chest heaving. Eyes wide. The gate opened to nothing. It was impossible. She was the last of Laijon's royal line.

Second swirled before Kiboro. Pulsing with fury.

She flung light into its maw—a weaker burst that still sent the creature scattering—and ran down the hill. Laijon's lightbearers surrounded her with the last of their light. We turned and retreated across the bridge. But Vispirios gave a shout and scrambled back up the hill to the Eternity Gate.

Second's living darkness swerved from us and circled the Pirthyian before he could reach the pedestal. The monster plucked Vispirios in its massive claws, tossed him far into the lake, and arced high to burst through our ranks. Screams split the air as many fell.

I held my torch high over Kiboro as we ran. Elites jostled us. I saw Father, but could not feel Geras's presence. There was splashing, shrieking, and scrambling. The cavern entrance yawned.

We escaped the chamber and slipped down the decline into the pool at the intersection. Someone led us into the refuge of the nearest tunnel. We who still held torches stood in front of the others in an exhausted, futile attempt to repel Second's pursuit. But the phantom did not come.

I looked at the other torchbearers. They were Laijonese, their hands emptied of light. Behind us, Father remained beside Kiboro. Perhaps ten of us survived, and there were none from the Brotherhood. I did not see the Nazakian woman. Or Geras.

My heart tore, then we tensed at splashing in the intersection. A large, hunched form approached. Geras carried Vispirios across his shoulders. He staggered into our midst, Father helped him lay Vispirios down, and they both knelt to hold the Pirthyian's head out of water. Vispirios still breathed, but in spasms. His coppery skin was gray, and torchlight revealed blood seeping from multiple wounds.

Father spoke urgently. "Tell us what to do."

"Physician, heal yourself?" Vispirios spoke in his mother tongue, and his attempt at a chuckle was garbled. "I could not reach the gate. To try my hand and distant, royal Laijonese blood, as promised." He labored to reach around his neck and put a token into Geras's gloved hand. His thin voice sputtered. "For my family. May the Father of Light receive me. Find my vows worthy and kept." Vispirios released his spirit, and silence fell.

Father sat back on his heels. Geras bowed over his friend while Kiboro, trained in the temple, voice soft and brittle, recited safety of passage across the Divide for those lost.

I should have joined her, but couldn't. Grief gripped me, and my thoughts rooted me to the watery tunnel floor. None of us should have lived. Not enough of us did. Father of Light, is this the greater sacrifice you spoke of? Is this your purpose? Lead us, for this cannot be all.

Kiboro finished her prayer and turned toward Father. "Daemu, the battle continues. I must go to my people."

Father rose, and the Laijonese rallied behind their queen. I dragged my feet through water to take my place beside Kiboro. My body grew taut. This felt wrong.

Geras did not rise.

Roaring reverberated through the tunnels and everyone froze. The sound was too vast to be Second. Did Pirthyians advance? Vedoans? But there was no marching. The reek of smoke and grease wafted through the still air.

Father rushed to the tunnel mouth, Kiboro and the others following.

Geras lifted his head. But I understood before seeing, and my heart turned over.

Brightness bounced across the atrium's walls. From cracks in the cave, shimmering oil and fire crawled across the surface of the pool. Vedoa sent hell to cut off our escape.

"To the Heart. Protect the queen," Father shouted.

The soldiers discarded their torches, formed a barrier around Kiboro, and we swept into the intersection. Oil-fed fire devoured half the lake. Warmth wafted over us in waves as Father led our evacuation toward the exit passage.

Water sloshed in the wrong direction.

I threw a glance backward. Geras charged toward the treasure chamber with a torch. Striving to outrun the encroaching flames. But he wouldn't.

I launched into the water and swam after Geras. I heard Father's cry, but I couldn't stop. Four lengths away. Three—

I gasped a breath and seized Geras's gloved hand with its cold manacles. In his surprise, he flinched, almost made eye contact. Then the wall of flames swept over us.

Geras jerked at the impact. I clung to his hand, and his fingers tightened around mine. The roar was unbearable. Overwhelmed by the force of fiery orange, yellow, and white consuming us, he stood still. Lost yet unburned.

I tugged him toward the treasure cavern and higher ground. Coming into fresh air, we climbed to evade the heat and looked back. Rippling flames filled the intersection. Thankfully, Father, Kiboro, and the soldiers had run ahead of the flames.

Geras sank to his knees, head down, pulling deep breaths. He held a dripping torch shaft with a trembling hand. Firelight danced off his da's sword, sheathed against his hip, and oractalm glowed from his wrist. My bracelet.

His brow creased with questions, but he did not ask them. Instead he said, "I am the last of the Brotherhood. I fight for my da Ortos, and I will keep my vow." He would not use his power even here.

My soul plummeted. He gave his life without hope. The torch wasn't enough, Second could not be slain, and the gate would not open to him. It hadn't even opened to Kiboro. This was futile.

But Geras knew this. He, cursed and marked, carried the last Brotherhood sword, forged during ancient times to defend the Eternity Gate, raised again to sever its dishonor. And his.

He reached to cover the top of my head with his palm. "Follow them."

My heart faltered. He would not need help crossing the flames again. But I stiffened and did not answer.

Geras stood and removed the rags covering his marked face and his gloves. The manacle chains clinked. Then he reached for the sword. Paused.

I endured the weight of his gaze and felt his division. Then I, also, rose and stepped back into the fiery pool.

Satisfied by my retreat, he turned, finished the ascent, and vanished with his flickering light into the chamber.

Trembling, I scooped a handful of fire from the pool and crept after him. Father of Light, you commanded me to follow and obey you. Let me also find redemption in what I began.

43

I PRESSED MYSELF AGAINST THE
wall of the chamber mouth, into shadows. The ore in the lake no
longer glowed.

Enveloped with thick quiet, Geras held his torch high and
threaded between high, darkened mounds. Piled treasure
shimmered with firelight before melting into darkness as he passed.
He halted to light a bonfire and stilled.

Snap. Plink. Metal breaking and falling upon metal.

Geras moved forward and lit a second bonfire.

The dim outline of the hill materialized in the far, faint light.
Second perched above the wooden doorframe, holding shining
pieces of something within its claws. It craned its humanlike head
to watch Geras. Then the monster dropped the fragments to join
the carpet of reflective metal scattered around the pedestal. The
broken hilts and blades of the Brotherhoods' swords. *Plink.*

Are you the one I search for?

Geras flinched, and my breath caught. The great Shadow's
unspoken words invaded my mind and twisted with translation.

*You escaped chains, like me. You suppress power. It stirs within
you. Does it give you confidence to approach me alone? What is it?* The
monster shook itself and scowled. *What is your lineage, Unknown?*

Geras did not answer and advanced toward the bridge.

I edged to the lake and released my handful of flaming oil into
water, then maneuvered around trash and rusted weaponry to the
first bonfire. I pulled a volcanic rock loose and fled to the next

dormant pyre, one in front of Geras, and helped new flames burst. I would light them all to deter the monster and fill the lake with Vedoa's fire. I cringed hearing Second's growl.

Forgery! Who stained your flesh with stolen symbols? Where do you come from? The phantom drew darkness to itself with rising agitation. *Do you seek to fight me or join me?*

Geras yelled and tore across the landing.

Second swooped into the air.

Geras dropped to his knees and lifted his da's sword just as Second dove. The monster swerved with a stripe across its torso.

Geras dove into a pile of coins, spraying glittering metal everywhere. Disoriented, Second chased the treasure before spying Geras and attacking again. Shrieking.

But Geras pierced him again and rolled away. He jumped to his feet and ran. Toward my fire.

I reached for him as Second wheeled in pursuit, and caught Geras's hand. He jumped into the flames with me, breathing hard and bewildered with surprise. "You're here."

Second swirled overhead to extinguish our fire and dove. I scooped my free hand full of burning, porous rocks and flung them overhead into the monster's face, causing Second to whirl away.

I scooped more volcanic stone and said, "Go."

Geras pulled from my grasp, and the fire, and made for the bridge.

I stepped into fresh air, exposed, and screamed for Second's attention. Circling the cavern, the monster swerved toward me. Unlimited power. Empty eyes.

Would it ask the lineage of a daughter of fire?

I hurtled more flaming rock and dove into the lake just before Second smothered the flames. I kicked deep toward the glowing ore blanketing the lake bottom. Could the phantom swim? I needed to breathe. But Second neared the water's surface, turned, and disappeared. Distracted by something.

Geras.

I broke the surface and gasped a breath full of flames. Oil and fire flowed from the chamber's mouth and devoured half the lake.

I fought to reach what used to be dry ground, scrambled over the submerged bank, and stood in ankle-deep water. My heart beat wildly. Ai'Biro had lost the pumps. The cavern was filling with water and fire. Soon, the tunnel mouth would be drowned, and we would be cut off from escape before the chamber flooded.

I looked to see Geras halfway up the hill, brandishing his sword. Second unveiled his form.

I scooped a handful of fire and raced toward the bridge. I was too far.

Second sprang.

Blue orbs of light blazed across the chamber and struck Second's hide. It screamed an unearthly sound that rumbled the atmosphere.

A dark shape winged across the cavern in lopsided flight. Gold collar gleaming.

Second trained its fathomless gaze on Jorai. *You dare to attack your master, counterfeit? How did you gain blue fire? You are far from Vedoa, and I do not know you.* It tore after the lesser Shadow.

Jorai wheeled and pumped his wings to keep ahead. Second followed. Taking its time before flinging Jorai against the cavern wall.

Geras held his side and reached the top of the hill.

Fiery water rose to my knees. I rushed across the bridge to the hill just as Second spotted Geras and veered with a scream.

Geras crossed the pile of sword fragments and gained the pedestal just before Second hurtled him to the ground. The monster raked claws across Geras's back, tearing cloth and skin. It smashed a fist into his head and seized his da's sword.

Breathless, I raced up the hill ahead of the flames.

Second lifted Geras's sword between talons and snapped the ancient blade in half. It tossed the pieces across Geras's body, then reached to finish him.

Jorai slammed into Second with an explosion of blue light. Second shrieked and sliced the air, but Jorai flew out of reach.

Geras struggled to his hands and knees. The oractalm bracelet glowed against his wrist. He seized his da's broken sword hilt and crawled toward the gate.

Second stalked Jorai. *Your blue fire dwindles, and it cannot kill me. Then you will die. With great difficulty.*

Somewhere, Jorai growled. "I will die battling you and prove that my monster's form has not yet overcome me."

Second lunged through the darkness, grasped Jorai's uninjured wing, and tore the appendage from his body. Jorai screeched, twisted in Second's grip, and smashed both claws filled with simmering blue fire into Second's eyes.

The phantom's roar thundered the atrium, and Jorai wriggled to the ground. He gasped, hopped, and darted awkwardly before Second snatched him again. It clutched Jorai's squirming form, broke his body, and tossed him aside.

My spirit splintered. I crossed the sea of broken blades, reached Geras, and fell to my palms and knees. Pushing myself under his arm, I helped him stand. He held onto my hand tightly as growing flames surrounded us.

Second wailed and clawed its face until fire spread around its feet. The monster shrieked at its touch and took flight.

Geras and I turned as inferno devoured the Eternity Gate.

44

FLAMES COVERED THE ANCIENT,
wooden door and licked the air.

A cry rose to my lips. Gripping his da's broken blade with one hand and my fingers with the other, Geras stared at the door as waves of fire swept against our legs.

But like us, the Eternity Gate did not burn.

Lengths away, Second flew, swerving around the blazing hill. It tasted the rising heat and recoiled before hunting again without sight.

We had to reach the door.

Second spun and hissed. *I feel you.* It wheeled toward us.

We crouched, and the monster toppled into flames and screamed. Geras tugged me to stand, and we dashed to the pedestal. He faced the fiery door, gasped a breath, and faltered. Second swirled frantically above.

I raised my voice, despite the phantom. "We have to try."

Geras shuddered, crushing my hand in his fist. Then he tore his fingers from mine, pressed his hand against my shoulder blades, and pushed me past the Eternity Gate.

I tumbled across shattered blades into piles of trash.

Fire climbed Geras's body. He gripped the doorknob, his back arching in agony, and cried the name of the Father of Light.

Second heard and swooped toward the gate with a terrible roar, outstretched claws and open fangs.

Burning, Geras faced the monster's assault. He looked the

sightless creature in the eye, turned the doorknob, and flung the Eternity Gate wide. Second crashed into him.

I screamed.

But then the monster shrieked and launched backward. Away from the Eternity Gate.

The doorframe bore light.

Presence older than time, brighter than day, poured into the cavern. Terrible and breathtaking, it raced across the hill, bridge, treasure, up walls, and replaced our air. Touching every corner and hiding place. Extinguishing fire.

The presence found me. I gasped and covered my face. Its otherness consumed me with intensity greater than flames or mountain rivers. But there was no pain. It invaded and knew every part of my body, spirit, and soul. It gave joy and terror, safety and quiet. Peace like the desert.

A rumble rose.

Divine beings flooded from the Eternity Gate. Quick, flaming warriors that carried swords like rays of light.

Second screeched at the warriors' advance. When he fled, they gave chase. But a handful broke away from the fight and sped toward me.

I pressed my face to the filthy ground as fleet footsteps thundered around me. One stopped close enough to touch. Terror overcame me, but I dared to lift my head.

The warrior stood in brilliant splendor, dulling all the lost treasure in comparison. Foreign and glorious, he studied me, too, as if he was as curious about me as I was about him. I almost bowed, but a whisper restrained me. Reminded me that this warrior, too, belonged to the Father of Light.

Weapon raised, his quick eyes surveyed the battles taking place across the risen water. His brothers and sisters who did not attack Second dashed through the chamber after other wraithlike beings, ones unseen before, and slayed them with swords of fire.

Second's cry rent the air. A multitude dragged the ancient monster to the ground and restrained its limbs. Second clawed and raged as the voices of warriors rang out, and their mighty arms drove heavenly blades into its chest. The phantom roared, thrashed, and fell still.

Could it be? I looked to my flaming guardian.

He offered a bow and hurried to join his kindred in their pursuit to join the war aboveground.

I trembled. Unable to grasp what I was experiencing. I looked toward the opened Eternity Gate. It shone brighter than the sun, and warriors began returning to it, hurtling over Geras's knelt form.

Geras.

He faced the doorway with his legs tucked underneath him, prone against the ground, arms wrapped over his head. He groaned as if unbearable weight pressed upon him, but then he nodded, as if speaking with someone. Something like a mighty hand lifted off his back, and Geras sat up, face streaming with tears. He looked into the open door and stared until his own eyes shone. Then the light left his gaze, and he bowed.

The final heavenly warriors reentered the gate. The presence intensified, held, and released. Darkness and quiet draped over the room as the Eternity Gate dimmed, until the doorway stood empty again.

With the fires extinguished, only the scarlet ore and Geras's glowing bracelet provided illumination. I took a shaky breath, gathered strength, and approached the pedestal. Beneath my feet, every Brotherhood blade lay whole again.

When I reached Geras's side, he stood. Markings still covered his exposed skin, but his chains had vanished. He stooped to reach in the ankle-high water for his da's sword.

I crouched and handed him the hilt. Geras jolted in surprise at its touch. He sheathed the blade before reaching toward me, mistakenly brushing my face before finding and gripping my shoulder.

What was wrong with him? My whisper sounded loud. "Geras?"

He looked me in the eye.

I suppressed a gasp. The swirling galaxies in his gaze, what

I saw in the Mirror Garden, were replaced by nut-brown irises. I felt no pain, no curse. His gaze failed to focus on mine. "Seyo, is it finished?"

My heart wrenched. He was blind. "Yes."

Geras exhaled. "We can't return to the tunnels."

"No." The water was too high. Now we would drown. Adrenaline coursed through me. "I can make a raft. Stay here." I pulled my hand from his, grabbed a blade from the water, and splashed toward the nearest chest. Then I stumbled and froze.

Second's body lay below the flood. Whole, but without life. Its monstrous, stretched wings blocked my path, but they outpaced the reconstructed size of its body. Indeed, I did not see Second's Shadow form, but someone almost human. A man? He was uncommonly handsome, except for the anguish etched in death across his face.

Farther off, I spotted a smaller wing arching out of the rising water.

My chest squeezed. I crept around Second's great wings and drew near.

Water caressed Jorai's face, also human again. The friend I used to know. But he appeared calm, as if asleep. The wing protruding from the flood was the one Second had torn and cast aside. I searched for the other wing, but I could not find it. Like Geras's chains, it was gone.

As I wiped tears from my cheeks, I remembered the large chest. I spotted it thrown on its side, the wooden lid broken by Pirthyians, gaping open to ruined manuscripts.

I summoned my strength, lifted the sword, and hewed the lid from its hinge. Yes, it would float, and was just large enough. I dragged our raft back to Geras who stood, waiting.

He steadied the rickety vessel and let me to climb in first. After he got in, he gripped my hand again. His bracelet continued to glow crimson.

Now the flood covered the hill and flowed through the Eternity Gate's empty, open door. Water covered the knob, and then reached the top of the frame. Balancing on our raft, we rose, too, into nothingness. It felt like the cavern went on forever until the walls narrowed.

My pulse raced. How much time did we have until reaching the ceiling? Despite the ore glowing below, I could not see the top.

Geras gripped my hand tighter. "I feel the water turning."

I looked into his eyes and bit back grief. "Yes." I could almost touch the rock walls. We were running out of space and time. "Geras." I hesitated and started again. "What was it like? When the Eternity Gate opened?"

Tension rolled off of him, and his hand tightened even more. For a moment, I didn't think he would tell me, but then, "He said I didn't kill my parents."

I stilled. The Father of Light spoke to him?

"Through the door," Geras went on with an expression of wonder, "I saw—"

Someone shouted orders above.

Our heads jerked up. High above the choking, narrowing walls, tendrils of light reached down toward us, like halos, blocked by something. I realized I breathed fresh air, and my soul leapt.

Geras's voice quickened. "What do you see?"

"There's an opening." Then I saw a shape overhead. "A bucket hanging from a rope." Careful not to upset our raft, I stretched my free arm high to seize the wooden container and passed it to Geras's own outstretched hand. "I see slivers of night sky."

I reached for the lip of the opening, made of rough stone, and guided Geras to his own handhold. First I, then he, clambered out of the hole onto grass, surrounded by an unkempt thicket and fencing. Nearby, the night-washed temple stood under a canopy of moon and stars.

We had escaped through a covered well. Father of Lights, was this really the Handprint of God? I shook my head, unable to believe. "We are at the temple."

Shouted commands drew closer. Soldiers speaking Laijonese.

"Hello!" I cried.

Soon five Laijonese soldiers found us and gaped.

I choked. "I am Historian Daemu's daughter, and serve Queen Kiboro. What has happened?"

The soldiers startled, and one spoke. "Srawa, Vedoa, Pirthyia, and their Shadows are routed. A mighty light appeared and has driven them from Laijon. Our army and Ai'Biro's army only needed to follow in victory. We have been sent to look for survivors, even for you. The rest gather in the castle." He bowed. "Please, follow us."

We cut across the temple paths, thick with leafy trees. I helped Geras as we climbed the cliffs into the trampled royal grounds.

Two of our escorting soldiers opened the palace's charred front doors to us, and we entered a world of dirt and ash. Laijonese and Ai'Biroan soldiers carried torches or light. The grand entry was destroyed, but we ignored this and passed the doors of the council chamber into a din of soldiers, nobility, allies, and commoners.

Our escort led us through the crowd. I gradually became aware of the falling quiet as I helped Geras avoid bumping into people and searched for familiar faces. We reached the throne, and there was Father.

He embraced me tightly. "Seyo. Praise the Father of Light, you survived. How did you—have you seen—" he broke off, eyes red with tears, and then he noticed that I still held Geras's hand and met Geras's sightless eyes.

Suddenly, the crowd erupted in a cheer.

Confused, I looked around and heard what the people said. They praised the Father of Light. They lifted Laijon's and the continent's freedom. They thanked those who gave their lives to open the Eternity Gate. The Brotherhood. Us.

I was overwhelmed and couldn't take it all in. I scanned the crowd again for those I knew, for Roji. Father pressed his hand against my back to lead me to the stairs of the throne.

I resisted, still holding on to Geras. He would be alone, the last of the Brotherhood. As if he read my mind, Father clasped Geras's forearm. I slowly released Geras's fingers and ascended the throne's steps. To Kiboro.

She stood at the top. Rips marred her soldier's disguise, short hair mussed. Bandaging covered her right arm, and her cheeks were pale. But her bright eyes fixed on me, and joy filled her gaze. She nodded.

I climbed the last stairs, bowed, and took my place behind her. Queen Kiboro watched the crowd until it hushed. I anticipated a speech, but instead, she lowered to her knees, and the rest of us did the same. When she lifted her hands, we expected her glorious gifting. But her palms were empty. Humble. Grateful.

We all did the same, and presented ourselves to the Father of Light. When Kiboro rose, we did, too, and raised a great shout. She lifted her gaze heavenward, bowed, and took her place upon her father's turquoise throne. Queen of victorious Laijon.

45

SUMMER ARRIVED. AT DUSK, GLOWING, golden butterflies painted the hills in numbers that astounded even our elders.

Monsoon season ended, but record flooding continued to fill the tunnels. After intense discussions between the queen, Chanji, and Ai'Biroan royalty, all agreed to wait a month for the waters to recede before excavating the treasure. Those who died aboveground were given burial. Kiboro attended all ceremonies, and I remained with her. Yet my thoughts strayed to those held in watery graves underground.

Roji didn't come home. I refused to mourn, fighting to believe he would stumble out of the woods or search parties would find him, that he had escaped the final battle. But he never returned, and no one found him among the corpses. Due to many factors, surfaced bodies rescued from the tunnel depths were impossible to identify. Yet I held onto hope for days, longer than Father, before surrendering to a pain I'd never felt before. One I knew would remain with me the rest of my life. Like Jorai.

While half our soldiers were routing Pirthyia and Vedoa, scouts reported sighting the mountain tribes. We prepared for border skirmishes, but the tribes disappeared.

On the second week after the Eternity Gate had opened, our armies returned from chasing Pirthyia and Vedoa back into the western deserts and southern plains. Some prisoners of war were taken. After a heated meeting with the Chanji, who thought the captives should be slain, Kiboro ordered that the Pirthyian captives be set free to return to their country to spread news of Laijon's victory. But she retained the Vedoans for further information. The desert people, despite their shameful defeat, remained proud and silent. At last, two Vedoans began to talk.

Vedoa had created Shadows from ancient incantations and lent this army to Pirthyia for an immense fee. To form these Shadows, Vedoa had captured Nazakians and some poor, northern Pirthyians. Few entered the experiment willingly, and there were no Vedoan Shadows and only a handful of Laijonese, like Jorai.

Second, the great Shadow, was one of the first monsters who'd helped to overtake Laijon during the Occupation, the only one that was not destroyed or did not escape back across the seas. The Vedoan prisoners of war trembled when they mentioned it and refused to believe it had been slain.

Under heavy guard, the Vedoan prisoners were forced to roam Laijon's hills and collect the fallen Shadows' bodies for burning. Once this dishonorable task was complete, the Vedoans, too, were released.

We continued to wait for the monsoon rains to recede and began the difficult process of healing the city and land from the scars of war. Our spring crop of grain was destroyed, but the hills remained wet late into the season. Farmers planted again. Harvest would be late, but by the will of the Father of Light, Laijon would be fed.

At last, it was time to return to the tunnels. The pumps churned again. Ai'Biroan and Laijonese soldiers, nobility, and scholars descended into the cavern to retrieve the lost treasure.

I did not go with them—I could not bear to return to that place. But Father did, and he told me that even in daylight, no one could see the opening to the Handprint of God in the ceiling. He also said that sighting the bounty illuminated the best and worst of Laijon and Ai'Biro. After much squabbling, negotiations, and with Father poring over records of riches, both nations took what was once theirs. At Kiboro's command, despite pushback, Nazak's wealth was set aside to be returned to the wilderness nation, even after ignoring our pleas for help.

As for the Eternity Gate, Father gained permission to retrieve the door for a museum. But when he climbed the hill, he only found a mound of rotted wood, as if the gate had been decaying for years.

Ai'Biro gathered their treasure and embalmed dead onto boats and sailed to the islands. Soon after, a special barge arrived bearing King Huari's coffin. Laijon ceased from reconstruction to bury its final dead.

Kiboro dedicated the royal portion of treasure to the poor and Laijon's restoration. She moved from the temple into the palace, where I, for the first time in my life, had my own quarters, near her royal chambers. After this, our queen began conducting business as usual, and the nation followed her example. One of her first acts was to restore Father as royal historian.

One night, she surprised me by calling Father to her room. She had both of us sit on a brocade couch and laid a short stack of books in front of us.

"These belong to the kings," she said. "I want you to look at them and help me find answers."

Eagerly, Father and I opened the tomes. Kiboro paced her room, one hand casting light, and listened to us read. After several evenings of this, the unsettling truth became clear. When the Occupation ended, Laijon's kings laid the stone slab in the center of the Heart to hide the Eternity Gate, which they feared as cursed. For generations, they kept this secret, until the knowledge died. When treasure continued to rise to the upper tunnels through the bellies of river serpents, the passages were locked. Only the most trusted and highest ranked soldiers were allowed to enter the tunnels, sworn to secrecy on pain of death. Like Faru.

Kiboro mourned Faru's involvement with Vedoa and the recent war. I listened and kept quiet. No one else needed to know about the vile blue flame Vedoa must have given him for his loyalty, and that he was Jorai's real father. All of that was over. Yet other questions continued to torment me.

First, when I walked through Vedoa's fire trial, the heavenly messenger who had placed her hands on my head and helped me endure the flames had appeared as Tol. Had I been hallucinating? Her last words haunted me. She said I would see Tol again soon. Where? In Vedoa? It didn't make any sense. Next, if Geras had lost his sight in the opening of the Eternity Gate, why could I still touch fire? How did Geras open the Eternity Gate? And what did he see inside before losing his sight? Lastly, all but one line of the prophecy appeared fulfilled. *And the one born of legend will slay her own soul to finish the age.* What in the continent did that mean?

Soldiers finished transporting Laijon's treasure to the palace and storehouses, including the chests of books. Father was put in charge of searching these tomes within the newly constructed Archives.

At one point, I would have begged for that position, but now I was far too busy. At the beginning of autumn, after a successful second harvest, Kiboro and I completed our temple training and received anointing as priestesses. Kiboro was the first Laijonese queen to do so. Instead of serving in the temple as queen, she threw herself into the recovery of her country, and I remained with her.

It was difficult to process. I always believed the temple would be my purpose, and the oddest realization struck me. In the corners of my heart, I knew I had trained as priestess to achieve worthiness. I knew now that nothing on this side of the Divide could make me worthy. And if I thought working in the temple would be glorious, especially after Laijon's miraculous victory, I was surprised. As prosperity returned, people began to belittle the Eternity Gate's opening. Such falling away was expected and recorded throughout history, but I was therefore glad not to serve in the temple, and this made me feel ashamed.

I had changed. Kiboro, my best friend, was also altered. I saw her less and less. I knew this would happen, but it did not ease the added loss.

Laijon's blossoming trade drew nations to her ports again. While Kiboro spoke with ambassadors and kings, I acted as interpreter and found myself continually answering questions about the Eternity Gate. These exchanges renewed my energy, but an inner restlessness multiplied. Why? Maybe because I was constantly talking about Geras after neglecting to visit him for weeks.

On my following blessed afternoon off, I entered the city, filled with fall colors, and reached Geras's whitewashed flat. The house was gifted to him by the crown.

I didn't know why I had avoided seeing him. He was a hero for opening the gate, and reportedly received scores of visitors, along with doctors and hired servants to help him navigate his new life.

I knocked.

There was bumbling inside, and then the knob twisted and his towering frame filled the doorway. I took in his marked face, bare hands, and the string tied to the knob. I opened my mouth to announce myself, but he spoke first, his brown eyes roaming. "Seyo?"

How in the continent did he know? "Yes." I swallowed. "Is this a good time to visit?"

He stepped back to allow my entry and led me to a small foyer, guided by a string pinched between his fingers. He bade me to sit in a wooden chair. I did and surveyed the sparse wall decorations—his da's sword mounted above the humble hearth—and a single window that opened to an impressive vegetable garden. He was Nazakian, one of the earth people. Wooden stakes marked cabbages, tares, and other Laijonese produce. Besides that and his presence, the loneliness of this place was strangling.

Geras knelt before the fireplace and prepared a kettle. "Will you take tea?"

A Laijonese pleasantry. "Please."

He threw himself into preparations, presented me with green tea, and felt his way to a second chair with his own cup. Out of habit, he bowed his head.

Quiet fell. My tongue refused to work.

Geras heaved a breath and rubbed his chin. He wore the oractalm bracelet I'd given him, and had added something else. A shard of mirror, from the Mirror Garden, with a hole made in its center, was added among the ancient, scarlet coins.

Tears burned my eyes.

He leaned forward and surprised me by talking in rough Laijonese. "Much hear . . . I." He shook his head and switched to Nazakian. "I was hoping to speak better by now."

I relaxed and, speaking in Nazakian, launched into conversations that I thought would interest him. When I spied his da's Nho on the table, I asked if he would like me to read aloud.

He did, and I fetched the book. When I read, he smiled. For a moment, I felt peace.

We read throughout the winter and enjoyed more tea and pickled vegetables from his garden. I expected to talk about the Eternity Gate, and wondered if he would ask about my Vedoan gifting. I was dying to know why the Father of Light had chosen him to open the door. But we never discussed these things. As time passed, a weight grew in Geras, although he was always happy to see me. I became worried and was determined to cheer him up.

One day, when Geras seemed especially downcast, I bounced the Nho against my knees. Now was a good time to tell him about a new kind of reading Ai'Biro was developing, accomplished through one's fingers. I planned to speak to their ambassador about acquiring a manuscript written in this sightless language. If only they could create a document in Nazakian—

Geras leaned forward, elbows to knees. "I hear that soldiers are preparing to transport Nazak's treasures within her borders this spring."

I nodded before catching myself. "Yes."

"The journey would be dangerous." He straightened. "I have asked to travel with them and find my da again."

My heart froze. "Of course," I said, and my mind scrambled through the implications of his statement. The trip would take months. *Qo'tah*, would he even come back?

Geras clasped his hands. "Your father is going as interpreter and to meet my da."

I blinked. What? Why hadn't Father told me this yet?

"I am hoping you will go too."

Mysteries of the continent. I sat back. What about my work here? Which currently consisted of little, now that Kiboro was queen. What about Father's translation of the manuscripts found among the treasure? He could bring some with him, and I could help with interpretation. Why shouldn't I go to Nazak? I'd always wanted to see that country. Maybe if I left for a while, I would feel less miserable when I returned.

"I want to go," I blurted.

Geras's expression gladdened.

But would Kiboro allow me to leave? When I asked her permission that evening, feeling like a deserter, Kiboro grasped my hands in hers and said she could not have chosen a better dignitary to send to Nazak. "Follow the Father of Light's guiding, wherever he directs you," she added.

Coming from her, that sounded dramatic. But I began making arrangements with more anticipation than I'd expected.

When winter ended, before spring monsoon rains, Laijon prepared a caravan with Nazak's treasure. Our transport and heavy guard were disguised as middleclass traders. Father, Geras with an accompanying soldier to guide him, other nobility, and I mounted horses as Queen Kiboro and our countrymen saw us off with shouts of, "May the Father of Light go with you!"

A new maiden attendance, a temple helper only months into her training, stood beside Kiboro. I had helped pick her, and seeing the girl standing in my place felt less odd than I thought it would. When Kiboro waved, I waved back and suppressed tears. What was wrong with me? No one anticipated that Pirthyia would attack us, at least not for another handful of years. Even if they did, Nazak, in full might, was joining us within her borders to receive their gift. Unless a strange turn of weather delayed us, we would return home before harvest.

Laijon's green hills gave way to Pirthyia's red earth. Though the mighty nation saw us, they called us "light warriors" and let us be.

We turned west, crossed the spine of mountains I had climbed with Geras, and met the wilderness of Nazak.

The dry, undisciplined land astounded me. I remembered tales of the Nazakians' ability to grow a bounty out of nothing, even after losing their gifting, but did not see evidence of that here. We spotted a silver snake tracing the horizon, Nazak's mighty river, given to them by the Father of Light through their own heavenly gate ages ago.

A great army neared on horseback in a cloud of dust, the Nazakian clan leaders come to receive their treasure. If not for my memories of the fallen Brotherhood, I would have despised this nation for ignoring our call to war and feared their rowdy appearance. Then I remembered Laijon's own shortcomings. What did we, lowly and disobedient, seem like to them?

After a week's worth of divvying of treasure and wild Nazakian camaraderie, we lapsed into the safety of a caravan carrying only travel supplies, and forged into the sparsely forested highlands toward Ortos's village. To a wattle-and-daub home gracing a breathtaking garden where Geras had grown up.

Geras brushed my side and stood too close, as was usual these days. His chest puffed and fell. After everything he had done, was he now afraid?

The front door opened to a bent, elderly man.

"He's here," I whispered, and looped my arm through Geras's.

He covered my hand with his. In another situation, maybe it would have appeared intimate. Rather, his halting steps and wandering gaze gave his difficulty away.

With surprising agility, Ortos met us halfway, flung his arms around his adopted son, and wept. Geras quickly relaxed and cried, too, with joy. Ortos searched his brown eyes again and again, and welcomed us joyously into his home.

Simple fare was shared, and stories flew. Ortos nodded and tears streamed down his face again as we gave our account of the Eternity Gate's opening and loss of the Brotherhood. Geras spoke last, slowly, humbly. I held my breath, waiting for him to describe what he saw within the Eternity Gate and what the Father of Light told him about his biological parents, but he didn't. Later, our Laijonese guard accepted Ortos's welcome to camp on his land, and Father and I were invited to sleep on pallets near the kitchen fire.

As we unpacked, the back door creaked open. A thin girl with large eyes and curly hair tied in a scarf entered the home.

I gaped as Cira greeted Ortos. How did she escape the Imperati's castle and find this place? How many orphans did Ortos take in?

"So many soldiers, *Taba*," she said, calling Ortos teacher. Her eyes flashed with annoyance, but her secret interest was clear. Then she glanced at me. No recognition flickered in her gaze. I suppose because I wasn't Laijon's princess anymore. Cira pranced to an upstairs loft and disappeared.

Several peaceful days passed. Ortos and Father talked daily for long hours. Our Laijonese soldiers enjoyed the reprieve. Cira never realized who I was, but I learned how she'd ended up here. While trying to sell a Laijonese copy of the Nho—mine that she had stolen—to Ortos, he had instead offered her a room and work with him, and she had ended up proving herself a good cook.

Geras quickly acclimated to his old home. He talked with Ortos and Father, took on some chores that used to be his, and showed me around the property he knew so well. We tended the garden together, and he encouraged me to continue our reading of the Nho for everyone in the household. I agreed, and translated the holy script into both Nazak and Laijonese. Soon, neighbors began crowding into Ortos's house to listen. Not for the first time, I wondered why Ortos, a leader of the Brotherhood, kept a Laijonese Nho that he could not read. Were there so few Nazakian copies, or was he illiterate, like Geras? But these times were the happiest, when I forgot my sorrows and enjoyed extending this skill I possessed. Yet, I knew it was too good to last.

Talk of our return to Laijon began. And when Ortos and Geras visited late into the night, I overheard conversations about the keeping of livestock because Geras's hunting days were possibly over.

Grief rose inside me. Geras wouldn't return to Laijon, where there was no life for him. Ortos needed him. I had suspected this, but facing its reality was a different matter.

The next day after morning meal, Ortos helped me wash and dry dishes. My new dislike of him embarrassed me. It wasn't his fault Geras was staying.

Ortos watched me from the corner of his wrinkled eye. "Geras speaks well of you, Lady Seyo. Thank you for what you have done for him."

What had I done that he hadn't already done for me? I merely dipped my head.

Ortos turned his attention to the wash basin. "Now that the Eternity Gate is fulfilled, I wonder if Laijon will return to her first call."

My ears pricked. "What do you mean, srolo?"

"Surely you know? Out of many nations, the Father of Light chose Laijon to be a seed of the knowledge of him and spread to all nations, such as Nazak, who has forgotten him. Your nightly reading reminds me of this."

My mouth felt dry. His words were too grand to accept. "May the Father of Light remind Nazak, as he did Laijon."

Ortos nodded, and we resumed our washing.

That evening, Father and the noblemen decided that we would depart in three days. While they and the soldiers shared excitement to return home, my insides churned. At night, as I rolled into rough blankets by the fire, long after the others slept, I imagined a joyful return to Kiboro—and only felt restlessness.

Father of Light, the Eternity Gate's opening had changed all of us, but would I ever feel like myself again? Did I have a purpose anymore?

I stared into the dying embers of the fireplace. I knew I could touch them and not be burned. Perhaps I hadn't changed at all, or didn't understand anything as well as I thought. Like the sea of questions I still needed to ask Geras. And the one task I had left.

The morning before our departure day, I passed through Ortos's garden under Nazak's bright sun. Around the guiding ropes he and Geras had strung between the fencing and house. Then I heard someone near and turned.

Geras walked through the garden, unaware of me.

If I was going to ask him about the Eternity Gate, there would never be a better time.

I cleared my throat to alert him to my presence, but Father and Ortos strode through the garden and hailed Geras. Both appeared sober, and then they saw me and waved.

My pulse quickened, and I hurried toward them. Father laid a hand on my shoulder, but did not speak. I knew something weighed on his heart, and the suspense was unbearable. What had happened?

At last, he sighed. "Seyo, your favorable reputation will be my undoing. Ortos has asked my permission to invite you to stay here—for a season—and assist in translating and sharing the Nho with Nazak."

What in the continent? Father nodded toward the Brotherhood leader.

"Yes, while the stories of the Eternity Gate ring in Nazak's ears and the people's hearts are receptive," Ortos said. "The neighbors have spread word of your readings, and nearby villages have asked for you to come and share with their communities. Many also ask to hear Geras's account of the Eternity Gate's opening." He gave a small smile. "I have my selfish reasons for asking you to do this too. I am an old man, Lady Seyo. Geras has always been the greatest help to me, perhaps now more than ever. However, he also needs assistance. I see that you offer this to him and have already aided his transition home. But as Historian Daemu said, you would need to stay months before I could arrange a safe return to Laijon."

"Is it possible to be safe between Pirthyia and Vedoa?" Father wondered. But he had allowed Ortos to make this offer.

I didn't know what to think. What about my life in Laijon? What would Roji say? Oh, how I missed him. Tears stung my eyes. What about my service to Kiboro?

Follow the Father of Light's guiding, wherever he directs you, she had said.

What about Father?

He gazed at me, and I could feel heaviness clinging to him. But there was something else too. Pride and hope.

Stay in Nazak and read the Nho to the people? They were a wild nation who would reject my message as often as they would listen. But the Brotherhood had belonged to this people, as did Geras. I looked and found him working in the garden, out of earshot.

Sureness like the desert flooded me, and I realized I wanted this opportunity.

I drew a breath. "I would be honored, Srolo Ortos."

Ortos clapped. "Wonderful! I took the liberty of already speaking with Cira, and she has agreed to share her room with you."

Rooming with Cira again? I almost laughed, then looked to Father. He drew me into a hug and said with a thickened voice, "We need to remove your belongings from the caravan, and perhaps a few recovered manuscripts. I could use your help with so much translation, even from afar."

The next and last day, Laijon rallied to depart. Farewells were exchanged between both cultures. Father embraced me for a long moment before accepting Ortos's escort to join the noblemen among the guards. Dry dust curled about their feet as they walked.

I wrapped my arms around my middle, and my heart quaked. It was only a year or so, but I felt like I was diving across the oceans. Was this the right decision? Or a mistake?

I was stepping through a new doorway.

A presence wafted over me, and Geras brushed my shoulder and stood beside me. Eyes searching, nervous hands playing with something. Wearing the oractalm bracelet around his wrist, he fingered a lump of red ore carved into the shape of a great bird.

I blinked. What—

"Vispirios gave this to me," Geras said, as if reading my mind. "He asked me to return it to his family."

Vispirios's wife and children lived in Pirthyia. I shivered at the thought of returning there.

"Seyo . . ." Geras fell silent.

I waited, eyes on his marked face, and remembered the question I wanted to ask him. The one that hounded me more than the rest.

The Laijonese caravan began to move, and all of us cheered and waved. My heart ached, and more tears fell down my face.

Geras expelled a breath. "I am glad you are here, Seyo."

I paused before smiling. What a pair we were. He was cursed, and I possessed my enemy's gifting. Unworthy vessels, yet used by the Father of Light to demonstrate that he alone possessed greatest power. And if He was with us, who could fight against us? So, it was time for me to be brave and ask.

"Geras," I said hesitantly, "when you looked inside the opened Eternity Gate, what did you see?"

Geras's marked brow creased. For a moment, I didn't think he would answer. "I saw an image of the gate, like a vision, but the frame was golden and lying on the ground. A girl stood in front of it. At first I thought it was you, but when she faced me, I realized it was someone else, someone I don't know. It confused me. I was planning to ask you about this."

"*Qo'tah.*" I covered my mouth. Missing pieces fell into place. The heavenly messenger. The last line of the prophecy. "We've only been half right this whole time. The full answer must be written in the recovered manuscripts or in the bimil. I have to catch Father and tell him. Geras, we opened the Eternity Gate, but it is only the beginning. There is a second gate."

ACKNOWLEDGEMENTS

With tear-filled eyes, thank you . . .

To my brainstormers, beta readers, critique partners, and fact-checkers: Jessica, Marissa, Irene, Meagan, Given, Susan, Liam, Susi, Scott, Frederick, and Michael.

To Given, Meagan, Lizzie, Candace, Karyne, and CJ, for writing beside me.

To DiAnn Mills, for taking me under your wing.

To Daniel Schwabauer, for teaching me about story.

To Jamie Foley, for sketching this world to life.

To Emilie Haney, for creating a masterpiece book cover.

To my students, for teaching me so much.

To Mom, Dad, Allison, Grandma, Memaw, and my extended family. Your love and support are an incredible gift.

To Jessica, for championing my dreams.

To John, for adventuring with me and being my strong, safe place. (Let's *snug*!)

To the wonderful Enclave Publishing and Oasis Family Media team, Steve, Lisa, Trissina, Jamie, Avily, Megan, Lisa, Steve, Charmagne, and Toni. Thank you for welcoming this debut author.

To C.S. Lewis, for writing *The Horse and His Boy* and helping me see Jesus.

To the Reader. This is for you.

ABOUT THE AUTHOR

Katherine Briggs crafted her first monster story at age three. Since graduating from crayons to laptop, she continues to devour and weave fantasy tales while enjoying chai tea. She, her coadventurer husband, and rescue dog reside outside Houston, where she classically educates amazing middle school students, teaches ESL to adults, and enjoys studying other languages.

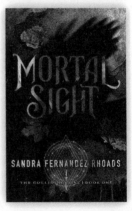